The Rex Stout Library

R E X
S T O U T

Black Orchids
&
The Silent Speaker

Introduction to Black Orchids
by Lawrence Block

Introduction to The Silent Speaker
by Walter Mosley

BANTAM BOOKS

2009 Bantam Books Trade Paperback Edition

Published in the United States by Bantam Books, an imprint of The Random House Publishing Group, a division of Random House, Inc., New York.

BANTAM BOOKS and the rooster colophon are registered trademarks of Random House, Inc.

Black Orchids was originally published in the United States by Farrar & Reinhart, New York, in 1942, and by Bantam Books, Random House, Inc., with a new introduction in 1992.

The Silent Speaker was originally published in the United States by The Viking Press, an imprint of Penguin Group (USA), New York, in 1946, and by Bantam Books, Random House, Inc., with a new introduction in 1994.

ISBN 978-0-553-38655-4

Printed in the United States of America

www.bantamdell.com

9

Cover art and design by Daniel Pelavin

Black Orchids

Black Orchids

Introduction

I n the early seventies I found myself at an impasse with a character named Chip Harrison. I had written two books about him. In the first he had lost his innocence, and in the second he was sort of looking around trying to figure out what had become of it. I wanted to write more about him, having found his voice an engaging one, but I didn't see how I could put the poor dope through another loss of innocence.

Inspiration struck, as it now and then does. Instead of having him contend with problems of his own, I'd let him stick his nose into those of other people. I'd put him to work for a private detective. Then, like all private eyes, he could stay the same age forever, and I could write about him till the cows came home.

His new employer, Leo Haig, had eked out a living in the Bronx as a small-time breeder of tropical fishes until a legacy allowed him to pursue a lifelong dream. He would become a private detective like his idol, Nero Wolfe.

Haig, a devout mystery fan, is secure in the knowledge that Nero Wolfe actually exists, not in fiction but in fact, and that the many books about him are indeed the subtly fictionalized reports of actual cases, written by Archie Goodwin himself and published under the painfully transparent pen name of "Rex Stout." (Look at the name itself, Haig says. Rex is Latin for king, Stout means fat, so what could the pseudonym be but a reference to the regal corpulence of the great detective?)

Of course, Haig would tell you, Goodwin has fictionalized things. He provides a number of addresses for the legendary brownstone, any of which would fall somewhere in the Hudson River. He calls the newspaper the *Gazette* and has Archie go dancing at the Flamingo or chasing around to the Hotel Churchill.

No doubt a man with a Wolfean concern for privacy would insist on such changes, he figures. The house is not on West Thirty-fifth Street at all, and very likely in another neighborhood altogether. Surely Wolfe's name is not Wolfe, nor Goodwin's Goodwin. But it is at least as certain that the two men exist, and Leo Haig lives in hope that, if he employs Nero Wolfe's method and principles in his chosen occupation as private detective, someday he will get his reward. Someday the telephone will ring, and someday he will be summoned to that famous house. (Perhaps in the East Eighties? Haig rather thinks it might be in the East Eighties.) There he will dine on something exquisite—shad roe, perhaps, if it's in season. And there, over postprandial coffee, Wolfe will provide the ultimate accolade.

"Satisfactory," he will say, inclining his head an eighth of an inch. "Satisfactory."

Leo Haig's character came easy to me, perhaps because it has always been effortless for me to share his idée fixe. Of course Nero Wolfe exists. Who could imagine a world without him?

I know several men and women who are forever rereading the Nero Wolfe canon. They read other things as well, of course, but every month or so they'll have another go at one of Rex Stout's books. Since there are forty, it may take four or five years at this pace to get through the cycle, at which time they can start in again at the beginning.

They do this not for the plots, which are serviceable, nor for the suspense, which is a good deal short of hairtrigger even on first reading. Nor, I shouldn't think, are they hoping for fresh insight into the human condition. No, those of us who reread Rex Stout do so for the pure joy of spending a few hours in the most congenial household in American letters, and in the always engaging company of Nero Wolfe and Archie Goodwin.

The relationship of these two men, Wolfe and Goodwin, genius and man of action, is endlessly fascinating. One quickly comes to delight in Wolfe's eccentricities—the orchids, the agoraphobia, the food and drink, the vast yellow pajamas, the refusal to countenance the use of "contact" as a verb. Ultimately, though, it is less these idiosyncracies than the pair's nuances of character that keep us transfixed. We know these two, and it is a joy to see them simply being themselves.

Rex Stout knew them, too, with such clarity that he was able to write the books almost effortlessly, in a matter of weeks. His first drafts went to the printer with no need to change so much as a comma. They seem as flawless today, and utterly timeless. For all that the world has changed, for all that New York City has changed, for all that the English language itself has changed, the books don't feel dated in the least. They are so wonderfully real within themselves that they allow us to forget what time it is outside.

It always seemed to me that the very first books were a little labored, with Wolfe tending to declaim pompously at the slightest provocation. So it often is with series; it takes a while to find out what you've got hold of. It didn't take very long at all for Stout to get a firm grasp, and he never let go. *Black Orchids* is vintage Wolfe, and long a particular favorite of mine. I especially like Wolfe's greedy obstinacy in the matter of his fee, and the part where—

Enough. Nero Wolfe needs no introduction, and has been encumbered with too much of one already. Read. Enjoy. And set the book aside when you're done. In a couple of years you'll want to read it again.

—Lawrence Block

Contents

Contents

I don't know how many guesses there have been in the past year, around bars and dinner tables, as to how Nero Wolfe got hold of the black orchids. I have seen three different ones in print—one in a Sunday newspaper magazine section last summer, one in a syndicated New York gossip column a couple of months ago, and one in a press association dispatch, at the time that a bunch of the orchids unexpectedly appeared at a certain funeral service at the Belford Memorial Chapel.

So here in this book are two separate Nero Wolfe cases, two different sets of people. The first is the low-down on how Wolfe got the orchids. The second tells how he solved another murder, but it leaves a mystery, and that's what's biting me. If anyone who knows Wolfe better than I do— but wait till you read it.

Archie Goodwin

Chapter 1

Monday at the Flower Show, Tuesday at the Flower Show, Wednesday at the Flower Show. Me, Archie Goodwin. How's that?

I do not deny that flowers are pretty, but a million flowers are not a million times prettier than one flower. Oysters are good to eat, but who wants to eat a carload?

I didn't particularly resent it when Nero Wolfe sent me up there Monday afternoon and, anyway, I had been expecting it. After all the ballyhoo in the special Flower Show sections of the Sunday papers, it was a cinch that some member of our household would have to go take a look at those orchids, and as Fritz Brenner couldn't be spared from the kitchen that long, and Theodore Horstmann was too busy in the plant rooms on the roof, and Wolfe himself could have got a job in a physics laboratory as an Immovable Object if the detective business ever played out, it looked as if I would be elected. I was.

When Wolfe came down from the plant rooms at six P.M. Monday and entered the office, I reported:

"I saw them. It was impossible to snitch a sample."

He grunted, lowering himself into his chair. "I didn't ask you to."

"Who said you did, but you expected me to. There are

three of them in a glass case and the guard has his feet glued."

"What color are they?"

"They're not black."

"Black flowers are never black. What color are they?"

"Well." I considered. "Say you take a piece of coal. Not anthracite. Cannel coal."

"That's black."

"Wait a minute. Spread on it a thin coating of open kettle molasses. That's it."

"Pfui. You haven't the faintest notion what it would look like. Neither have I."

"I'll go buy a piece of coal and we'll try it."

"No. Is the labellum uniform?"

I nodded. "Molasses on coal. The labellum is large, not as large as aurea, about like truffautiana. Cepals lanceolate. Throat tinged with orange—"

"Any sign of wilting?"

"No."

"Go back tomorrow and look for wilting on the edges of the petals. You know it, the typical wilting after pollination. I want to know if they've been pollinated."

So I went up there again Tuesday after lunch. That evening at six I added a few details to my description and reported no sign of wilting.

I sat at my desk, in front of his against the wall, and aimed a chilly stare at him.

"Will you kindly tell me," I requested, "why the females you see at a flower show are the kind of females who go to a flower show? Ninety per cent of them? Especially their legs? Does it have to be like that? Is it because, never having any flowers sent to them, they have to go there in order to see any? Or is it because—"

"Shut up. I don't know. Go back tomorrow and look for wilting."

I might have known, with his mood getting blacker every hour, all on account of three measly orchid plants, that he was working up to a climax. But I went again Wednesday, and didn't get home until nearly seven o'clock. When I entered the office he was there at his desk with two empty beer bottles on the tray and pouring a third one into the glass.

"Did you get lost?" he inquired politely.

I didn't resent that because I knew he half meant it. He has got to the point where he can't quite understand how a man can drive from 35th Street and Tenth Avenue to 44th and Lexington and back again with nobody to lead the way. I reported no wilting, and sat at my desk and ran through the stuff he had put there, and then swiveled to face him and said:

"I'm thinking of getting married."

His half-open lids didn't move, but his eyes did, and I saw them.

"We might as well be frank," I said. "I've been living in this house with you for over ten years, writing your letters, protecting you from bodily harm, keeping you awake, and wearing out your tires and my shoes. Sooner or later one of my threats to get married will turn out not to be a gag. How are you going to know? How do you know this isn't it?"

He made a noise of derision and picked up his glass.

"Okay," I said. "But you're enough of a psychologist to know what it means when a man is irresistibly impelled to talk about a girl to someone. Preferably, of course, to someone who is sympathetic. You can imagine what it means when I want to talk about her to *you*. What is uppermost in my mind is that this afternoon I saw her washing her feet."

He put the glass down. "So you went to a movie. In the afternoon. Did it occur—"

"No, sir, not a movie. Flesh and bone and skin. Have you ever been to a flower show?"

Wolfe closed his eyes and sighed.

"Anyway," I went on, "you've seen pictures of the exhibits, so you know that the millionaires and big firms do things up brown. Like Japanese gardens and rock gardens and roses in Picardy. This year Rucker and Dill, the seed and nursery company, have stolen the show. They've got a woodland glade. Bushes and dead leaves and green stuff and a lot of little flowers and junk, and some trees with white flowers, and a little brook with a pool and rocks; and it's inhabited. There's a man and a girl having a picnic. They're there all day from eleven to six thirty and from eight to ten in the evening. They pick flowers. They eat a picnic lunch. They sit on the grass and read. They play mumblety-peg. At four o'clock the man lies down and covers his face with a newspaper and takes a nap, and the girl takes off her shoes and stockings and dabbles her feet in the pool. That's when they crowd the ropes. Her face and figure are plenty good enough, but her legs are absolutely artistic. Naturally she has to be careful not to get her skirt wet, and the stream comes tumbling from the rocks into the pool. Speaking as a painter—"

Wolfe snorted. "Pah! You couldn't paint a—"

"I didn't say painting as a painter, I said speaking as a painter. I know what I like. The arrangement of lines into harmonious composition. It gets me. I like to study—"

"She is too long from the knees down."

I looked at him in amazement.

He wiggled a finger at a newspaper on the desk. "There's a picture of her in the *Post*. Her name is Anne Tracy. She's a stenographer in Rucker and Dill's office. Her favorite dish is blueberry pie with ice cream."

"She is not a stenographer!" I was on my feet. "She's a secretary! W. G. Dill's!" I found the page in the *Post*. "A damn important job. I admit they look a little long here, but it's a bad picture. Wrong angle. There was a better one in the *Times* yesterday, and an article—"

"I saw it. I read it."

"Then you ought to have an inkling of how I feel." I sat down again. "Men are funny," I said philosophically. "That girl with that face and figure and legs has been going along living with her pop and mom and taking dictation from W. G. Dill, who looks like a frog in spite of being the president of the Atlantic Horticultural Society—he was around there today—and who knew about her or paid any attention to her? But put her in a public spot and have her take off her shoes and stockings and wiggle her toes in a man-made pool on the third floor of Grand Central Palace, and what happens? Billy Rose goes to look at her. Movie scouts have to be chased off the grass of the woodland glade. Photographers engage in combat. Lewis Hewitt takes her out to dinner—"

"Hewitt?" Wolfe opened his eyes and scowled at me. "Lewis Hewitt?"

I knew that the sound of that name would churn his beer for him. Lewis Hewitt was the millionaire in whose greenhouse, on his Long Island estate, the black orchids had been produced—thereby creating in Wolfe an agony of envy that surpassed any of his previous childish performances.

"Yep," I said cheerfully. "Lew himself, in his two hundred dollar topcoat and Homburg and gloves made of the belly-skin of a baby gazelle fed on milk and honey, and a walking stick that makes your best Malacca look like a piece of an old fishing pole. I saw her go out with him less than an hour ago, just before I left. And pinned to her left shoulder was a black orchid! He must have cut it for her himself. She becomes the first female in captivity to wear a black orchid. And only last week she was typing with her lovely fingers, 'Yours of the ninth received and contents noted.'"

I grinned at him. "But Lew will have to get out the spray for the insects. Men are flocking in there who don't know a stamen from a stigma. The guy having the picnic with her inside the ropes smirks fatuously. His name is Harry Gould and he is one of Dill's gardeners. A gray-haired geezer that needs a shave gazes at her as if he was about to say his prayers—I've seen him twice. A whole-some young fellow with a serious chin wanders by and pretends he's not looking at her. His name is Fred Updegraff. Updegraff Nurseries, Erie, Pennsylvania. They've got an exhibit not far off. And there's a lot more, but chiefly there's me. Your friend Lew is going to have me to contend with. She smiled at me today without mean-ing to, and I blushed from head to foot. My intentions are honorable but they are not vague. Look at that picture of her and then take a slant at this." I lifted a heel to the corner of the desk and pulled my trouser leg up to the knee. "In your mind's eye strip off the shoe and sock and garter and apply your knowledge of cross-pollination. What would be the result—"

"Pfui," Wolfe said. "Don't scar the desk. You will re-turn there tomorrow and look for edge-wilt, and you will be here at six o'clock."

But it didn't work out that way. At lunch the next day his envy and curiosity finally foamed up to the climax. He put down his coffee cup, assumed the expression of a man prepared to brave all hardship or hazard for the sake of a Cause, and told me:

"Please bring the sedan around. I'm going up there and look at those confounded freaks myself."

Chapter 2

So Thursday was my fourth day at the Flower Show in a row. It was the biggest mob of the week, and getting Nero Wolfe through and up to the fourth floor where the orchids were was like a destroyer making a way through a mine field for a battleship. We were halted a couple of times by acquaintances who wanted to exchange greetings, and as we passed the Rucker and Dill woodland glade on the third floor Wolfe stopped to look it over. There was a line of spectators three deep all the way around the ropes. Harry and Anne were playing mumblety-peg. When a flash bulb made a flare she didn't flicker an eyelash.

"Look at her teeth when she smiles," I said. "Look at her hair like fine-spun open kettle molasses. She was more self-conscious the first day or two. A year of this would spoil her. Look at the leaves on the peony bushes, turning yellow, pining away because she'll be with them only one more day—"

"They are not peonies. They are azaleas and laurel, and they have a disease."

"Call it a disease if you want to. They're pining—"

He had started off, and I nearly knocked three women down getting around in front of him for interference.

At the orchid benches up on the fourth floor he disregarded everything else—though there was, for one thing, the finest display of B. thorntoni I had ever seen—and planted himself in front of the glass case. A card in the corner said, "Unnamed hybrid by Mr. Lewis Hewitt. The only three plants in existence." They certainly were something different, and I had been through all the big establishments several times, not to mention the twenty thousand plants Wolfe had, with hundreds of varieties. I stood to one side and watched Wolfe's face. He mumbled something to himself, and then just stood and looked, with his expanse of face five inches from the glass of the case. His emotions didn't show, but from the twitching of a muscle on his neck I knew he was boiling inside. For a quarter of an hour he didn't budge, not even when women bumped against him trying to get a peek at the orchids, though ordinarily he hates to have anyone touching him. Then he backed away and I thought he was through.

"It's hot in here," he said, and was taking off his overcoat. I took it to hold for him.

"Ah, Mr. Wolfe," a voice said. "This is indeed a compliment! What do you think of them?"

It was Lewis Hewitt. Wolfe shook hands with him. He had on another hat and topcoat and gloves, but the same walking stick as the day before—a golden-yellow Malacca with reddish-brown mottles. Any good appraiser would have said $830 as is, on the hoof. He was tall enough to look down at Wolfe with a democratic smile below his aristocratic nose.

"They're interesting," Wolfe said.

Interesting. Ha ha.

"Aren't they marvelous?" Hewitt beamed. "If I had time I'd take one from the case so you could have a good look, but I'm on my way upstairs to judge some roses and

I'm already late. Will you be here a little later? Please do?—Hello, Wade. I'm running."

He went. The "Wade" was for a little guy who had come up while he was talking. As this newcomer exchanged greetings with Wolfe I regarded him with interest, for it was no other than W. G. Dill himself, the employer of my future wife. In many ways he was the exact opposite of Lewis Hewitt, for he looked up at Wolfe instead of down, he wore an old brown suit that needed pressing, and his sharp gray eyes gave the impression that they wouldn't know how to beam.

"You probably don't remember me," he was telling Wolfe. "I was at your house one day with Raymond Plehn—"

"I remember. Certainly, Mr. Dill."

"I just saw Plehn downstairs and he told me you were here. I was going to phone you this afternoon. I wonder if you'd do something for me?"

"That depends—"

"I'll explain. Let's step aside away from this jostling." They moved, and I followed suit. "Do you know anything about the Kurume yellows?"

"I've heard of them." Wolfe was frowning but trying to be courteous. "I've read of them in horticultural journals. A disease fatal to broad-leaved evergreens, thought to be fungus. First found two years ago on some Kurume azaleas imported from Japan by Lewis Hewitt. You had some later, I believe, and so did Watson in Massachusetts. Then Updegraff lost his entire plantation, several acres, of what he called rhodaleas."

"You do know about them."

"I remember what I read."

"Did you see my exhibit downstairs?"

"I glanced at it as I passed." Wolfe grimaced. "The crowd.

I came to see these hybrids. That's a fine group of Cypripedium pubescens you have. Very fine. The Fissipes—"

"Did you see the laurel and azaleas?"

"Yes. They look sick."

"They are sick. They're dying. The Kurume yellows. The underside of the leaves shows the typical brown spots. Some scoundrel deliberately infected those plants, and I'd give a good deal to know who it was. I intend to know who it was!"

Wolfe looked sympathetic, and he really was sympathetic. Between plant growers a fatal fungus makes a bond. "It's too bad your exhibit was spoiled," he said. "But why a personal devil? Why a deliberate miscreant?"

"It was."

"Have you evidence?"

"No. Evidence is what I want."

"My dear sir. You are a child beating the stick it tripped on. You had that disease once on your place. A nest of spores in a bit of soil—"

Dill shook his head. "The disease was at my Long Island place. These plants came from my place in New Jersey. The soil could not possibly have become contaminated."

"With fungi almost anything is possible. A tool taken from one place to the other, a pair of gloves—"

"I don't believe it." Dill's voice indicated that nothing was going to make him believe it. "With the care we take. I am convinced it was done deliberately and maliciously, to ruin my exhibit. And I'm going to know who it was. I'll pay you a thousand dollars to find out for me."

Wolfe abandoned the ship. Not physically, but mentally. His face went bland and blank. "I don't believe I could undertake it, Mr. Dill."

"Why not? You're a detective, aren't you? Isn't that your business?"

"It is."

"This is a job for a detective. Isn't it?"

"No."

"Why not?"

"Because you wouldn't walk across the continent to take a swim in the Pacific Ocean. The effort and expense are out of proportion to the object sought. You say you have no evidence. Do you suspect anyone in particular?"

"No. But I absolutely intend—"

I butted in. I said to Wolfe, "I've got to go and judge some brussels sprouts," and I beat it.

I did have a destination in mind, but mostly I wanted to be somewhere else. What with a couple of lucrative cases we had handled since the first of the year, the budget was balanced for months to come, but even so it always gave me the nettles to hear Wolfe turn down a job, and I didn't want to start riding him right there in front of Hewitt's hybrids. To avoid the mob, I opened a door marked PRIVATE and descended a flight of stairs. This part was not open to the public. On the floor below I made my way through a jungle of packing cases and trees and bushes and spraying equipment and so on, and went along a corridor and turned right with it. This stretch of the corridor extended almost the length of the building, but I knew there was an exit halfway. Along the left wall were cluttered more trees and shrubs and paraphernalia, surplus from the exhibits, and along the right wall, which was the partition between the corridor and the main room, were doors with cards on them, all closed, leading into the exhibits themselves from the back. As I passed the one with a card tacked on it saying RUCKER AND DILL, I threw a kiss at it.

Through the door further on I entered the main room. There was even more of a crowd than when Wolfe and I had passed by half an hour earlier. I dodged through the

field as far as the rustic scene which had labels on the
rope-posts reading UPDEGRAFF NURSERIES, ERIE, PENNA. The
exhibits on this side were a series of peninsulas jutting
into the main room, with aisles between them extending
back to the partition, on which they were based. I skirted
the band of spectators taking in the Updegraff arrangement and halted beside a runty specimen who was standing there by the rope scowling at the foliage.

"Hello, Pete," I said.

He nodded and said hello.

I had met Pete day before yesterday. I didn't really
like him. In fact I disliked him. His eyes didn't match and
that, together with a scar on his nose, made him look
unreliable. But he had been hospitable and made me at
home around the place.

"Your peonies look nice," I said socially.

Someone tittered on my left and made a remark which
probably wasn't intended for my ear but I have good ears.
I turned and saw a pair of vintage Helen Hokinsons from
Bronxville. I stared and compelled an eye.

"Yes, madam, peonies," I said. "What's a Cymbidium
miranda? You don't know. I've known that since I was
knee-high to a grasshopper. What's a Phalaenopsis? Do
you know?"

"No, I don't, but I know those are rhododendrons.
Peonies! Come, Alice."

I watched them waddle off and turned back to Pete.
"Excuse me for chasing your audience, but it's none of her
business if I prefer to call them peonies. What were you
scowling at? Looking for the Kurume yellows?"

His head jerked around at me. "What about the
Kurume yellows?" he demanded.

"Nothing. Just conversation. I heard Dill saying his
woodland glade has got it and I wondered if it was spreading. You don't need to look at me like that. I haven't got it."

His left eye blinked but the off-color one didn't. "When did you hear Dill say that?"

"Just a while ago."

"So. What I suspected." He stretched himself as high as he could up on his toes, looking in all directions at the throng. "Did you see my boss?"

"No. I just came—"

Pete darted off. Apparently I had started something. But he went off to the left, towards the front, so I didn't follow him. I turned right, past a rose garden and a couple of other exhibits to Rucker and Dill's.

The crowd was about the same as before; it was only a quarter past three and they wouldn't begin surging against the ropes until four o'clock, when Harry would lie down for a nap and Anne would take off her shoes and stockings, positively never seen before at a flower show in the history of the world. I got behind some dames not tall enough to obstruct the view. Mumblety-peg was over, and Harry was making a slingshot and Anne was knitting. What she was working on didn't look as if it might be something I would be able to use, but anyway what I was interested in was her and not her output, which is a normal and healthy attitude during courtship. She sat there on the grass knitting as if there were no one within miles. Harry was nothing like as good an actor as she was. He didn't look at the spectators' faces, and of course he said nothing, since it was all pantomime and neither of them ever spoke, but by movements and glances he gave it away that he was conscious of the audience every minute.

Naturally I was jealous of him, but aside from that he impressed me as a good deal of a wart. He was about my age and he put something on his hair to make it slick. His hair and eyes were dark and he smirked. Also he was cocky. One reason I had picked Anne was that while they were eating lunch Tuesday Harry had put his hand on her arm and she had pulled away, and it wasn't an invitation to try it again. There had been further indications that she was resolved to keep herself innocent and unsullied for me, though of course she had no way of knowing that it was for me until I got a chance to speak to her. I admit her letting Hewitt decorate her with orchids and take her to dinner had been a bitter pill to swallow, but after all I had no right to expect her to be too spiritual to eat, with her legs.

All of a sudden Harry jumped to his feet and yelled, "Hey!"

It was the first word I had ever heard him utter.

Everyone, including me, looked in the direction of his stare.

"You, Updegraff!" Harry yelled. "Get out of that!"

It was the wholesome young man with the serious chin who had been identified for me as Pete's boss, Fred Updegraff, by Pete himself. At the right corner where the exhibit ended at the partition, he had straddled the rope, stretched an arm and snipped off a peony twig or maybe laurel with a pruning shears, picked up the twig, and was making off with it.

"I'll report that!" Harry yelled.

The crowd muttered and ejaculated with indignation, and for a second I thought we might see a lynching as an added attraction for the most dramatic flower show on record, but all that happened was that two women and a man trotted after Updegraff and started remonstrating with him as he kept going. Believe it or not, Anne never looked up and didn't miss a stroke with her needles. A born actress.

My watch said 3:25. It would be over half an hour before the big scene started, and I didn't dare leave Wolfe alone that long in a strange place, so I regretfully dragged myself away. Retracing my steps, I kept an eye out for

Pete, thinking to tell him that his boss had resorted to crime, but he wasn't visible. Taking the corridor again as a short cut, I saw it was inhabited by a sample who didn't strike me as the flower show type, either for backstage or out front. She was standing there not far from the door with the RUCKER AND DILL card on it, a fancy little trick in a gray coat with 14th Street squirrel on the collar, with a little blue hat and a blue leather handbag under her arm, and as I approached she looked at me with an uneasy eye and a doubtful smile.

I asked her, "You lost, sister?"

"No," she said, and the smile got confident. "I'm waiting for someone."

"Me?"

"Nothing like you."

"That's good. It could have been me a week ago, but now I'm booked."

I went on.

Upstairs I found that Wolfe had stayed put, and W. G. Dill was still with him. Apparently the question of tracking down the gazook who had spoiled Dill's exhibit had been settled one way or the other, for they were arguing about inoculated peat and sterile flasks for germination. I sat down on a vacant spot on a bench. After a while Dill departed and Wolfe went back to the glass case and started peering again, and a few minutes later here came Lewis Hewitt, with his topcoat over his arm. He glanced around as if he was looking for something and asked Wolfe:

"Did I leave my stick here?"

"I haven't seen it. Archie?"

"No, sir."

"Damn it," Hewitt said. "I do leave sticks around, but I wouldn't like to lose that one. Well. Do you want to inspect one of those beauties?"

"Very much. Even without an inspection, I'd like to buy one."

"I imagine you would." Hewitt chuckled. "Plehn offered ten thousand for one the other day." He took a key from his pocket and leaned over the case. "I'm afraid I'm going to be regarded as a miser, but I can't bear to let one go."

"I'm not a commercial grower," Wolfe said ingratiatingly. "I'm an amateur like you."

"I know," Hewitt conceded, lifting out one of the pots as if it was made of star bubbles and angels' breath, "but, my dear fellow, I simply couldn't part with one."

From there on the scene was painful. Wolfe was so damn sweet to him I had to turn my head away to conceal my feelings. He flattered him and yessed him and smiled at him until I expected any minute to hear him offer to dust off his shoes, and the worst of it was, it was obvious he wasn't getting anywhere and wasn't going to. When Hewitt went on and on with a discourse about ovules and pollen tubes, Wolfe beamed at him as if he was fascinated and, finally, when Hewitt offered to present him with a couple of C. hassellis, Wolfe thanked him as if they were just what he asked Santa Claus for, though he had twenty specimens as good or better under his own glass. At a quarter past four I began to fidget. Not only would I have liked to give Wolfe a kick in the fundament for being such a sap, but also I wanted to conduct him past the woodland glade and prove to him that he was wrong when he said my affianced was too long from the knees down, and the big scene would end at four thirty, when Anne would flip water out of the pool onto her co-picnicker to wake him from his nap. That always got a big laugh.

So I was relieved when they started off. Ordinarily Wolfe would have had me carry the two pots of C. hassellis, but he toted them himself, one in each hand, to show

Hewitt how precious he thought they were. The big toad-eater. But the worst was yet to come. We went by the back stairs, and, at my suggestion, along the corridor on the floor below, and there on the floor at the base of the door to Rucker and Dill's exhibit, I saw an object I recognized. I halted and told Hewitt:

"There's your cane."

Hewitt stood and looked at it and demanded, "How in the name of heaven did it get there?"

And by gum, Wolfe told me to pick it up for him! I should have resigned on the spot, but I didn't want to make a scene in front of Hewitt, so I stopped and grabbed it. There was a piece of green string looped on the crook and I brushed it off and extended the crook end toward Hewitt, controlling an impulse to jab him in the ribs. He thanked me democratically and we went on.

"Curious," Hewitt said. "I certainly didn't leave it there. Very odd."

A door ahead of us opened and a man emerged. The door had a card on it, UPDEGRAFF NURSERIES, and the man was the twig-snitcher, Fred Updegraff. At sight of us he stopped, and stood there as we went by. A little farther on, after passing two more doors with exhibitors' cards on them, I swerved to one that wasn't labeled and turned the knob and opened it.

"Where are you going?" Wolfe demanded.

"The water nymph. The pool episode. I thought you might—"

"Bosh. That bedlam—"

"It's really worth seeing," Hewitt declared. "Charming. Perfectly charming. Really delightful. I'll come too."

He headed for the door I was holding open, and Wolfe followed him like an orderly after a colonel, his hands full of potted plants. It would have been comical if it hadn't been disgusting. I kept in front so as not to have to look at him.

At the glade the audience was five and six deep around the ropes to the point on either side where the bushes were in the way, but all three of us were tall enough to get a good view. Anne was putting on a swell performance, dabbling with her toes and swishing around. Her knees were beautiful. I was proud of her. Harry was stretched out in the usual spot for his nap, his head on a grassy mound alongside the rocks and bushes, with a newspaper over his face. The audience was chattering. Anne kicked water onto a cluster of flowers that hung over the pool, and glistening drops fell from the petals.

"Charming," Hewitt said.

"Delightful," Wolfe said. "Archie, will you kindly take these plants? Be very careful—"

Pretending not to hear him, I moved off to the right. Partly I thought he needed some ignoring, but also I wanted to get a better look at Harry's right leg and foot. They were twisted into a strange and unnatural position for a man pretending to take a nap. I stretched tiptoe to get a good look over heads and hats and decided that either his shoe hurt him or he was doing a yogi leg exercise, and went back to Anne just as she took another glance at her wrist watch. She swished once more, swung her feet out of the pool, cast a mischievous eye on her companion, reached into the pool with her cupped hand, and sloshed water over Harry's shirt. The audience screeched with glee.

But Harry didn't take his cue. He was supposed to jerk himself up and blink and look mad, but he didn't move. Anne stared at him in astonishment. Someone called:

"Douse him again!"

I had a quick hunch it wasn't funny, with his leg twisted like that. Pushing through to the front, I got over the rope. As I started across the grass a guard yelled at me, and so did some of the spectators, but I kept going and was bent over Harry when the guard grabbed my arm.

"Hey, you—"

"Shut up." I shook him off and lifted the newspaper enough to see Harry's face, and after one glimpse dropped the paper back over it. As I did that I sniffed. I thought I smelled something, a faint something that I recognized.

"What is it? What's the matter?" a voice above me asked.

It was the first time I had ever heard Anne's voice, but I didn't reply or look up at her because I was seeing something about the moss which clung to the face of the rocks just back of Harry's head. On account of the shrubs and rocks I couldn't get around to see the top of his head, so I reached a hand to feel of it, and the end of my finger went right into a hole in his skull, away in, and it was like sticking your finger into a warm apple pie. I pulled away and started wiping my finger off on the grass, and realized with a shock that the two white things there were Anne's bare feet. I nearly got blood on them.

Chapter 3

I stood up and told Anne, "Put on your shoes and stockings."

"What—"

"Do as I tell you." I had the guard by the sleeve and stabbed into his sputtings, "Get a cop." By the way his mouth fell open I saw he was too dumb even for something as simple as that without a fireside chat, so I turned to call to Hewitt and there was Fred Updegraff inside the ropes headed for us. His eyes were on Anne, but when I intercepted him and told him to get a cop he about-faced without a word and went. Wolfe's voice barked above the din:

"What the devil are you doing in there?"

I ignored him again and raised my voice to address the multitude: "Ladies and gentlemen. That's all for today. Mr. Gould has had an attack. If you're sensible you'll go and look at flowers. If you're morbid or have got the itch you'll stay where you are—outside the ropes—"

A flash bulb flared at the left. Sympathetic murmurs arose, but they seemed to be a hundred percent morbid. At the right a guy with a camera came diving under the rope, but that was something for which arrangements had already been made inside the guard's head and he responded promptly and adequately. I was gratified to see that Anne appeared to have a modicum of wits. She must have seen the color of what I had wiped from my finger, but she was sitting on the grass getting her feet shod, hastily but efficiently.

"Archie!" Wolfe's voice came in his most menacing tone. I knew what was eating him. He wanted me to get out of there and drive him home, and he thought I was showing off, and he knew I was sore. As he called my name again I turned my back on him to welcome the law. A big flatfoot with no neck shoved through the crowd to the rope and got over it and strode across the grass. I blocked his way at Harry's feet.

"What's wrong with him?" he asked gruffly.

I moved aside and let him pass. He stopped and got a corner of the newspaper and jerked it off.

"Archie!" Wolfe bellowed.

Some of the spectators could see Harry's face and they were reacting. The ropes were bellied in, taut, with the pressure from behind. The guard was charging across the grass at them and Anne was on her feet again and Fred Updegraff was there.

"Hell, he's dead," the cop said.

"You guessed it," I conceded. "Shall I get some help?"

"Go ahead."

I won't say that I already knew things I didn't know, but I already had stirrings above the ears and, besides, I didn't want Wolfe to bust a lung, so I went that way and found him standing with Hewitt a few paces to the rear of the throng.

"Hold everything," I muttered to him.

"Confound you—"

"I said hold everything." I cantered off to the phone booths at the front of the room, parted with a nickel and dialed a number and got connected with Extension 19, gave my name and asked for Inspector Cramer. His voice came:

"What do you want?"

"Me? Nothing. I'm helping with the chores. Wolfe and I are up at the Flower Show—"

"I'm busy!"

"Okay. Now you're busier. Rucker and Dill's exhibit, third floor, Flower Show. Man murdered. Shot through the top of the head. Lying there on the grass guarded by one bull-necked bull who will never be an inspector. That's all."

"Wait a min—"

"Can't. I'm busy."

I slid out of the booth and dodged through the traffic back across the room. In that short time the mob surrounding the glade had doubled in size. A glance showed me that the cop and the guard had got reinforcements and Anne and Fred Updegraff were not in sight, and Wolfe and Hewitt had retreated to the other side of the rose garden next door. W. G. Dill was with them. Wolfe glared at me as I approached. He was still hanging onto those measly plants and was speechless with rage.

". . . feel a sort of responsibility," Hewitt was saying. "I am Honorary Chairman of the Committee. I don't like to shirk responsibility, but what can I do—just look at them—"

"That policeman," Dill said. "Imbecile. Wouldn't let me in my own exhibit. Broke my shoulder blade. It feels like it." He worked his shoulder up and down, grimacing. "There's the doctor—no—"

"A doctor won't help any. He's dead."

They looked at me. Dill stopped working his shoulder. "Dead? Dead!" He darted off and burrowed into the crowd.

"You said he had an attack," Hewitt regarded me accusingly. "How can he be dead? What did he die of?"

"He ceased breathing."

"Archie," Wolfe said in his most crushing tone. "Stop that. I asked you an hour ago to take these plants. Take them, and take me home."

"Yes, sir." I took the plants. "But I can't leave yet. I'm looking—"

"Good heavens," Hewitt said. "What a calamity . . . poor Dill . . . I must see . . . excuse me . . ." He marched off towards the main stair.

At that instant I caught sight of an object I had been halfway expecting to see. I only got a glimpse of the gray coat with its collar of 14th Street squirrel, for she came from the other side and disappeared into the crowd. I put the pots on the floor at the edge of the rose garden and dashed off before Wolfe could say a word. I didn't care how sore it made him because he had it coming to him after his degrading performance with Hewitt, but I admit I glanced back over my shoulder as I went to see if he was throwing something. His face was purple. I'll bet he lost ten pounds that afternoon.

I skirted the throng and went into it on the other side. In a minute I saw her, squirming through to the front. I took it easy working through to her because I didn't want to make myself conspicuous, and, getting right behind her, saw that the blue leather bag was under her right arm. I shifted Wolfe's coat to my own right arm and under its cover got my fingers on the end of the bag and pulled gently. It started coming, and she was so interested in what she was trying to see around the people still in front of her that she didn't notice it even when the bag was out from under her arm and safely under Wolfe's coat. I kept an eye on her as I backed out, apologizing to the flower lovers as I went, and as soon as I was in the clear turned and made for the stairs.

In the men's room on the second floor I spent a nickel to achieve privacy and sat down and opened the bag, which was monogrammed "RL." It inventoried about as usual, handkerchief and compact and purse and so on, but it also had what I was after, her name and address. They were on an envelope addressed to Miss Rose Lasher, 326 Morrow Street, New York City, which checked with the RL on the bag. I copied it in my notebook. The letter inside was from Ellie and explained why she hadn't paid back the two dollars. And another item was more than I had bargained for. It was a clipping from the *Gazette* of a picture of Harry and Anne playing mumblety-peg. It had cut edges, not torn, and was neatly folded.

I put everything back in, went back to the third floor, worked my way into the crowd, not taking it so easy this time, found her in the front row against the rope, and put my hand on her shoulder. Her head twisted around.

"Will you please—" she began indignantly.

"Okay, sister. It's me. Here's your bag."

"My bag!"

"You dropped it and I risked life and limb to get it. It's yours, isn't it?"

"Sure it's mine!" She grabbed it.

"Say think you."

She mumbled something and was through with me. I glanced at the scene. The cast had been augmented. The contents of two radio police cars, four of them in uniform, were there in the glade, one of them standing at Harry's feet watching a doctor, who was on his knees applying a stethoscope. W. G. Dill stood at the cop's side, his hands in his pockets, scowling. There was no sign that anyone had got interested in the moss on the rocks. I backed out again without bruising anyone seriously and circled around to the rose garden to rejoin Wolfe.

He wasn't there.

He was gone. The two pots were there on the floor, but he wasn't anywhere.

The damn hippopotamus, I thought. He'll get lost. He'll be kidnapped. He'll fall in a hole. He'll catch cold.

I went back down to the men's room on the second floor and yelled his name in front of the private apartments, but no soap. I went up to the fourth, to the orchid benches. No. I went down to the ground floor and out the main exit and to where I had parked the car on 46th Street, but he wasn't in it. It was trying to snow in March gusts. I spat at a snowflake as it sailed by. Our little Nero, I thought, out on such a night and no coat. The bag fat flumpus. I'll put salt on his grapefruit. It was a quarter past five.

I stood and applied logic to it. Had he taken a taxi home? Not the way he hated taxis. What, as I had left him standing there, what had been his most burning desires? That was easy. To shoot me, to sit down, and to drink beer. He couldn't shoot me because I wasn't there. Where might he have found a chair?

I went back and paid four bits to get in again, mounted one flight, and made my way across the grain of the traffic to the corner of the room where a door said OFFICE. People were standing around, and one of them plucked at my sleeve as I put my hand on the knob, and I recognized him. It was the gray-haired geezer I had seen on previous days looking at Anne from a distance as if he was saying his prayers. He looked worried under an old felt hat, and his fingers on my sleeve were trembling.

"Please," he said, "if you're going in there will you please give this to Miss Anne Tracy?"

"Is she in there?"

"Yes, she went in—I saw her go in—"

I took the folded piece of paper and said I'd see that Miss Tracy got it, opened the door and entered, and was in an anteroom containing a tired-looking woman at a desk. I smiled at her irresistibly to keep her quiet, unfolded the piece of paper, and read what it said.

Dear daughter,

I hope there is no serious trouble. I am outside here. If there is anything I can do let me know.

Your father.

It was written with a pencil on cheap white paper. I folded it up again, thinking that one of the first jobs to tackle would be to buy my father-in-law a new hat.

"Do you want something?" the woman at the desk asked in a sad and skeptical tone. I told her I had an important message for Miss Anne Tracy, and she opened her mouth and then decided not to use it any more and motioned to one of three doors. I opened it and passed through, and the first thing I saw was Nero Wolfe sitting in a chair almost big enough for him, with a tray on a table beside him holding four beer bottles, and a glass in his hand.

You can't beat logic.

On another chair right in front of him, facing him, was Anne. Propped against a desk at the left was Lewis Hewitt. A man I didn't know was at another desk writing something, and another one was standing by a window with Fred Updegraff.

Wolfe saw me enter. I saw him see me. But he went on talking to Anne without dropping a stitch:

". . . a matter of nerves, yes, but primarily it depends on oxygenation of the blood. The most remarkable case of self-control I ever saw was in Albania in 1915, displayed by a donkey, I mean a four-legged donkey, which toppled over a cliff—"

I was standing by him. "Excuse me," I said icily. "For you, Miss Tracy." I extended the paper.

She looked up at me, looked at the paper, took it, unfolded it, and read it.

"Oh," she said. She glanced around and looked up at me again. "Where is he?"

"Outside."

"But I . . ." Her brow wrinkled. "Would you tell him . . . no . . . I'll go . . ."

She got up and started for the door. I went to open it for her, saw that Hewitt had the same intention, quickened my step, beat him to the knob, and swung it open. Anne was walking through, and then she wasn't. A man barging through from the other side ran smack into her and nearly knocked her over, and I grabbed her arm to help her get her balance. I beat Hewitt to that too.

"Pardon me," the intruder said. His eyes swept the room and everything in it and went back to Anne. "Are you Anne Tracy?"

"She is Miss Anne Tracy," Hewitt said, "and that is scarcely the way—"

Anne was sidling by to get to the door. The man put an arm out to stop her.

"Where are you going?"

"I'm going to see my father."

"Where is he?"

Another arm got in on it. Fred Updegraff arrived and his hand came out and contacted the intruder's ribs and gave a healthy shove.

"Learn some manners," he said gruffly. "What business is—"

"Permit me," I interposed. "This is Inspector Cramer

of the Homicide Squad." I indicated another man on the door sill. "And Sergeant Purley Stebbins."

"Even so," Lewis Hewitt said in a tone of displeasure. "It is scarcely necessary to restrain Miss Tracy by force. She merely wishes to speak with her father. I am Lewis Hewitt, Inspector. May I ask—"

"Where is your father?"

"Just outside the door," I said.

"Go with her, Purley. All right, Miss Tracy. Come back in here, please."

Purley went out at her heels. That cleared the doorway for another man to enter, W. G. Dill. His lips were in a thinner line than ever, and without looking at anybody or saying anything he crossed to a chair by the rear wall and sat down.

"Hello, Wolfe," Cramer said.

"How do you do, Inspector." With only two grunts, one under par, Wolfe got to his feet and moved forward. "Come, Archie. We'll only be in the way."

"No," Cramer said meaningly.

"No?" Wolfe halted. "No what?"

"Goodwin won't be in the way. On the contrary. At least until I get through with him."

"He's going to drive me home."

"Not now he isn't."

"May I ask what this is all about?" Hewitt was still displeased. "This surveillance of Miss Tracy? This attitude—"

"Certainly, Mr. Hewitt. Sit down." Cramer waved at chairs, of which there were plenty. "Everybody sit down. This is going to be—ah, Miss Tracy, did you find your father? Good. Pull that chair around for Miss Tracy, Purley. Sit down, Goodwin."

I attended to the chair for Anne myself, then turned to face the Inspector.

"No, thanks. I'm nervous."

"You are," Cramer growled. "The day you're nervous I'll shave with a butter knife. How did you know that man had been shot in the top of the head when you called me on the phone?"

Some of them made noises, but Anne didn't. Her head jerked up and her nostrils tightened, but that was all. I admired her more all the time. Hewitt exclaimed, "Shot!" and Fred Updegraff demanded, "What man?"

"Harry Gould," I told him. I grinned at Cramer. "As you see, I didn't blab around. I saved it for you—"

"How did you know?"

"Good heavens," Hewitt said blankly. He rose half out of his chair and then dropped back again.

"It was nothing to write home about," I said. "I looked at his face and he looked dead. I smelled cordite. I saw a jagged hole in the moss at the back of his head, and the moss was puffed out. I couldn't see the top of his head from where I was, but I felt of it, and my finger went in a hole. By the way, don't build a theory from some blood on the grass about where his knees were. I wiped my finger there."

I saw Anne gulp.

"Confound you," Wolfe said angrily, "I might have known."

"Why did you go to him in the first place?" Cramer demanded. "You climbed the ropes and ran to him. Why did you do that?"

"Because he didn't move when Miss Tracy threw water on him, and because I had already noticed that his leg and foot were twisted in an unnatural position."

"Why did you notice that?"

"Ah," I said, "now you've got me. I give up. I'm trapped. Why does anybody notice anything?"

"Especially a nervous man like you," he said sarcastically. "What were you doing there? Why did you come here?"

"I brought Mr. Wolfe."

"Did he come here on a case?"

"You know damn well he didn't. He never goes anywhere on a case. He came to look at flowers."

"Why were you there at that particular exhibit?"

"For the same reason that other people were. To watch Miss Tracy dabble her feet in the pool."

"Did you know Miss Tracy? Or Gould?"

"No."

"Did you, Wolfe?"

"No," Wolfe said.

Cramer resumed with me. "And smelling the cordite and seeing the hole in the moss and feeling the one in his head, how did you figure someone had shot him? By lying hidden in the bushes and aiming through a crack in the rocks?"

"Now have a heart, Inspector." I grinned at him. "If you're not careful you'll trap me again. At the moment I didn't do much figuring, but that was over an hour ago and you know what my brain is when it gets started. Gould took his nap at the same hour each day, and he put his head in exactly the same spot—"

"How do you know that?"

"Mr. Wolfe has been sending me here to look at orchids. That's a matter I'd rather not dwell on. The pile of rocks was only eight or nine inches from his head. Place a gun among the rocks at the right height, wedge it in, aimed the right way, and replace the moss. The rocks and the moss would muffle the report so that no one would notice it in that big noisy room—or what if they did notice it? Fasten a string to the trigger—make it green string so it won't be seen among the foliage. At the proper time, which will be anywhere between four and four thirty, pull the string."

"Pull the string how? From where?"

"Oh, suit yourself." I waved a hand. "Hide in the bushes and after you've pulled it sneak out the door at the back of the exhibit that leads to the corridor. Or if the string's long enough, run it through the crack at the bottom of the door and then you can pull it from the corridor, which would be safer. Or if you want to be fancy, tie the string to the doorknob and it will be pulled by whoever opens the door from the corridor side. Or if you want to be still fancier, run the string around the trunk of a bush and have its end a loop dangling into the pool, and take off your shoes and stockings and swish your feet around in the pool, and catch the loop with your toes and give it a jerk, and who would ever suspect—"

"That's a lie!"

That blurted insult came from Fred Updegraff. He confronted me, and his chin was not only serious, it was bigoted, and anyone might have thought I was a caterpillar eating his best peony.

"Nonsense!" came another blurt, from W. G. Dill, who didn't leave his chair.

"It seems to me—" Lewis Hewitt began sarcastically.

"Pooh," I said. "You cavaliers. I wouldn't harm a hair of her head. Don't you suppose the Inspector had thought of that? I know how his mind works—"

"Can it," Cramer growled. "The way your mind works." His eyes were narrowed at me. "We'll discuss that a little later, when I'm through with Miss Tracy. The gun was wedged among the rocks and covered with the moss, and the string was tied to the trigger, and the string was green, so you're quite a guesser—"

"How long was the string?"

"Long enough to reach. What else do you know?"

I shook my head. "If you can't tell guessing from logic—"

"What else do you know?"

"Nothing at present."

"We'll see." Cramer looked around. "If there's a room where I can go with Miss Tracy—"

The man who had been writing at a desk stood up. "Certainly, Inspector. That door there—"

"Who are you?"

"I'm Jim Hawley of the house staff. I don't think there's anyone in there—I'll see—"

But there was an interruption. The door to the anteroom opened, and in came a delegation of four. In front was a dick whom I recognized as a member of the squad, next came a lady, next my friend Pete with unmatched eyes, and bringing up the rear a cop in uniform. The lady wore a gray coat with a squirrel collar and had a blue leather bag under her arm, but I didn't presume on old acquaintance by speaking to her.

Chapter 4

Cramer took in the influx with a glance and asked, "What have you got, Murphy?"

"Yes, sir." The dick stood with his shoulders straight. He was the military type. "At or about half past four o'clock this young woman was seen in the corridor opening the door leading to the Rucker and Dill exhibit."

"Who saw her?"

"I did," Pete spoke up.

"Who are you?"

"I am Pete Arango. I work for Updegraff Nurseries. That's my boss there, Mr. Updegraff. I went through the door at the back of our exhibit, into the corridor, to get some cookies, and I—"

"To get what?"

"Cookies. I eat cookies. In my locker in the corridor."

"Okay. You eat cookies. And saw what?"

"I saw her opening that door. Rucker and Dill. After all what happened I remembered it and I told a cop—"

"Did she go inside?"

Pete shook his head. "She saw me and she shut the door."

"Did she say anything?"

"No, she didn't have anything to say."

"Did you?"

"No, I went to my locker and got the cookies, and she must have gone away because when I came back she wasn't there. Then when I got back on the floor and saw—"

Cramer turned to the young woman. "What's your name?"

"None of your business!" she snapped.

"Yes, sir," the dick said. "She won't co-operate."

"What do you mean, I won't co-operate?" She was indignant, but I wouldn't have said she looked scared. "I admit I opened the door and looked in, don't I? I got into the corridor by mistake and I was looking for a way out. And why should I have to tell you my name and get my name in the papers—"

"Why didn't you get out the way you got in?"

"Because I got in away around at the other side, and I just thought . . . hey! Hello there!"

Everyone looked the way she was looking, which resulted in all of us looking at Fred Updegraff. Fred himself turned red and was turning redder, as he met her gaze.

"Well," he said, and seemed to think he had said something.

"It was you," she said, "there with the door open, stooping down there peeking in when you heard me."

"Sure," Fred acknowledged, "sure it was me."

"The Rucker and Dill door?" Cramer demanded.

"Yes."

"Were you looking for a way out too?"

"No."

"What were you looking for?"

"I was—" Fred swallowed it. He looked red and flustered, and then all of a sudden he looked relieved. There was no telling what sort of idea had popped into his head that relieved him and pleased him so much, but he certainly showed it. He spoke louder as if he didn't want anyone to miss it: "I was looking at Miss Tracy. I've been doing that all week. My name is Fred Updegraff and I'm an exhibitor here. I was looking at Miss Tracy!" It sounded as if he almost thought he was singing it.

Cramer was unimpressed. "I'll have a talk with you later, Mr. Updegraff." He turned to the Sergeant. "Purley, you stay here with Mr. Updegraff and Goodwin and this young woman and this man Pete. Murphy, come with me and Miss Tracy. The rest of you can go if you want—"

"Just a minute." Hewitt, who hadn't sat down again, moved a step. "I am Lewis Hewitt."

"So I understand," Cramer grunted.

"And I have responsibilities here as the Honorary Chairman of the Committee. Without any wish to interfere with the performance of your duties, I feel that Miss Tracy, who is only a young girl, should properly be protected from any undue annoyance or unpleasantness—"

"Allow me, Hewitt," W. G. Dill had got up and walked over. He faced Cramer. "I'm Miss Tracy's employer and I suppose I ought to look after her. If you don't mind I'll go along with her."

I was keeping tabs on Anne, knowing that the best time to get the lowdown on a woman is when she's under stress. I thought she was doing fine. After four straight days in a glaring spotlight as the star attraction of a flower show, with such by-products as having her picture taken with Billy Rose and dining out with Lewis Hewitt, here she was kerplunk in the mire with murder-mud ready to splatter all over her, and so far she had done nothing to forfeit my respect, even when I had explained how you could pull a trigger with your toes. But at this juncture she wasn't so hot. She might have spoken up with something suitable about being armored in her virtue and not needing to be looked after by any sourpuss employer or millionaire orchid fancier, but all she did was deadpan W. G. Dill without opening her trap. I began to suspect she either had depths I hadn't plumbed or was a bit limited in the mental area—but don't get me wrong, I was still faithful. Even as a deadpan, the sight of her face—for the mental side of life you can go to the library.

She went off with Cramer. Cramer informed both Hewitt and Dill that it wasn't necessary for them to protect her against annoyance, and took her and Murphy through the door that had been indicated to an inner room. But not without another brief delay.

"Mr. Cramer! If you please?"

It was Nero Wolfe speaking. I concealed a grin. Of course he was going to request, or demand, depending on which he thought would work best, that I be allowed to drive him home. I hope Cramer would say yes. Then, after we got in the sedan and he started raving, I would let him rave, and when he was through I would stick my little dagger in his ribs and give it a twist. It wasn't often I had a chance like that.

Cramer had turned. "What do you want?"

"I want," Wolfe said, "to finish a discussion I was having with Mr. Hewitt about orchids."

"Go ahead—"

"And not in a menagerie. In decent privacy. We can find a room somewhere."

"Go ahead. I said the rest of you could go—"

"And Mr. Goodwin must be present to take notes. He will be available when you want him. You can't legally detain him, anyhow, unless you are prepared—"

Cramer snorted in exasperation. "Oh, for God's sake. Discuss orchids. All I want is Goodwin when I want him."

He crossed the sill with the other two, and the door was closed behind them. I glared at Wolfe without any attempt to cover it, and Purley Stebbins gazed at him suspiciously. Neither of us was making any impression on Wolfe, who had got up from his chair and was speaking to Lewis Hewitt in an undertone. Hewitt, frowning, nodded without enthusiasm, and moved toward the door to the anteroom with Wolfe at his heels.

"Come, Archie," Wolfe said.

Purley blocked me. "Where you going?"

"The other end of the anteroom," Hewitt said. "A room there."

Purley hated it. He did hate it. Me detained and going through doors like that. He didn't even smile when I playfully stuck a thumb in his ribs as I went by.

The room at the other end of the anteroom wasn't much more than a cubbyhole, with one window, a couple of small wooden tables, and four wooden chairs. The sad woman in the anteroom came in and turned on the light and went out again and closed the door. Wolfe scowled at the skimpy chairs and darted a glance at me, but I ignored it because I was in no mood to lug in the comfortable seat he had left in the other room. He compressed his lips and sat down, taking care to center himself on what seat there was.

"Sit down, Mr. Hewitt," he invited.

Hewitt stood. "This is an odd performance." He looked at me and back at Wolfe. "What you can possibly have to say to me so confidential as to require—"

"I have," Wolfe said brusquely. "I assure you."

"About orchids? That seems hardly—"

"Not orchids. Murder. I know who shot that man."

Hewitt's eyes opened wide. "You know who shot him?"

"I do."

"But my dear Mr. Wolfe." Hewitt was displeased but courteous. "That is scarcely a matter to discuss confidentially with me. The proper authorities—"

"I prefer to discuss it with you first. I suggest that we

keep our voices as low as possible. It's quite possible that a policeman has his ear at the door—"

"Bosh! This melodramatic—"

"Please, Mr. Hewitt. Don't sneer at melodrama; that's only a point of view. I wish to give you a fresh point of view on the death of Harry Gould. The shot was fired by my assistant, Mr. Goodwin. —Please let me finish. First to establish the fact. Archie?"

I had sat down. The fat bum had taken my dagger away from me. I looked at him and said bitterly, "What if I let you down?"

"You won't. Anyway, you can't. I saw the piece of string you brushed off of it. And I wish to say that your performance this afternoon has been satisfactory. Completely satisfactory throughout. Was there a tug when you picked it up? That's the only detail I lack."

"What the devil is all this?" Hewitt demanded without courtesy. "If you actually—"

"Please, Mr. Hewitt. And keep your voice down. I'll state the situation as briefly as possible. Should I report it to Mr. Cramer—"

"There was a tug," I said. "A little jerk. I didn't especially notice it at the time because I was sore as hell."

Wolfe nodded. "I know you were. My report to Mr. Cramer would be this: that Lewis Hewitt said he had lost his cane. A little later, in the corridor on the third floor, we saw the cane lying on the floor with its crook against the crack under the door leading to the Rucker and Dill exhibit. That was at twenty minutes past four. Mr. Goodwin picked up the cane, and as he did so felt a tug. He calls it a little jerk, but he is exceptionally strong and was in a savage emotional state. Looped on the crook of the cane was a piece of green string which he brushed off before he handed it to its owner."

"I saw no string," Hewitt snapped.

"Maybe not," Wolfe admitted. "People who inherit wealth don't have to bother to see things. But certainly Mr. Goodwin saw it, and so did I, and he felt the tug. The tug was unquestionably the pulling of the trigger and the breaking of the string. That would be my report to Mr. Cramer, since those are the facts."

"I tell you I saw no string!"

"But we did. Keep your voice down, Mr. Hewitt. And Mr. Goodwin touched it. Surely you don't suppose we cooked this up?"

"I don't—" Hewitt looked at the door, and then at me, and then back at Wolfe. "No. I don't suppose you did. But it's inconceivable—" He stopped and stared. "What's that?"

"The piece of string," Wolfe said.

The son of a gun had pulled it out of his vest pocket. I got up for a look, and it was it. I said, "Good here," and sat down. Hewitt sat down too. He looked as if he had to do something and that was all he could think of.

"You and Mr. Dill and Mr. Goodwin left me there," Wolfe said. "Standing there alone. He left those plants there on the floor—and by the way, I have better hassellis than those, much better, my own growing. At a certain point my head began to work, which was remarkable under the circumstances. I don't say that I foresaw this moment precisely, but I saw enough to impel me to go to the corridor and find this piece of string on the floor and pick it up. It is indubitably the piece that was looped on the crook of your cane. By comparing it with the piece left attached to the trigger, Mr. Cramer can establish our surmise as a certainty. That is, he can if I let him have it. Do you think I should do that?"

"Good heavens," Hewitt muttered. "My stick. Good heavens, do you realize—*my* stick!"

"Exactly," Wolfe agreed. "Don't talk so loud. I do

realize. Whoever rigged up that affair made a loop at the end of the string that could be passed under the door. It may have been an afterthought, ad libbing, suggested by the sight of your cane where you had left it, to pass the loop over the cane and leave it lying there for the first passer-by to pick up. If that hadn't happened before half past four I imagine he would have attended to it himself. I do realize what a story that will be for the newspapers. I doubt if it would lead to any official suspicion that you rigged it up yourself, but the public mind—at least some of it—is even less subtle than Mr. Crammer's."

"Good heavens," Hewitt moaned. "This . . ." He clenched his fingers, and released them, and clenched them again. "This is horrible."

"Oh, I wouldn't say horrible. Disagreeable."

"Horrible. For me. For a Hewitt. Horrible!"

"Perhaps for a Hewitt," Wolfe conceded. "Then all the more reason why this may interest you. I want those orchid plants. All three of them."

That changed things entirely. The change, showing itself on Hewitt's face, took perhaps two seconds all told. Up to then nothing had been threatened but his peace of mind or maybe his reputation, at most his life and liberty. But this was something else again; this threatened his property. It put stone in his heart and steel in his jaw. He eyed Wolfe with a shrewd and stubborn stare.

"I see," he hissed. "So that's it. To put it plainly, blackmail. Blackmail! No! I won't do it!"

Wolfe sighed. "You won't?"

"No!"

"Very well. Then I won't get the orchids, but I'll be saved a lot of trouble. Archie, get Mr. Cramer in here. Tell him it's urgent. I'll not perch on this confounded milking stool any longer than I have to."

I arose and started for the door, not hastily. I knew it

was in the bag because Hewitt hadn't raised his voice. It was only a war of nerves.

"Blackmail," Hewitt said through his teeth.

"Go on, Archie," Wolfe said. I put my hand on the knob.

"Wait a minute," Hewitt said. I turned my head but kept my hand on the knob.

"One of them," Hewitt said. "Select any one."

I went back and sat down.

Wolfe sighed and shook his head. "All three. I won't haggle. I'm going to have to work for them. You may call it blackmail to relieve your feelings, but what about me? It's possible that this evidence I'm withholding from Mr. Cramer is vital evidence, and I don't intend to shield a murderer. If I withhold it I'll have to find the murderer myself, and enough evidence to convict him without this. And if I fail I'll have to tell Mr. Cramer all about it, which would be deplorable, and shall have to return the plants to you, which would be unthinkable. So I shan't fail."

"Two of them," Hewitt said. "Two plants. To be delivered to you when you have satisfactorily performed your part of the bargain." He may have inherited it, but he certainly knew how to hang onto it.

"No," Wolfe said. "All three, and I take them home with me now. You can trust me, I can't trust you, because if it turns out that you killed the man yourself and I get you for it, I'd never get them."

"Do you—" Hewitt was goggle-eyed. "You have the effrontery—you dare to suggest—"

"Not at all. I suggest nothing. I consider contingencies, and I'd be a fool if I didn't." Wolfe put a hand on the edge of the table for leverage and lifted himself from the milking stool. "I'm going home where there is a chair to sit on, and go to work. If you'll please take Mr. Goodwin upstairs and give him the plants so I can take them with me . . ."

Chapter 5

Of course I had a card up my sleeve. Wolfe had taken my dagger away and done the twisting himself in Hewitt's ribs instead of his own, but I still had a card.

I had a chance to make arrangements for playing it while Wolfe went around, after we returned to the other room, inviting people to lunch. That was actually what he did. Anyhow he invited W. G. Dill and Fred Updegraff; I heard that much. Apparently he intended to spend the evening thinking it out, and have them all to lunch the next day to announce the result. Hewitt declined my help on the orchid portage from upstairs. It seemed as if he didn't like me. When Wolfe had finished the inviting he calmly opened, without knocking, the door into the room where Cramer had gone with Anne, and disappeared within.

I approached Purley Stebbins, stationed on a chair near the door to the anteroom, and grinned at him reassuringly. He was always upset in the presence of either Wolfe or me, and the two of us together absolutely gave him the fidgets. He gave me a glancing eye and let out a growl.

"Look, Purley," I said cordially, "here's one for the notebook. That lady over there." She was sitting by the far wall with her coat still on and the blue leather bag under her arm. "She's a phony. She's really a Chinese spy. So am I. We were sent to do this job by Hoo Flung Dung. If you don't believe it watch us talk code."

"Go to hell," Purley suggested.

"Yeah? You watch."

I ambled across the room and stood right in front of her so Purley couldn't see her face.

"Hello, dear old friend," I said not too loud.

"You've got a nerve," she said. "Beat it."

"Nerve? Me?"

"Beat it. 'Dear old friend!' I never saw you before."

"Aha!" I smiled down at her. "Not a chance in the world. If I tell them I saw you in that corridor at half past three waiting for someone, they'll believe me, don't think they won't, and you'll have to start all over again about opening that door at half past four because you got there by mistake and were looking for a way out. Think fast and don't tell me to beat it again or we part forever. And control your face and keep your voice down."

Her fingers were twisting under a fold of the coat. "What do you want?"

"I want to get to know you better. I'll be leaving here in a minute to drive my boss home, but I'll be back before long for a little talk with the Inspector. Then I'll go to the news movie in Grand Central and you'll be there in the back row. Won't you?"

"Yes."

"You're sure."

"Yes."

"You'd better be. If you are, it's all right that you never saw me before. If you put over your song and dance there may be a tail on you when you leave. Don't try to shake him. We'll take care of that when we leave the movie. Understand?"

"Yes."

"Righto. Stick to me and you'll wear black orchids."

I started to go back to Purley to kid him out of any suspicions that might be pecking at the shell, but a door opened and Wolfe emerged, and Cramer stood on the sill and spoke:

"Purley! Goodwin's taking Wolfe home and will be back in half an hour."

"Yeah," Purley said disrespectfully.

"Come, Archie," Wolfe said.

We waited in the anteroom, and in a few minutes here came Lewis Hewitt, followed by a guard balancing the glass case on his upper limbs. The transfer was made to me without ceremony, after Wolfe peered through the glass for a good gloating look, and off we went. When we got to where I had parked the car Wolfe got in the back, always a major operation, and I deposited the case on the floor at his feet. Ten minutes later we arrived at the old house on West 35th Street near the river, and the sigh he heaved as he deposited his weight and volume in a chair that had been made for them was a record for both depth and duration.

"You'd better get back up there," he said. "I regret it and I resent it, but I gave Mr. Cramer my word. Theodore will attend to the plants. Get back for dinner if you can. We're having saucisse minuit."

He was being sweet. "I didn't give Cramer my word," I suggested.

"No." He wiggled a finger at me. "Archie! No shenanigan."

"I'll see. But I need refreshment."

I went to the kitchen and put two bowls of crackers and milk where they belonged, meanwhile chinning with Fritz and getting sniffs of the sausage he was preparing. Eating crackers and milk and smelling saucisse minuit simultaneously is like sitting with your arm around a country lass while watching Hedy Lamarr raise the temperature. I told Fritz to save some for me if I was late getting back, and departed.

It was 7:15 when I entered the big inside room of the offices on the second floor of Grand Central Palace. There were a dozen or more people in there, most of whom were new to me, but including W. G. Dill and Lewis Hewitt. Updegraff wasn't in sight, and neither was Anne Tracy, and neither was the girl friend I had a date with. Her absence made it desirable to get troublesome without delay, but it wasn't necessary because in a couple of minutes the door to the inner room opened and Pete Arango came out, and I got a sign from Purley and went in. Cramer was there with a dick I had never seen and Murphy with a notebook. His unlighted cigar was chewed halfway to the end and he looked unjubilant.

"Now," I said brightly, taking a seat, "what can I do to help?"

"Join a circus," Cramer said. "By God, you'll clown at your own funeral. What have you been hanging around here all week for?"

That was all it amounted to, a bunch of whats and whys and whens and four pages of the notebook filled, and my wit wasted on the homicide squad as usual. As a matter of fact, the wit was below par because I wanted to get out of there for my date, since it appeared that she had had her session and been turned loose. So I kept it fairly succinct and tried to co-operate on details, and we were about running out of material when the door opened and in came an undersized dick with a flat nose. Cramer looked at him and demanded:

"What the hell are you doing back here?"

The dick's mouth opened and shut again. It didn't want to say what it had to say. On the second try it got it out:

"I lost her."

Cramer groaned and looked speechless.

"It wasn't my fault," the dick said, "I swear it wasn't, Inspector. That damn subway. A local rolled in and stopped and she hung back like waiting for an express and then the last second she dived through—"

"Can it," Cramer said. "Choke on it. My God. The wonder to me is that—what does it matter what the wonder to me is? What's that name and address?"

Murphy flipped back through the pages of his notebook and stopped at one. "Ruby Lawson. One fourteen Sullivan Street."

The dick got out his memo book and wrote it down. "I don't think it was deliberate," he said. "I think she just changed her mind. I think she just—"

"You think? You say you think?"

"Yes, Inspector, I—"

"Get out. Take another man, take Dorsey, and go to that address and look into her. Don't pick her up. Keep on her. And for God's sake don't think. It's repulsive, the idea of you thinking."

The thinker made himself scarce. Naturally I was now itching to be on my way, so I leaned back comfortably and crossed my legs and began, "You know, when I am tailing someone and they go into a subway station, it is my invariable custom—"

"You can go," Cramer snapped. "On out. If I want you, which God forbid, I know where to get you."

"But I think—"

"I said go!"

I got up leisurely and went out leisurely, and on my way through the outer room paused for a friendly word with Purley, but when I got to the stairs outside I stepped on it. It was at least a hundred to one that I had been stood up, but nevertheless I hotfooted it to the Lexington Avenue entrance of Grand Central Station and on to the newsreel theater, parted with money, and entered. She wasn't in the back row, and I didn't waste time inspecting any other rows. Since she had given a phony name and address to Cramer, and had been smart enough to make it one that matched the RL on her bag, I figured she probably wouldn't be letting grass come up between her toes. Out in the lighted corridor I took a hasty glance at a page in my memo book, considered patronizing the subway and decided no, and headed for 46th Street where I had parked the car.

My high-hatting the subway nearly lost me a trick, for it was slow work at that hour getting around on to Park Avenue, but once headed downtown I made good time.

Number 326 Morrow Street, down at the southern fringe of Greenwich Village, was one of those painted brick fronts that were painted too long ago. There were supposed to be two lights on black iron brackets at the entrance to the vestibule, but only one was working. I parked across the street and moseyed over. Inside the vestibule was the usual row of mailboxes and bell pushes, and the card below one of them had LASHER printed on it. That was okay, but what made it interesting was that on the same card, above LASHER, another name was printed: GOULD. I was leaning over looking at it when the inside door opened and there she was.

It was easy to see that high-hatting the subway had nearly cost me a trick, because she had a traveling bag in her hand and was stooping to pick up a suitcase with the hand she had used to open the door with.

"Allow me," I said, extending a hand. "That looks heavy."

She gave me one startled glance and dropped the suitcase and sat down on it and started to cry. She didn't cover her face with her hands or anything like that, she just burst.

I waited a minute for a lull. "Look," I said, "you're blocking the way in case anyone wants to come in or go out. Let's take these things—"

"You dirty—" The crying interfered with it. "You lousy—"

"No," I said firmly. "No, sister. You stood me up. You humiliated me." I picked up the traveling bag which she had also dropped. "Let's go."

"He's dead," she said. She wasn't bothering about small things like tears. "He's dead, ain't he? Hasn't anybody got any heart at all? The way I had to sit up there—sit there and pretend—" She stopped and chewed her lip, and all of a sudden she stood up and blazed at me. "Who are you, anyway? How did you know who I was? How did you get here so quick? You're a detective, that's what you are, you're a lousy detective—"

"No." I gripped her arm. "If you mean a city employee, no. My name is Archie Goodwin and I work for Nero Wolfe. My car's outside and I'm taking you up to Wolfe's place for a little conference. He's got one of the biggest hearts in the world, encased in a ton of blubber."

Of course she balked. She even defied me to call a cop, but then she started to cry again, and during that deluge I picked up the bag and suitcase and herded her out and across the street to the car. All the way up to 35th Street she cried and I had to lend her a handkerchief.

With my hands full of luggage, I had her precede me up the stoop and ring the bell for Fritz to let us in. He did so, and helped her off with her coat like a head waiter helping the Duchess of Windsor, one of the nicest things about Fritz being that to him anything in a skirt is a lady.

"Mr. Wolfe is at dinner," he announced.

"I'll bet he is. Take Miss Lasher to the office."

I took the luggage with me to the dining room, set it down against the wall, and approached the table. There he was, floating in clouds of bliss. He looked from the luggage to me.

"What's that? Those aren't your bags."

"No, sir," I agreed. "They are the property of an object I brought with me named Rose Lasher, who may help you hang onto those orchids. She is bereaved and hungry and I'm hungry. Shall I stay with her in the office—"

"Hungry? Bring her in here. There's plenty."

I went to the office and returned with her. She had stopped crying but sure was forlorn.

"Miss Lasher," I said, "this is Nero Wolfe. He never discusses business at the table, so we'll eat first and go into things later." I held a chair for her.

"I don't want to eat," she said in a thin voice. "I can't eat."

She ate seven sausages, which was nothing against her grief. Fritz's saucisse minuit would make Gandhi a gourmet.

Chapter 6

"And now," Wolfe demanded, "what is Miss Lasher here for?"

Dinner was over and we were settled in the office. Wolfe was seated behind his desk, leaning back with his fingers laced over his sausage mausoleum, his eyes half closed. I was at my desk, and Rose was in a red leather chair facing Wolfe. The set of her lips didn't indicate that the meal had made her one of us.

I recited particulars, briefly but completely.

"Indeed." Wolfe inclined his head a sixteenth of an inch. "Satisfactory, Archie." The head turned. "You must have a lot to tell, Miss Lasher. Tell it, please."

She looked sullen. "Tell what?"

"Start at the end. Where did you hide in that corridor from half past three to half past four and who and what did you see?"

"I didn't hide. I went out and went back and the second time I saw that man opening that door. Then I went—"

"No. That won't do. You were waiting to intercept Mr. Gould when he came out, and you hid. The police won't like it that you lied to them and gave them a false name and address and were running away. So I may not tell the police if you tell me the truth."

"I wasn't running away. I was merely going to visit a friend."

It was certainly a job to steam her off the envelope. She stuck for ten minutes in spite of all Wolfe said, and she didn't loosen up until after I brought the luggage from the dining room and went through it. I had to dig the keys out of her handbag, and at one point I thought she was going to start clawing and kicking, but finally she stopped squealing and only sat in the chair and made holes in me with her eyes.

I did it thoroughly and methodically. When I got through, the suitcase was nearly filled with female garments and accessories, mostly intimate, and piled on Wolfe's desk was a miscellaneous collection not so female. Shirts and ties, three photographs of Harry Gould, a bunch of snapshots, a bundle of letters tied with string, the top one addressed to Rose, various other items, among them a large Manila envelope fastened with a clasp.

I opened the envelope and extracted the contents. There were only two things in it and neither of them made my heart jump. One was a garage job-card with grease smears on it. At the top was printed, "Nelson's Garage, Salamanca, New York," and judging from the list of repairs required the car must have had an argument with a mountain. It was dated 4–11–40. The other item was sheets of printed matter. I unfolded them. They had been torn from the *Garden Journal*, which I would have recognized from the page and type without the running head, and the matter was an article entitled "Kurume Yellows in America" by Lewis Hewitt. I lifted the brows and handed it to Wolfe. Then my eye caught something I had missed on the garage job-card, something written in pencil on the reverse side. It was a name, "Pete Arango," and it was written in a small fine hand quite different from the scribbling on the face of the card. There was another sample of a similar small fine hand there in front of me, on the envelope at the top of the bundle addressed to Rose Lasher, and I untied the string and got out the letter and found that it was signed "Harry."

I passed the outfit to Wolfe and he looked it over.

He grunted. "This will interest the police." His eyes went to Rose. "Even more than your—"

"No!" she cried. She was wriggling. "You won't . . . oh, for God's sake, you mustn't—"

"Where did you hide in that corridor?"

She unloaded. She had hid in the corridor, yes, from the time I saw her there until some time after she had opened the door of the exhibit to look in. She had hid behind the packing cases and shrubs against the rear wall of the corridor. The sound of commotion had alarmed her, and she had sneaked out and gone to the main room and pushed into the crowd around the exhibit and I had returned her bag to her, which she had dropped without knowing it.

What and whom had she seen while hiding in the corridor?

Nothing. Maybe a few people, she didn't know who, passing by. Nothing and no one she remembered, except Fred Updegraff.

Of course she was lying. She must have seen Wolfe and Hewitt and me go by and me pick up the stick. The stick was there at the door that she was watching. And she must have seen someone leave the stick there, stoop down to pass the crook through the loop of the string, probably open the door to get hold of the loop which was ready inside, hidden among the foliage. But Wolfe was handicapped. He didn't dare mention the stick. That was out. But boy, did he want her to mention it, and incidentally mention who had walked in there with it and left it there?

Didn't he? He did. But she wouldn't. She was stuck

tight again, and I never saw Wolfe try harder and get nowhere. Finally he pulled the bluff of phoning Cramer, and even that didn't budge her. Then he gave up and rang for Fritz to bring beer.

At that point the phone rang and I answered it, and heard a familiar voice:

"Archie? Saul Panzer. May I speak to Mr. Wolfe?"

Wolfe took it on his phone, and I learned that during my absence he had got hold of Saul and sent him to the Flower Show. After getting a report he told Saul to drop the line he was on and come to the office. He hung up and leaned back and heaved a sigh, and regarded Rose with no sign of esteem.

"That," he said, "was a man I sent to collect facts about Mr. Gould. I'd rather get them from you. I'll allow you until tomorrow to jog your memory about what you saw in that corridor this afternoon, but you'll tell me about him now. We've got all night. How long had you known him?"

"About two years," she said sullenly.

"Are you his wife? His widow?"

She flushed and her lips tightened. "No. He said he wasn't the marrying kind. That's what he said."

"But he lived on Morrow Street with you?"

"No, he didn't. He only came there. He had a room in one of the houses on the Dill place on Long Island. No one ever knew about Morrow Street—I mean no one out there." She suddenly perked forward and her eyes flashed, and I was surprised at her spunk. "And no one's going to know about it! You hear that? Not while I'm alive they're not!"

"Do you have relatives on Long Island? Do your folks live there?"

"None of your business!"

"Perhaps not," Wolfe conceded. "I wouldn't want it to be. When and where did you meet Mr. Gould?"

She shut her mouth.

"Come," Wolfe said sharply. "Don't irritate me beyond reason. The next time I tell Mr. Goodwin to get Mr. Cramer on the phone it won't be a bluff."

She swallowed. "I was clerking in a store at Richdale and he—I met him there. That was nearly two years ago, when he was working at Hewitt's."

"Do you mean Lewis Hewitt's."

"Yes, the Hewitt estate."

"Indeed. What did he do there?"

"He was a gardener and he did some chauffeuring. Then he got fired. He always said he quit, but he got fired."

"When was that?"

"Over a year ago. Winter before last, it was. He was a good greenhouse man, and it wasn't long before he got another job at Dill's. That's about two miles the other side of Richdale. He went to live there in one of the houses."

"Did you live there with him?"

"Me?" She looked shocked and indignant. "I certainly didn't! I was living at home!"

"I beg your pardon. How long have you been living at the place on Morrow Street?"

She shut her mouth.

"Come, Miss Lasher. Even the janitor could tell me that."

"Look here," she said. "Harry Gould was no good. He never was any good. I knew that all the time. But the trouble is you get started, that's what makes the trouble, you get started and then you keep it up—even if I knew he was no good there was something about him. He always said he wasn't the marrying kind, but when he took me to that place on Morrow Street one day—that was last June, June last year—and said he had rented it, that looked like he wanted a home and maybe to get married after a while, so I quit my job and went there to live. That's how long

I've been living there, nine months. At first I was scared, and then I wasn't. There wasn't much money, but there was enough, and then I got scared again on account of the money. I didn't know where he got it."

The seam had ripped and the beans were tumbling out, and Wolfe sat back and let them come.

"He came there one night—he came four or five nights a week—that was one night in December not long before Christmas—and he had over a thousand dollars. He wouldn't let me count it, but it must have been, it might have been two or three thousand. He bought me a watch, and that was all right, but all the money did to me, it scared me. And he began to act different and he didn't come so often. And then about a month ago he told me he was going to get married."

Her lips went tight and after a moment she swallowed.

"Not to you," Wolfe said.

"Oh, no." She made a noise. "Me? Not so you could notice it. But he wouldn't tell me her name. And he kept having money. He didn't show it to me any more, but several times at night I looked in his pockets and he had a bankbook with over three thousand dollars in it and he always had a big roll of bills. Then yesterday I saw a picture of him in the paper, at the Flower Show with that girl. He hadn't said a word to me about it, not a word. And he hadn't been to Morrow Street for nearly a week, and he didn't come last night, so I went there today to see, and there he was in there with her. When I saw him in there with her I wanted to kill him, I tell you that straight, I wanted to kill him!"

"But you didn't," Wolfe murmured.

Her face worked. "I wanted to!"

"But you didn't."

"No," she said, "I didn't."

"But someone did." Wolfe's voice was silky. "He was

murdered. And naturally you are in sympathy with the effort to find the murderer. Naturally you intend to help—"

"I do not!"

"But my dear Miss Lasher—"

"I'm not your dear Miss Lasher." She leaned to him from the edge of the chair. "I know what I am, I'm a bum, that's what I am and I know it. But I'm not a complete dumbbell, see? Harry's dead, ain't he? Who killed him I don't know, maybe you did, or maybe it was that ten-cent Clark Gable there that thinks he's so slick he can slide uphill. Whoever it was, I don't know and I don't care, all I care about now is one thing, my folks aren't going to know anything about all this, none of it, and if it gets so I can't help it and they find out about it, all they'll have left to do with me is bury me."

She straightened up. "It's my honor," she said. "It's my family's honor."

Whether that came from the movies or wherever it came from, that's exactly what she said. I suspected the movies, considering her cheap crack about me being a ten-cent Clark Gable, which was ridiculous. He simpers, to begin with, and to end with no one can say I resemble a movie actor, and if they did it would be more apt to be Gary Cooper than Clark Gable.

Anyhow, that's what she said. And apparently she meant it, for although Wolfe went on patiently working at her he didn't get much. She didn't know why Harry had been fired from Hewitt's, or where his sudden wealth had come from, or why he had carefully saved that garage job-card, or why he had been interested in the Kurume yellows, which she had never heard of, and above all she couldn't remember anyone or anything she had seen while she was hiding in the corridor. Wolfe kept at her, and it looked as if she was in for a long hard night.

Around eleven o'clock an interruption arrived in the shape of Saul Panzer. I let him in and he went to the office. With one glance of his sharp gray eyes he added Rose to his internal picture gallery, which meant that she was there for good, and then stood there in his old brown suit—he never wore an overcoat—with his old brown cap in his hand. He looked like a relief veteran, whereas he owned two houses in Brooklyn and was the best head *and* foot detective west of the Atlantic.

"Miss Rose Lasher, Mr. Saul Panzer," Wolfe said. "Archie, get me the atlas."

I shrugged. One of his favorite ways of spending an evening was with the atlas, but with company there? Muttering, "Mine not to reason why," I took it to him, and sat down again while he went on his trip. Pretty soon he closed it and shoved it aside, and addressed Rose:

"Was Mr. Gould ever in Salamanca, New York?"

She said she didn't know.

"Those letters, Archie," Wolfe said.

I got the pile and gave him half and kept half for myself and ran through the envelopes. I was nearly at the bottom when Wolfe emitted a grunt of satisfaction.

"Here's a postcard he sent you from Salamanca on December 14th, 1940. A picture of the public library. It says, 'Will be back tomorrow or next day. Love and kisses. Harry.'"

"Then I guess he was there," Rose admitted sullenly.

"Archie, give Saul a hundred dollars." Wolfe handed Saul the postcard and the garage job-card. "Go to Salamanca. Take a plane to Buffalo and hire a car. Do you know what Harry Gould looked like?"

"Yes, sir."

"Note the dates—but I don't need to tell you. Go up there and get all you can. Phone me on arrival."

"Yes, sir. If necessary do I pay for it?"

Wolfe grimaced. "Within reason. I want all I can get. Make it two hundred, Archie."

I counted ten twenties into Saul's hand from the stack I got from the safe, and he stuffed it into his pocket and went, as usual, without any foolish questions.

Wolfe resumed with Rose, after ringing for beer. First he spent five minutes trying to get her to remember what Harry had gone to Salamanca for, or anything he had said to her about it, but that was a blank. No savvy Salamanca. Then he returned to former topics, but with a series of flanking movements. He discussed cooking with her. He asked about Harry's abilities and experience as a gardener, his pay, his opinion of Hewitt and Dill, his employers, his drinking habits and other habits.

I was busy getting it down in my notebook, but I certainly wasn't trembling with excitement. I knew that by that method, by the time dawn came Wolfe could accumulate a lot of facts that she wouldn't know he was getting, and one or two of them might even mean something, but among them would not be the thing we wanted most to know, what and who she had seen in the corridor. As it stood now we didn't dare to let the cops get hold of her even if we felt like it, for fear Cramer would open her up by methods of his own, and if he learned about the stick episode his brain might leap a barricade and spoil everything. And personally I didn't want to toss her to the lions anyhow, even after that Clark Gable crack.

It was a little after midnight when the doorbell rang again, and I went to answer it and got an unpleasant surprise. There on the stoop was Johnny Keems. I never resented any of the other boys being called in to work on a case, and I didn't actually resent Johnny either, only he gave me a pain in the back of my lap with his smirking around trying to edge in on my job. So I didn't howl with delight at sight of him, and then I nearly did howl, not with delight, when I saw he wasn't alone and what it was that kept him from being alone.

It was Anne Tracy standing behind him. And standing behind her was Fred Updegraff.

"Greetings," I said, concealing my emotions, and they all entered. And the sap said to her, "This way, Miss Tracy," and started for the office with her!

I stepped around and blocked him. "Some day," I said, "you'll skin your nose. Wait in the front room."

He smiled at me the way he does. I waited until all three of them had gone through the door to the front room and it had closed behind them, and then returned to the office and told Wolfe:

"I didn't know you had called out the army while I was gone. Visitors. The guy who wants my job and is welcome to it at any time, and my future wife, and the wholesome young fellow with the serious chin."

"Ah," Wolfe said. "That's like Johnny. He should have phoned." He grunted. He leaned back. His eyes rested on Rose an instant, then they closed, and his lips pushed out, and in, and out and in.

His eyes opened. "Bring them in here."

"But—" Rose began, starting from her chair.

"It's all right," he assured her.

I wasn't so darned sure it was all right, but it was him that wanted the black orchids, not me, so I obeyed orders, went to the front room by the connecting doors, and told them to come in. Johnny, who is a gentleman from his skin out, let Anne and Fred pass through ahead of him. She stopped in the middle of the room.

"How do you do," Wolfe said politely. "Forgive me for not rising; I rarely do. May I introduce—Miss Rose Lasher, Miss Anne Tracy. By the way, Miss Lasher has just been telling me that you were engaged to marry Mr. Gould."

"That's a lie," Anne said.

She looked terrible. At no time during the afternoon, when the turmoil had started or when Cramer had announced it was murder or when he had marched her out for examination, had she shown any sign of sag or yellow, but now she looked as if she had taken all she could. At least she did when she entered, and maybe that is why she reacted the way she did to Wolfe's statement and got rough.

"Marry Harry Gould?" she said. "That isn't true!" Her voice trembled with something that sounded like scorn but might have been anything.

Rose was out of her chair and was trembling all over. All right, I thought, Wolfe arranged for it and now he'll get it. She'll scratch Anne's eyes out. I moved a step. But she didn't. She even tried to control her voice.

"You bet it ain't true!" she cried, and that *was* scorn. "Harry wasn't marrying into *your* family! He wasn't marrying any daughter of a thief!"

Anne gawked at her.

Rose spat. "You with your stuckup nose! Why ain't your father in jail where he belongs? And you up there showing your legs like a ten-cent floozie—"

"Archie," Wolfe said sharply. "Take her upstairs."

Rose went on, not even hearing him. I got her suitcase in one hand and gripped her arm with the other and turned her around, and the idea of her nonmarrying Harry marrying another girl, in spite of his being dead, occupied her brain so that she kept right on spitting compliments without even knowing I was propelling her out of the room until we were in the hall. Then she went flat-footed and shut her mouth and glared at me.

"On up two flights," I said. "Or I know how to carry you so you can't bite." I still had her arm. "Up we go, sister."

She came. I took her into the spare room on the same

floor as mine, switched on the lights, and put her suitcase on a chair.

I pointed. "Ten-cent bathroom there. Ten-cent bed there. You won't be needed—"

She sat down on the bed and started to bawl.

I went down to the kitchen and told Fritz, "Lady guest in the south room. She has her own nightie, but would you mind seeing about towels and flowers in her room? I'm busy."

Chapter 7

Anne slept in my bed that night.

It went like this. When I got back to the office Anne was in my chair with her elbows on the desk and her hands covering her eyes. That was a favorite trick of Johnny's, putting someone else in my chair. He hadn't tried putting himself in it again since the day a couple of years back when I found him there looking at my notebook and sort of lost my temper.

Fred Updegraff was on a chair against the wall and Johnny was standing in front of Wolfe's desk. Evidently Wolfe had made some pointed remarks, for Johnny didn't look at all cocky.

"Yes, sir," he was saying in a hurt tone, "but the Tracys live in humble circumstances and have no phone, so I used my best judgment—"

"You were at the Tracy home? Where is it?"

"In Richdale, Long Island, sir. My instructions were to investigate Anne Tracy. I learned that she lives in Richdale, where the Dill nurseries and offices are. You know she works there—"

"I was aware of that. Be brief."

"Yes, sir. I went out to Richdale and made inquiries. I

contacted a young woman—as you know, I am especially effective with young women—-"

"Contact is not a verb and I said be brief."

"Yes, sir. The last time you told me that I looked it up in the dictionary and I certainly don't want to contradict you but it says contact is a verb. Transitive or intransitive."

"Contact is not a verb under this roof."

"Yes, sir. I learned that Miss Tracy's father had worked at Dill's for many years, up to about a year ago. He was assistant superintendent in charge of broad-leaved evergreens. Dill discovered he was kiting shipments and fired him."

"Kiting shipments?"

"Yes, sir. On shipments to a big estate in Jersey, the Cullen place. He would ship two hundred rhododendrons instead of one hundred and collect from Cullen for the extra hundred personally, at half price. It amounted to several thousand dollars."

Anne lifted her head and turned it and made a noise of protest.

"Miss Tracy says it was only sixteen hundred dollars," Johnny said. "I'm telling you what I was told. People exaggerate, and this never was made public, and Tracy wasn't arrested. He stole it to pay a specialist for fixing his son's eyes, something wrong with his son's eyes. He can't get another job. His daughter was Dill's secretary and still is. She gets fifty a week and pays back twenty on what her father stole, so I was told. She refuses to verify those figures."

Wolfe looked at Anne.

"It doesn't matter," Anne said, looking at me. "Does it?"

"I suppose not," Wolfe said, but if it's wrong, correct it."

"It's wrong. I get twenty dollars a week and I pay back ten."

"Good God," I blurted, "you need a union."

That was probably Freudian. Probably subconsciously I meant she needed a union with me. So I added hastily, "I mean a labor union. Twenty bucks a week!"

Johnny looked annoyed. He's a conservative. "So of course that gave me an in. I went to Miss Tracy's home and explained to her confidentially the hole she was in. That this murder investigation would put the police on to her father's crime, and that she and Dill were compounding a felony, which is against the law, and that the police would have to be fixed or they'd all be in jail, and there was only one man I knew of who could fix it because he was on intimate terms with high police officials, and that was Mr. Nero Wolfe. I said she'd better come and see you immediately, and she came. It was nearly eleven o'clock and there was no train in from Richdale, so we took a taxi."

Johnny shot me a glance, as much as to say, "Try and match that one."

"How far is it to Richdale?" Wolfe demanded.

"From here? Oh, twenty-five miles."

"How much was the taxi fare?"

"Eight dollars and forty cents counting the tip. The bridge—"

"Don't put it on expense. Pay it yourself."

"But—but, sir—Archie always brings people here—"

"Pay it yourself. You are not Archie. Thank God. One Archie is enough. I sent you to get facts, not Miss Tracy— certainly I didn't send you to coerce her with preposterous threats and fables about my relations with the police. Go to the kitchen—no. Go home."

"But, sir—"

"Go home. And for God's sake quit trying to imitate Archie. You'll never make it. Go home."

Johnny went.

Wolfe asked the guests if they would like some beer and they shook their heads. He poured a glass for himself, drank some, wiped his lips, and leaned back.

"Then—" Anne began, but it got caught on the way out. She cleared her throat and swallowed, and tried again. "Then what he said—you said his threat was preposterous. You mean the police won't do that—won't arrest my father?"

"I couldn't say, Miss Tracy. The police are unpredictable. Even so, that is highly improbable." Wolfe's eyes left her. "And you, Mr. Updegraff? By what bold stroke did Mr. Keems bring you along?"

"He didn't bring me." Fred stood up. "I came."

"By pure coincidence? Or automatism?"

Fred moved forward and put a hand on the back of my chair, which Anne was still sitting in. "I'm protecting Miss Tracy."

"Oh. From what?"

"From everything," he said firmly. He appeared to have a tendency to talk too loud, and he looked more serious than ever, and the more serious he looked the younger he looked. At that moment he might even have passed for Anne's younger brother, which was okay, since I had no objection if she wanted to be a sister to him.

"That's quite a job," Wolfe said. "Are you a friend of hers?"

"I'm more than a friend!" Fred declared defiantly. Suddenly he got as red as a peony. "I mean I—she let me take her home."

"You were there when Mr. Keems arrived?"

"Yes. We had just got there. And I insisted on coming along. It sounded to me like a frame-up. I thought he was lying; I didn't think he was working for you. It didn't sound—I've heard my father talk about you. He met you once—you probably don't remember—"

Wolfe nodded. "At the Atlantic States Exposition. How is he?"

"Oh, he's—not very good." Fred's color was normal again. "He gave up when we lost the plantation of rhodaleas—he just sat down and quit. He had spent his whole life on it, and of course it was an awful wallop financially too. I suppose you know about it."

"I read of it, yes. The Kurume yellows." Wolfe was sympathetic but casual. "And by the way, someone told me, I forget who, that your father was convinced that his plantation was deliberately infected by Lewis Hewitt, out of pique—or was it Watson or Dill he suspected?"

"He suspected all of them." Fred looked uncomfortable. "Everybody. But that was just—he was hardly responsible, it broke him up so. He had been holding back over thirty varieties, the best ones, for ten years, and was going to start distribution this spring. It was simply too much for Dad to take."

Wolfe grunted. "It seems to be still on your mind too. Mr. Goodwin tells me you invaded Rucker and Dill's exhibit this afternoon and made off with an infected twig. As a souvenir?"

"I—" Fred hesitated. "I guess that was dumb. Of course it's still on my mind—it darned near ruined us. I wanted to test that twig and see if it was Kurume yellows that had somehow got into the exhibits."

"And investigate the how?"

"I might have. I might have tried to."

"You never traced the infection of your plantation?"

"No. We hadn't had a thing for two years from any of the people that had had Kurume yellows, except a few Ilex crenata as a gift from Hewitt, and they were from no-where near his infected area and we had them half a mile from the rhodaleas." Fred gestured impatiently. "But that's old prunings. What I was saying, I didn't think you'd pull a trick like that on Miss Tracy." A look came into his eyes. "Now I can take her back home."

The look in his eye took me back to high school days. It was the hand-holding look. Flutter, my heart, bliss looms and ecstasy, I shall hold her little hand in mine! I looked at Anne with pride. A girl who could enkindle Lewis Hewitt to the extent of a black orchid and a dinner on Tuesday, and on Thursday forment the hand-holding hankering in a pure young peony-grower—a girl with a reach like that was something.

At that moment, I admit, she wasn't so overwhelming. She looked pretty dilapidated. She said to Wolfe, "I have to be at the District Attorney's office at ten in the morning. I said I would. I don't mind them asking me questions about that—what happened there today—but what I'm afraid of now, I'm afraid they'll ask me about my father. If they do, what am I going to say? Am I going to admit—" She stopped and her lip started to tremble and she put her teeth on it.

"You need a lawyer," Fred declared. "I'll get one. I don't know any in New York—"

"I do," Wolfe said. "Sit down, Mr. Updegraff." His eyes moved to Anne. "There's a bed here, Miss Tracy, and you'd better use it. You look tired. I doubt if the police will ask you about your father. If they do, don't answer. Refer them to Mr. Dill. They're much more apt to be inquisitive about your engagement to marry Mr. Gould."

"But I wasn't!"

"Apparently he thought you were."

"But he couldn't. He knew very well I didn't like him! And he—" She stopped.

"He what?"

"I won't say that. He's dead."

"Had he asked you to marry him?"

"Yes, he had."

"And you refused?"

"Yes."

"But you consented to perform that rustic charade at the Flower Show with him?"

"I didn't know he was going to be in it—not when Mr. Dill asked me to do it, about two months ago, when he first thought of it. It was going to be another man, a young man in the office. Then Mr. Dill told me Harry Gould was going to do it. I didn't like him, but I didn't want to object because I couldn't afford to offend—I mean Mr. Dill had been so kind about my father—not having him arrested and letting me pay it off gradually—"

"Call it kind if you want to," Fred blurted indignantly. "My lord, your father had worked for him for twenty years!"

Wolfe ignored him. "Was Mr. Gould pestering you? About marrying him?"

"Not pestering me, no. I was—" Anne bit her lip. "I just didn't like him."

"Had you known him long?"

"Not very long. I'm in the office and he was outside. I met him, I don't know, maybe three months ago."

"Did your father know him?"

She shook her head. "I don't think they ever met. Father was—had left before Harry came to work there. Harry used to work on the Hewitt estate on the other side of Richdale."

"So I understand. Do you know why he quit?"

"No, I didn't know him then."

"Have you any idea who killed him?"

"No," she said.

I lifted a brow, not ostentatiously. She said it too quick and she shaded it wrong. There was enough change in tempo and tone to make it at least ten to one that she was telling a whopper. That was bad. Up to that everything had been wholesome and straightforward, and all of a sudden without any warning that big fly plopped in the milk. I cocked an eye at Fred, and of course he hadn't caught it. But Wolfe had. His eyes had gone nearly shut.

He started after her. He kept it polite and friendly, but he went at her from every angle and direction. And for the second time that night he got the can sent back empty by a juvenile female. After a solid hour of it he didn't have even a hint of what it was she was keeping tucked away under her hair, whether it was a suspicion or a fact or a deduction she had made from a set of circumstances. Neither did I. But she was sitting on some kind of lid, and she was smart enough to see that Wolfe knew it and was trying to jostle her off.

It was half past one when Fred Updegraff looked at his watch and stood up again and said it was late and he would take Miss Tracy home.

Wolfe shook his head. "She's exhausted and it's twenty-five miles and there are no trains. She can sleep here. I want to speak to her in the morning before she goes to the District Attorney's office. Archie, will you please see that the north room is in order?"

That meant my room and my bed. Anne started to protest, but not with much spirit, and I went and got Fritz and took him upstairs with me to help change sheets and towels. As I selected a pajama suit for her from the drawer, tan with brown stripes, and put it on the turned down sheet, I reflected that things were moving pretty fast, considering that it was less than ten hours since she had first spoken to me and we never had actually been introduced. Fritz took my sheets and pillow and a blanket downstairs and I went up one flight to the plant rooms and cut three black orchids, one from each plant, and returned and put them in a vase on the bed table. Hewitt had given her one.

On my way downstairs I stopped at the door to the south room and listened. No sound. I tried the door; it was bolted on the inside. I knocked, not very loud. Rose's voice came:

"Who is it?"

"Clark Gable," I called. "Good night, Ruby."

In the lower hall I met Anne coming out of the office, escorted by Fritz. I suppose it would have been more genteel to take her up myself, but it would have been a temptation to get sentimental there among my own furniture, so I told her good night and let her go. In the office Wolfe was alone, in his chair with his arms folded and his chin down; evidently Fred had departed. I began taking cushions from the couch and tossing them into a corner, getting ready to fix my bed.

"Two of them," Wolfe growled.

"Two of what?"

"Women. Nannygoats."

"Not Anne. She's more like a doe. More like a gazelle."

"Bah."

"More like a swan." I flipped a sheet over the couch and tucked it in. "I put three black orchids at her bedside. One from each plant."

"I told Theodore to put them in the fumigating room."

"He did. That's where I found them." I spread the blanket. "I thought we might as well get all the pleasure we can put out of them before they're returned to Hewitt."

"They're not going to be returned."

"Oh, I expect they are." I hung my coat and vest over a chair and sat down to take off my shoes. "It seems a pity.

Two girls up there in bed, and if you knew what they know, or probably what either one of them knows, you'd have it sewed up. Rose actually saw the murderer set the trap. I don't know what Anne saw or heard, but she sure does. It's a darned shame. With all your finesse . . ." I got my pants off. ". . . all your extraordinary gifts . . ." I removed my shirt. ". . . all your acknowledged genius, your supreme talent in the art of inquest . . ."

He got up and stalked from the room without a word. I called a cheery good night after him but heard no reply, and after performing a few bedtime chores such as bolting the front door, I laid me down to sleep.

I overdid it. With the house full of company, I intended to be up and about bright and early, but when something jangled my brain alive and I realized it was the phone ringing, I opened my eyes and glanced at my wrist and saw it was after eight o'clock. It was Saul Panzer on the phone calling from Salamanca. I put him through to Wolfe's room and was told by Wolfe that no record would be required, which was his polite way of telling me to hang up, so I did. A trip to Fritz in the kitchen got me the information that Wolfe already had his breakfast tray, and so did Anne and Rose. I washed and dressed in a hurry, returned to the kitchen for my morning refreshment of grapefruit, ham and eggs, muffins and coffee, and was finishing my second cup when the doorbell rang. Fritz was upstairs at the moment, so I went for it, and through the glass panel saw it was Inspector Cramer, unattended.

The situation had aspects. Rose might come trotting downstairs any minute, and if she chose the minute that Cramer was in the hall, that would be the last we would see of Rose. But any delay in opening up would make Cramer suspicious. I swung the door open.

"Law and order forever," I said cordially. "Come in."

"Nuts," he said, entering.

So for that incivility I let him hang up his hat and coat himself. By the time he had done that I had the door closed and was on the other side of him. He screwed up his face at me and demanded:

"Where is she?"

Chapter 8

I grinned to the best of my ability. "Now wait a minute," I said in a grieved tone. "I've been up less than an hour and my brain's not warmed up. In the first place, how could I know she was married? In the second—"

He made a noise and moved. I moved, sort of backward. The maneuver ended with me covering the foot of the stairs, which was across the hall from the door to the office, and him pressing forward without actually touching me. There I stopped and he had to.

"I'm going up to see Wolfe," he said as if he meant it. "I am aware that he spends the morning with his goddamn posies and refuses to come down before eleven o'clock. So I'm going up. Stand aside."

He moved again and we made contact (noun), but I merely held it. "This," I said, "is pretty damn silly. I didn't have to let you in and you know it, but I did. What do you think this is, the den of the White Slave King? This is Nero Wolfe's home, and there's his office where he receives callers, and for last year his income tax was eleven thousand four hundred and twelve dollars and eighty-three cents and he paid it last week. Do you remember what happened the time Purley took me down and charged me with interfering with an officer in the performance of his duty? Wasn't that a picnic?"

He swung on his heel and tramped into the office. I followed, and shut the door, and stayed between him and it until he had sat down. Then, knowing I could move at least twice as fast as he could, I went to my desk.

"Now," I inquired pleasantly, "where is who?"

He regarded me with a mean eye. "Last night," he said, "one of Wolfe's men took Anne Tracy from her home in Richdale. My man covering the house recognized him and phoned in. I had a man out front when they arrived here. Your man soon left, and so did the Updegraff boy, later, but she hasn't left up to now. Where is she?"

So our little Rose was still safe. I locked my relief in my breast and looked crestfallen.

"I guess it's your trick, Inspector," I admitted. "Miss Tracy is upstairs in my bed. She spent the night there."

He got red. He's a terrible prude. "See here, Goodwin—"

"No no no no," I said hastily. "Rinse your mind out. I slept here on the couch. And I doubt if she's in my bed at that, because she's probably up and dressed. She has a date at the D.A.'s office at ten o'clock, and it's nine thirty now."

"Then you admit she's here."

"Admit it? I'm proud of it."

"Where is she, up with Wolfe?"

"I don't know. I got up late. I just finished breakfast."

"Find out. Tell her the appointment at the D.A.'s office is off. I want to see her as soon as I finish with you."

I plugged in the plant room extension and gave it a buzz. In a minute Wolfe's voice was in my ear:

"Archie? It's about time. Get Mr. Hewitt—"

"Hold it," I put in. "Reporting bad luck. Inspector Cramer is sitting here glaring at me. Johnny was spotted last night, and Miss Tracy is not to go to the D.A.'s office because Cramer wants to see her as soon as he gets through with me. He seems to be disgruntled about something."

"Does he know who slept in the south room?"

"I think not. I'm sure not."

"Very well. I'll attend to that. Miss Tracy is here with me. She can go down whenever. Mr. Cramer is ready for her. Get Mr. Hewitt on the phone."

"Right out loud?"

"Certainly."

I disconnected and told Cramer, "Miss Tracy is up helping with the orchids and will be available when wanted. Excuse me." I found Hewitt's Long Island number and requested it, and finally got him via two butlers and a secretary, and put him through to Wolfe. Then I swiveled around and crossed my legs and clasped my hands back of my head.

"Okay, Inspector. I'm disengaged for the moment. What shall we talk about?"

"Murder."

"Fine. Any particular murder?"

Cramer took a cigar from his pocket and put it in his mouth and took it out again. He was controlling himself. "I hand it to you," he said. "For barefaced lying I'd play you on the nose. Up there yesterday. You didn't know anyone or anything. But—" He put the cigar back in his mouth. "But you've been hanging around there all week. Every day. And then a man gets murdered and there you are. You *and* Nero Wolfe."

I nodded sympathetically. "I admit it looks sinister. But as I told you yesterday, Wolfe sent me there to look at orchids."

"There were no orchids in the Rucker and Dill exhibit."

"No, but there was—you know what there was. You've seen her. And I'm only a man after all—"

"All right, clown it. Yesterday afternoon about twenty minutes past four you were seen by young Updegraff, with Wolfe and Lewis Hewitt, in the corridor back of the Rucker and Dill exhibit. What were you doing there?"

"Well." I hesitated. "If I told you I was pulling the string that fired the shot that killed Harry Gould, would you believe me?"

"No."

"Then I won't. We were walking from one place to another place."

"You didn't mention yesterday that you were in that corridor at that time."

"Excuse it. Oversight."

"Maybe. What were you saying to Ruby Lawson yesterday?"

"Ruby—?" I frowned. "Oh. Her. You mean after I told Purley she was a Chinese spy. I was trying to date her up. You see, looking at Miss Tracy so much had aroused—"

"I'll bet it had. Did you date her?"

"Yes."

"When is it?"

"Not is it, was it. She didn't keep it."

"That's too bad. What was in the note Miss Tracy's father gave you to take to her?"

"Now, Inspector," I said reprovingly. "I didn't write the note and it wasn't addressed to me."

"Had you met her father before?"

"Never. Didn't know him from Adam."

"Wasn't it peculiar that he entrusted a perfect stranger with an important message to his daughter at a time like that?"

"Not very. He saw me entering the office. People trust me on sight. It's my face, especially my eyes."

"I see. That talk Wolfe had to have with Lewis Hewitt.

So important he had to have it then and there, murder or no murder."

Cramer chewed his cigar.

"Yes, sir," I said.

"So important he had to have you to take notes of it."

"Yes, sir."

"I'd like to see the notes you took."

I shook my head regretfully. "Sorry, confidential business. Ask Wolfe."

"I intend to. You won't show me the notes?"

"Certainly not."

"Very well. Now. Last but not least. Why did Wolfe send a man out to Richdale last night to get Anne Tracy?"

"Search me. I wasn't here when he sent him."

"Were you here when she came?"

"Yes."

"Well?"

I grinned at him. "When I was a kid out in Ohio we had a swell comeback for that. If someone said 'Well?' to you, you said, 'Enough wells will make a river.' Wasn't that a stunner?"

"You bet it was. Had Lewis Hewitt engaged Wolfe to arrange for payment to W. G. Dill of the amount Anne Tracy's father had stolen, and get a release?"

I stared at him. "By golly, that's an idea," I said enthusiastically. "That's pretty cute. Hewitt took her to dinner—"

The door opened and Fritz entered. I nodded at him.

"A young man," Fritz said, being discreet.

"Who?" I asked. "Don't mind the Inspector; he already knows everything in the world—"

Fritz didn't get a chance to tell me, because the young man came bouncing in. It was Fred Updegraff. He stopped in the middle of the room, saw Cramer, said, "Oh," looked at me and demanded:

"Where's Miss Tracy?"

I surveyed him disapprovingly. "That's no way to behave," I told him. "Inspector Cramer is grilling me. Go to the front room and wait your turn—"

"No." Cramer stood up. "Get Miss Tracy down here and I'll take her to the front room. I want to see her before I have a talk with Wolfe, and then we can all go to the D.A.'s office together."

"The hell we can," I remarked.

"The hell we can. Send for her."

I sent Fritz. He used the elevator, since a lady was involved. In the office you could hear it creaking and groaning up, and pretty soon it came down again and jolted to a stop. When Anne entered Fred looked at her the way a blind man looks at the sun. I hoped I wasn't that obvious, and anyway she wasn't very sunny. She tried to greet us with a kind of smile, but with the red-rimmed eyes and the corners of the mouth down it certainly wasn't the face that had stolen the show from a million flowers.

Cramer took her to the front room and shut the sound-proof door behind him. I went to my desk and took advantage of this first chance to open the morning mail. Fred wandered around restlessly, looking at the titles of books on the shelves, and finally sat down and lit a cigarette.

"Am I in the way?" he asked.

"Not at all," I assured him.

"Because if I am I can wait outdoors. Only I got a little chilly. I've been out there since eight o'clock."

I abandoned the mail to swivel around and stare at him in awe.

"Good God," I said, stupefied. "You win." I waved a hand. "You can have her."

"Have her?" He flushed. "What are you talking about? Who do you think you are?"

"Brother," I said, "who I am can be left to the worms

that eventually eat me, but I know who I am not. I am not a guy who swims the Hellespont, nor him who—he who flees the turmoil of battle to seek you know what on the silken cushions of Cleopatra's barge. I'm not the type—"

The phone rang and I put the receiver to my ear and heard Wolfe's voice: "Archie, come up here."

"Right away," I said, and arose and asked Fred, "Which do you want, whisky or hot coffee?"

"Coffee, if it's not—"

"Righto. Come with me."

I turned him over to Fritz in the kitchen and mounted the three flights to the plant rooms. It was a sunny day and some of the mats were drawn, but mostly the glass was clear, especially in the first two rooms, and the glare and blaze of color was dazzling. In the long stretch where the germinating flasks were, of course the glass was painted. Theodore Horstmann was there examining the flasks. I opened the door into the potting room, and after taking one step stopped and sniffed. My nose is good and I knew that odor. One glance at Wolfe there on his special stool, which is more like a throne, showed me that he was alive, so I dived across to the wall and grabbed the valve to turn it. It was shut tight.

"What's the matter?" Wolfe inquired peevishly.

"I smelled ciphogene. I still do."

"I know. Theodore fumigated those plants a little while ago and opened the door too soon. There's not enough to do any harm."

"Maybe not," I muttered, "but I wouldn't trust that stuff on top of the Empire State Building on a windy day." The door to the fumigating room was standing open and I glanced inside. The benches were empty, as well as I could tell in the half dark. It had no glass. The smell didn't seem any stronger inside. I returned to Wolfe.

"How's Mr. Cramer?" he asked. "Stewing?"

I looked at him suspiciously. His asking that, and the tone of his voice, and the expression on his face—any one would have been enough for me the way I knew him, and the three together made it so obvious that the only question was how he got that way.

I confronted him. "Which one did you crack?" I demanded. "Rose or Anne?"

"Neither," he replied complacently. "I had an hour's talk with Miss Lasher while you were still sleeping, and later some conversation with Miss Tracy. They still clutch their secrets. When Mr. Hewitt—"

"Then where did you lap up all the cream? What are you gloating about?"

"I'm not gloating." He cocked his massive head on one side and rubbed his nose with a forefinger. "It is true that I have conceived a little experiment."

"Oh, you have. Goody. Before or after Cramer carts us off to the D.A.'s office?"

Wolfe chuckled. "Is that his intention? Then it must be before. Is Miss Tracy with him?"

"Yes. The youthful Updegraff is in the kitchen. He's going to marry Anne provided your experiment doesn't land him in the coop for murder."

"I thought you were affianced to Miss Tracy."

"That's off. If I married her he'd stand around in front of the house and make me nervous. He's started it already."

"Well, that saves us the trouble of sending for him. Keep him. When Mr. Hewitt arrives send him up to me immediately. Go down and get Mr. Dill on the phone and put him through to me. On your way make sure that Miss Lasher is in her room and going to stay there and not have hysterics. Except for Mr. Dill, and Mr. Hewitt when he comes, don't disturb me. I have some details to work out. And by the way, do not mention ciphogene."

His tone and look of smug self-satisfaction were absolutely insufferable. Not only that, as I well knew, they were a sign of danger for everyone concerned. When he was in that mood God alone could tell what was going to happen.

I went back through the plant rooms to the door to the stairs with my fingers crossed.

Chapter 9

It was nearly an hour later, 11:45, and I was alone in the office, when the door to the front room opened and Anne and Cramer entered. She looked mad and determined, and Cramer didn't appear to be exactly exultant, so I gathered that no great friendship had burst its bud.

"Where's Updegraff?" Cramer asked.

"Upstairs."

"I want to see Wolfe."

I buzzed the house phone, got an answer, held a brief conversation, and told the Inspector:

"He says to come up. Hewitt and Dill are up there."

"I'd rather see him down here."

That irritated me, and anyway I was already jumpy, waiting for Wolfe's experiment to start exploding. "My God," I said, "you're fussy. On arrival you insist on going upstairs right through me or over me. Now you have to be coaxed. If you want him down here go up and get him."

He turned. "Come, Miss Tracy, please."

She hesitated. I said, "Fred's up there. Let's all go."

I led the way and they followed. I took the elevator because the stairway route went within ten feet of the door to the south room and Rose might pick that moment to sneeze.

I was half expecting to see one of the peony-growers tied up and the other three applying matches to his bare feet, but not at all. We single-filed through twenty thousand orchids in the four plant rooms and entered the potting room, and there they were in the fumigating room, with the lights turned on, chatting away like pals. In the potting room Theodore was sloshing around with a hose, washing old pots.

"Good morning, Mr. Cramer!" Wolfe called. "Come in!"

Theodore was so enthusiastic with the hose that spray was flying around, and we all stepped into the fumigating room. Fred and Dill were there, seated on the lower tier of a staggered bench, and Wolfe was showing Hewitt a sealed joint in the wall. He was leaning on the handle of an osmundine fork, like a giant shepherd boy resting on his staff, and was expounding with childish enthusiasm:

". . . so we can stick them in here and close the door, and do the job with a turn of the valve I showed you in the potting room, and go on with our work outside. Twice a year at the most we do the whole place, and we use ciphogene for that, too. It's a tremendous improvement over the old methods. You ought to try it."

Hewitt nodded. "I think I will. I've been tempted to, but I was apprehensive about it, such deadly stuff."

Wolfe shrugged. "Anything you use is dangerous. You can't kill bugs and lice and eggs and spores with incense. And the cost of installation is a small item, unless you include a sealed chamber, which I would certainly advise—"

"Excuse *me*," Cramer said sarcastically.

Wolfe turned. "Oh, yes, you wanted to speak to me." He sidled around the end of a bench, sat down on a packing box, gradually giving it his weight, and kept himself upright with nothing to lean against, holding the osmundine fork perpendicular, with the handle-end resting on the floor, like Old King Cole with his scepter. He simpered at the Inspector, if an elephant can simper.

"Well, sir?"

Cramer shook his head. "I want you and Goodwin and Miss Tracy. So does the District Attorney. At his office."

"You don't mean that, Mr. Cramer."

"And why the hell—why don't I mean it?"

"Because you know I rarely leave my home. Because you know that citizens are not obligated to regulate their movements by the caprice of the District Attorney or to dart around frantically at your whim. We've had this out before. Have you an order from a court?"

"No."

"Then if you have questions to ask, ask them. Here I am."

"I can get an order from a court. And the D.A. is sore and probably will."

"We've had that out before, too. You know what you'll get if you try it." Wolfe shook his head regretfully. "Apparently you'll never learn. Confound you, you can't badger me. No one on earth can badger me except Mr. Goodwin. Why the devil do you rile me by trying it? It's a pity, because I'm inclined to help you. And I could help you. Do you want me to do you a favor?"

If the man who knew Wolfe best was me, next to me came Inspector Cramer. Over and over again through the years, he tried bluster because it was in his system and had to come out, but usually he knew when to drop it. So after narrowing his eyes at Wolfe without answering, he kicked a packing box a couple of feet to where there was more leg room, sat down and said calmly:

"Yeah, I'd love to have you do me a favor."

"Good, Archie, bring Miss Lasher up here."

I went. On my way downstairs I thought, so here she

goes to the wolves. I didn't like it. I wasn't especially fond of her, but my pride was hurt. It wasn't like Wolfe; it wasn't like us at all.

She was standing looking out of a window, biting her nails. The minute she saw me she started on a torrent. She couldn't stand it any longer, cooped up like that, she had to get out of there, she had to use a telephone—

"Okay," I said, "come up and say good-bye to Wolfe."

"But where am I going—what am I doing—"

"Discuss it with him."

I steered her up the one flight and through to the potting room. I had left the door to the fumigating room nearly closed so she couldn't see the assemblage until she was on the threshold, and as I opened it and ushered her in I took a better hold on her arm as a precaution in case she decided to go for Wolfe's eyes as souvenirs. But the reaction was the opposite of what I expected. She saw Cramer and went stiff. She stood stiff three seconds and then turned her head to me and said between her teeth:

"You lousy bastard."

They all stared at her.

Especially Cramer. Finally he spoke not to her but to Wolfe, "This is quite a favor. Where did you get her?"

"Sit down, Miss Lasher," Wolfe said.

"You might as well," I told her. "It's a party."

Her face white and her lips tight, she went and dropped onto a bench. The others were all sitting on benches or packing boxes.

"I told you this morning," Wolfe said, "that unless you told me what you saw in that corridor I would have to turn you over to the police."

She didn't say anything and didn't look as if she intended to.

"So, your name's Lasher," Cramer growled. "You might as well—"

"I think," Wolfe put in, "I can save you some time. Details can be supplied later. Her name is Rose Lasher. Yesterday at the Flower Show she saw Miss Tracy and Mr. Gould in Mr. Dill's exhibit. She wished to discuss an extremely important matter with Miss Tracy, so—"

"With me?" It popped out of Anne. She looked indignant. "There was nothing she could possibly—"

"Please, Miss Tracy." Wolfe was peremptory. "This will go better without interruptions. So, to intercept Miss Tracy on her exit, Miss Lasher found her way to the corridor and hid among the shrubs and packing cases along the rear wall opposite the door labeled 'Rucker and Dill.' That was at or about half past three. She remained concealed there until after half past four, and she was watching that door. Therefore she must have seen whatever went on there during that hour or more."

There were stirrings and sounds, then silence, except for the hissing of Theodore's hose in the potting room and the slapping and sloshing of the water against the pots. Wolfe told me to shut the door, and I did so, and then sat on the bench next to W. G. Dill.

"Okay," Cramer said dryly, "details later. What did she see?"

"She prefers not to say. Will you tell us now, Miss Lasher?"

Rose's eyes moved to him and away again, and that was all.

"Sooner or later you will," Wolfe declared. "Mr. Cramer will see to that. He can be—persuasive. In the meantime, I'll tell you what you saw, at least part of it. You saw a man approach that door with a cane in his hand. He was furtive, he kept an eye on the corridor in both directions, and he was in a hurry. You saw him open the door and close it again, and kneel or stoop, doing something with his hands, and when he went away he left the cane there on the floor, its crook against the crack at the bottom of the door. You saw that, didn't you?"

Rose didn't even look at him.

"Very well. I don't know what time that happened, except that it was between four and four-twenty. Probably around four o'clock. The next episode I do know. At twenty minutes past four you saw three men come along the corridor. They saw the cane and spoke about it. One of them picked it up, brushed a loop of green string from the crook, and handed it to one of the others. I don't know whether you saw the string or not. I'm certain that you didn't know that it was part of a longer string that had been tied to the trigger of a revolver, and that by picking up the cane the man had fired the revolver and killed Harry Gould. Nor did you know their names, though you do now. Mr. Goodwin picked up the cane and handed it to Mr. Hewitt. The man with them was myself."

Wolfe took something from his vest pocket, with his left hand, because his right was holding the osmundine fork for support. "Here's the piece of string that was looped on the cane. Not that I would expect you to identify it. I may as well say here that the cane was handed to Mr. Hewitt because it was his property."

He handed the string to Cramer.

I was sunk. Ordinarily, in such circumstances, I would have been watching faces and movements, and hearing what sounds were made or words blurted, but this time he had me. He looked as if he was in his right mind, with all the assured arrogance of Nero Wolfe salting away another one, but either he was cuckoo or I was. He was not only spilling the beans; he was smashing the dish. In any conceivable case it was good-bye orchids. I looked at Hewitt.

And Hewitt should have been half astonished and half sore, and he wasn't. He was pale, and he was trying to pretend he wasn't pale. He was staring at Wolfe, and he licked his lips—the end of his tongue came out and went in, and then came out again.

Uh-uh, I thought. So that's it. But my God, then—

Cramer was looking at the string. W. G. Dill asked, "May I see it?" and held out a hand, and Cramer gave it to him but kept his eyes on it.

"Of course," Wolfe said, "the point is, not who picked the cane up, but who put it there. Miss Lasher, who saw him do it, could tell us but prefers not to. She claims she didn't see him. So we'll have to get at it by indirection. Here are some facts that may help—but it isn't any too comfortable in here. Shall we move downstairs?"

"No," Hewitt said. "Go ahead and finish."

"Go ahead," Cramer said. He reached for the string and Dill handed it to him and he stuffed it in his pocket.

"I'll make it as brief as possible," Wolfe promised. "Harry Gould had an employer. One day he found a garage job-card in one of his employer's cars—possibly it had slipped under a seat and been forgotten—I don't know. Anyhow he found it and he kept it. I don't know why he kept it. He may have suspected that his employer had been on a trip with a woman, for the card was from a garage in Salamanca, New York, which is quite a distance from Long Island. A man with the blackmailing type of mind is apt to keep things. It is understandable that he kept the card. It is less understandable that his employer had been careless enough to leave it in the car." Wolfe turned his head suddenly and snapped at Hewitt:

"Was it just an oversight, Mr. Hewitt?"

But Hewitt had stuff in him at that. He was no longer pale and he wasn't licking his lips. His eyes were steady and so was his voice:

"Finish your story, Mr. Wolfe. I am inclined—but no matter. Finish your story."

"I prefer to use your name instead of clumsy circumlocutions like 'his employer.' It's neater."

"By all means keep it neat. But I warn you that merely because I acknowledged ownership of that cane—"

"Thank you. I appreciate warnings. So I'll say Hewitt hereafter. The time came when Harry Gould's suspicions regarding the card became more definite. Again I don't know why, but my surmise is that he learned about the loss of the most valuable plantation of broad-leaved evergreens in the country—the rhodalea plantation of the Updegraff Nurseries of Erie, Pennsylvania—by an attack of the Kurume yellows. He knew that Hewitt was inordinately proud of his own broad-leaved evergreens, and that he was capable of abnormal extremes in horticultural pride and jealousy. He also, being a gardener, knew how easy it would be, with a bag or two of contaminated peat mulch, to infect another plantation if you had access to it. At any rate, his suspicion became definite enough to cause him to go to Salamanca, which is in the western part of New York near the Pennsylvania border, not far from Erie, and see the proprietor of the Nelson Garage. That was in December. He learned that when Hewitt had gone there with his car months before, damaged in an accident, he had been accompanied not by a woman, but by a man of a certain description, with a cast in his eye. He went to Erie and found the man among the employees of the Updegraff Nurseries. His name was Pete Arango."

Fred Updegraff started up with an ejaculation.

Wolfe showed him a palm. "Please, Mr. Updegraff, don't prolong this." He turned. "And Mr. Hewitt, I'm being fair. I'm not trying to stampede you. I admit that much of this detail is surmise, but the main fact will soon be established beyond question. I sent a man to Salamanca last night, partly to learn why Harry Gould had so carefully preserved an old garage job-card, and partly because he had written on the back of it that name Pete Arango, and I knew that Pete Arango was in the employ of the Updegraff Nurseries. My man phoned me this morning to say that he will be back here at one o'clock, and the proprietor of the Nelson Garage will be with him. He'll tell us whether you were there with Pete Arango. Do you suppose you'll remember him?"

"I'll—" Hewitt swallowed. "Go ahead."

Wolfe nodded. "I imagine you will. I wouldn't be surprised if Gould even got a written confession from Pete Arango that you had bribed him to infect the rhodalea plantation, by threatening to inform Mr. Updegraff that he had been at Salamanca, not far away, in your company. At least he got something that served well enough to put the screws on you. You paid him something around five thousand dollars. Did he turn the confession over to you? I suppose so. And then—may I hazard a guess?"

"I think," Hewitt said evenly, "you've done too much guessing already."

"I'll try one more. Gould saw Pete Arango at the Flower Show, and the temptation was too much for him. He threatened him again, and made him sign another confession, and armed with that made another demand on you. What this time? Ten thousand? Twenty? Or he may even have got delusions of grandeur and gone to six figures. Anyhow, you saw that it couldn't go on. As long as ink and paper lasted for Pete Arango to write confessions with, you were hooked. So you—by the way, Mr. Updegraff, he's up there at your exhibit, isn't he, and available? Pete Arango? We'll want him when Mr. Nelson arrives."

"You're damn right he's available," Fred said grimly.

"Good."

Wolfe's head pivoted back to Hewitt. He paused, and the silence was heavy on us. He was timing his climax, and just to make it good he decorated it.

"I suppose," he said to Hewitt in a tone of doom, "you are familiar with the tradition of the drama? The three traditional knocks to herald the tragedy?"

He lifted the osmundine fork and brought it down again, thumping the floor with it, once, twice, thrice.

Hewitt gazed at him with a sarcastic smile, and it was a pretty good job with the smile.

"So," Wolfe said, "you were compelled to act, and you did so promptly and effectively. And skillfully, because, for instance, Mr. Cramer has apparently been unable to trace the revolver, and no man in the world is better at that sort of thing. As Honorary Chairman of the Committee, naturally you had the run of the exhibit floors at any hour of the day; I suppose you chose the morning, before the doors were opened to the public, to arrange that primitive apparatus. I don't pretend to be inside of your mind, so I don't know when or why you decided to use your own cane as the homicide bait for some unsuspecting passer-by. On the theory that—"

The door opened and Theodore Horstmann was on the threshold.

"Phone call for Mr. Hewitt," he said irritably. Theodore resented his work being interrupted by anything whatever. "Pete Arando or something?"

Hewitt stood up.

Cramer opened his mouth, but Wolfe beat him to it by saying sharply, "Wait! You'll stay here, Mr. Hewitt! Archie—no, I suppose he would recognize your voice. Yours too, Mr. Cramer. Mr. Dill. You can do it if you pitch your voice low. Lead him on, get him to say as much as you can—"

Hewitt said, "That phone call is for me," and was moving for the door. I got in front of him. Dill arose, looking uncertain.

"I don't know whether I can—"

"Certainly you can," Wolfe assured him. "Go ahead. The phone is there on the potting bench. Theodore, confound it, let him by and come in here and close the door."

Theodore obeyed orders. When Dill had passed through Theodore pulled the door shut and stood there resenting us. Hewitt sat down again and put his elbows on his knees and covered his face with his hands. Anne had her head turned not to look at him. That made her face Fred Updegraff, who was next to her, and I became aware for the first time that he was holding her hand. Hardly as private as in a taxi, but he had her hand.

"While we're waiting," Wolfe observed, "I may as well finish my speculations about the cane. Mr. Hewitt may have decided to use it on the theory that the fact of its being his cane would divert suspicion away from him instead of toward him. Was that it, Mr. Hewitt? But in that case, why did you submit to my threat to divulge the fact that it was your cane? I believe I can answer that too. Because you mistrusted my acumen? Because you were afraid my suspicions would be aroused if you failed to conform to the type of the eminent wealthy citizen zealously guarding his reputation from even the breath of scandal? Things like that gather complications as they go along. It's too bad."

Wolfe looked at Hewitt, and shook his head as though regretfully. "But I have no desire to torment you. Theodore, try the door."

"I don't have to," Theodore said, standing with his back to the door. "I heard the bolt. The lower one squeaks."

I stood up. Not that there was anything I intended to do or could do, but I was coming to in a rush and I couldn't stay sitting. Cramer did, but his eyes, on Wolfe, were nothing but narrow slits.

"Try it anyway," Wolfe said quietly.

Theodore turned and lifted the latch and pushed, and turned back again. "It's bolted."

"Indeed," Wolfe said with a tingle in his voice. His head turned. "Well, Miss Lasher, what do you think of it?" His eyes swept the faces. "I ask Miss Lasher because she knew all along that I was lying. She knew it couldn't have been Mr. Hewitt who put that cane there on the floor of the corridor, because she saw Mr. Dill do it. Mr. Hewitt, let me congratulate you on a superb performance—you can't force it, Mr. Cramer, it's a sturdy door—"

Cramer was at it, lifting the latch, assaulting the panel with his shoulder. He turned, his face purple, blurted, "By God, I might have known—," jumped across and grabbed up a heavy packing-box.

"Archie!" Wolfe called sharply.

In all my long and varied association with Inspector Cramer I had never had an opportunity to perform on him properly. This, at last, was it. I wrapped myself around him like cellophane around a toothbrush and turned on the pressure. For maybe five seconds he wriggled, and just as he stopped Fred Updegraff sprang to his feet and gasped in horror:

"Ciphogene! For God's sake—"

"Stop it!" Wolfe commanded. "I know what I'm doing! There is no occasion for panic. Mr. Cramer, there is an excellent reason why that door must not be opened. If Archie releases you, will you listen to it? No? Then, Archie, hold him. This is a fumigating room where we use ciphogene, a gas which will kill a man by asphyxiation in two minutes. The pipe runs from a tank in the potting room and the valve is in there. This morning I closed the outlet of the pipe in this room, and removed the plug from an outlet in the potting room. So if Mr. Dill has opened that valve in the potting room, he is dead, or soon will be. And if you batter a hole in that door I won't answer for the consequences. We might get out quickly enough and we might not."

"You goddamn balloon," Cramer sputtered helplessly. It was the first and only time I ever heard him cuss in the presence of ladies.

I unwrapped myself from him and stepped back. He shook himself and barked at Wolfe:

"Are you going to just sit there? Are we going to just sit here? Isn't there—can't you call someone—"

"I'll try," Wolfe said placidly. He lifted the osmundine fork and thumped the floor with it, five times, at regular intervals.

Lewis Hewitt murmured, believe it or not, apparently to Theodore, "I was in the dramatic club at college."

Chapter 10

"All right, I'll buy you a medal," Inspector Cramer said in utter disgust.

Five hours had passed. It was six thirty that evening, and the three of us were in the office. I was at my desk, Cramer was in the red leather chair, and Wolfe was seated behind his own desk, leaning back with his fingertips touching on top of his digestive domain. He looked a little creasy around the eyes, which were almost open.

Cramer went on sputtering: "Dill was a murderer, and he's dead, and you killed him. You maneuvered him into the potting room with a fake phone call, and he took the bait and bolted the door to the fumigating room and opened the valve. And then why didn't he walk out and go home? How did you know he wouldn't do that?"

"Pfui," Wolfe said lazily. He grunted. "Without waiting four minutes to make sure the ciphogene had worked? And leaving the door bolted, and the valve open? Mr. Dill was a fool, but not that big a fool. After a few minutes he would have closed the valve and opened the door, held his nose long enough to take a look at us and make sure we were finished, and departed, leaving the door closed but not bolted to give it the appearance of an accident. And probably leaving the valve a bit loose so it would leak a little." Wolfe grunted again. "No. That wasn't where the thin ice was. It was next thing to a certainty that Mr. Dill wouldn't decamp without having a look inside at us."

"You were sure of that."

"I was."

"You admit it."

"I do."

"Then you murdered him."

"My dear sir." Wolfe wiggled a finger in exasperation. "If you are privately branding me to relieve your feelings, I don't mind. If you are speaking officially, you are talking gibberish. I could be utterly candid even to a jury, regarding my preparations. I could admit that I plugged the outlet in the fumigating room, and opened the one in the potting room, so that it would be the latter, and not the former, that would be filled with ciphogene if Mr. Dill bolted that door and opened that valve. I could admit that I arranged with Mr. Hewitt to play his part, appealing to him in the interest of justice. He is a public-spirited man. And I discovered his weakness; he has always wanted to be an actor. He even gave me permission to mention his cane, and to recite that wild tale about him—which of course was true, though not true about him, but about Mr. Dill.

"I could admit that I arranged with Theodore also to play his part. He works for me and obeyed orders. I could admit that I had Fritz stationed in the room below, and my three thumps on the floor were a signal to him to make the telephone call for Mr. Hewitt, and the five thumps, later, told him to come upstairs and start the ventilating blowers in the potting room, which can be done from the hall. I could admit that I deliberately postponed the second signal to Fritz for three minutes after I learned that the door had been bolted; that I had previously released a minute quantity of ciphogene in the potting room and fumigating room so that Mr. Dill's nose would be accustomed to the smell and would not take alarm at any sudden odor in the potting room after he turned on the valve; that all my arrangements were made with the idea that if Mr. Dill should open that valve, thinking to murder all eight of us, he would die, I could admit all that to a jury."

Wolfe sighed. "But the fact would remain that Mr. Dill opened the valve of his own volition, intending to exterminate eight people, including you. No jury would find against me even for damage to your self-esteem."

"To hell with my self-esteem," Cramer growled. "Why don't you send a bill to the State of New York for the execution of a murderer f.o.b. your potting room? That's the only thing you've left out. Why don't you?"

Wolfe chuckled. "I wonder if I could collect. It's worth trying. I may tell you privately, Mr. Cramer, that there were several reasons why it would have been unfortunate for Mr. Dill to be brought to trial. One, it might have been difficult to convict him. Only a fairly good case. Two, the part played by Mr. Hewitt's cane would have been made public, and I had undertaken to prevent that. Three, Archie would have been embarrassed. He pulled the trigger and killed the man. Four, Miss Lasher would have committed suicide, or tried to. She's not very bright, but she's stubborn as the devil. She had decided that if she admitted having seen anything from her hiding-place in the corridor, she would have to testify to it publicly, her relations with Mr. Gould would have been exposed, and her family would have been dishonored."

"They would have been exposed anyway."

"Certainly, once you got hold of her. When Archie brought her to the potting room, with you there, she was a goner. That was the beauty of it. Mr. Dill knew she was bound to crack, and that coupled with the threat of being confronted with the garage man was what cracked him. It was a delicate situation. Among many others was the danger that during my recital Miss Lasher might blurt out that it was Dill, not Hewitt, who had placed the cane there by the door, and that would have spoiled everything."

"Wasn't it Hewitt's cane?"

"Yes. A fact as I have told you, not for publication."

"Where did Dill get it?"

"I don't know. Hewitt had mislaid it, and no doubt Dill spied it and decided to make use of it. By the way, another item not for publication is Miss Lasher's statement. Don't forget you promised that. I owe it to her. If she hadn't included that garage job-card when she packed Mr. Gould's belongings in her suitcase I wouldn't have got anywhere."

"And another thing," I put in. "A public airing of the little difficulty Miss Tracy's father got into wouldn't get you an increase in salary."

"Nothing in God's world would get me an increase in salary," Cramer declared feelingly. "And Miss Tracy's father—" He waved it away.

Wolfe's eyes came to me. "I thought you were no longer affianced to her."

"I'm not. But I'm sentimental about my memories. My lord, but she'll get sick of Fred. Peonies! Incidentally, while you're sweeping up, what was Annie's big secret?"

"Not so big." Wolfe glanced up at the clock, saw that it would be nearly an hour till dinner, and grimaced. "Miss Tracy admitted the soundness of my surmises this morning. Mr. Gould was as devious as he was ruthless. He told her that unless she married him he would force Mr. Dill to have her father arrested, and assured her that he had it in his power to do that. He also spoke of large sums of money. So naturally, when he was murdered Miss Tracy suspected that Mr. Dill was concerned in it, but she refused to disclose her suspicions for obvious reasons—the fear of consequences to her father."

Wolfe put his fingertips together again. "It is surprising that Mr. Gould lived as long as he did, in view of his character. He bragged to Miss Lasher that he was going to marry another girl. That was silly and sadistic. He let Miss Tracy know that he had a hold on Mr. Dill. That was rashly indiscreet. He even infected the Rucker and Dill exhibit with Kurume yellows, doubtless to dramatize the pressure he was exerting on Dill for his big haul—at least I presume he did. That was foolish and flamboyant. Of course Dill was equally foolish when he tried to engage me to investigate the Kurume yellows in his exhibit. He must have been unbalanced by the approaching murder he had arranged for, since bravado was not in his normal character. I suppose he had a hazy idea that hiring me to investigate in advance would help to divert suspicion from him. He really wasn't cut out for a murderer. His nerves weren't up to it."

"Yours are." Cramer stood up. "I've got to run. One thing I don't get, Dill's going clear to Pennsylvania to bribe a guy to poison some bushes. I know you spoke about extremes in horticultural jealousy, but have they all got it? Did Dill have it too?"

Wolfe shook his head. "I was then speaking of Mr. Hewitt. What Mr. Dill had was a desire to protect his investment and income. The prospect of those rhodaleas appearing on the market endangered the biggest department of his business." He suddenly sat up and spoke in a new tone. "But speaking of horticultural jealousy—I had a client, you know. I collected a fee in advance. I'd like to show it to you. Archie, will you bring them down, please?"

I was tired after all the hubbub and the strain of watching Wolfe through another of his little experiments, but he had said please, so I went up to the plant rooms and got them, all three of them, and brought them down and put them side by side on Wolfe's desk. He stood up and bent over them, beaming.

"They're absolutely unique," he said as if he was in church. "Matchless! Incomparable!"

"They're pretty," Cramer said politely, turning to go. "Kind of drab, though. Not much color. I like geraniums better."

That's the first of the two cases. That's how he got the black orchids. And what do you suppose he did with them? I don't mean the plants; it would take the lever Archimedes wanted a fulcrum for to pry one of those plants loose from him (just last week Cuyler Ditson offered him enough for one to buy an antiaircraft gun); I mean a bunch of the blossoms. I saw them myself there on a corner of the casket, with a card he had scribbled his initials on, "N.W." That was all.

I put this case here with the other one only on account of the orchids. As I said, it's a totally different set of people. If, when you finish it, you think the mystery has been solved, all I have to say is you don't know a mystery when you see one.

A. G.

CORDIALLY INVITED
TO MEET DEATH

Chapter 1

That wasn't the first time I ever saw Bess Huddleston.

A couple of years previously she had phoned the office one afternoon and asked to speak to Nero Wolfe, and when Wolfe got on the wire she calmly requested him to come at once to her place up at Riverdale to see her. Naturally he cut her off short. In the first place, he never stirred out of the house except in the direction of an old friend or a good cook; and secondly, it hurt his vanity that there was any man or woman alive who didn't know that.

An hour or so later here she came, to the office—the room he used for an office in his old house on West 35th Street, near the river—and there was a lively fifteen minutes. I never saw him more furious. It struck me as an attractive proposition. She offered him two thousand bucks to come to a party she was arranging for a Mrs. Somebody and be the detective in a murder game. Only four or five hours' work, sitting down, all the beer he could drink, and two thousand dollars. She even offered an extra five hundred for me to go along and do the leg work. But was he outraged! You might have thought he was Napoleon and she was asking him to come and deploy the tin soldiers in a nursery.

After she had gone I deplored his attitude. I told him that after all she was nearly as famous as he was, being the most successful party-arranger for the upper brackets that New York had ever had, and a combination of the talents of two such artists as him and her would have been something to remember, not to mention what I could do in the way of fun with five hundred smackers, but all he did was sulk.

That had been two years before. Now, this hot August morning with no air conditioning in the house because he distrusted machinery, she phoned around noon and asked him to come up to her place at Riverdale right away. He motioned to me to dispose of her and hung up. But a little later, when he had gone to the kitchen to consult with Fritz about some problem that had arisen in connection with lunch, I looked up her number and called her back. It had been as dull as a blunt instrument around the office for nearly a month, ever since we had finished with the Nauheim case, and I would have welcomed even tailing a laundry boy suspected of stealing a bottle of pop, so I phoned and told her that if she was contemplating a trip to 35th Street I wanted to remind her that Wolfe was incommunicado upstairs with his orchid plants from nine to eleven in the morning, and from four to six in the afternoon, but that any other time he would be delighted to see her.

I must say he didn't act delighted, when I ushered her in from the hall around three o'clock that afternoon. He didn't even apologize for not getting up from his chair to greet her, though I admit no reasonable person would have expected any such effort after one glance at his dimensions.

"You," he muttered pettishly, "are the woman who came here once and tried to bribe me to play the clown."

She plopped into the red leather chair I placed for her,

got a handkerchief out of her large green handbag, and passed it across her forehead, the back of her neck, and her throat. She was one of those people who don't look much like their pictures in the paper, because her eyes made her face and made you forget the rest of it when you looked at her. They were black and bright and gave you the feeling they were looking at you when they couldn't have been, and they made her seem a lot younger than the forty-seven or forty-eight she probably was.

"My God," she said, "as hot as this I should think you would sweat more. I'm in a hurry because I've got to see the Mayor about a Defense Pageant he wants me to handle, so I haven't time to argue, but your saying I tried to bribe you is perfectly silly. Perfectly silly! It would have been a marvelous party with you for the detective, but I had to get a policeman, an inspector, and all he did was grunt. Like this." She grunted.

"If you have come, madam, to—"

"I haven't. I don't want you for a party this time. I wish I did. Someone is trying to ruin me."

"Ruin you? Physically, financially—"

"Just ruin me. You know what I do. I do parties—"

"I know what you do," Wolfe said curtly.

"Very well. My clients are rich people and important people, at least they think they're important. Without going into that, they're important to me. So what do you suppose the effect would be—wait, I'll show it to you—"

She opened her handbag and dug into it like a terrier. A small bit of paper fluttered to the floor, and I stepped across to retrieve it for her, but she darted a glance at it and said, "Don't bother, wastebasket," and I disposed of it as indicated and returned to my chair.

Bess Huddleston handed an envelope to Wolfe. "Look at that. What do you think of that?"

Wolfe looked at the envelope, front and back, took

from it a sheet of paper which he unfolded and looked at, and passed them over to me.

"This is confidential," Bess Huddleston said.

"So is Mr. Goodwin," Wolfe said dryly.

I examined the exhibits. The envelope, stamped and postmarked and slit open, was addressed on a typewriter:

> Mrs. Jervis Horrocks
> 902 East 74th Street
> New York City

The sheet of paper said, also typewritten:

> Was it ignorance or something else that caused Dr.
> Brady to prescribe the wrong medicine for your
> daughter? Ask Bess Huddleston. She can tell you if
> she will. She told me.

There was no signature. I handed the sheet and envelope back to Wolfe.

Bess Huddleston used her handkerchief on her forehead and throat again. "There was another one," she said, looking at Wolfe but her eyes making me feel she was looking at me, "but I haven't got it. That one, as you see, is postmarked Tuesday, August 12th, six days ago. The other one was mailed a day earlier, Monday, the 11th, a week ago today. Typewritten, just like that. I've seen it. It was sent to a very rich and prominent man, and it said—I'll repeat it. It said: 'Where and with whom does your wife spend most of her afternoons? If you knew you would be surprised. My authority for this is Bess Huddleston. Ask her.' The man showed it to me. His wife is one of my best—"

"Please." Wolfe wiggled a finger at her. "Are you consulting me or hiring me?"

"I'm hiring you. To find out who sent those things."

"It's a mean kind of a job. Often next to impossible. Nothing but greed could induce me to tackle it."

"Certainly." Bess Huddleston nodded impatiently. "I know how to charge too. I expect to get soaked. But where will I be if this isn't stopped and stopped quick?"

"Very well. Archie, your notebook."

I got it out and got busy. She reeled it off to me while Wolfe rang for beer and then leaned back and closed his eyes. But he opened one of them halfway when he heard her telling me about the stationery and the typewriter. The paper and envelopes of both the anonymous letters, she said, were the kind used for personal correspondence by a girl who worked for her as her assistant in party-arranging, named Janet Nichols; and the letters and envelopes had been typed on a typewriter that belonged to Bess Huddleston herself which was used by another girl who worked for her as her secretary, named Maryella Timms. Bess Huddleston had done no comparing with a magnifying glass, but it looked like the work of that typewriter. Both girls lived with her in her house at Riverdale, and there was a large box of that stationery in Janet Nichols' room.

Then if not one of the girls—one of the girls? Wolfe muttered, "Facts, Archie." Servants? No use to bother about the servants, Bess Huddleston said; no servant ever stayed with her long enough to develop a grudge. I passed it with a nod having read about the alligators and bears and other disturbing elements in newspaper and magazine pieces. Did anyone else live in the house? Yes, a nephew, Lawrence Huddleston, also on the payroll as an assistant party-arranger, but, according to Aunt Bess, not on any account to be suspected. That all? Yes. Any persons sufficiently intimate with the household to have had access to the typewriter and Janet Nichols' stationery?

Certainly, as possibilities, many people.

Wolfe grunted impolitely. I asked, for another fact, what about the insinuations in the anonymous letters? The wrong medicine and the questionable afternoons? Bess Huddleston's black eyes snapped at me. She knew nothing about those things. And anyway, they were irrelevant. The point was that some malicious person was trying to ruin her by spreading hints that she was blabbing guilty secrets about people, and whether the secrets happened to be true or not had nothing to do with it. Okay, I told her, forget about where Mrs. Rich Man spends her afternoons, maybe at the ball game, but as a matter of record did Mrs. Jervis Horrocks have a daughter, and had she been sick, and had Dr. Brady attended her? Yes, Bess Huddleston said impatiently, Mrs. Horrocks' daughter had died a month ago and Dr. Brady had been her doctor. Died of what? Tetanus. How had she got tetanus? By scratching her arm on a nail in a riding-academy stable.

Wolfe muttered, "There is no wrong medicine—"

"It was terrible," Bess Huddleston interrupted, "but it has nothing to do with this. I'm going to be late for my appointment with the Mayor. This is perfectly simple. Someone wanted to ruin me and conceived this filthy way of doing it, that's all. It has to be stopped, and if you're as smart as you're supposed to be, you can stop it. Of course, I ought to tell you, I know who did it."

I cocked my head at her. Wolfe's eyes opened wide.

"What? You know?"

"Yes, I think I know. No, I do know."

"Then why, madam, are you annoying me?"

"Because I can't prove it. And she denies it."

"Indeed." Wolfe shot a sharp glance at her. "You seem to be less intelligent than you look. If, having no proof, you charged her with it."

"Did I say charged her with it? I didn't. I discussed it

with her, and also with Maryella, and my nephew, and Dr. Brady, and my brother. I asked them questions. I saw I couldn't handle it. So I came to you."

"By elimination—the culprit is Miss Nichols."

"Yes."

Wolfe was frowning. "But you have no proof. What do you have?"

"I have—a feeling."

"Pfui. Based on what?"

"I know her."

"You do." Wolfe continued to frown, and his lips pushed out, once, and in again. "By divination? Phrenology? What specific revelations of her character have you observed? Does she pull chairs from under people?"

"Cut the glitter," Bess Huddleston snapped, frowning back at him. "You know quite well what I mean. I say I know her, that's all. Her eyes, her voice, her manner—"

"I see. Flatly, you don't like her. She must be either remarkably stupid or extremely clever, to have used her own stationery for anonymous letters. Had you thought of that?"

"Certainly. She is clever."

"But knowing she did this, you keep her in your employ, in your house?"

"Of course I do. If I discharged her, would that stop her?"

"No. But you say you think her guilty because you know her. That means you knew a week ago, a month ago, a year ago that she was the sort of person who would do this sort of thing. Why didn't you get rid of her?"

"Because I—" Bess Huddleston hesitated. "What difference does that make?" she demanded.

"It makes a big difference to me, madam. You've hired me to investigate the source of those letters. I am doing so now. I am considering the possibility that you sent them yourself."

Her eyes flashed at him. "I? Nonsense."

"Then answer me." Wolfe was imperturbable. "Since you knew what Miss Nichols was like, why didn't you fire her?"

"Because I needed her. She's the best assistant I've ever had. Her ideas are simply . . . take the Stryker dwarf and giant party . . . that was her idea . . . this is confidential . . . some of my biggest successes . . ."

"I see. How long has she worked for you?"

"Three years."

"Do you pay her adequately?"

"Yes. I didn't, but I do now. Ten thousand a year."

"Then why does she want to ruin you? Just cussedness? Or has she got it in for you?"

"She has—she thinks she has a grievance."

"What about?"

"Something . . ." Bess Huddleston shook her head. "That's of no importance. A private matter. It wouldn't help you any. I am willing to pay your bill for finding out who sent those letters and getting proof."

"You mean you will pay me for fastening the guilt on Miss Nichols."

"Not at all. On whoever did it."

"No matter who it is?"

"Certainly."

"But you're sure it's Miss Nichols."

"I am not sure. I said I have a feeling." Bess Huddleston stood up and picked up her handbag from Wolfe's desk. "I have to go. Can you come up to my place tonight?"

"No. Mr.—"

"When can you come?"

"I can't. Mr. Goodwin can go—" Wolfe stopped himself. "No. Since you have already discussed it with all of those people, I'd like to see them. First the young women. Send them down here. I'll be free at six o'clock. This is a nasty job and I want to get it over with."

"My God," Bess Huddleston said, her eyes snapping at him, "you would have made a wonderful party! If I could sell it to the Crowthers I could make it four thousand—only there won't be many more parties for me if we don't get these letters stopped. I'll phone the girls—"

"Here's a phone," I said.

She made the call, gave instructions to one she called Maryella, and departed in a rush.

When I returned to the office after seeing the visitor to the door, Wolfe was out of his chair. There was nothing alarming about that, since it was one minute to four and therefore time for him to go up to the orchids, but what froze me in my tracks was the sight of him stooping over, actually bending nearly double, with his hand in my wastebasket.

He straightened up.

"Did you hurt yourself?" I inquired anxiously.

Ignoring that, he moved nearer the window to inspect an object he held between his thumb and forefinger. I stepped over and he handed it to me and I took a squint at it. It was a snapshot of a girl's face, nothing special to my taste, trimmed off so it was six-sided in shape and about the size of a half dollar.

"Want it for your album?" I asked him.

He ignored that too. "There is nothing in the world," he said, glaring at me as if I had sent him an anonymous letter, "as indestructible as human dignity. That woman makes money killing time for fools. With it she pays me for rooting around in mud. Half of my share goes for taxes which are used to make bombs to blow people to pieces. Yet I am not without dignity. Ask Fritz, my cook. Ask Theodore, my gardener. Ask you, my—"

"Right hand."

"No."

"Prime minister."

"No."

"Pal."

"No!"

"Accomplice, flunkey, Secretary of War, hireling, comrade . . ." He was on his way out to the elevator. I tossed the snapshot onto my desk and went to the kitchen for a glass of milk.

Chapter 2

Y ou're late," I told the girls reproachfully as I showed them into the office. "Mr. Wolfe supposed you would be here at six o'clock, when he comes down from the plant rooms, and it's twenty after. Now he's gone to the kitchen and started operations on some corned beef hash."

They were sitting down and I was looking them over.

"You mean he's eating corned beef hash?" Maryella Timms asked.

"No. That comes later. He's concocting it."

"It's my fault," Janet Nichols said. "I didn't get back until after five, and I was in riding clothes and had to change. I'm sorry."

She didn't look much like a horseback rider. Not that she was built wrong, she had a fairly nice little body, with good hips, but her face was more of a subway face than a bridle-path face. Naturally I had been expecting something out of the ordinary, one way or another, since according to Bess Huddleston she was an anonymous letter writer and had thought up the Stryker dwarf and giant party, and to tell the truth I was disappointed. She looked more like a school teacher—or maybe it would be more accurate to say that she looked like what a school teacher looks like before the time comes that she absolutely looks like a school teacher and nothing else.

Maryella Timms, on the other hand, was in no way disappointing, but she was irritating. Her hair started far back above the slant of her brow, and that made her brow look even higher and broader than it was, and noble and spiritual. But her eyes were very demure, which didn't fit. If you're noble and spiritual you don't have to be demure. There's no point in being demure unless there's something on your mind to be demure about. Besides, there was her accent. Cawned beef ha-a-sh. I am not still fighting the Civil War, and anyway my side won, but these Southern belles—if it sounds like a deliberate come-on to me then it does. I was bawn and braht up in the Nawth.

"I'll see if I can pry him loose," I said, and went to the hall and through to the kitchen.

The outlook was promising for getting Wolfe to come and attend to business, because he had not yet got his hands in the hash. The mixture, or the start of it, was there in a bowl on the long table, and Fritz, at one side of the table, and Wolfe, at the other, were standing there discussing it. They looked around at me as I would expect to be looked at if I busted into a Cabinet meeting at the White House.

"They're here," I announced. "Janet and Maryella."

From the expression on his face as his mouth opened it was a safe bet that Wolfe was going to instruct me to tell them to come back tomorrow, but he didn't get it out. I heard a door open behind me and a voice floated past:

"Ah heah yawl makin' cawned beef ha-a-sh. . . ."

That's the last time I try to reproduce it.

The owner of the voice floated past me too, right up beside Wolfe. She leaned over to peer into the bowl.

"Excuse me," she said, which I couldn't spell the way

she said it anyhow, "but corned beef hash is one of my specialties. Nothing in there but meat, is there?"

"As you see," Wolfe grunted.

"It's ground too fine," Maryella asserted.

Wolfe scowled at her. I could see he was torn with conflicting emotions. A female in his kitchen was an outrage. A woman criticizing his or Fritz's cooking was an insult. But corned beef hash was one of life's toughest problems, never yet solved by anyone. To tone down the corned flavor and yet preserve its unique quality, to remove the curse of its dryness without making it greasy—the theories and experiments had gone on for years. He scowled at her, but he didn't order her out.

"This is Miss Timms," I said. "Mr. Wolfe. Mr. Brenner. Miss Nichols is in—"

"Ground too fine for what?" Wolfe demanded truculently. "This is not a tender fresh meat, with juices to lose—"

"Now you just calm down." Maryella's hand was on his arm. "It's not ruined, only it's better if it's coarser. That's far too much potatoes for that meat. But if you don't have chitlins you can't—"

"Chitlins!" Wolfe bellowed.

Maryella nodded. "Fresh pig chitlins. That's the secret of it. Fried shallow in olive oil with onion juice—"

"Good heavens!" Wolfe was staring at Fritz. "I never heard of it. It has never occurred to me. Fritz? Well?"

Fritz was frowning thoughtfully. "It might go," he conceded. "We can try it. As an experiment."

Wolfe turned to me in swift decision. "Archie, call up Kretzmeyer and ask if he has pig chitlins. Two pounds."

"You'd better let me help," Maryella said. "It's sort of tricky. . . ."

That was how I came to get so well acquainted with Janet that first day. I thought I might as well have company driving down to the market for chitlins, and Maryella was glued to Wolfe, and as far as that's concerned Wolfe was glued to her for the duration of the experiment, so I took Janet along. By the time we got back to the house I had decided she was innocent in more ways than one, though I admit that didn't mean much, because it's hard for me to believe that anyone not obviously a hyena could pull a trick like anonymous letters. I also admit there wasn't much sparkle to her, and she seemed to be a little absent-minded when it came to conversation, but under the circumstances that wasn't surprising, if she knew why she had been told to go to Nero Wolfe's office, as she probably did.

I delivered the chitlins to the hash artists in the kitchen and then joined Janet in the office. I had been telling her about orchid hybridizing on the way back up-town, and when I went to my desk to get a stack of breeding cards I was going to show her, I noticed something was missing. So I gave her the cards to look at and excused myself and returned to the kitchen, and asked Wolfe if anyone had been in the office during my absence. He was standing beside Maryella, watching Fritz arrange the chitlins on a cutting board, and all I got was a growl.

"None of you left the kitchen?" I insisted.

"No," he said shortly. "Why?"

"Someone ate my lollipop," I told him, and left him with his playmates and returned to the office. Janet was sitting with the cards in her lap, going through them. I stood in front of her and inquired amiably:

"What did you do with it?"

She looked up at me. That way, with her head tilted up, from that angle, she looked kind of pretty.

"What did I—what?"

"That snapshot you took from my desk. It's the only picture I've got of you. Where did you put it?"

"I didn't—" Her mouth closed. "I didn't!" she said defiantly.

I sat down and shook my head at her. "Now listen," I said pleasantly. "Don't lie to me. We're comrades. Side by side we have sought the chitlin in its lair. The wild boar chitlin. That picture is my property and I want it. Let's say it fluttered into your bag. Look in your bag."

"It isn't there." With a new note of spunk in her voice, and a new touch of color on her cheeks, she was more of a person. Her bag was beside her on the chair, and her left hand was clutching it.

"Then I'll look in your bag." I started for her.

"No!" she said. "It isn't there!" She put a palm to her stomach. "It's here."

I stopped short, thinking for a second she had swallowed it. Then I returned to my chair and told her, "Okay. You will now return it. You have three alternatives. Either dig it out yourself, or I will, or I'll call in Maryella and hold you while she does. The first is the most ladylike. I'll turn my back."

"Please." She kept her palm against her stomach. "Please! It's my picture!"

"It's a picture of you, but it's not your picture."

"Miss Huddleston gave it to you."

I saw no point in denying the obvious. "Say she did."

"And she told you . . . she . . . she thinks I sent those awful letters! I know she does!"

"That," I said firmly, "is another matter which the boss is handling. I am handling the picture. It is probably of no importance except as a picture of the girl who thought up the Stryker dwarf and giant party. If you ask Mr. Wolfe for it he'll probably give it to you. It may even be that Miss Huddleston stole it; I don't know. She didn't say where she got it. I do know that you copped it from my desk and I want it back. You can get another one, but I can't. Shall I call Maryella?" I turned my head and looked like a man about to let out a yell.

"No!" she said, and got out of her chair and turned her back and went through some contortions. When she handed me the snapshot I tucked it under a paperweight on Wolfe's desk and then went to help her collect the breeding cards from the floor where they had tumbled from her lap.

"Look what you did," I told her, "mixed them all up. Now you can help me put them in order again. . . ."

It looked for a minute as if tears were going to flow, but they didn't. We spent an hour together, not exactly jolly, but quite friendly. I avoided the letter question, because I didn't know what line Wolfe intended to take.

When he finally got at it there was no line to it. That was after nine o'clock, when we assembled in the office after the hash and trimmings had been disposed of. The hash was okay. It was good hash. Wolfe had three help-ings, and when he conversed with Maryella, as he did through most of the meal, he was not only sociable but positively respectful. There was an unpleasant moment at the beginning, when Janet didn't take any hash and Fritz was told to slice some ham for her, and Maryella told her resentfully:

"You won't eat it because I cooked it."

Janet protested that that wasn't so, she just didn't like corned beef.

In the office, afterwards, it became apparent that there was no love lost between the secretary and the assistant party-arranger. Not that either accused the other of writing the poison-pen letters; there were no open hostilities, but a few glances I observed when I looked up from my notebook, and tones of voice when they ad-dressed each other, sounded as if there might be quite a blaze if somebody touched a match to it. Wolfe didn't get anything, as far as I could see, except a collection of unimportant facts. Both the girls were being discreet, to put it mildly. Bess Huddleston, according to them, was a very satisfactory employer. They admitted that her celebrated eccentricities made things difficult sometimes, but they had no kick coming. Janet had worked for her three years, and Maryella two, and they hadn't the slightest idea who could have sent those dreadful letters, and Bess Huddleston had no enemies that they knew of . . . oh, of course, she had hurt some people's feelings, but what did that amount to, and there were scores of people who could have got at Janet's stationery during the past months but they couldn't imagine who, and so forth and so on. Yes, they had known Mrs. Jervis Horrocks' daughter, Helen; she had been a close friend of Maryella's. Her death had been a shock. And yes, they knew Dr. Alan Brady quite well. He was fashionable and successful and had a wonderful reputation for his age. He often went horseback riding with one of them or with Bess Huddleston. Riding academy? No, Bess Huddleston kept horses in her stable at her place at Riverdale, and Dr. Brady would come up from the Medical Center when he got through in the afternoon—it was only a ten-minute drive.

And Bess Huddleston had never been married, and her brother Daniel was some kind of a chemist, not in society, very much not, who showed up at the house for dinner about once a week; and her nephew, Larry, well, there he was, that was all, a young man living there and getting paid for helping his aunt in her business; and there were no other known relatives and no real intimates, except that Bess Huddleston had hundreds of intimates of both sexes and all ages. . . .

It went on for nearly two hours.

After seeing them out to their car—I noticed Maryella was driving—I returned to the office and stood and watched Wolfe down a glass of beer and pour another one.

"That picture of the culprit," I said, "is there under your paperweight if you want it. She did. I mean she wanted it. In my absence she swiped it and hid it in a spot too intimate to mention in your presence. I got it back—no matter how. I expected her to ask you for it, but she didn't. And if you think you're going to solve this case by—"

"Confound the case." Wolfe sighed clear to the beer he had swallowed. "I might have known better. Tomorrow go up there and look around. The servants, I suppose. Make sure of the typewriter. The nephew. Talk with him and decide if I must see him; if so, bring him. And get Dr. Brady here. After lunch would be best."

"Sure," I said sarcastically.

"Around two o'clock. Please get your notebook and take a letter. Get it off tonight, special delivery. To Professor Martingale of Harvard. Dear Joseph. I have made a remarkable discovery, comma, or rather, comma, have had one communicated to me. You may remember our discussion last winter regarding the possibility of using pig chitlins in connection with . . ."

Chapter 3

Ever since an incident that occurred when Wolfe sent me on an errand in February, 1935, I automatically ask myself, when leaving the office on a business chore, do I take a gun? I seldom do; but if I had done so that Tuesday afternoon I swear I would have found use for it. As sure as my name is Archie and not Archibald, I would have shot that goddamn orangutan dead in his tracks.

Formerly it took a good three-quarters of an hour to drive from 35th Street to Riverdale, but now, with the West Side Highway and the Henry Hudson Bridge, twenty minutes was ample. I had never seen the Huddleston place before, but since I read newspapers and magazines the trick fence was no surprise to me. I parked the roadster at a wide space on the drive which ran parallel with the fence, got a gate open and went through, and started up a path across the lawn towards the house. There were trees and bushes around, and off to the right an egg-shaped pool.

About twenty paces short of the house I suddenly stopped. I don't know where he had appeared from, but there he was straddling the path, big and black, his teeth flashing in a grin if you want to call it that. I stood and looked at him. He didn't move. I thought to myself, nuts, and moved forward, but when I got closer he made a certain kind of a noise and I stopped again. Okay, I thought, if this is your private path why didn't you say so, and I sashayed off to the right, seeing there was another path the other side of the pool. I didn't actually turn but went sort of sidewise because I was curious to see what he was going to do, and what he did was stalk me, on all fours. So it happened that my head was twisted to keep an eye on him when I backed into a log there on the grass at the edge of the pool and went down flat, nearly tumbling into the water, and when I sprang to my feet again the log was crawling along the ground length-wise towards me. It was one of the alligators. The orangutan was sitting down laughing. I don't mean he was making a laughing noise, but by his face he was laughing. That's when I would have shot him. I circled around the pool and got to the other path and headed for the house, but there he was, strad-dling the path ten yards ahead of me, making the noise again, so I stopped.

A man's voice said, "He wants to play tag."

I had been too preoccupied to see the man, and anyway he had just stepped from behind a shrub at the end of a terrace. With a glance I saw that he was clad in a green shirt and brick-colored slacks, was about my age or a little younger, and seemed to be assuming a supercilious atti-tude.

He said, "He wants to play tag."

I said, "I don't."

He said, "If you offend him he'll bite you. Start past him on the grass and dodge when he goes to touch you. Dodge three times and then let him tag you, and say 'Mister' in an admiring voice. That's all. His name is Mis-ter."

"I could turn around and go home."

"I wouldn't try that. He would resent it."

"I could sock him one."

"You might. I doubt it. If you hurt him and my aunt ever catches you . . . I suppose you're Archie Goodwin? I'm Larry Huddleston. I didn't send those letters and don't know who did or who might. My aunt will be down later, she's upstairs arguing with Brother Daniel. I can't invite you in until you get past Mister."

"Does everyone who comes here have to play tag with this damn overgrown orangutan?"

"He's not an orangutan; he's a chimpanzee. He doesn't often play with strangers. It means he likes you."

I had to go through with it. I took to the grass, was intercepted, dodged three times, said 'Mister' in as admiring a tone of voice as I could manage, and was by. Mister emitted a little squeal and scampered off to a tree and bounded up to a limb. I looked at the back of my hand and saw blood. The nephew asked, not with great concern:

"Did he bite you?"

"No, I fell down and must have scratched it. It's just a scratch."

"Yeah, I saw you trip over Moses. I'll get you some iodine."

I said it wasn't worth bothering about, but he took me across the terrace into the house, into a large living room, twice as long as it was broad, with big windows and a big fireplace, and enough chairs and divans and cushions for a good-sized party right there. When he opened a cupboard door in the wall near the fireplace a shelf was disclosed with a neat array of sterilized gauze, band-aids, adhesive tape, and salve. . . .

As I dabbed iodine on the scratch I said, for something to say, "Handy place for a first-aid outfit."

He nodded. "On account of Mister. He never bites

deep, but he often breaks somebody's skin. Then Logo and Lulu, sometimes they take a little nip—"

"Logo and Lulu?"

"The bears."

"Oh, sure. The bears." I looked around and then put the iodine bottle on the shelf and he closed the door. "Where are they now?"

"Having a nap somewhere. They always nap in the afternoon. They'll be around later. Shall we go out to the terrace? What'll you have, scotch, rye, bourbon?"

It was a nice spot, the terrace, on the shady side of the house with large irregular flagstones separated by ribbons of turf. I sat there for an hour with him, but about all I got out of it was three highballs. I didn't cotton to him much. He talked like an actor; he had a green handkerchief in the breast pocket of his shirt, to match the shirt; he mentioned the Social Register three times in less than an hour; and he wore an hexagonal wrist watch, whereas there's no excuse for a watch to be anything but round. He struck me as barely bright enough for life's simplest demands, but I admit he might have been a darb at a party. I must say he didn't turn loose any secrets. He was pretty indignant about the letters, but about all I learned from him was that he knew how to use a typewriter, that Maryella had gone downtown on some errands, and that Janet was out horseback riding with Dr. Brady. He seemed to be a little cynical about Dr. Brady, but I couldn't get the slant.

When it got five o'clock and his aunt hadn't come down, he went to inquire, and in a moment returned and said I was to go up. He led me upstairs and showed me a door and beat it. I entered and found I was in an office, but there was no one there. It was a mess. Phone books were heaped on a chair. The blotters had been used since the Declaration of Independence. The typewriter wasn't covered. I was frowning around when I heard steps, and Bess Huddleston trotted in, with a skinny specimen behind her. His eyes were as black as hers, but everything else about him was shrunk and faded. As she breezed past me she said:

"Sorry. How are you. My brother. Mr. Goldwyn."

"Goodwin," I said firmly, and shook brother's hand. I was surprised to find he had a good shake. Sister was sitting at a desk, opening a drawer. She got out a checkbook, took a pen from a socket, made out a check, tried to blot it and made a smudge, and handed it to brother Daniel. He took one look at it and said:

"No."

"Yes," she snapped.

"I tell you, Bess, it won't—"

"It will have to, Dan. At least for this week. That's all there is to it. I've told you a thousand times—"

She stopped, looked at me, and looked at him.

"All right," he said, and stuck the check in his pocket, and sat down on a chair, shaking his head and looking thoughtful.

"Now," Bess turned to me, "what about it?"

"Nothing to brag about," I told her. "There's a slew of fingerprints on that letter and envelope, but since you discussed it with your brother and nephew and the girls and Dr. Brady, I suppose they all handled it. Did they?"

"Yes."

I shrugged. "So. Maryella showed Mr. Wolfe how to make corned beef hash. The secret is chitlins. Aside from that, nothing to report. Except that Janet knows that you think she's it. Also she wanted that picture."

"What picture?"

"The snapshot of her you told me to throw in the wastebasket. It caught her eye and she wanted it. Is there any objection to her having it?"

"Certainly not."

"Is there anything you want to say about it? That might help?"

"No, that picture has nothing to do with it. I mean that wouldn't help you any."

"Dr. Brady was requested to call at our office at two o'clock today but was too busy."

Bess Huddleston went to a window and looked out and came back. "He wasn't too busy to come and ride one of my horses," she said tartly. "They ought to be back soon—I thought I heard them at the stable. . . ."

"Will he come to the house?"

"He will. For cocktails."

"Good. Mr. Wolfe told me to say that there is a remote chance there might be prints on the other letter. The one the rich man got."

"It isn't available."

"Couldn't you get it?"

"I don't think so."

"Has he turned it over to the police?"

"Good heavens, no!"

"Okay. I've played tag with Mister and had a talk with your nephew. Now if I could see where Janet keeps her stationery, and take a sample from that typewriter. Is that the one?"

"Yes. But first come to Janet's room. I'll show you."

I followed her. It was at the other end of the house, on that floor, one flight up, a pleasant little room and nice and neat. But the stationery was a washout. It wasn't in a box. It was in a drawer of a writing table with no lock on it, and all you had to do was open the drawer with a metal ring for a puller, which couldn't possibly have had a print, and reach in and take what you wanted, paper and envelopes both. Bess Huddleston left me there, and after a look around where there was nothing to look for, I went back to the office. Daniel was still there on the chair where we had left him. I ran off some sample lines on the typewriter, using a sheet of Janet's paper, and was putting it in my pocket when Daniel spoke:

"You're a detective."

I nodded. "That's what they tell me."

"You're finding out who sent those anonymous letters."

"Right." I snapped my fingers. "Just like that."

"Anyone who sends letters like that deserves to be immersed to the chin in a ten percent solution of hydrofluoric acid."

"Why, would that be painful?"

Daniel shuddered. "It would. I stayed here because I thought you might want to ask me something."

"Much obliged. What shall I ask you?"

"That's the trouble." He looked dismal. "There's nothing I can tell you. I wish to God there was. I have no information to offer, even no suspicions. But I would like to offer a comment. Without prejudice. Two comments."

I sat down and looked interested. "Number one?" I said receptively.

"You can pass them on to Nero Wolfe."

"I can and will."

Daniel eyed me, screwing up his lips. "You mentioned five people to my sister just now. Her nephew, Larry—mine too—Miss Nichols and Miss Timms, Dr. Brady, and me. It is worth considering that four of us would be injured by anything that injured my sister. I am her brother and I have a deep and strong affection for her. The young ladies are employed by her and they are well paid. Larry is also well paid. Frankly—I am his uncle—too well. But for his aunt, he might earn four dollars a day as a helper on a coal barge. I know of no other occupation that would not strain his faculties beyond their limit. But the point is, his prosperity depends entirely on hers. So it is conceivable—I offer this merely as a comment—that we four may properly be eliminated from suspicion."

"Okay," I said. "That leaves one."

"One?"

"Sure, Doc Brady. Of the five I mentioned, you rule out four. Pointing straight at him."

"By no means." Daniel looked distressed. "You misunderstand me. I know very little about Dr. Brady, though it so happens that my second comment concerns him. I insist it is merely a comment. You have read the letter received by Mrs. Horrocks? Then you have probably realized that while it purports to be an attack on Dr. Brady, it is so manifestly absurd that it couldn't possibly damage him. Mrs. Horrocks' daughter died of tetanus. There is no such thing as a wrong medicine for tetanus, nor a right one either, once the toxin has reached the nerve centers. The antitoxin will prevent, but never, or very rarely, will it cure. So the attack on Dr. Brady was no attack at all."

"That's interesting," I admitted. "Are you a doctor?"

"No, sir. I'm a research chemist. But any standard medical treatise—"

"Sure. I'll look it up. What reason do you suppose Doc Brady might have for putting your sister on the skids?"

"So far as I know, none. None whatever."

"Then that lets him out. With everyone else out, there's no one left but your sister."

"My sister?"

I nodded. "She must have sent the letters herself."

That made him mad. In fact he rather blew up, chiefly because it was too serious a matter to be facetious about, and I had to turn on the suavity to calm him down. Then he went into a sulk. After fooling around with him for another ten minutes and getting nothing for my trouble, I decided to move on and he accompanied me downstairs and out to the terrace, where we heard voices.

If that was a sample of a merry gathering arranged by Bess Huddleston, I'll roll my own, though I admit that isn't fair, since she hadn't done any special arranging. She was lying on a porch swing with her dress curled above her knees by the breeze, displaying a pair of bare legs that were merely something to walk with, the feet being shod with high-heeled red slippers, and I don't like shoes without stockings, no matter whose legs they are. Two medium-sized black bears were sitting on the flagstones with their backs propped against the frame of the swing, licking sticks of candy and growling at each other. Maryella Timms was perched on the arm of a chair with her hand happening to rest on the shoulder of Larry Huddleston, who was sitting at careless ease in the chair the way John Barrymore would. Janet Nichols, in riding clothes, was in another chair, her face hot and flushed, which made her look better instead of worse as it does most people, and standing at the other end of the swing, also in riding clothes, was a wiry-looking guy with a muscular face.

When Bess Huddleston introduced us, Dr. Brady and me, I started to meet him halfway for the handshake, but I had taken only two and a half steps when the bears suddenly started for me as if I was the meal of their dreams. I leaped sideways half a mile in one bound and their momentum carried them straight on by, but as I whirled to faced them another big black object shot past me from behind like a bat out of hell and I jumped again, just at random. Laughter came from two directions, and from a third Bess Huddleston's voice:

"They weren't after you, Mr. Goldwin, they smelled Mister coming and they're afraid of him. He teases them."

The bears were not in sight. The orangutan jumped up on the swing and off again. I said savagely, "My name is Goolenwangel."

Dr. Brady was shaking my hand. He said with a laugh, "Don't mind her, Mr. Goodwin. It's a pose. She pretends she can't remember the name of anyone not in the Social Register. Since her entire career is founded on snobbery—"

"Snob yourself," Bess Huddleston snorted. "You were born to it and believe in it. With me it's business. But for heaven's sake let's not—Mister, you devil, don't you dare tickle my feet!"

Mister went right ahead. He already had the red slippers off, and, depositing them right side up on a flagstone, he proceeded to tickle the sole of her right foot. She screamed and kicked him. He tickled the other foot, and she screamed again and kicked him with that. That appeared to satisfy him, for he started off, but his next performance was unpremeditated. A man in a butler's jacket, approaching with a tray of glasses and bottles, had just reached the end of the swing when Mister bumped him, and bumped him good. The man yelled and lost control, and down went the works. Dr. Brady caught one bottle on the fly, and I caught another, but everything else was shattered on the stones. Mister went twenty feet through the air and landed in a chair and sat there and giggled, and the man was trembling all over.

"For God's sake, Haskell," Bess Huddleston said, "don't leave now, with guests coming for dinner. Go to your room and have a drink and lie down. We'll clean this up."

"My name is Hoskins," the man said in a hollow tone.

"So it is. Of course it is. Go and have a drink."

The man went, and the rest of us got busy. When Mister got the idea, which was at once, he waddled over to help, and I'll say this much for him, he was the fastest picker-up of pieces of broken glass I have ever seen. Janet went and came back with implements, among them a couple of brooms, but the trouble was that you couldn't make a comprehensive sweep of it on account of the strips of turf between the flagstones. Larry went for another outfit of drinks, and finally Maryella solved the problem of the bits of glass in the grass strips by bringing a vacuum cleaner. Bess Huddleston stayed on the swing. Dr. Brady carried off the debris, and eventually we got back to normal, everybody with a drink, including Mister, only his was non-alcoholic, or I wouldn't have stayed. What that bird would have done with a couple of Martinis under his fur would have been something to watch from an airplane.

"This seems to be a day for breaking things," Bess Huddleston said, sipping an old-fashioned. "Someone broke my bottle of bath salts and it splattered all over the bathroom and just left it that way."

"Mister?" Maryella asked.

"I don't think so. He never goes in there. I didn't dare ask the servants."

But apparently at the Huddleston place there was no such thing as settling down for a social quarter of an hour, whether Mister was drunk or sober, only the next disturbance wasn't his fault, except indirectly. The social atmosphere was nothing to brag about anyhow, because it struck me that certain primitive feelings were being felt and not concealed with any great success. I'm not so hot at nuances, but it didn't take a Nero Wolfe to see that Maryella was working on Larry Huddleston, that the sight of the performance was giving Dr. Brady the fidgets in his facial muscles, that Janet was embarrassed and trying to pretend she didn't notice what was going on, and that Daniel was absent-mindedly drinking too much because he was worrying about something. Bess Huddleston had her ear cocked to hear what I was saying to Dr. Brady, but I was merely dating him to call at the office. He couldn't make it that evening, but tomorrow perhaps . . . his schedule was very crowded. . . .

The disturbance came when Bess Huddleston said she guessed she had better go and see if there was going to be any dinner or anyone to serve it, and sat up and put on her slippers. That is, she put one on; the second one, she stuck her foot in, let out a squeak, and jerked the foot out again.

"Damn!" she said. "A piece of glass in my slipper! Cut my toe!"

Mister bounced over to her, and the rest of us gathered around. Since Brady was a doctor, he took charge of matters. I didn't amount to much, a shallow gash half an inch long on the bottom of her big toe, but it bled some, and Mister started whining and wouldn't stop. Brother Daniel brought first-aid materials from the living room, and after Brady had applied a good dose of iodine, he did a neat job with gauze and tape.

"It's all right, Mister," Bess Huddleston said reassuringly. "You don't—hey!"

Mister had swiped the iodine bottle, uncorked it, and was carefully depositing the contents, drop by drop, onto one of the strips of turf. He wouldn't surrender it to Brady or Maryella, but he gave it to his mistress on demand, after re-corking it himself, and she handed it to her brother.

It was after six o'clock, and I wasn't invited to dinner, and anyway I had had enough zoology for one day, so I said good-bye and took myself off. When I got the roadster onto the highway and was among my fellows again, I took a long deep breath of the good old mixture of gasoline and air and the usual odors.

When I got back to the office Wolfe, who was making marks on a big map of Russia he had bought recently, said he would take my report later, so, after comparing the type on my sample with that on the Horrocks letter and finding they were written on the same machine, I went up to my room for a shower and a change. After dinner, back in the office, he told me to make it a complete recital, leaving out nothing, which meant that he had made no start and formed no opinion. I told him I preferred a written report, because when I delivered it verbally he threw me off the track by making faces and irritating me, but he leaned back and shut his eyes and told me to proceed.

It was nearly midnight when I finished, what with the usual interruptions. When he's doing a complete coverage, he thinks nothing of asking such a question as, "Did the animal pour the iodine on the grass with its right paw or its left?" If he were a movable object and went places himself it would save me a lot of breath, but then that's what I get paid for. Partly.

He stood up and stretched, and I yawned. "Well," I asked offensively, "got it sewed up? Including proof?"

"I'm sleepy," he said, starting off. At the door he turned. "You made the usual quantity of mistakes, naturally, but probably the only one of importance was your failure to investigate the matter of the broken bottle in Miss Huddleston's bathroom."

"Pah," I said. "If that's the best you can do. It was not a bottle of anonymous letters. Bath salts."

"All the same it's preposterous. It's even improbable. Break a bottle and simply go off, leaving it scattered around? No one would do that."

"You don't know that orangutan. I do."

"Not orangutan. Chimpanzee. It might have done it, yes. That's why you should have investigated. If the animal did not do it, there's something fishy about it. Highly unnatural. If Dr. Brady arrives by eight fifty-nine, I'll see him before I go up to the plant rooms. Good night."

Chapter 4

That was Tuesday night, August 19th. On Friday the 22nd Bess Huddleston got tetanus. On Monday the 25th she died. To show how everything from war to picnics depends on the weather, as Wolfe remarked when he was discussing the case with a friend the other day, if there had been a heavy rainfall in Riverdale between the 19th and 26th it would have been impossible to prove it was murder, let alone catch the murderer. Not that he showed any great—oh, well.

On Wednesday the 20th Dr. Brady came to the office for an interview with Wolfe, and the next day brother Daniel and nephew Larry came. About all we got out of that was that among the men nobody liked anybody. In the meantime, upon instructions from Wolfe, I was wrapping my tentacles about Janet, coaxing her into my deadly embrace. It really wasn't an unpleasant job, because Wednesday afternoon I took her to a ball game and was agreeably surprised to find that she knew a bunt from a base on balls, and Friday evening we went to the Flamingo Roof and I learned that she could dance nearly as well as Lily Rowan. She was no cuddler and a little stiff, but she went with the music and always knew what we were going to do. Saturday morning I reported to Wolfe regarding her as follows:

1. If she was toting a grievance against Bess Huddleston, it would take a smarter man than me to find out what it was.
2. There was nothing fundamentally wrong with her except that she would rather live in the country than the city.
3. She had no definite suspicion about who had sent the anonymous letters or anyone's motive for sending them.

Wolfe said, "Try Miss Timms for a change."

I didn't try to date Maryella for Saturday or Sunday, because Janet had told me they were all going to Saratoga for the weekend. Monday morning, I thought, was no time to start a romance, so I waited until afternoon to phone, got Maryella, and got the news. I went up to the plant rooms, where Wolfe was a sight to behold in his undershirt, cutting the tops from a row of vandas for propagation, and told him:

"Bess Huddleston is dead."

"Let me alone," he said peevishly. "I'm doing all I can. Someone will probably get another letter before long, and when—"

"No, sir. No more letters. I am stating facts. Friday evening tetanus set in from that cut on her toe, and about an hour ago she died. Maryella's voice was choked with emotion as she told me."

Wolfe scowled at me. "Tetanus?"

"Yes, sir."

"That would have been a five thousand dollar fee."

"It would have been if you had seen fit to do a little work instead of—"

"It was no good and you know it. I was waiting for another letter. File it away, including the letter to Mrs. Horrocks, to be delivered to her on request. I'm glad to be rid of it."

I wasn't. Down in the office, as I checked over the folder, consisting of the Horrocks letter, the snapshot of Janet, a couple of reports I had made and some memos Wolfe had dictated, I felt as if I was leaving a ball game in the fourth inning with the score a tie. But it looked as if nothing could be done about it, and certainly there was no use trying to badger Wolfe. I phoned Janet to ask if there was anything I could do, and she told me in a weak tired voice that as far as she knew there wasn't.

According to the obit in the *Times* the next morning, the funeral service was to be Wednesday afternoon, at the Belford Memorial Chapel on 73rd Street, and of course there would be a big crowd, even in August, for Bess Huddleston's last party. Cordially invited to meet death. I decided to go. Not merely, if I know myself, for curiosity or another look at Janet. It is not my custom to frequent memorial chapels to look at girls even if they're good dancers. Call it a hunch. Not that I saw anything criminal, only something incredible. I filed past the casket with the throng because from a distance I had seen it and couldn't believe it. But when I got close there it was. Eight black orchids that could have come from nowhere else in the world, and a card with his initials the way he scribbled them, "N.W."

When I got home, and Wolfe came down from the plant rooms at six o'clock, I didn't mention it. I decided it wasn't advisable. I needed to devote some thought to it.

It was that evening, Wednesday evening after the funeral, that I answered the doorbell, and who should I see on the stoop but my old colleague Inspector Cramer of the Homicide Squad. I hailed him with false enthusiasm and ushered him into the office, where Wolfe was making more marks on the map of Russia. They exchanged greetings, and Cramer sat in the red leather chair, took out a handkerchief and wiped perspiration from his exposed surfaces, put a cigar between his lips and sank his teeth in it.

"Your hair's turning gray," I observed. "You look as if you weren't getting enough exercise. A brain-worker like you—"

"God knows why you keep him," he said to Wolfe.

Wolfe grunted. "He saved my life once."

"Once!" I exclaimed indignantly. "Beginning—"

"Shut up, Archie. What can I do for you, Inspector?"

"You can tell me what you were doing for Bess Huddleston."

"Indeed." Wolfe's brows went up a shade. "You? The Homicide Bureau? Why do you want to know?"

"Because a guy is making himself a pest down at Headquarters. Her brother. He says she was murdered."

"He does?"

"Yes."

"Offering what evidence?"

"None at all."

"Then why bother me about it? Or yourself either?"

"Because we can't shut him up. He's even been to the Commissioner. And though he has no evidence, he has an argument. I'd like to tell you his argument."

Wolfe leaned back and sighed. "Go ahead."

"Well. He started on us last Saturday, four days ago. She got tetanus the day before. I don't need to tell you about that cut on her toe, since Goodwin was there—"

"I've heard about it."

"I'll bet you have. The brother, Daniel, said she

couldn't have got tetanus from that cut. He said it was a clean piece of glass that dropped into her slipper when the tray of glasses fell on the terrace. He saw it. And the slipper was a clean house slipper, nearly new and clean. And she hadn't been walking around barefooted. He claimed there couldn't possibly have been any tetanus germs in that cut, at least not enough to cause so violent an attack so soon. I sent a man up there Saturday night, but the doctor wouldn't let him see her, and of course he had no evidence—"

"Dr. Brady?"

"Yes. But the brother kept after us, especially when she died, and yesterday morning I sent a couple of men up to rub it off. I want to ask you, Goodwin, what was the piece of glass like? The piece in her slipper that cut her?"

"I knew you really came to see me," I told him genially. "It was a piece from one of the thick blue glasses that they had for old-fashioneds. Several of them broke."

Cramer nodded. "So they all say. We sent the slippers to the laboratory, and they say no tetanus germs. Of course there was another possibility, the iodine and the bandage. We sent all the stuff on that shelf to the laboratory, and the gauze was sterile, and it was good iodine, so naturally there were no germs in it. Under the circum—"

"Subsequent dressings," Wolfe muttered.

"No. The dressing Brady found on it when he was called up there Friday night was the one he had put on originally."

"Listen," I put in, "I know. By God. That orangutan. He tickled her feet. He rubbed germs on her—"

Cramer shook his head. "We went into that too. One of them suggested it—the nephew. That seems to be a possibility. It sounds farfetched to me, but of course it's possible. Now what the doctor says. Brady."

"Excuse me," Wolfe said. "You talked to those people.

Had Miss Huddleston nothing to say to them before she died? Any of them?"

"Not much. Do you know what tetanus does?"

"Vaguely."

"It does plenty. Like strychnine, only worse because there are no periods of relaxation and it lasts longer. When Brady got there Friday night her jaw was already locked tight. He gave her avertin to relieve her, and kept it up till the end. When my man was there Saturday night she was bent double backwards. Sunday she told Brady through her teeth she wanted to tell people good-bye, and he took them in one at a time. I've got their statements. Nothing significant, what you'd expect. Of course she only said a few words to each one—she was in bad shape. Her brother tried to tell her that her approaching death wasn't an accident, it was murder, but Brady and the nurse wouldn't let him."

"She herself had no such suspicion?"

"Not in evidence. You realize what she was like." Cramer shifted the cigar to the other side of his mouth. "What Brady says about the tetanus, one three-hundredth of a grain of the toxin is fatal. The bacilli and spores are more or less around everywhere, but of course especially in the neighborhood of horses. The soil around a barnyard reeks with it. I asked Brady what about his infecting the cut or the bandage with his own fingers when he dressed it, since he had just been riding, but he said he had washed his hands, and so had the Nichols girl, and she corroborated it. He said it was highly unlikely that there should have been tetanus bacilli on the piece of glass or her slipper or the skin of her toe or that animal's paw, at least enough of them to cause such a quick and virulent attack, but he said it was also unlikely that when a man walks across a street at a corner with a green light he should get run over, but sometimes he does. He says that he deeply regrets he didn't return Tuesday evening or

Wednesday and give her an injection of antitoxin, but he doesn't blame himself because no doctor alive would have done so. After the poison reached the nerve centers, as it had when Brady arrived Friday night, it was too late for antitoxin, though he tried it. Everything Brady said has been checked with the Examiner and is okay."

"I don't like his analogy," Wolfe declared. "A man crossing a street is extremely likely to get run over. That's why I never undertake it. However, that doesn't impeach Dr. Brady. I ask you again, Mr. Cramer, why do you bother me with all this, or yourself either?"

"That's what I came here to find out."

"Not the proper place. Try the inside of your head."

"Oh, that's all right," Cramer asserted. "I'm satisfied. It was accidental. But that damn brother won't let go. And before I get through with him and toss him out on his ear. I thought I'd better have a word with you. If there was anyone around there with murder in his heart, you ought to know. You would know. Since you had just started on a job for her. You're not interested in petty larceny. So I'd like to know what the job was."

"No doubt," Wolfe said. "Didn't any of those people tell you?"

"No."

"None of them?"

"No."

"Then how did you know she had hired me?"

"The brother told me about Goodwin being there, and that led me to question him. But he doesn't seem to know what your job was about."

"Neither do I."

Cramer took the cigar from his mouth and said vehemently, "Now look! How's it going to hurt you? Loosen up for once! I want to cross this off, that's all. I've got work to do! All I want to know—"

"Please!" Wolfe said curtly. "You say you are satisfied that the death was accidental. You have no shred of evidence of a crime. Miss Huddleston hired me for a confidential job. Her death does not release me, it merely deprives me of the job. If you had an action you could summon me, but you haven't. Will you have some beer?"

"No." Cramer glared. "My God, you can be honorable when you want to be! Will you answer a plain question? Do you think she was murdered?"

"No."

"Then you think it was purely accidental?"

"No."

"What the hell do you think?"

"Nothing at all. About that. I know nothing about it. I have no interest in it. The woman died, as all women do, may she rest in peace, and I lost a fee. Why don't you ask me this: if you knew what I know, if I told you all about the job she hired me for, would you feel that her death required further investigation?"

"Okay. I ask it."

"The answer is no. Since you have discovered no single suspicious circumstance. Will you have some beer?"

"Yes, I will," Cramer growled.

He consumed a bottle, got no further concessions either in information or in hypothetical questions, and departed.

I saw him to the door, returned to the office and remarked:

"Old Frizzle-top seems to be improving with age. Of course he has had the advantage of studying my methods. He seems to have covered the ground up there nearly as well as I could."

"Pfui." Wolfe pushed the tray aside to make room for the map. "Not that I don't agree with you. Nearly as well as you could, yes. But either he didn't have sense enough to learn everything that happened that afternoon, or he missed his best chance to expose a crime, if there was one. It hasn't rained the past week, has it? No."

I cocked an eye at him. "You don't say. How many guesses can I have?"

But he left it at that and got busy with the map, ignoring my questions. It was one of the many occasions when it would have been a pleasure to push him off of the Empire State Building, if there had been any way of enticing him there. Of course there was a chance that he was merely pulling my leg, but I doubted it. I know his tones of voice.

It ruined my night for me. Instead of going to sleep in thirty seconds it took me thirty minutes, trying to figure out what the devil he meant, and I woke up twice with nightmares, the first time because it was raining on me through the roof and each raindrop was a tetanus germ, and the second time I was lost in a desert where it hadn't rained for a hundred years. Next morning, after Wolfe had gone up to the plant rooms at nine o'clock, I got stubborn. I sat at my desk and went over that party at Riverdale in my mind, second by second, as I had reported it to Wolfe. And I got it. I would have hit it sooner if it hadn't been for various interruptions, phone calls and so on, but anyway finally there it was, as obvious as lipstick.

Provided one thing. To settle that I phoned Doc Vollmer, whose home and office were in a house down the street, and learned that tetanus, which carried death, had a third as many lives as a cat—one as a toxin, one as a bacillus, and one as a spore. The bacillus or the spore got in you and manufactured the toxin, which did the dirty work, traveling not with the blood but with the nerves. The bacillus and spore were both anaerobic, but could live in surface soil or dust for years and usually did, especially the spore.

And now what? Just forget it? Wolfe had, but then he wasn't human, whereas I was and am. Besides, it would be very neat if it got results, and it would teach Wolfe a lesson. It was nearly eleven o'clock, and I wanted to get out before he came downstairs, so I phoned up to him that I was leaving on an errand, and walked to the garage on Tenth Avenue and got the roadster. Heading uptown, I stopped at a hardware store near 42nd Street and went in and bought a long-bladed kitchen knife, a narrow garden trowel, and four paper bags. Then I went to a phone booth in a drug store at the corner and called the Huddleston number.

Maryella's voice answered, and I asked to speak to Miss Nichols. In a minute she was on, and I told her I was thinking she might be leaving there soon and I'd like to have her address.

"It's nice of you to call," she said. "It's a—pleasant surprise. Naturally I thought you—last week, I mean—I thought you were just being a detective."

"Don't kid me," I told her. "Anyone that dances the way you do being surprised at a phone call. Not that I suppose you're doing any dancing at present."

"Not now. No."

"Will you be leaving there soon?"

"Not this week. We're trying to help Mr. Huddleston straighten things up."

"Will you send me your address when you go?"

"Why—yes. Certainly. If you want it."

"I do you know. How would it be if I drove up there? Just to say hello?"

"When? Now?"

"Right now. I can be there in twenty minutes. I'd kind of like to see you."

"Why—" Silence. "That would be all right. If you want to take the trouble."

I told her it would be no trouble at all, hung up, went out to the roadster, and made for the entrance to the West Side Highway at 46th Street.

I admit my timing was terrible. If I had arrived, say, between twelve thirty and one, they might have been in the house having lunch, and I could have said I had already eaten and waited for Janet on the terrace, which would have been a perfect opportunity. Of course as it turned out that would have made a monkey of me, so it was just as well that I dubbed it. As it was, leaving the car outside the fence, with the knife in one hip pocket and the trowel in the other, and the folded paper bags in the side pocket of my coat, I walked across the lawn to where Larry stood near the pool, glowering at it. When he heard me coming he transferred the glower to me.

"Hello," I said amiably. "What, no alligators?"

"No. They're gone."

"And Mister? And the bears?"

"Yes. What the hell are you doing here?"

I suppose it would have been sensible to appease him, but he was really quite irritating. Tone and look both. So I said, "I came to play tag with Mister," and started for the house, but Janet appeared, cutting across the lawn. She looked prettier than I remembered her, or maybe not so much prettier as more interesting. Her hair was done differently or something. She said hello to me and let me have a hand to shake, and then told Larry:

"Maryella says you'll have to help her with those Corliss bills. Some of them go back before she came, and she doesn't seem to trust my memory."

Larry nodded at her, and, moving, was in front of me. "What do you want?" he demanded.

"Nothing special," I said. "Freedom of speech, freedom of religion, freedom—"

"If you've got a bill, mail it. You'll get about three percent."

I suppressed impulses and shook my head. "No bill. I came to see Miss Nichols."

"Yes you did. You came to snoop—"

But Janet had her hand on his arm. "Please, Larry. Mr. Goodwin phoned and asked to see me. Please?"

I would have preferred smacking him, and it was irritating to see her with her hand on his arm looking up at him the way she did, but when he turned and marched off towards the house I restrained myself and let him go.

I asked Janet, "What's eating him?"

"Well," she said, "after all, you are a detective. And his aunt has died—terrible, it was terrible—"

"Sure. If you want to call that grief. What was the crack about three per cent?"

"Oh . . ." She hesitated. "But there's nothing secret about it, goodness knows. Miss Huddleston's affairs are tangled up. Everybody thought she was rich, but apparently she spent it as fast as she made it."

"Faster, if the creditors are going to get three percent." I got started towards the terrace, and she came beside me. "In that case, the brother and the nephew are out of luck. I apologize to Larry. He's probably overcome by grief, after all."

"That's a mean thing to say," Janet protested.

"Then I take it back." I waved it away. "Let's talk about something else."

I was thinking the best plan was to sit with her on the terrace, with the idea of getting her to leave me alone there for a few minutes, which was all I needed, but the hot noon sun was coming straight down, and she went on into the house with me behind her. She invited me to sit on a couch with her, but with the tools in my hip pockets I thought it was safer to take a chair facing her. We had a conversation.

Of course the simplest thing would have been to tell her what I wanted to do and then go ahead and do it, and I deny that it was any suspicion of her, either as a letter writer or as a murderess, that kept me from doing that. It was the natural desire I had not to hurt her feelings by letting her know that my real purpose in coming was not just to see her. If things should develop it was good policy to have her friendly. So I played it for a solo. I was thinking it was about time to get on with it, and was figuring out an errand for her, preferably upstairs, that would be sure to keep her five minutes, when suddenly I saw something through the window that made me stare.

It was Daniel Huddleston on the terrace with a newspaper bundle under his arm and a long-bladed knife in one hand and a garden trowel in the other!

I stood up to see better.

"What is it?" Janet asked, and stood up too. I shushed her and whispered in her ear, "First lesson for a detective. Don't make any noise."

Brother Daniel stopped near the center of the terrace, in front of the swing, knelt down on a flagstone, deposited the newspaper bundle and some folded newspapers beside him, and the trowel, and plunged the knife into the strip of turf at the edge of the flagstone. There was nothing furtive about it; he didn't do any glancing over his shoulder, but he worked fast. With the trowel he scooped out a hunk of the turf, the width of the strip, about six inches long and three inches deep, and rolled it in a piece of newspaper. Then a second one, to the right of the first hole, and then a third one, to the left, wrapping each separately.

"What on earth does he think he's doing?" Janet whispered. I squeezed her arm.

He was about done. Opening the package he had

brought with him, he produced three strips of turf the size and shape of those he had just dug out, fitted them into the trench he had made, pressed them with his foot until they were level with the flagstone, remade the package with the three hunks he had removed, and the knife and trowel, and went off as if he were bound somewhere.

I took Janet's hand and gave her an earnest eye. "Listen, girlie," I said, "my one fault is curiosity. Otherwise I am perfect. Don't forget that. It's time for your lunch anyway."

She said something to my back as I made for the door. I emerged onto the terrace cautiously, slid across and into the hedge of shrubbery, made a hole and looked through. Daniel was forty paces away, going across the lawn not in the direction of the drive where my car was but the other way, off to the right. I decided to give him another twenty paces before emerging, and it was well that I did, for suddenly a voice sounded above me:

"Hey, Uncle Dan! Where you going?"

Daniel stopped in his tracks and whirled. I twisted my neck, and through the leaves got a glimpse of Larry's head sticking out of an upper window, and Maryella's beside it.

Larry shouted, "We need you!"

"See you later!" Daniel yelled.

"But it's time for lunch!" Maryella called.

"See you later!" Daniel turned and was off.

"Now that's a performance," Maryella said to Larry.

"Cuckoo," Larry declared.

Their heads went in. But they might still have been looking out, so I scooted along the side of the house to the corner, and from there circled wide around evergreens and similar obstructions before swinging into the direction Daniel had taken. He wasn't in sight. This part of the premises was new to me, and the first thing I knew I ran smack into the fence in the middle of a thicket. I couldn't fight my way through on account of noise, so I doubled around, dashed along the edge of the thicket, and pretty soon hit a path. No sight of Daniel. The path took me to a series of stone steps up a steep bank, and up I went. Getting to the top, I saw him. A hundred feet ahead was a gate in the fence, and he was shutting the gate and starting down a lane between rows of little trees. The package was under his arm. In a way I was more interested in the package than I was in him. What if he threw it down a sewer? So I closed up more than I would have for an ordinary tailing job, and proceeding through the gate, followed him down the lane. At the end of the lane, not far ahead, he stopped, and I dived into the trees.

He had stopped at a curb, a paved street. The way cars were rolling by, apparently it was a main traffic street; and that point was settled when a double-decker bus jerked to a stop right square in front of Daniel, and he climbed on and off the bus went.

I hotfooted it to the corner. It was Marble Avenue. Riverdale is like that. The bus was too far away to read its number, and no taxi was in sight in either direction. I stepped into the street, into the path of the first car coming, and held up a commanding palm. By bad luck it was occupied by the two women that Helen Hokinson used for models, but there was no time to pick and choose. I hopped into the back seat, gave the driver a fleeting glimpse of my detective license, and said briskly:

"Police business. Step on it and catch up with a bus that's ahead."

The one driving emitted a baby scream. The other one said, "You don't look like a policeman. You get out. If you don't we'll drive to a police station."

"Suit yourself, madam. While we sit and talk the most dangerous gangster in New York is escaping. He's on the bus."

"Oh! He'll shoot at us."

"No. He isn't armed."

"Then why is he dangerous?"

"For God's sake," I reached for the door latch, "I'll take a car with a man in it!"

But the car started forward. "You will not," the driver said fiercely. "I'm as good a driver as any man. My husband says so."

She was okay at that. Within a block she had it up to fifty, and she was good at passing, and it wasn't long before we caught up with the bus. At least, a bus. When it stopped at a corner I told her to get alongside, which she did neatly, and with my hand over my face I looked for him and there he was.

"I'm shadowing him," I told the ladies. "I think he's on his way to meet a crooked politician. The first empty taxi we see you can let me out if you want to, but of course he might suspect a taxi, whereas he never would suspect a car like this with two good-looking well-dressed women in it."

The driver looked grim. "In that case," she declared, "it is our duty."

And by gum she crawled along behind that bus for a good three-quarters of an hour, to Riverside Drive, the whole length of the Drive, over to Broadway, and on downtown. I thought the least I could do was furnish diversion, which I did with tales of my experiences with gangsters and kidnappers and so forth. When Daniel was still on the bus after crossing 42nd Street I decided in disgust that he was probably bound for Headquarters, and I was so deeply considering the feasibility of intercepting him before he got there that I nearly missed it when he hopped to the sidewalk at 34th Street. Paying the ladies with thanks and a cordial smile, I jumped out and dodged

through the midday shopping mob, and almost lost him. I
picked him up going west on 34th.

At Eighth Avenue he turned uptown. I kept twenty
yards behind.

At 35th he turned west again.

That was when I got suspicious. Naturally. On he
went, straight as a bullet. When he kept on west of Ninth
Avenue, there was no question about it. I closed up. He
began looking at the numbers on buildings, and came to
the stoop and started up. Boy, I'm telling you, they don't
get away from me. I get my man. I had trailed this one the
length of New York, hanging on like a bulldog, right to
Nero Wolfe's door.

Chapter 5

I had been thinking fast the last two blocks. I had considered, and rejected, three different maneuvers to keep Wolfe from finding out. They all seemed good, but I knew damn well none of them was good enough. He would find out all right, no matter what I did. So I bounded up the steps past Daniel, greeted him, let us in with my key, and took him to the office.

Wolfe, at his desk, frowned at us. "How do you do, Mr. Huddleston. Archie. Where have you been?"

"I know," I said, "it's about lunch time, so I'll make it brief. First cast a glance at this." I took the knife, the trowel, and the paper bags from my pockets and put them on his desk.

Daniel stared and muttered something.

"What is this flummery?" Wolfe demanded.

"No flummery," I asserted. "Tools. It still didn't rain last night. So I went to Riverdale to get the piece of turf where the orangutan poured the iodine. Brother Daniel had the same idea. He was just ahead of me. He's got it in that newspaper. I thought he might be going to toss it in the river, so I tailed him and he led me here. So I look foolish but not dumb. Now you can laugh."

He didn't. He looked at Daniel. "Is that what you have in that package, Mr. Huddleston?"

"It is," Daniel said. "I want—"

"Why did you bring it to me? I'm not a chemist. You are."

"Because I want to authenticate it. I want—"

"Take it to the police."

"No." Daniel looked and sounded determined. "They think I'm nothing but a nuisance. Maybe I am. But if I analyze this myself, without someone to—"

"Don't analyze it yourself. You have colleagues, friends, haven't you?"

"None I would want to give this to."

"Are you sure you have the piece where the iodine was poured?"

"I am. A few drops were on the edge of the flagstone. I also have pieces taken from each side of that piece, for comparison."

"Naturally. Who suggested this step to you?"

"No one. It occurred to me this morning, and I immediately went up there—"

"Indeed. I congratulate you. Take it to the Fisher Laboratories. You know them, don't you?"

"Certainly." Daniel flushed. "I happen not to have any cash at the moment. They are expensive."

"Establish credit. Your sister's estate. Aren't you her nearest relative?"

"There is no estate. The liabilities greatly exceed the assets."

Wolfe looked annoyed. "You are careless not to have cash. Confound it, you should have cash. You understand, sir, my finger is not in this pie. I am not concerned. My lunch is ready. I should bid you good day. But you seem to be capable of using your brains, and that is so rare a phenomenon it is a pity to waste it. Archie, phone

Mr. Weinbach at the Fisher Laboratories. Tell him to expect Mr. Huddleston, to rush the analysis he requires, and to charge it to me. You can pay the bill, sir, at your convenience."

Daniel hesitated. "I have a habit—I am extremely backward about paying bills—"

"You'll pay this one. I'll see that you do. What is argyrol?"

"Argyrol? Why—it's a silver-protein compound. Silver vietllin."

"It stains like iodine. Could tetanus bacilli live in it?"

Daniel considered. "I believe they could. It's far weaker—"

Wolfe nodded impatiently. "Tell Mr. Weinbach to try for it." He got up. "My lunch is waiting."

After I had finished the phone call and ushered Daniel out, with his package, I joined Wolfe in the dining room. Since no discussion of business was permitted at meals, I waited until we were back in the office again before observing:

"I ought to tell you that Janet saw him lifting that turf, and Maryella and the nephew—"

"There is no reason to tell me. I am not concerned." He pointed to the knife and trowel, still on his desk. "Where did you get those things?"

"Bought them."

"Please put them somewhere. They are not to appear on the expense account."

"Then I'll keep them in my room."

"Do so. By all means. Please take a letter to Mr. Hoehn."

His tone said, and that's the end of Miss Huddleston and her affairs for this office, for you, and for me.

No doubt it would have been, except for his vanity. Or perhaps it wasn't vanity; it may be that the reason he permitted his privacy to be invaded again by brother Daniel was that he wanted to impress on him the desirability of getting the bill of the Fisher Laboratories paid as soon as possible. At any rate, when Daniel turned up some hours later, a little before seven that evening, Fritz was told to bring him to the office. At first sight of him I knew he had something, by the look in his eye and the set of his jaw. He tramped over to Wolfe's desk and announced:

"My sister was murdered."

He got an envelope from his pocket, took out a paper and unfolded it, and fumbled the job because his hands were trembling. He swayed a little, steadied himself with a hand on the edge of the desk, looked around for a chair, and sat down.

"I guess I'm a little weak from excitement," he said apologetically. "Then I had only an apple for breakfast, and I haven't eaten anything since."

It was probably the one thing in the world he could have said to keep Wolfe from telling him to go to the police and telling me to bounce him out. The one kind of man that never gets the gate at that house is one with an empty stomach. Glaring at him, not sympathetically but indignantly, Wolfe pushed a button and, when Fritz appeared, inquired:

"How far along is the soup?"

"Quite ready, sir, except for the mushrooms."

"Bring a bowl of it, crackers, cottage cheese, and hot tea."

Daniel tried to protest, but Wolfe didn't even listen. He heaved a deep sigh and leaned back and shut his eyes, a man who had eaten nothing but an apple for twenty-four hours being too painful an object to look at. When Fritz came with the tray I had a table ready in front of Daniel, and he wolfed a couple of crackers and blew on a spoonful of soup and swallowed it.

I had acquired the sheet of paper he had taken from the envelope, a report sheet from Fisher Laboratories, and was looking it over. After some more spoonfuls Daniel said:

"I knew it. I was sure of it. There couldn't—"

"Eat!" Wolfe commanded sternly.

"I'm eating. I'm all right. You were correct about the argyrol. That was a good guess. Argyrol and nothing else." A fork conveyed a hunk of cottage cheese to Daniel's mouth, but he went on, "Not a trace of iodine. And millions of tetanus bacilli, hundreds of millions. Weinbach said he never saw anything like it. And they were all concentrated on the one piece of turf, on the grass stems and the soil surface. The other two pieces had no sign either of the silver vietllin or the tetanus. Weinbach said . . ."

The doorbell rang, but I kept my seat and left it for Fritz because I had no reason to expect any undesirable intrusions. As it turned out, however, it was exactly the kind of invasion Wolfe resents more than anything else. An insurance salesman or a wife wanting her husband tailed is merely a mosquito to be brushed off, with me to do the brushing, but this wasn't as simple as that. The sound of Fritz's voice came from the hall, in indignant protest, and then the door flew open and Inspector Cramer strode in. I mean strode. His first glance caught me, and was it withering. Then he saw who Daniel was, emitted a triumphal grunt, spread his feet apart, and rasped out:

"Come along, you!" And to me: "You too, bud! Come on!"

I grinned at him. "If you ever find time to glance over an interesting document called the Constitution of the United—"

"Shut up, Archie," Wolfe snapped. "Mr. Cramer. What in the name of heaven is the matter with you?"

"Not a thing," Cramer said sarcastically. "Matter with

me? Not a damn thing." I never saw him sorer or sourer.
"Listen!" he said. He stepped to the desk and tapped a
heavy finger on it, sounding like a hammer. "Last night,
sitting right at this desk, what did you say? What did you
tell me?"

Wolfe was grimacing with distaste. "Your tone and
manner, Mr. Cramer—"

"You said, in case you've forgotten, that you weren't
interested in the death of Bess Huddleston! Knew nothing
about it! Weren't interested!" Cramer went on tapping
the desk. "Well, this afternoon somebody in my office got
an idea—we do that once in a while! I sent a man up there,
and young Huddleston showed him where the monkey
poured some of that iodine, and when he went to take some
of that turf for analysis, he found it had already been
taken! It had been carefully filled up with other turf, but
the grass didn't match. He asked questions, and he
learned that Daniel Huddleston had done it, taken the turf
away, and Goodwin had been there and gone with him!"

"Not with him," I corrected emphatically. "After him."

Cramer ignored me. "We went for Huddleston and
couldn't find him. So I come to see you. You and Goodwin.
And what do I find? By God! I find Huddleston! Sitting
here eating! This is the rawest one you've ever pulled!
Removing evidence, destroying evidence—"

"Nonsense," Wolfe said curtly and coldly. "Stop shout-
ing. If you wish to know the purpose of Mr. Huddleston's
visit—"

"Not from you I don't! I'll get it from him! And from
Goodwin! And separately! I'm taking them downtown."

"No," Wolfe said. "Not from my office."

That was the central point of the situation. Twenty
minutes earlier Daniel's empty stomach was all that had
kept Wolfe from chasing him to the police, and it wouldn't
have hurt his appetite any if I had gone along to keep

Daniel company, but this was different. For a cop to remove persons from the house, any person whatever, with
or without a charge or a warrant, except at Wolfe's insti-
gation, was an intolerable insult to his pride, his vanity,
and his sense of the fitness of things. So as was to be
expected, he acted with a burst of energy amounting to
violence. He sat up straight in his chair.

"Mr. Cramer," he said, "sit down."

"Not a chance." Cramer meant it. "You're not going to
take me in with one of your goddamn—"

"Archie, show Mr. Cramer that report from the Fisher
Laboratories."

I stuck it under his nose. His impulse was to push it
away, but no cop, not even an Inspector, dares to refuse to
look at a paper. So he snatched it and scowled at it. Daniel
started to say something, but Wolfe shushed him, and
Daniel finished off the cheese and the last cracker, and put
sugar in his tea and began to stir it.

"So what?" Cramer growled. "How do I know—"

"I sometimes doubt if you know anything," Wolfe said
shortly. "I was not and am not interested in Miss Huddleston's death, though you and Mr. Huddleston and
Archie keep pestering me about it. I have no client. My
client died. You are even affronted to find Mr. Huddleston
here eating. If he's hungry, why the devil shouldn't he eat?
When he appeared here at one o'clock with that turf, I told
him to take it to the police. He said they regarded him as a
nuisance. Why he returned here with the laboratory report, I do not know; I only know he was hungry. If you
are disgruntled because you have no assurance that the
piece of turf examined by the laboratory is the piece onto
which the chimpanzee poured some of the contents of the
bottle of supposed iodine, I can't help it. Why didn't you
get the turf yourself when Mr. Huddleston first called on
you, five days ago? It was an obvious thing to do."

"I didn't know then that the chimpanzee had poured—"

"You should have. Proper questioning would have got it. Either it was worth investigating competently, or not at all. Well, sir, there's your report. Keep it. You'll get a bill for it from the Fisher Laboratories. Archie, make a note of that. It wasn't iodine in that bottle; it was argyrol, and it was reeking with tetanus bacilli. An uncommonly ugly thing to do. I have never heard of a more objectionable way of committing murder, nor of an easier or simpler one. I trust, sir, that you'll make an arrest. You should, since you have only five people to deal with—the five who were there, not counting Archie—"

"Wait a minute," Daniel protested. "You're wrong. That bottle could have been put there any time—"

Wolfe shook his head. "No. Only that afternoon. If we had to we could argue that it is not credible that it was left in the cupboard for an extended period, for just anyone to use, but we don't have to. The bottle in that cupboard contained good iodine at four o'clock that afternoon."

Cramer growled. Daniel demanded, "How do you know that?"

"Because it was used at that hour. By Archie. He tripped on an alligator and scratched his hand."

"By God," Cramer said, and sat down. Daniel looked at me, and I nodded at him.

Daniel looked at Wolfe, his jaw hanging open and his face gray. "Then it c-couldn't have been—" he stammered.

"Couldn't have been what?" Cramer demanded.

"It couldn't have been someone—" Daniel shook his head weakly, as if trying to reject something. Suddenly he exclaimed fiercely, "I can't believe that! One of them? Those two girls or Larry or Brady?"

"Or you, sir," Wolfe said dryly. "You were there. As for your trying to get the police started on it, you may be more devious than you look. Save your indignation. Calm yourself. Your digestive processes will make a botch of that soup and cheese if you don't. So, Mr. Cramer, I give you that. It was an impromptu job. Not that it was unpremeditated; far from it; it was carefully prepared; an iodine bottle had been emptied and washed and replenished with argyrol and an army of tetanus germs."

Wolfe compressed his lips. "Very ugly. It would take an extremely unattractive person to think of that, let alone do it. It was done. I presume a situation was to be created requiring the use of the iodine; in fact, there is reason to believe that it had been created, or was in process; but the accident on the terrace provided an opportunity too good to be missed. From the standpoint of technique, it was brilliantly conceived and managed. Only two things needed to be done: drop a piece of glass into Miss Huddleston's slipper, which was quite simple with everyone jostling around picking up the pieces, and substitute the bottle of bogus iodine for the one that was in the cupboard. With no risk whatever. If Miss Huddleston shook the glass out of her slipper before putting it on, if for any reason she didn't cut herself, the bottle could be switched again and nothing lost. There is a point, of course: if the bottle in the cupboard had a different kind of label—"

"They all had the same label," Cramer rumbled.

"All?"

"Yes. There were seven bottles of iodine in that house, counting the kitchen, and they were all the same, size and shape and label."

"They bought it wholesale," I explained, "on account of Mister and the bears."

"That," Wolfe said, "is precisely the sort of thing you would know, Mr. Cramer. Seven. Not eight. Seven. And of course you had it all analyzed and it was all good iodine."

"It was. And what the hell is there in that to be sarcastic about? It clears up your point, don't it? And I might mention another point. The murderer had to leave the terrace, go in the house, between the time the glasses got broken and the time Miss Huddleston cut herself, to switch the iodine bottles."

Wolfe shook his head. "That offers nothing. They all went in the house during that period. Miss Nichols went for brooms and pans. The nephew went for another tray of supplies. Miss Timms went for a vacuum cleaner. Dr. Brady carried off the debris."

Cramer stared at him in exasperation. "And you know nothing about it! Jesus. You're not interested!"

"I didn't," Daniel put in. "I didn't leave the terrace during that period."

"So far as I know," Wolfe agreed, "that is correct. But if I were you I wouldn't brag about it. You went for the iodine. It was the bottle you handed to Dr. Brady that he used. Your jaw is loose again. You bounce, Mr. Huddleston, from wrath to indignation, with amazing agility. Frankly, I doubt if it is possible to suspect you of murdering your sister. If you did it, your facial dexterity surpasses anything in my experience. If you'll stay and dine with me, I'll reach a decision on that before the meal is finished. Partridges in marinade. *En escabeche.*" His eyes gleamed. "They are ready for us." He pushed back his chair and got himself onto his feet. "So, Mr. Cramer, it seems likely that it is limited to four, which simplifies your task. You'll excuse me, I'm sure—"

"Yeah," Cramer said, "glad to." He was up too. "But you'll enjoy your partridges alone. Huddleston and Goodwin are going with me." His glance took us in. "Let's go."

Wolfe looked displeased. "I have already cleared away the brush for you. If you insist on seeing them this evening, they can call at your office—say at ten o'clock?"

"No. They're coming now."

Wolfe's chin went up. His mouth opened and then closed again. It was an interesting sight, especially for me, knowing as I do how hard he is to flabbergast, next to impossible, but I can't truthfully say I enjoyed it, because of who was doing it. So I spoke up:

"I'm staying for the partridges. And I may or may not show up at ten o'clock, depending—"

"To hell with you," Cramer rumbled. "I'll deal with you later. We'll go, Mr. Huddleston."

Wolfe took a step, and his voice was as close to trembling with rage as it ever got. "Mr. Huddleston is my invited guest!"

"I've uninvited him. Come, Mr. Huddleston."

Wolfe turned to Daniel. He was controlling himself under insufferable provocation. "Mr. Huddleston. I have invited you to my table. You are under no compulsion, legal or moral, to accompany this man on demand. He struts and blusters. Later Mr. Goodwin will drive you—"

But Daniel said firmly, "I guess I'll go along with him, Mr. Wolfe. After the days I've spent trying to get them started on this . . ."

The partridge was swell, and I ate nearly as much as Wolfe did. Otherwise it was one of the dullest meals I had ever had under Wolfe's roof. He didn't say a word, clear to the coffee.

Chapter 6

I described that scene in detail, because if it hadn't been for that I doubt if the murderer of Bess Huddleston would ever have been caught. One of Cramer's bunch might possibly have doped it out, but they never in the world would have got enough evidence for an arrest. And Wolfe, with no client and no commitment, was through with it, or would have been if Cramer hadn't kidnapped a dinner guest right under his nose and made him so damn mad he had to take Amphojel twice that evening.

Twice. The first dose was right after dinner, when he sent me up to his room for the bottle. The second was long after midnight, when I got home after my call on Inspector Cramer downtown. I sneaked quietly up the two flights to my room, but was just starting to undress when the house phone on my table buzzed, and, answering it and getting a summons, I descended to Wolfe's room and entered. The light was on and he wasn't in his bed, and, proceeding to his bathroom, I found him taking another shot of Amphojel, with a scowl on his face that would have scared Joe Louis right out of the ring. He was a spectacle anyway, draped in the ten yards of yellow silk that it took to make him a suit of pajamas.

"Well?" he demanded.

"Nothing. Routine. Questions and a signed statement."

"He'll pay for this." Wolfe made a face like an infuriated gargoyle and put the Amphojel bottle back in the cabinet. "I haven't had to take this stuff since that hideous experiment with eels in the spring. He'll pay for it. Go to Riverdale early in the morning. Consult the stableman and learn—"

"I doubt if there is one. The horses are gone. The creditors get two percent."

"Find him. Wherever he is. I wish to know whether anyone has recently removed anything, any material, from the vicinity of the stable. A small paper bag filled at the manure pile would have been ideal. Question him. If he's difficult, bring him here. Also—is there a servant on the place?"

I nodded. "The butler. I think he's hanging on hoping to get paid."

"Ask him about that bottle that Miss Huddleston found broken in her bathroom. Whatever he knows about it. Ask any other servant who was there at the time. All details possible—"

"The others too? Maryella, Janet, Larry—"

"No. Mention it to no one but the servants. Phone before returning. Before you go, leave phone numbers on my desk—Riverdale, Mr. Huddleston, Dr. Brady—that's all. He'll pay for this. Good night."

So we had a case. We had no client, no retainer, and no fee in sight, but at least we had a case, which was better than sitting around on my tail listening to the radio.

I made six hours' sleep do me, and before eight o'clock next morning I was up at Riverdale. I didn't phone in advance, since I had to go anyway to get my car which I had left on the driveway the day before. Greeted at the door by Hoskins, I was told that the stableman was gone and maybe Maryella had his address. I would have preferred asking Janet or even Larry, but Hoskins said they were both late sleepers and Maryella was already eating breakfast, so I got the address from her, and by good luck it wasn't Bucyrus, Ohio, but merely Brooklyn. Whatever else you want to say about Brooklyn, and so do I, it does have one big advantage, it's close.

That errand was one of the simplest I have ever performed, once I found the address and the stableman. His name was Tim Lavery and a scar on his cheek made him look mean until he grinned. I started with him cautiously, pretending that my mind was on something else, but soon saw that it wasn't necessary to sneak up on him, and put it to him straight.

"Sure," he said, "one day about a month ago, maybe a little more, Doc Brady filled up a box he brought, an empty candy box. I helped him. He said he wanted it for a test. One of his patients had died of tetanus—I forget her name—"

I pretended there was nothing to be excited about. "Where'd he take it from? The stall?"

"No. The pile. I dug into the middle of the pile for him."

"Who was with him that day? One of the girls?"

Tim shook his head. "He was alone when he did that. They had been riding—I forget who was with him that day—and they went to the house and then he came back alone with that box and said what he wanted."

"Do you remember the day? The date?"

The best he could do on that was the last week in July. I got the details all filled in, made sure that he would be available if and when needed, and, leaving, stopped at the first phone booth and called Wolfe. Answering from the plant rooms and therefore with his mind occupied, he displayed no exultation, which he wouldn't anyway, and informed me that my discovery made no change in the rest of my assignment.

Arriving at the Huddleston place in Riverdale a little

after ten o'clock, my luck still held. Instead of stopping by the side gate, I continued along the drive, where another gate opened onto a path leading to the back door, and Hoskins was there in the kitchen having a conversation with a depressed-looking female in a maid's uniform. They acted reserved but not hostile; in fact, Hoskins invited me to have a cup of coffee, which I accepted. Taking an inventory as a precaution against any unwelcome interruptions, I was told that Larry and Maryella had both gone out, Daniel hadn't shown up that morning, no city employees were on the premises, and Janet had just had breakfast in bed. The field was clear, but I had a hunch that a delegation from Cramer's office might be appearing any minute, so I got down to business without wasting any time.

They both remembered all about it. Shortly after lunch that Tuesday afternoon Hoskins had been summoned to Miss Huddleston's room upstairs and requested to take a look at the bathroom. Broken glass was everywhere, in the tub, on the floor, the remnants of a large bottle of bath salts that had been kept on a high shelf above the bathtub. Miss Huddleston hadn't done it. Hoskins hadn't done it. The maid, summoned, said she hadn't done it, and then she and Hoskins cleaned up the mess. I asked what about the orangutan. Possibly, they said, with that beast anything was possible, but it had not been permitted upstairs and seldom went there, and had not been observed inside the house that day.

I filled in details all I could, even asking to view the remains of the broken bottle, which they said had been thick and heavy and creamy yellow in color, but that had been carted away. Then I asked Hoskins to let me take a look at the bathroom, and when we started for the stairs the maid came along, mumbling something about Miss

Nichols' breakfast tray. Bess Huddleston's room was more like a museum than a bedroom, the walls covered with framed autographed photographs and letters, and all the available space filled with everything from a lady manikin in an Eskimo suit to a string of Chinese lanterns, but what I was interested in was the bathroom. It was all colors, the World War camouflage type, or Devil's Rainbow. It made me too dizzy to do a decent job of inspection, but I managed to note such details as the position of the shelf on which the bottle of bath salts had stood. There was a new bottle there, nearly full, and I was reaching for it to take it down to look at it when I suddenly jerked around and cocked an ear and stepped to the door. Hoskins was standing in the middle of the room in a state of suspended animation, his back to me.

"Who screamed?" I demanded.

"Down the hall," he said without turning. "There's nobody but Miss Nichols—"

There had been nothing ear-piercing about it, in fact I had barely heard it, and there were no encores, but a scream is a scream. I marched past Hoskins and through the door, which was standing open, to the hall, and kept going.

"Last door on the right," Hoskins said behind me. I knew that, having been in Janet's room before. The door was shut. I turned the knob and went in, and saw no one, but another door, standing open, revealed a corner of a bathroom. As I started for it the maid's voice came out:

"Who is it?"

"Archie Goodwin. What—"

The maid appeared in the doorway, looking flustered. "You can't come in! Miss Nichols isn't dressed!"

"Okay." I halted out of delicacy. "But I heard a scream. Do you need any rescuing, Janet?"

"Oh, no!" the undressed invisible Janet called, in a voice so weak I could just hear it. "No, I'm all right!" The voice was not only weak, it was shaky.

"What happened?" I asked.

"Nothing serious," the maid said. "A cut on her arm. She cut herself with a piece of glass."

"She what?" I goggled. But without waiting for an answer, I stepped across and walked through the maid into the bathroom. Janet, undressed in the fullest sense of the word and wet all over, was seated on a stool. Ignoring protests and shaking off the maid, who was as red as a beet having her modesty shocked by proxy, I got a towel from a rack and handed it to Janet.

"Here," I said, "this will protect civilization. How the dickens did you do that?"

I lifted her left arm for a look. The cut, nearly an inch long, halfway between the wrist and the elbow, looked worse than it probably was on account of the mixture of blood and iodine. It certainly didn't seem to be worth fainting for, but Janet's face looked as if she might be going to faint. I took the iodine bottle out of her hand and put the cork in it.

"I never scream," Janet said, holding the towel up to her chin. "Really, I never do. But it seemed so . . . cutting myself with glass . . . so soon after Miss Huddleston . . ." She swallowed. "I didn't scream when I cut myself; I'm not quite that silly, really I'm not. I screamed when I saw the piece of glass in the bath brush. It seemed so—"

"Here it is," the maid said.

I took it. It was a piece of jagged glass, creamy yellow, not much bigger than my thumbnail.

"It's like a piece of that bottle that was broke in Miss Huddleston's room that you was asking about," the maid said.

"I'll keep it for a souvenir," I announced, and dropped it into the pocket where I had put the iodine bottle, and picked up the bath brush from the floor. It was soaking wet. "You mean you got in the tub and got soaped, and started to use the brush and cut yourself, and looked at the brush and saw the piece of glass wedged in the bristles, and screamed. Huh?"

Janet nodded. "I know it was silly to scream—"

"I was in the room," the maid said, "and I ran in and—"

"Okay," I cut her off. "Get me some gauze and bandages."

"There in the cabinet," Janet said.

I did a neat job on her, using plenty of gauze because the cut was still trying to bleed. Where she needed the blood was in her face, which was still white and scared, though she tried to smile at me when she thanked me.

I patted her on a nice round shoulder. "Don't mention it, girlie. I'll wait downstairs until you get dressed. I like you in that towel, but I think it would be sensible to go to a doctor and get a shot of antitoxin. I'll drive you. When you—"

"Anitoxin?" she gasped.

"Sure." I patted her again. "Just a precaution. Nothing to worry about. I'll be waiting downstairs."

Hoskins, hovering around in the hall, was relieved when I told him there was nothing for him to do except to get me a piece of paper to wrap the bath brush in. I waited till I was alone, down in the living room, to take the iodine bottle from my pocket, uncork it, and smell it. Whatever it was, it wasn't iodine. I put the cork back in good and tight, went to a lavatory across the hall and washed my hands, and then found a telephone and dialed Wolfe's number.

He answered himself, from the plant rooms since it wasn't eleven o'clock yet, and I gave it to him, all of it. When I finished he said immediately and urgently:

"Get her away from there!"

"Yes, sir, that is my intention—"

"Confound it, at once! Why phone me? If Mr. Cramer goes—"

"Please," I said firmly. "She was naked. I have no white horse, and she hasn't got much hair, at least not that much. As soon as she's dressed we're off. I was going to suggest that you phone Doc Vollmer and tell him to have a dose of antitoxin ready. We'll be there in about half an hour. Or I can phone him from here—"

"No. I will. Leave as soon as possible."

"Righto."

I went upstairs to the door of Janet's room and called to her that I'd be waiting by the side gate, and then went out and turned the car around and took it that far back down the drive. I was debating what course to follow if a police car put in an appearance, when here she came down the path, a little wobbly on her pins and far from pert but her buttons all buttoned. I helped her in and tore out of there with the gravel flying.

She didn't seem to feel like talking. I explained to her about Doc Vollmer being an old friend of ours, with his home and office on the same block as Nero Wolfe's house, so I was taking her there, and I tried a few leading questions, such as whether she had any idea how the piece of glass got into the bristles of her bath brush, but she didn't seem to be having any ideas. What she needed was a strong man to hold her hand, but I was driving. She had simply had the daylights scared out of her.

I had no explaining to do at Doc Vollmer's, since Wolfe had talked to him on the phone, and we weren't in there more than twenty minutes altogether. He cleaned the cut thoroughly, applied some of his own iodine, gave her the antitoxin in that arm, and then took me to an inside room and asked me for the iodine bottle I had. When I gave it to him he uncorked it, smelled it, frowned, poured a little of the contents into a glass vial, corked it again even tighter than I had, and handed it back to me.

"She'll be all right," he said. "What a devilish trick! Tell Mr. Wolfe I'll phone him as soon as possible."

I escorted Janet back out to the car. It was only a

couple of hundred feet from there to Wolfe's door, and I
discovered that I couldn't drive the last thirty of them
because two cars were parked in front. Janet hadn't even
asked why I was taking her to Wolfe's house. Apparently
she was leaving it up to me. I gave her a reassuring grin as
I opened the door with my key and waved her in.

Not knowing who the callers might be, the owners of
the cars in front, instead of taking her straight to the office
I ushered her into the front room. But one of them was
there, sprawled in a chair, and when Janet saw him she
emitted an exclamation. It was Larry Huddleston. I
greeted him, invited Janet to sit, and not wanting to use
the connecting door to the office, went around by the hall.
Wolfe wasn't in the office, but two more visitors were, and
they were Dr. Brady and Daniel Huddleston, evidently,
judging from their attitudes, not being chummy.

Oho, I thought, we're having a party, and went to the
kitchen, and there was Wolfe.

He was standing by the long table, watching Fritz rub
a spice mixture into slices of calf's liver, and watching with
him, standing beside him, closer to him than I had ever
seen any woman or girl of any age tolerated, with her hand
slipped between his arm and his bulk, was Maryella.

Wolfe gave me a fleeting glance. "Back, Archie? We're
doing mock terrapin. Miss Timms had a suggestion." He
leaned over to peer at the liver, straightened, and sighed
clear to the bottom. He turned to me: "And Miss Nichols?"

"In front. Doc Vollmer took a sample and will phone as
soon as possible."

"Good. On the coldest shelf, Fritz; the time is uncertain; and leave the door to Archie. Archie, we are busy and
not available. All of us. Come, Miss Timms."

She couldn't cling to him as they went through the
door, because there wasn't room.

Chapter 7

D r. Brady said sharply, "I've been waiting here over half an hour. How long will this take? I'm due at my office at one o'clock."

I was at my desk and he was nearby, on one of the straight-backed chairs. Next to him was Maryella, in the wing chair that I like to read in, and on the other side of her was Larry. Then Daniel Huddleston; and ending the arc was Janet in the red leather chair, her shoulders sagging, looking as if she were only about half there. As far as that goes, none of them looked very comfortable, not even Maryella; she would glance at one of them and then look back at Wolfe, and set her teeth on her lip and clear her throat again.

Wolfe's half-open eyes were directed at Brady. "I'm afraid you may be a little late at your office, doctor. I'm sorry—"

"But what kind of a performance is this? You said on the telephone—"

"Please," Wolfe interrupted sharply. "I said that to get you here." His glance went around. "The situation is no longer as I represented it on the phone, to any of you. I told you that it was definitely known that Miss Huddleston had been murdered. Now we're a little further along. I know who murdered her."

They stared at him. Maryella's teeth went deeper into her lip. Janet gripped the arms of her chair and stopped breathing. Daniel leaned forward with his chin stuck out like a halfback waiting for a signal. Brady made a noise in his throat. The only one who uttered anything intelligible was Larry. He said harshly:

"The hell you do."

Wolfe nodded. "I do. That is one change in the situation. The other is that an attempt has been made to murder Miss Nichols.—Please! There is no cause for alarm. The attempt was frustrated—"

"When?" Brady demanded. "What kind of an attempt?"

"To murder Janet!" Maryella exclaimed incredulously.

Wolfe frowned at them. "This will go more quickly and smoothly with no interruptions. I'll make it as brief as possible; I assure you I have no wish to prolong the unpleasantness. Especially since I find less than enjoyable the presence in this room of an extremely unattractive person. I shall call that person X. As you all know, X began with an effort to injure Miss Huddleston by sending anonymous letters—"

"Nothing of the sort!" Larry blurted indignantly. "We don't know that one of us sent those letters! Neither do you!"

"Put it this way, Mr. Huddleston." Wolfe wiggled a finger at him. "I make statements. You suspect belief. In the end there will be a verdict, and you will concur or not. X sent those letters. Then he—I am forced thus to exclude women, at least temporarily, by the pronominal inadequacy of our language—then he became dissatisfied with the results, or something happened, no matter which. In any case, X decided on something more concrete and conclusive. Murder. The technique was unquestionably suggested by the recent death of Miss Horrocks by teta-nus. A small amount of material procured at the stable, immersed in water, furnished the required emulsion. It was strained and mixed with argyrol, the mixture was put in a bottle with an iodine label, and the bottle was substi-tuted for the iodine bottle in the cabinet in Miss Hud-dleston's bathroom. But—"

"Her bathroom?" Maryella was incredulous again.

"Yes, Miss Timms. But X was not one to wait indefi-nitely for some accidental disjunction in Miss Hud-dleston's skin. He carried the preparations further, by smashing her bottle of bath salts and inserting a sliver of glass among the bristles of her bath brush. Beautifully simple. It would be supposed that the sliver lodged there when the bottle broke. If she saw it and removed it, no harm done, try again. If she didn't see it, she would cut herself, and there was the iodine bottle—"

"Nuts!" Larry exploded. "You can't possibly—"

"No?" Wolfe snapped. "Archie, if you please?"

I took it from my pocket and handed it to him, and he displayed it to them between his thumb and forefinger. "Here it is. The identical piece of glass."

They craned their necks. Brady stretched clear out of his chair, demanding, "How in the name of God—"

"Sit down, Dr. Brady. How did I get it? We'll come to that. Those were the preparations. But chance inter-vened, to make better ones. That very afternoon, on the terrace, a tray of glasses was upset and the pieces flew everywhere. X conceived a brilliant improvisation on the spot. Helping to collect the pieces, he deposited one in Miss Huddleston's slipper, and, entering the house on an errand, as all of you did in connection with that minor catastrophe, he ran upstairs and removed the sliver of glass from the bath brush, and got the bogus bottle of iodine, took it downstairs, and placed it in the cupboard in the living room, removing the genuine one kept there. For an active person half a minute, at most a minute, did for that."

Wolfe sighed. "As you know, it worked. Miss Huddleston stuck her foot in the slipper and cut her toe, her brother brought the iodine, Dr. Brady applied it, and she got tetanus and died." His eyes darted to Brady. "By the way, doctor, that suggests a question. Is it worthy of remark that you failed to notice the absence of the characteristic odor of iodine? I merely ask."

Brady was looking grim. "As far as I am concerned," he said acidly, "it remains to be proven that the bottle did not contain iodine, and therefore—"

"Nonsense. I told you on the phone. The piece of turf where the chimpanzee poured some of the contents has been analyzed. Argyrol, no iodine, and a surfeit of tetanus germs. The police have it. I tell you, I tell all of you, that however disagreeable you may find this inquiry as I pursue it, it would be vastly more disagreeable if the police were doing it. Your alternative—"

The doorbell called me away, since Fritz had been told to leave it to me. I dashed out, not wanting to miss anything crucial, and naturally took the precaution, under the circumstances, of pulling the curtain aside for a peek through the glass. It was well that I did. I never saw the stoop more officially populated. Inspector Cramer, Lieutenant Rowcliff, and Sergeant Stebbins! I slipped the chain bolt in place, which would let the door come only five inches, turned the lock and the knob and pulled, and spoke through the crack:

"They don't live here any more."

"Listen, you goddamn squirt," Cramer said impolitely. "Open the door!"

"Can't. The hinge is broke."

"I say open up! We know they're here!"

"You do in a pig's eye. The things you *don't* know. If you've got one, show it. No? No warrant? And all the judges out to lunch—"

"By God, if you think—"

"I don't. Mr. Wolfe thinks. All I have is brute force. Like this—"

I banged the door to, made sure the lock had caught, went to the kitchen and stood on a chair and removed a screw, bolted the back door and told Fritz to leave it that way, and returned to the office. Wolfe stopped talking to look at me. I nodded, and told him as I crossed to my chair:

"Three irate men. They'll probably return with legalities."

"Who are they?"

"Cramer, Rowcliff, Stebbins."

"Ha." Wolfe looked gratified. "Disconnect the bell."

"Done."

"Bolt the back door."

"Done."

"Good." He addressed them: "An inspector, a lieutenant, and a sergeant of police have this building under siege. Since they are investigating murder, and since all of the persons involved have been collected here by me and they know it, my bolted doors will irritate them almost beyond endurance. I shall let them enter when I am ready, not before. If any of you wish to leave now, Mr. Goodwin will let you out to the street. Do you?"

Nobody moved or spoke, or breathed.

Wolfe nodded. "During your absence, Archie, Dr. Brady stated that outdoors on that terrace, with a breeze going, it is not likely that the absence of the iodine odor would have been noticed by him, or by anyone. Is that correct, doctor?"

"Yes," Brady said curtly.

"Very well. I agree with you." Wolfe surveyed the group. "So X's improvisation was a success. Later, of course, he replaced the genuine iodine in the cupboard and removed the bogus. From his standpoint, it was next to perfect. It might indeed have been perfect, invulnerable to any inquest, if the chimpanzee hadn't poured some of that mixture on the grass. I don't know why X didn't attend to that; there was plenty of time, whole days and nights; possible he hadn't seen the chimpanzee doing it, or maybe he didn't realize the danger. And we know he was foolhardy. He should certainly have disposed of the bogus iodine and the piece of glass he had removed from Miss Huddleston's bath brush when it was no longer needed, but he didn't. He—"

"How do you know he didn't?" Larry demanded.

"Because he kept them. He must have kept them, since he used them. Yesterday he put the bogus iodine in the cabinet in Miss Nichols' bathroom, and the piece of glass in her bath brush."

I was watching them all at once, or trying to, but he or she was too good for me. The one who wasn't surprised and startled put on so good an imitation of it that I was no better off than I was before. Wolfe was taking them in too, his narrowed eyes the only moving part of him, his arms folded, his chin on his necktie.

"And," he rumbled, "it worked. This morning. Miss Nichols got in the tub, cut her arm, took the bottle from the cabinet, and applied the stuff—"

"Good God!" Brady was out of his chair. "Then she must—"

Wolfe pushed a palm at him. "Calm yourself, doctor. Antitoxin has been administered."

"By whom?"

"By a qualified person. Please be seated. Thank you. Miss Nichols does not need your professional services, but

I would like to use your professional knowledge. First—Archie, have you got that brush?"

It was on my desk, still wrapped in the paper Hoskins had got for me. I removed the paper and offered the brush to Wolfe, but instead of taking it he asked me:

"You use a bath brush, don't you? Show us how you manipulate it. On your arm."

Accustomed as I was to loony orders from him, I merely obeyed. I started at the wrist and made vigorous sweeps to the shoulder and back.

"That will do, thank you.—No doubt all of you, if you use bath brushes, wield them in a similar manner. Not, that is, with a circular motion, or around the arm, but lengthwise, up and down. So the cut on Miss Nichols's arm, as Mr. Goodwin described it to me, runs lengthwise, about halfway between the wrist and the elbow. Is that correct, Miss Nichols?"

Janet nodded, cleared her throat, and said, "Yes," in a small voice.

"And it's about an inch long. A little less?"

"Yes."

Wolfe turned to Brady. "Now for you, sir. Your professional knowledge. To establish a premise invulnerable to assault. Why did Miss Nichols carve a gash nearly an inch long on her arm? Why didn't she jerk the brush away the moment she felt her skin being ruptured?"

"Why?" Brady was scowling at him. "For the obvious reason that she didn't feel it."

"Didn't feel it?"

"Certainly not. I don't know what premise you're trying to establish, but with the bristles rubbing her skin there would be no feeling of the sharp glass cutting her. None whatever. She wouldn't know she had been cut until she saw the blood."

"Indeed." Wolfe looked disappointed. "You're sure of that? You'd testify to it?"

"I would. Positively."

"And any other doctor would?"

"Certainly."

"Then we'll have to take it that way. Those, then, are the facts. I have finished. Now it's your turn to talk. All of you. Of course this is highly unorthodox, all of you together like this, but it would take too long to do it properly, singly."

He leaned back and joined his finger tips at the apex of his central magnificence. "Miss Timms, we'll start with you. Talk, please."

Maryella said nothing. She seemed to be meeting his gaze, but she didn't speak.

"Well, Miss Timms?"

"I don't know—" she tried to clear the huskiness from her voice—"I don't know what you want me to say."

"Nonsense," Wolf said sharply. "You know quite well. You are an intelligent woman. You've been living in that house two years. It is likely that ill feeling or fear, any emotion whatever, was born in one of these people and distended to the enormity of homicide, and you were totally unaware of it? I don't believe it. I want you to tell me the things that I would drag out of you if I kept you here all afternoon firing questions at you."

Maryella shook her head. "You couldn't drag anything out of me that's not in me."

"You won't talk?"

"I can't talk." Maryella did not look happy. "When I've got nothing to say."

Wolfe's eyes left her. "Miss Nichols?"

Janet shook her head.

"I won't repeat it. I'm saying to you what I said to Miss Timms."

"I know you are." Janet swallowed and went on in a thin voice, "I can't tell you anything, honestly I can't."

"Not even who tried to kill you? You have no idea who tried to kill you this morning?"

"No—I haven't. That's what frightened me so much. I don't know who it was."

Wolfe grunted, and turned to Larry. "Mr. Huddleston?"

"I don't know a damn thing," Larry said gruffly.

"You don't. Dr. Brady?"

"It seems to me," Brady said coolly, "that you stopped before you were through. You said you know who murdered Miss Huddleston. If—"

"I prefer to do it this way, doctor. Have you anything to tell me?"

"No."

"Nothing with any bearing on any aspect of this business?"

"No."

Wolfe's eyes went to Daniel "Mr. Huddleston, you have already talked, to me and to the police. Have you anything new to say?"

"I don't think I have," Daniel said slowly. He looked more miserable than anyone else. "I agree with Dr. Brady that if you—"

"I would expect you to," Wolfe snapped. His glance swept the arc. "I warn all you, with of course one exception, that the police will worm it out of you and it will be a distressing experience. They will make no distinction between relevancies and irrelevancies. They will, for example, impute significance to the fact that Miss Timms has been trying to captivate Mr. Larry Huddleston with her charms—"

"I have not!" Maryella cried indignantly. "Whatever—"

"Yes, you have. At least you did on Tuesday, August

19th. Mr. Goodwin is a good reporter. Sitting on the arm of his chair. Ogling him—"

"I wasn't! I wasn't trying to captivate him—"

"Do you love him? Desire him? Fancy him?"

"I certainly don't!"

"Then the police will be doubly suspicious. They will suspect that you were after him for his aunt's money. And speaking of money, some of you must know that Miss Huddleston's brother was getting money from her and dissatisfied with what he got. Yet you refuse to tell me—"

"I wasn't dissatisfied," Daniel broke in. His face flushed and his voice rose. "You have no right to make insinuations—"

"I'm not making insinuations." Wolfe was crisp. "I am showing you the sort of thing the police will get their teeth into. They are quite capable of supposing you were blackmailing your sister—"

"Blackmail!" Daniel squealed indignantly. "She gave it to me for research—"

"Research!" his nephew blurted with a sneer. "Research! The Elixir of Life! Step right up, gents . . ."

Daniel sprang to his feet, and for a second I thought his intention was to commit mayhem on Larry, but it seemed he merely was arising to make a speech.

"That," he said, his jaw quivering with anger, "is a downright lie! My motivation and my methods are both strictly scientific. Elixir of Life is a romantic and inadmissible conception. The proper scientific term is 'catholicon.' My sister agreed with me, and being a woman of imagination and insight, for years she generously financed—"

"Catholicon!" Wolfe was staring at him incredulously. "And I said you were capable of using your brains!"

"I assure you, sir—"

"Don't try. Sit down." Wolfe was disgusted. "I don't care if you wasted your sister's money, but there are some things you people know that I do care about, and you are foolish not to tell me." He wiggled a finger at Brady. "You, doctor, should be ashamed of yourself. You ought to know better. It is idiotic to withhold facts which are bound to be uncovered sooner or later. You said you had nothing to tell me with any bearing on any aspect of this business. What about the box of stable refuse you procured for the stated purpose of extracting tetanus germs from it?"

Daniel made a noise and turned his head to fix Brady with a stare. Brady was taken aback, but not as much as might have been expected. He regarded Wolfe a moment and then said quietly, "I admit I should have told you that."

"Is that all you have to say about it? Why didn't you tell the police when they first started to investigate?"

"Because I thought there was nothing to investigate. I continued to think so until this morning, when you phoned me. It would have served no useful purpose—"

"What did you do with that stuff?"

"I took it to the office and did some experiments with two of my colleagues. We were settling an argument. Then we destroyed it. All of it."

"Did any of these people know about it?"

"I don't—" Brady frowned. "Yes, I remember—I discussed it. Telling them how dangerous any small cut might be—"

"Not me," Daniel said grimly. "If I had known you did that—"

They glared at each other. Daniel muttered something and sat down.

The phone rang, and I swiveled and got it. It was Doc Vollmer, and I nodded to Wolfe and he took it. When he hung up he told them:

"The bottle from which Miss Nichols treated her wound this morning contained enough tetanus germs to destroy the population of a city, properly distributed." He focused on Brady. "You may have some idea, doctor, how the police would regard that episode, especially if you had withheld it. It would give you no end of trouble. In a thing like this evasion or concealment should never be attempted without the guidance of an expert. By the way, how long had you known Miss Huddleston?"

"I had known her casually for some time. Several years."

"How long intimately?"

"I wouldn't say I knew her intimately. A couple of months ago I formed the habit of going there rather often."

"What made you form the habit? Did you fall in love with her?"

"With whom?"

"Miss Huddleston."

"Certainly not." Brady looked not only astonished but insulted. "She was old enough to be my mother."

"Then why did you suddenly start going there?"

"Why—a man goes places, that's all."

Wolfe shook his head. "Not in an emotional vacuum. Was it greed or parsimony? Free horseback rides? I doubt it; your income is probably adequate. Mere convenience? No; it was out of your way, quite a bother. My guess, to employ the conventional euphemism, is love. Had you fallen in love with Miss Nichols?"

"No."

"Then what? I assure you, doctor, I am doing this much more tactfully than the police would. What was it?"

A funny look appeared on Brady's face. Or a series of looks. First it was denial, then hesitation, then embarrassment, then do or die. All the time his eyes were straight at Wolfe. Suddenly he said, in a voice louder than he had been using, "I had fallen in love with Miss Timms. Violently."

"Oh!" Maryella exclaimed in amazement. "You certainly never—"

"Don't interrupt, please," Wolfe said testily. "Had you notified Miss Timms of your condition?"

"No, I hadn't." Brady stuck to his guns. "I was afraid to. She was so—I didn't suppose—she's a terrible flirt—"

"That's not true! You know mighty well—"

"Please!" Wolfe was peremptory. His glance shot from right to left and back again. "So all but one of you knew of Dr. Brady's procuring that box of material from the stable, and all withheld the information from me. You're hopeless. Let's try another one, more specific. The day Miss Huddleston came here, she told me that Miss Nichols had a grievance against her, and she suspected her of sending those anonymous letters. I ask all of you—including you, Miss Nichols—what was that grievance?"

No one said a word.

"I ask you individually. Miss Nichols?"

Janet shook her head. Her voice was barely audible. "Nothing. It was nothing."

"Mr. Huddleston?"

Daniel said promptly, "I have no idea."

"Miss Timms?"

"I don't know," Maryella said, and by the way Wolfe's eyes stayed with her an instant, I saw that he knew she was lying.

"Dr. Brady?"

"If I knew I'd tell you," Brady said, "but I don't."

"Mr. Huddleston?"

Larry was waiting for him with a fixed smile that twisted a corner of his mouth. "I told you before," he said harshly, "that I don't know a damn thing. That goes right down the line."

"Indeed. May I have your watch a moment, please?"

Larry goggled at him.

"That hexagonal thing on your wrist," Wolfe said. "May I see it a moment?"

Larry's face displayed changes, as Brady's had shortly before. First it was puzzled, then defiant, then he seemed to be pleased about something. He snarled:

"What do you want with my watch?"

"I want to look at it. It's a small favor. You haven't been very helpful so far."

Larry, his lips twisted with the smile again, unbuckled the strap and arose to pass the watch across the desk to Wolfe, whose fingers closed over it as he said to me:

"The Huddleston folder, Archie."

I went and unlocked the cabinet and got out the folder and brought it. Wolfe took it and flipped it open and said:

"Stay there, Archie. As a bulwark and a witness. Two witnesses would be better. Dr. Brady, if you will please stand beside Mr. Goodwin and keep your eyes on me? Thank you."

Wolfe's eyes went through the gap between Brady and me to focus on Larry. "You are a very silly young man, Mr. Huddleston. Incredibly callow. You were smugly gratified because you thought I was expecting to find a picture of Miss Nichols in your watch case and would be chagrined not to. You were wrong. Now, doctor, and Archie, please observe. Here is the back of the watch. Here is a picture of Miss Nichols, trimmed to six sides, and apparently to fit. The point could be definitely determined by opening the watch case, but I'm not going to, because it will be opened later and microscopically compared with the picture to prove that it did contain it—Archie!"

I bulwarked. I owed Larry a smack anyhow, for bad manners if nothing else, but I didn't actually deliver it, since all he did was shoot off his mouth and try to shove through Brady and me to make a grab for the watch. So I merely stiff-armed him and propelled him backwards into his chair and stood ready.

"So," Wolfe went on imperturbably, "I put the watch and picture inside separate envelopes for safekeeping. Thus. If, Mr. Huddleston, you are wondering how I got that picture, your aunt left it here. I suggest that it is time for you to help us a little, and I'll start with a question that I can make a test of. When did your aunt take that picture from you?"

Larry was trying to sneer, but it wasn't working very well. His face couldn't hold it because some of the muscles were making movements of their own.

"Probably," Wolfe said, "it's time to let the police in. I suppose they'll get along faster with you—"

"You fat bastard!" But the snarl in Larry's voice had become a whine.

Wolfe grimaced. "I'll try once more, sir. You are going to answer these questions, if not for me then for someone less fat but more importunate. Would you rather have it dug out of the servants and your friends and acquaintances? It's shabby enough as it is; that would only make it worse. When did your aunt take that picture from you?"

Larry's jaw worked, but his tongue didn't. Wolfe waited ten seconds, then said curtly:

"Let them in, Archie."

I took a step, but before I took another one Larry blurted:

"Goddamn you! You know damn well when she took it! She took it the day she came down here!"

Wolfe nodded. "That's better. But that wasn't the first time she objected to your relations with Miss Nichols. Was it?"

"No."

"Did she object on moral grounds?"

"Hell, no. She objected to our getting married. She

ordered me to break off the engagement. The engagement was secret, but she got suspicious and questioned Janet, and Janet told her, and she made me call it off."

"And naturally you were engaged." Wolfe's voice was smooth, silky. "You burned for revenge—"

"I did not!" Larry leaned forward, having trouble to control his jaw. "You can come off that right now! You're not going to pin anything on me! I never really wanted to marry her, and what's more, I never intended to! I can prove that by a friend of mine!"

"Indeed." Wolfe's eyes were nearly shut. "A man like you has friends? I suppose so. But after your aunt made you break the engagement you still kept the picture in your watch?"

"Yes. I had to. I mean I had Janet to deal with too, and it wasn't easy, living right there in the house. I was afraid of her. You don't know her. I opened the watch case purposely in front of my aunt so she'd take that damn picture. Janet seemed to think the picture meant something, and I thought when she knew it was gone—"

"Did you know that Miss Nichols sent the anonymous letters?"

"No, I didn't. Maybe I suspected, but I didn't know."

"Did you also suspect, when your aunt—"

"Stop! Stop it!"

It was Janet.

She didn't raise her voice. She didn't have to. The tone alone was enough to stop anything and anybody. It was what you would expect to come out of an old abandoned grave, if you had such expectations. Except her mouth, no part of her moved. Her eyes were concentrated on Wolfe's face, with an expression in them that made it necessary for me to look somewhere else. Apparently it had the same effect on the others, for they did the same as me. We gazed at Wolfe.

"Ha," he said quietly. "A little too much for you, is it, Miss Nichols?"

She went on staring at him.

"As I expected," he said, "you're all rubble inside. There's nothing left of you. The simplest way is for me to dictate a confession and you sign it. Then I'll send a copy of it to a man I know, the editor of the *Gazette*, and it will be on his front page this evening. He would like an exclusive picture of you to go with it, and Mr. Goodwin will be glad to take it. I know you'll like that."

Uh-huh, I thought, he's not only going to make a monkey of Cramer, he's going to give him a real black eye. Daniel muttered something, and so did Brady, but Wolfe silenced them with a gesture.

"For your satisfaction," he went on, "I ought to tell you, Miss Nichols, that your guilt was by no means obvious. I became aware of it only when Mr. Goodwin telephoned me from Riverdale this morning, though I did of course notice Mr. Larry Huddleston's hexagonal watch when he came here nine days ago, and I surmised your picture had been in it. But your performance today was the act of a nitwit. I presume you were struck with consternation yesterday when you saw that turf being removed, realized what the consequences would be, and attempted to divert suspicion by staging an attack on yourself. Did you know what I was getting at a while ago when I asked Dr. Brady why you didn't jerk the brush away the instant you felt the glass puncture your skin? And he replied, as of course he would, that you didn't feel the glass cutting you?"

She didn't answer.

"That," Wolfe said, "was precisely the point, that you did jerk the brush away when you had pulled it along your arm less than an inch, because you knew the glass was there and was cutting you, having put it there yourself.

Otherwise the cut would have been much longer, probably half the length of your arm. You saw Mr. Goodwin wield the brush as an illustration, sweeping from wrist to shoulder. Everyone does that. At least, no one moves the brush less than an inch and stops. But even without that, your performance today was fantastic, if you meant—as you did—to make it appear as an attempt by some other person to kill you. Such a person would have known that after what had happened, even if you used the bogus iodine, you would certainly have antitoxin administered, which would have made the attempt a fiasco. Whereas you, arranging the affair yourself, knew that a dose of antitoxin would save you from harm. You really—"

"Stop it!" Janet said, in exactly the same tone as before. I couldn't look at her.

But that was a mistake, not looking at her. For completely without warning she turned into a streak of lightning. It was so sudden and swift that I was still in my chair when she grabbed the sliver of glass from Wolfe's desk, and by the time I got going she had whirled and gone through the air straight at Larry Huddleston, straight at his face with the piece of glass in her fingers. Everyone else moved too, but no one fast enough, not even Larry. Daniel got his arms around her, her left arm pinned against her, and I got her other arm, including the wrist, but there was a red streak across Larry's cheek from beneath his eye nearly to his chin.

Everybody but Janet was making noises, some of which were words.

"Shut up!" Wolfe said gruffly. "Archie, if you've finished your nap—"

"Go to hell," I told him. "I'm not a genius like you." I gave Janet's wrist a little pressure. "Drop it, girlie."

She let the piece of glass fall to the floor and stood rigid, watching. Brady examined Larry's cheek.

"Only skin deep," Brady said, unfolding a handkerchief. "Here, hold this against it."

"By God," Larry blurted, "if it leaves a scar—"

"That was a lie," Janet said. "You lied!"

"What?" Larry glared at her.

"She means," Wolfe put in, "that you lied when you said you neither desired nor intended to marry her. I agree with her that the air was already bad enough in here without that. You fed her passion and her hope. She wanted you, God knows why. When your aunt intervened, she struck. For revenge? Yes. Or saying to your aunt, preparing to say, 'Let me have him or I'll ruin you?' Probably. Or to ruin your aunt and then collect you from the debris? Possibly. Or all three, Miss Nichols?"

Janet, her back to him, still facing Larry, did not speak. I held onto her.

"But," Wolfe said, "your aunt came to see me, and that frightened her. Also, when she herself came that evening and found that picture here, the picture you had carried in your watch, she was not only frightened but enraged. Being a very sentimental young woman—"

"Good God," Brady muttered involuntarily. "Sentimental!"

A shudder ran over Janet from top to bottom. I pulled her around by the arm and steered her to the red leather chair and she dropped into it. Wolfe said brusquely:

"Archie, your notebook. No—first the camera—"

"I can't stand it!" Maryella cried, standing up. She reached for something to hold onto, and as luck would have it, it was Brady's arm. "I can't!"

Wolfe frowned at them. "Take her up and show her the orchids, doctor. Three flights. And take that casualty along and patch it up. Fritz will get what you need. I advise you to smell the iodine."

———

At six o'clock that evening I was at my desk. The office was quiet and peaceful. Wolfe had done it up brown. Cramer had come like a lion with a squad and a warrant, and had departed like a lamb with a flock of statements, a confession, a murderer, and apoplexy. Despite all of which, loving Cramer as I do, when I heard the elevator bringing Wolfe down from the plant rooms I got too busy with my desk work to turn around. Intending not even to acknowledge his presence. The excuse he had given for keeping Maryella there was that it was impossible for her to return to Riverdale as things stood, and there was no place else for her to go. Phooey.

But I got no chance to freeze them out, for they went right on by the office door, to the kitchen. I stuck to my desk. Time went by, but I was too irritated to get any work done. Towards seven o'clock the bell rang, and I went to the front door and found Doc Brady. He said he had been invited, so I took him to the kitchen.

The kitchen was warm, bright, and full of appetizing smells. Fritz was slicing a ripe pineapple. Wolfe was seated in the chair by the window, tasting out of a steaming saucepan. Maryella was perched on one end of the long table with her legs crossed, sipping a mint julep. She fluttered the fingers of her free hand at Brady for a greeting. He stopped in astonishment, and stood and blinked at her, at Wolfe and Fritz, and back at her.

"Well," he said. "Really. I'm glad you can be so festive. Under the circumstances—"

"Nonsense!" Wolfe snapped. "There's nothing festive about it; we're merely preparing a meal. Miss Timms is much better occupied. Would you prefer hysterics? We had a discussion about spoon bread, and there are two batches in the oven. Two eggs, and three eggs. Milk at a hundred and fifty degrees, and boiling. Take that julep she's offering you. Archie, a julep?"

Brady took the julep from her, set it down on the table without sampling it, wrapped his arms around her, and made it tighter. She showed no inclination to struggle or scratch. Wolfe pretended not to notice, and placidly took another taste from the saucepan. Fritz started trimming the slices of pineapple.

Maryella gasped, "Ah think, Ah'd bettah breathe."

Wolfe asked amiably, "A julep, Archie?"

I turned without answering, went to the hall and got my hat, slammed the door from the outside, walked to the corner and into Sam's place, and climbed onto a stool at the counter. I didn't know I was muttering to myself, but I must have been, for Sam, behind the counter, demanded:

"Spoon bread? What the hell is spoon bread?"

"Don't speak till you're spoken to," I told him, "and give me a ham sandwich and a glass of toxin. If you have no toxin, make it milk. Good old wholesome orangutan milk. I have been playing tag with an undressed murderess. Do you know how to tell a murderess when you see one? It's a cinch. Soak her in iodine over night, drain through cheesecloth, add a pound of pig chitlins—what? Oh. Rye and no pickle. Ah think Ah'd bettah breathe."

I have never mentioned it to him, and I don't intend to. I've got a dozen theories about it. Here are a few for samples:

1. He knew I would go to the funeral, and he sent that bunch of orchids purely and simply to pester me.

2. Something from his past. When he was young and handsome, and Bess Huddleston was ditto, they might have been—uh, acquainted. As for her not recognizing him, I doubt if his own mother would, as is. And there's no doubt he has fifteen or twenty pasts; I know that much about him.

3. He was paying a debt. He knew, or had an idea, that she was going to be murdered, from something someone said that first day, and was too damn lazy, or too interested in corned beef hash with chitlins, to do anything about it. Then when she was ready for burial he felt he owed her something, so he sent her what? Just some orchids, any old orchids? No, sir. Black ones. The first black orchids ever seen on a coffin anywhere on the globe since the dawn of history. Debt canceled. Paid in full. File receipted bills.

4. I'll settle for number three.

5. But it's still a mystery, and when he catches me looking at him a certain way he knows darned well what's on my mind.

A. G.

The Silent
Speaker

Introduction

I love Nero Wolfe. I love his house, his orchids, his sour disposition, and his shrouded past. I love his reading habits, his unabashed fear of women, and his incredible appetite; that is to say, I love *his love* of food.

When Nero Wolfe spoke, I learned. He taught me, when I was just a teenager, to look closely at the world because what might be apparent to us everyday kind of guys was probably just fluff. I'm not talking so much about the crimes he solved as the way he exercised his mind on whatever came before him. The way he read books or the petty arguments he had with his clients, his employees, and the police. Nero Wolfe was always thinking, always distrustful, and almost always right.

Wolfe was lazy, agoraphobic, prejudiced against many different kinds of people (most notably women), and a glutton. He was arrogant, vengeful, spiteful, and sometimes cruel. Any manners he had came from a personal sense of decorum and never from common civility. But I always knew that he had high moral values and that people sitting before him could trust him if they themselves could be trusted.

Wolfe was never a hero in the American sense. No gunslinger or karate master he. He never subdued the bad guy or ran a merry chase. As a matter of fact, Nero Wolfe was a coward when it came to things physical.

He was afraid of traffic.

Again, instead of condemning Mr. Wolfe for his cowardice, I learned from him. I learned that the American ideal of heroism is no more than a bad movie; that real heroes rarely exist—if, indeed, they ever do. I learned that life is not so much the struggle of good against evil as it is the struggle to survive.

Wolfe struggled for comfort. A great meal and a solid brownstone, that was the prize; a brief respite in this all too short, all too painful life.

Wolfe didn't care about crime and its eradication. He was a philosopher. "As long as there is man there will be murder, adultery, and theft," he might have said. And he knew that his efforts would make little difference in that equation. His job was to pay the rent and buy the groceries. All the liars and murderers and saints that passed through his house over the decades meant little or nothing to Wolfe's heart. He was a man doing his job.

And now that I think of it—what could be more heroic than that?

All of that said, I still haven't touched on why I've read all of the Nero Wolfe mysteries. As a matter of fact, you would be justified in asking why anyone would read about such a rude and unredeemed character.

The answer is, of course, Archie Goodwin.

Archie's voice is at once so humorous and so

revealing that I often felt I was being addressed by a spirit rather than just some normal human being. Archie, it seemed, was sprung fully grown from the mind of that twentieth-century god, New York City. He's a footloose New Yorker who sees the whole world from Thirty-fifth Street. He can tell you about a cop's gait, a pretty woman's choice of a particular hue of lipstick, an unusual texture in Fritz's corn fritters, or the angle of a dead man's arm—all with wit and humor that keep you reading for more.

Archie is the leg man. He's the one who carries out Wolfe's plans and errands. He drives the car, romances the ladies, and applies the pike to Nero's rear end when the rent is due and there's a paying client downstairs.

Archie has no dark moods, no real fears, and no concerns beyond what it takes to keep three hundred and fifty pounds of genius going. He loves women (Lily Rowan especially), but he's married to his work.

All the years I read the Nero Wolfe mysteries it was because of Archie. Archie talking about walking up Madison; Archie cracking wise with Cramer; Archie amazed by the detecting abilities of Saul Panzer (the second or third greatest detective in New York—and, therefore, the world).

Archie Goodwin was the real gumshoe. He was willing to get out there and work. He wasn't daunted by traffic or sunlight or possibility of death.

Archie Goodwin is the distilled optimism of America as it was for more than half of this century. Ebullient and proud, he still had to be humble because of the great brain of his employer.

I read about Nero Wolfe because it was Archie who told the tale. His voice is the voice of all the hope and humor of a new world. This bright light shines upon the darkness of Wolfe's deep fears and genius and upon the craven and criminal minds that infest the world.

This juxtaposition of light and dark is much more satisfying than the struggle between good and evil. It is the essence of positive and negative space in literature.

Rex Stout, through the voice of Archie telling us about his world (a full third of which was occupied by Nero Wolfe), raised detective fiction to the level of art with these books. He gave us genius of at least two kinds, and a strong realist voice that was shot through with hope.

—Walter Mosley

Chapter 1

Seated in his giant's chair behind his desk in his office, leaning back with his eyes half closed, Nero Wolfe muttered at me:

"It is an interesting fact that the members of the National Industrial Association who were at that dinner last evening represent, in the aggregate, assets of something like thirty billion dollars."

I slid the checkbook into place on top of the stack, closed the door of the safe, twirled the knob, and yawned on the way back to my desk.

"Yes, sir," I agreed with him. "It is also an interesting fact that the prehistoric Mound Builders left more traces of their work in Ohio than in any other state. In my boyhood days—"

"Shut up," Wolfe muttered.

I let it pass without any feeling of resentment, first because it was going on midnight and I was sleepy, and second because it was conceivable that there might be some connection between his interesting fact and our previous conversation, and that was not true of mine. We had been discussing the bank balance, the reserve against taxes, expectations as to bills and burdens, one of which was my salary, and related matters. The exchequer had not swung for the third strike, but neither had it knocked the ball out of the park.

After I had yawned three more times Wolfe spoke suddenly and decisively.

"Archie. Your notebook. Here are directions for tomorrow."

In two minutes he had me wide awake. When he had finished and I went upstairs to bed, the program for the morning was so active in my head that I tossed and turned for a full thirty seconds before sleep came.

Chapter 2

That was a Wednesday toward the end of the warmest March in the history of New York. Thursday it was more of the same, and I didn't even take a topcoat when I left the house on West Thirty-fifth Street and went to the garage for the car. I was fully armed, prepared for all contingencies. In my wallet was a supply of engraved cards reading:

ARCHIE GOODWIN

With Nero Wolfe
922 West 35th Street   PRoctor 5–5000

And in the breast pocket of my coat, along with the routine cargo, was a special item just manufactured by me on the typewriter. It was on a printed Memo form and, after stating that it was FOR Nero Wolfe and FROM Archie Goodwin, it went on:

*Okay from Inspector Cramer for inspection of
the room at the Waldorf. Will report later by
phone.*

At the right of the typing, scribbled in ink, also my
work and worthy of admiration, were the initials LTC.

Since I had got an early start and the office of the
Homicide Squad on Twentieth Street was less than a
mile downtown, it was only a little after nine-thirty
when I was admitted to an inside room and took a
chair at the end of a crummy old desk. The man in the
swivel chair, frowning at papers, had a big round red
face, half-hidden gray eyes, and delicate little ears that
stayed close to his skull. As I sat down he transferred
the frown to me and grunted:

"I'm busy as hell." His eyes focused three inches
below my chin. "What do you think it is, Easter?"

"I know of no law," I said stiffly, "against a man's
buying a new shirt and tie. Anyhow, I'm in disguise as
a detective. Sure you're busy, and I won't waste your
time. I want to ask a favor, a big favor. Not for me, I'm
quite aware that if I were trapped in a burning
building you would yell for gasoline to toss on the
flames, but on behalf of Nero Wolfe. He wants permission for me to inspect that room at the Waldorf where
Cheney Boone was murdered Tuesday evening. Also
maybe to take pictures."

Inspector Cramer stared at me, not at my new tie.
"For God's sake," he said finally in bitter disgust. "As
if this case wasn't enough of a mess already. All it
needed to make it a carnival was Nero Wolfe, and by
God here he is." He worked his jaw, regarding me
sourly. "Who's your client?"

I shook my head. "I have no information about any

client. As far as I know it's just Mr. Wolfe's scientific curiosity. He's interested in crime—"

"You heard me, who's your client?"

"No, sir," I said regretfully. "Rip me open, remove my heart for the laboratory, and you'll find inscribed on it—"

"Beat it," he grated, and dug into his papers.

I stood up. "Certainly, Inspector, I know you're busy. But Mr. Wolfe would greatly appreciate it if you'll give me permission to inspect—"

"Nuts." He didn't look up. "You don't need any permission to inspect and you know damn well you don't. We're all through up there and it's public premises. If what you're after is authority, it's the first time Wolfe ever bothered to ask for authority to do anything he wanted to do, and if I had time I'd try to figure out what the catch is, but I'm too busy. Beat it."

"Gosh," I said in a discouraged tone, starting for the door. "Suspicious. Always suspicious. What a way to live."

Chapter 3

In appearance, dress, and manner, Johnny Darst was about as far as you could get from the average idea of a hotel dick. He might have been taken for a vice-president of a trust company or a golf club steward. In a little room, more a cubbyhole than a room in size, he stood watching me deadpan while I looked over the topography, the angles, and the furniture, which consisted of a small table, a mirror, and a few chairs. Since Johnny was not a sap I didn't even try to give him the impression that I was doing something abstruse.

"What are you really after?" he asked gently.

"Nothing whatever," I told him. "I work for Nero Wolfe just as you work for the Waldorf, and he sent me here to take a look and here I am. The carpet's been changed?"

He nodded. "There was a little blood, not much, and the cops took some things."

"According to the paper there are four of these rooms, two on each side of the stage."

He nodded again. "Used as dressing rooms and resting rooms for performers. Not that you could call Cheney Boone a performer. He wanted a place to look over his speech and they sent him in here to be alone. The Grand Ballroom of the Waldorf is the best-equipped—"

"Sure," I said warmly. "You bet it is. They ought to pay you extra. Well, I'm a thousand times obliged."

"Got all you want?"

"Yep, I guess I've solved it."

"I could show you the exact spot where he was going to stand to deliver his speech if he had still been alive."

"Thanks a lot, but if I find I need that I'll come back."

He went with me down the elevator and to the entrance, both of us understanding that the only private detectives hotels enjoy having around are the ones they hire. At the door he asked casually:

"Who's Wolfe working for?"

"There is never," I told him, "any question about that. He is working first, last, and all the time for Wolfe. Come to think of it, so am I. Boy, am I loyal."

Chapter 4

It was a quarter to eleven when I parked the car in Foley Square, entered the United States Court House, and took the elevator.

There were a dozen or more FBI men with whom Wolfe and I had had dealings during the war, when he was doing chores for the government and I was in G-2. It had been decided that for the present purpose G. G. Spero, being approximately three per cent less tight-lipped than the others, was the man, so it was to him I sent my card. In no time at all a clean efficient girl took me to a clean efficient room, and a clean efficient face, belonging to G. G. Spero of the FBI, was confronting me. We chinned a couple of minutes and then he asked heartily:

"Well, Major, what can we do for you?"

"Two little things," I replied. "First, quit calling me Major. I'm out of uniform, and besides, it stimulates my inferiority complex because I should have been a colonel. Second is a request from Nero Wolfe, sort of confidential. Of course he could have sent me to the Chief, or phoned him, but he didn't want to bother him about it. It's a little question about the Boone murder case. We've been told that the FBI is mixing in, and of course you don't ordinarily touch a local murder. Mr. Wolfe would like to know if there is something about the FBI angle that would make it undesirable for a private detective to take any interest."

Spero was still trying to look cordial, but training and habit were too much for him. He started to drum on the desk, realized what he was doing, and jerked his hand away. FBI men do not drum on desks.

"The Boone case," he said.

"That's right. The Cheney Boone case."

"Yes, certainly. Putting aside, for the moment, the FBI angle, what would Mr. Wolfe's angle be?"

He went at me and kept after me from forty different directions. I left half an hour later with what I had expected to leave with, nothing. The reliance on his three per cent under par in lip tightness was not for the sake of what he might tell me, but what he might tell about me.

Chapter 5

The last number on the program proved to be the most complicated, chiefly because I was dealing with total strangers. I didn't know a soul connected with the National Industrial Association, and so had to start from scratch. The whole atmosphere, from the moment I entered the offices on the thirtieth floor of a building on Forty-first Street, made a bad impression on me. The reception room was too big, they had spent too much money on rugs, upholstery had been carried to extremes, and the girl at the desk, though not a bad specimen from the standpoint of design, had been connected up with a tube running from a refrigerating unit. She was so obviously congealed for good that there wasn't the slightest temptation to start thawing her out. With females between twenty and thirty, meeting a certain standard in contour and coloring, I do not believe in being distant, but I was with that one as I handed her a card and said I wanted to see Hattie Harding.

The hurdles I had to make, you might have thought Hattie Harding was the goddess of a temple and this was it, instead of merely the Assistant Director of Public Relations for the NIA, but I finally made the last jump and was taken in to her. Even she had space, rugs, and upholstery. Personally, she had quality, but the kind that arouses one or two of my most dangerous instincts, and I do not mean what some may think I mean. She was somewhere between twenty-six and forty-eight, tall, well put together, well dressed, and had skeptical, competent dark eyes which informed you with the first glance that they knew everything in the world.

"This is a pleasure," she declared, giving me a firm and not cold handshake. "To meet *the* Archie Goodwin, coming direct from *the* Nero Wolfe. Really a great pleasure. At least, I suppose you do? Come direct, I mean?"

I concealed my feelings. "On a beeline, Miss Harding. As the bee from the flower."

She laughed competently. "What! Not to the flower?"

I laughed back. We were chums. "I guess that's nearer the truth, at that, because I admit I've come to get a load of nectar. For Nero Wolfe. He thinks he needs a list of the members of the NIA who were at that dinner at the Waldorf Tuesday evening, and sent me here to get it. He has a copy of the printed list, but he needs to know who is on it that didn't come and who came that isn't on it. What do you think of my syntax?"

She didn't answer that, and she was through laughing. She asked, not as chum to chum, "Why don't we sit down?"

She moved toward a couple of chairs near a window, but I pretended not to notice and marched across to one for visitors at the end of her desk, so she would have to take her desk chair. The Memo from me to Wolfe, initialed for Inspector Cramer by me, was now in the side pocket of my coat, destined to be left on the

floor of Miss Harding's office, and with the corner of
her desk between us the operation would be simple.

"This is very interesting," she declared. "What
does Mr. Wolfe want the list for?"

"Being honest," I smiled at her, "I can but tell you
an honest lie. He wants to ask them for their auto-
graphs."

"I'm honest too," she smiled back. "Look, Mr.
Goodwin. You understand of course that this affair is
in the highest degree inconvenient for my employers.
Our guest of the evening, our main speaker, the
Director of the Bureau of Price Regulation, murdered
right there just as the dinner was starting. I am in a
perfectly terrible spot. Even if for the past ten years
this office has done the best public relations job on
record, which I am not claiming for it, all its efforts
may have been destroyed by what happened there in
ten seconds. There is no—"

"How do you know it happened in ten seconds?"

She blinked at me. "Why—it must—the way—"

"Not proven," I said conversationally. "He was hit
four times on the head with the monkey wrench. Of
course the blows could all have been struck within ten
seconds. Or the murderer could have hit him once and
knocked him unconscious, rested a while and then hit
him again, rested some more and hit him the third—"

"What are you doing?" she snapped. "Just trying to
see how objectionable you can be?"

"No, I'm demonstrating what a murder investigation is like. If you made that remark to the police, that
it happened in ten seconds, you'd never hear the last of
it. With me it goes in one ear and out the other, and
anyhow I'm not interested, since I'm here only to get
what Mr. Wolfe sent me for, and we'd greatly appreciate it if you would give us that list."

I was all set for quite a speech, but stopped on seeing her put both hands to her face, and I was thinking my lord she's going to weep with despair at the untimely end of public relations, but all she did was press the heels of her palms against her eyes and keep them there. It was the perfect moment to drop the Memo on the rug, so I did.

She kept her hands pressed to her eyes long enough for me to drop a whole flock of memos, but when she finally removed them the eyes still looked competent.

"I'm sorry," she said, "but I haven't slept for two nights and I'm a wreck. I'll have to ask you to go. There's to be another conference in Mr. Erskine's office about this awful business, it starts in ten minutes and I'll have to do myself for it, and anyway you know perfectly well I couldn't give you that list without approval from higher up, and besides if Mr. Wolfe is as intimate with the police as people say, why can't he get it from them? Talk about your syntax, look at the way I'm talking. Only one thing you might tell me, I sincerely hope you will, who has engaged Mr. Wolfe to work on this?"

I shook my head and got upright. "I'm in the same fix you are, Miss Harding. I can't do anything important, like answering a plain simple question, without approval from higher up. How about a bargain? I'll ask Mr. Wolfe if I may answer your question, and you ask Mr. Erskine if you may give me the list. Good luck at your conference."

We shook hands, and I crossed the rugs to the door without lingering, not caring to have her find the Memo in time to pick it up and hand it to me.

The midtown midday traffic being what it was, the short trip to West Thirty-fifth Street was a crawl all the way. I parked in front of the old stone house, owned by Nero Wolfe, that had been my home for over ten years, mounted the stoop, and tried to get myself in with my key, but found that the bolt was in and had to ring the bell. Fritz Brenner, cook, housekeeper, and groom of the chambers, came and opened up, and, informing him that the chances looked good for getting paid Saturday, I went down the hall to the office. Wolfe was seated behind his desk, reading a book. That was the only spot where he was ever really comfortable. There were other chairs in the house that had been made to order, for width and depth, with a guaranty for up to five hundred pounds—one in his room, one in the kitchen, one in the dining room, one in the plant rooms on the roof where the orchids were kept, and one there in the office, over by the two-foot globe and the book-shelves—but it was the one at his desk that nearly always got it, night and day.

As usual, he didn't lift an eye when I entered. Also as usual, I paid no attention to whether he was paying attention.

"The hooks are baited," I told him. "Probably at this very moment the radio stations are announcing that Nero Wolfe, the greatest living private detective when he feels like working, which isn't often, is wrapping up the Boone case. Shall I turn it on?"

He finished a paragraph, dog-eared a page, and put the book down. "No," he said. "It's time for lunch." He eyed me. "You must have been uncommonly transparent. Mr. Cramer has phoned. Mr. Travis of the FBI has phoned. Mr. Rohde of the Waldorf has phoned. It seemed likely that one or more of them would be coming here, so I had Fritz bolt the door."

That was all for the moment, or rather for the hour or more, since Fritz entered to announce lunch, which that day happened to consist of corn cakes with breaded fresh pork tenderloin, followed by corn cakes with a hot sauce of tomatoes and cheese, followed by corn cakes with honey. Fritz's timing with corn cakes was superb. At the precise instant, for example, that one of us finished with his eleventh, here came the twelfth straight from the griddle, and so on.

Chapter 6

I called it Operation Payroll. That name for the preliminary project, the horning-in campaign, was not, I admit, strictly accurate. In addition to the salaries of Fritz Brenner, Charley the cleaning man, Theodore Horstmann the orchid tender, and me, the treasury had to provide for other items too numerous to mention. But on the principle of putting first things first, I called it Operation Payroll.

It was Friday morning before we caught the fish we were after. All that happened Thursday afternoon was a couple of unannounced visits, one from Cramer and one from G. G. Spero, and Wolfe had told me not to let them in, so they went away without crossing the sill. To show how sure I felt that the fish would sooner or later bite. I took the trouble Thursday afternoon and evening to get up a typed report of the Boone case as I knew it, from newspaper accounts and a talk I had had Wednesday with Sergeant Purley Stebbins. I've just read that report over again and decided not to copy it all down here but only hit the high spots.

Cheney Boone, Director of the government's Bureau of Price Regulation, had been invited to make the main speech at a dinner of the National Industrial

Association on Tuesday evening at the Grand Ballroom of the Waldorf-Astoria. He had arrived at ten minutes to seven, before the fourteen hundred guests had gone to their tables, while everyone was still milling around drinking and talking. Taken to the reception room reserved for guests of honor, which as usual was filled with over a hundred people, most of whom weren't supposed to be there, Boone, after drinking a cocktail and undergoing a quantity of greetings and introductions, had asked for a private spot where he could look over his speech, and had been taken to a small room just off the stage. His wife, who had come with him to the dinner, had stayed in the reception room. His niece, Nina Boone, had gone along to the private spot to help with the speech if required, but he had almost immediately sent her back to the reception room to get herself another cocktail and she had remained there.

Shortly after Boone and his niece had departed for the murder room, as the papers called it, Phoebe Gunther had showed up. Miss Gunther was Boone's confidential secretary, and she had with her two can openers, two monkey wrenches, two shirts (men's), two fountain pens, and a baby carriage. These were to be used as exhibits by Boone for illustrating points in his speech, and Miss Gunther wanted to get them to him at once, so she was escorted to the murder room, the escort, a member of the NIA, wheeling the baby carriage, which contained the other items, to the astonished amusement of the multitude as they passed through. Miss Gunther remained with Boone only a couple of minutes, delivering the exhibits, and then returned to the reception room for a cocktail. She reported that Boone had said he wanted to be alone.

At seven-thirty everybody in the reception room

was herded out to the ballroom, to find their places on the dais and at the tables, where the fourteen hundred were settling down and the waiters were ready to hurl themselves into the fray. About seven forty-five Mr. Alger Kates arrived. He was from the Research Department of the BPR, and he had some last-minute statistics which were to be used in Boone's speech. He came to the dais looking for Boone, and Mr. Frank Thomas Erskine, the President of NIA, had told a waiter to show him where Boone was. The waiter had led him through the door to backstage and pointed to the door of the murder room.

Alger Kates had discovered the body. It was on the floor, the head battered with one of the monkey wrenches, which was lying nearby. The implication of what Kates did next had been hinted at in some newspapers, and openly stated in others: namely, that no BPR man would trust any NIA man in connection with anything whatever, including murder. Anyhow, instead of returning to the ballroom and the dais to impart the news, Kates had looked around backstage until he found a phone, called the hotel manager, and told him to come at once and bring all the policemen he could find.

By Thursday evening, forty-eight hours after the event, something like a thousand other details had been accumulated, as for instance that nothing but smudges were found on the handle of the monkey wrench, no identifiable prints, and so forth and so forth, but that was the main picture as it had been painted when I was typing my report.

Chapter 7

Friday we got the bite. Since Wolfe spends every morning from nine to eleven up in the plant rooms, I was in the office alone when the call came. The call took the regular routine in this Land of the Secretary.

"Miss Harding calling Mr. Wolfe. Put Mr. Wolfe on, please."

If I put it all down it would take half a page to get me, not Mr. Wolfe, just me, connected with Miss Harding. Anyhow I made it, and got the idea across that Wolfe was engaged with orchids and I would have to do. She wanted to know how soon Wolfe could get up there to see Mr. Erskine, and I explained that he seldom left the house for any purpose whatever, and never merely on business.

"I know that!" she snapped. She must have missed another night's sleep. "But this is *Mr. Erskine!*"

I knew we had him now, so I snooted her. "To you," I agreed, "he is all of that. To Mr. Wolfe he is nothing but a pest. Mr. Wolfe hates to work, even at home."

Instructed to hold the wire, I did so, for about ten minutes. Finally her voice came again:

"Mr. Goodwin?"

"Still here. Older and wiser, but still here."

"Mr. Erskine will be at Mr. Wolfe's office at four-thirty this afternoon."

I was getting exasperated. "Listen, Public Relations," I demanded, "why don't you simplify it by connecting me with this Erksine? If he comes at four-thirty he'll wait an hour and a half. Mr. Wolfe's hours with orchids are from nine to eleven in the morning and from four to six in the afternoon, and nothing short of murder—I mean nothing—has ever changed it or ever will."

"That's ridiculous!"

"Sure it is. So is this ring-around-the-rosy method for a man communicating with another man, but I stand for it."

"Hold the wire."

I never got connected with Erskine, that was too much to expect, but in spite of everything we finally completed an arrangement, fighting our way through the obstacles, so that when Wolfe come downstairs at eleven o'clock I was able to announce to him:

"Mr. Frank Thomas Erskine, President of the National Industrial Association, with outriders, will be here at ten minutes past three."

"Satisfactory, Archie," he muttered.

Frankly, I wish I could make my heart quit doing an extra thump when Wolfe says satisfactory, Archie. It's childish.

Chapter 8

When the doorbell rang that afternoon right on
the dot at three-ten and I left my chair to
answer it, I remarked to Wolfe:

"These people are apt to be the kind that you often
walk out on or, even worse, tell me to eject. It may be
necessary to control yourself. Remember the payroll.
There is much at stake. Remember Fritz, Theodore,
Charley, and me."

He didn't even grunt.

The catch was above expectations, for in the delegation of four we got not one Erskine but two. Father
and son. Father was maybe sixty and struck me as not
imposing. He was tall and bony and narrow, wearing a
dark blue ready-made that didn't fit, and didn't have
false teeth but talked as if he had. He handled the
introductions, first himself and then the others. Son
was named Edward Frank and addressed as Ed. The
other two, certified as members of the NIA Executive
Committee, were Mr. Breslow and Mr. Winterhoff.
Breslow looked as if he had been born flushed with
anger and would die, when the time came, in character.
If it had not been beneath the dignity of a member of
the NIA Executive Committee, Winterhoff could have

snagged a fee posing as a Man of Distinction for a whisky ad. He even had the little gray mustache.

As for Son, not yet Ed to me, who was about my age, I reserved judgment because he apparently had a hangover and that is no time to file a man away. Unquestionably he had a headache. His suit had cost at least three times as much as Father's.

When I had got them distributed on chairs, with Father on the red leather number near the end of Wolfe's desk, at his elbow a small table just the right size for resting a checkbook on while writing in it, Father spoke:

"This may be time wasted for us, Mr. Wolfe. It seemed impossible to get any satisfactory information on the telephone. Have you been engaged by anyone to investigate this matter?"

Wolfe lifted a brow a sixteenth of an inch. "What matter, Mr. Erskine?"

"Uh—this—the death of Cheney Boone."

Wolfe considered. "Let me put it this way. I have agreed to nothing and accepted no fee. I am committed to no interest."

"In a case of murder," Breslow sputtered angrily, "there is only one interest, the interest of justice."

"Oh, for God's sake," son Ed growled.

Father's eyes moved. "If necessary," he said emphatically, "the rest of you can leave and I'll do this alone." He returned to Wolfe. "What opinion have you formed about it?"

"Opinions, from experts, cost money."

"We'll pay you for it."

"A reasonable amount," Winterhoff put in. His voice was heavy and flat. He couldn't have been cast as a Man of Distinction with a sound-track.

"It wouldn't be worth even that," Wolfe said,

"unless it were expert, and it wouldn't be expert unless I did some work. I haven't decided whether I shall go that far. I don't like to work."

"Who has consulted you?" Father wanted to know.

"Now, sir, really." Wolfe wiggled a finger at him. "It is indiscreet of you to ask, and I would be a blather-skite to answer. Did you come here with the notion of hiring me?"

"Well—" Erskine hesitated. "That has been discussed as a possibility."

"For you gentlemen as individuals, or on behalf of the National Industrial Association?"

"It was discussed as an Association matter."

Wolfe shook his head. "I would advise strongly against it. You might be wasting your money."

"Why? Aren't you a good investigator?"

"I am the best. But the situation is obvious. What you are concerned about is the reputation and standing of your Association. In the public mind the trial has already been held and the verdict rendered. Everyone knows that your Association was bitterly hostile to the Bureau of Price Regulation, to Mr. Boone, and to his policies. Nine people out of ten are confident that they know who murdered Mr. Boone. It was the National Industrial Association." Wolfe's eyes came to me. "Archie. What was it the man at the bank said?"

"Oh, just that gag that's going around. That NIA stands for Not Innocent Atall."

"But that's preposterous!"

"Certainly," Wolfe agreed, "but there it is. The NIA has been convicted and sentence has been pronounced. The only possible way of getting that verdict reversed would be to find the murderer and convict him. Even if it turned out that the murderer was a member of the NIA, the result would be the same; the interest and the odium would be transferred to the individual, if not altogether, at least to a great extent, and nothing else would transfer any of it."

They looked at one another. Winterhoff nodded gloomily and Breslow kept his lips compressed so as not to explode. Ed Erskine glared at Wolfe as if that was where his headache had come from.

"You say," Father told Wolfe, "that the public has convicted the NIA. But so have the police. So has the FBI. They are acting exactly like the Gestapo. The members of such an old and respectable organization as the NIA might be supposed to have some rights and privileges. Do you know what the police are doing? In addition to everything else, do you know that they are actually communicating with the police in every city in the United States? Asking them to get a signed statement from local citizens who were in New York at that dinner and have returned home?"

"Indeed," Wolfe said politely. "But I imagine the local police will furnish paper and ink."

"What?" Father stared at him.

"What the hell has that got to do with it?" Son wanted to know.

Wolfe skipped it and observed, "The deuce of it is that the probability that the police will catch the murderer seems somewhat thin. Not having studied the case thoroughly, I can't qualify as an expert on it, but I must say it looks doubtful. Three days and nights have passed. That's why I advise against your hiring me. I admit it would be worth almost any amount to your Association to have the murderer exposed, even if he proved to be one of you four gentlemen, but I would tackle the job, if at all, only with the greatest reluctance. I'm sorry you had your trip down here for nothing.—Archie?"

The implication being that I should show them what good manners we had by taking them to the front door, I stood up. They didn't. Instead they exchanged glances.

Winterhoff said to Erskine, "I would go ahead, Frank."

Breslow demanded, "What else can we do?"

Ed growled, "Oh, God, I wish he was alive again. That was better than this."

I sat down.

Erskine said, "We are businessmen, Mr. Wolfe. We understand that you can't guarantee anything. But if we persuade you to undertake this matter, exactly what would you engage to do?"

It took them nearly ten minutes to persuade him, and they all looked relieved, even Ed, when he finally gave in. It was more or less understood that the clinching argument was Breslow's, that they must not let justice down. Unfortunately, since the NIA had a voucher system, the check-writing table did not get used. As a substitute I typed a letter, dictated by Wolfe, and Erskine signed it. The retainer was to be ten thousand dollars, and the ultimate charge, including expenses, was left open. They certainly were on the ropes.

"Now," Erskine said, handing me back my fountain pen, "I suppose we had better tell you all we know about it."

Wolfe shook his head. "Not right now. I have to get my mind adjusted to this confounded mess. It would be better for you to return this evening, say at nine o'clock."

They all protested. Winterhoff said he had an appointment he couldn't break.

"As you please, sir. If it is more important than

this. We must get to work without delay." Wolfe turned to me: "Archie, your notebook. A telegram. 'You are invited to join in a discussion of the Boone murder at the office of Nero Wolfe at nine o'clock this evening Friday March twenty-ninth.' Sign it with my name. Send it at once to Mr. Cramer, Mr. Spero, Mr. Kates, Miss Gunther, Mrs. Boone, Miss Nina Boone, Mr. Rohde, and perhaps to others, we'll see later.— Will you gentlemen be here?"

"My God," Ed grumbled, "with that mob, why don't you hold it in the Grand Ballroom at the Waldorf?"

"It seems to me," Erskine said in a grieved tone, "that this is a mistake. The first principle—"

"I," Wolfe said, in a tone used by NIA men only to people whose names were never on the letterhead, "am handling the investigation."

I started banging the typewriter, and since the telegrams were urgent, and since Wolfe took long walks only in emergencies, Fritz was sent for to escort them to the door. All I was typing was the text of the telegram and a list of the names and addresses, because the phone was the quickest way to send them. Some of the addresses were a problem. Wolfe was leaning back in his chair with his eyes closed, not to be bothered about trivialities, so I called Lon Cohen on the city desk at the *Gazette* and got the addresses from him. He knew everything. They had come up from Washington for the big speech that was never delivered and had not gone back. Mrs. Boone and the niece were at the Waldorf, Alger Kates was staying with friends on Eleventh Street, and Phoebe Gunther, who had been Boone's confidential secretary, had a room-and-bath on East Fifty-fifth Street.

When I had that job done I asked Wolfe who else

he wanted to invite. He said no one. I stood up and stretched, and looked at him.

"I presume," I observed, "that the rest is merely routine collection of evidence. Ed Erskine has calluses on his hands. Will that help?"

"Confound it." He sighed clear down. "I was going to finish that book this evening. Now this infernal mishmash."

He heaved the bulk forward and rang for beer.

I, standing at the cabinet filing the germination records that Theodore had brought down from the plant rooms, was compelled to admit that he had earned my admiration. Not for his conception of the idea of digging up a paying customer; that was merely following precedent in times of drought. Not for the method he had adopted for the digging; I could have thought that up myself. Not for the execution, his handling of the NIA delegation; that was an obvious variation of the old hard-to-get finesse. Not for the gall of those telegrams; admiring Wolfe's gall would be like admiring ice at the North Pole or green leaves in a tropical jungle. No. What I admired was his common sense. He wanted to get a look at those people. What do you do when you want to get a look at a man? You get your hat and go where he is. But what if the idea of getting your hat and going outdoors is abhorrent to you? You ask the man to come where you are. What makes you think he'll come? That was where the common sense entered. Take Inspector Cramer. Why would he, the head of the Homicide Squad, come? Because he didn't know how long Wolfe had been on the case or how deep he was in it, and therefore he couldn't afford to stay away.

At four sharp Wolfe had downed the last of his beer and taken the elevator up to the plant rooms. I finished the filing and gathered up miscellaneous loose ends around the office, expecting to be otherwise engaged for at least a day or two, and then settled down at my desk with a stack of newspaper clippings to make sure I hadn't missed anything important in my typed summary of the Boone situation. I was deep in that when the doorbell rang, and I went to the front and opened up, and found confronting me a vacuum cleaner salesman. Or anyhow he should have been. He had that bright, friendly, uninhibited look. But some of the details didn't fit, as for example his clothes, which were the kind I would begin buying when my rich uncle died.

"Hello!" he said cheerfully. "I'll bet you're Archie Goodwin. You came to see Miss Harding yesterday. She told me about you. Aren't you Archie Goodwin?"

"Yep," I said. It was the easiest way out. If I had said no or tried to evade he would have cornered me sooner or later.

"I thought so," he was gratified. "May I come in? I'd like to see Mr. Wolfe. I'm Don O'Neill, but of course that doesn't mean anything to you. I'm president of O'Neill and Warder, Incorporated, and a member of that godforsaken conglomeration of antiques, the NIA. I was Chairman of the Dinner Committee for that affair we had at the Waldorf the other evening. I guess I'll never live that one down. Chairman of a Dinner Committee, and let the main speaker get murdered!"

Of course my reaction was that I had got along fairly well for something like thirty years without knowing Don O'Neill and saw no reason for a change in policy, but my personal feelings could not be permitted to dominate. So I let him in and steered him to the office and into a chair before I even explained that he would have to wait half an hour because Wolfe was engaged. For a brief moment he seemed irritated, but he realized instantly that that was no way to sell vacuum cleaners and said sure, that was all right, he didn't mind waiting.

He was delighted with the office and got up and went around looking. Books—what a selection! The big globe was marvelous, just what he had always wanted and never took the trouble to get one, now he would . . .

Wolfe entered, saw him, and gave me a dirty look. It was true that I was supposed to inform him in advance of any waiting caller and never let him come in cold like that, but it was ten to one that if I had told him about O'Neill he would have refused to see him and had me invite him for the nine o'clock party, and I saw no necessity for another three-hour rest for Wolfe's brains. He was so sore that he pretended he didn't believe in shaking hands, acknowledged the introduction with a nod that wouldn't have spilled a drop if he had had a jar of water on his head, sat down and regarded the visitor unsympathetically, and asked curtly:

"Well, sir?"

O'Neill wasn't at all taken aback. He said, "I was admiring your office."

"Thank you. But I assume that wasn't what you came for."

"Oh, no. Being the Chairman of that Dinner Committee, I'm in the middle of this thing whether I like it or not—this business of Boone's murder. I wouldn't say I'm involved, that's too strong a word—make it concerned. I'm certainly concerned."

"Has anyone suggested that you are involved?"

"Suggested?" O'Neill looked surprised. "That's

putting it mildly. The police are taking the position that everyone connected with the NIA is involved. That's why I claim that the line the Executive Committee is taking is sentimental and unrealistic. Don't get me wrong, Mr. Wolfe." He took time out for a friendly glance at me, to include me in the Society of United Citizens for Not Getting Don O'Neill Wrong. "I am one of the most progressive members of the NIA. I was a Willkie man. But this idea of co-operating with the police the way they're acting, and even spending our own money to investigate, that's unrealistic. We ought to say to the police, all right, there's been a murder, and as good citizens we hope you catch the guilty man, but we had nothing to do with it and it's none of our business."

"And tell them to quit bothering you."

"That's right. That's exactly right." O'Neill was pleased to find a kindred spirit. "I was at the office when they came back an hour ago with the news that they had engaged you to investigate. I want to make it plain that I am not doing anything underhanded. I don't work that way. We had another argument, and I told them I was coming to see you."

"Admirable." Wolfe's eyes were open, which meant that he was bored and was getting nothing out of it. Either that, or he was refusing to turn on the brain until nine o'clock. "For the purpose of persuading me to call it off?"

"Oh, no. I saw that was hopeless. You wouldn't do that. Would you?"

"I'm afraid not without some excellent reason. As Mr. Breslow put it, the interest of justice is paramount. That was his position. Mine is that I need the money. Then what did you come for?"

O'Neill grinned at me, as if to say, your boss is

really a card, isn't he? He shifted the grin intact to Wolfe. "I'm glad to see you stick to the point. With me you need to, the way I go floundering around. What brought me down here, frankly, was a sense of my responsibility as Chairman of the Dinner Committee. I've seen a copy of the letter Frank Erskine gave you, but I didn't hear the conversation you had, and ten thousand dollars as a retainer on a straight inquiry job is away above the clouds. I hire detectives in my business, things like labor relations and so on, and I know what detectives get, so naturally the question occurs to me, is it really a straight inquiry job? I asked Erskine point-blank, have you hired Wolfe to protect the NIA members by—uh—getting attention shifted to other directions, and he said no. But I know Frank Erskine, and I wasn't satisfied, and I told him so. The trouble with me is I've got a conscience and a sense of responsibility. So I came to ask you."

Wolfe's lips twitched, but whether with amusement or fierce indignation I couldn't tell. The way he takes an insult never depends on the insult but on how he happens to be feeling. At the peak of one of his lazy spells he wouldn't have exerted himself to bat an eyelash even if someone accused him of specializing in divorce evidence.

His lips twitched. "I also say no, Mr. O'Neill. But I'm afraid that won't help you much. What if Mr. Erskine and I are both lying? I don't see what you can do about it, short of going to the police and charging us with obstructing justice, but then you don't like the police either. You're really in a pickle. We have invited some people to meet here this evening at nine o'clock and talk it over. Why don't you come and keep an eye on us?"

"Oh, I'm coming. I told Erskine and the others I'm coming."

"Good. Then we won't keep you now.—Archie?"

It wasn't as simple as that. O'Neill was by no means ready to go, on account of his sense of responsibility. But we finally got him out without resorting to physical violence. After wrangling him to the stoop, I returned to the office and asked Wolfe:

"Exactly what did he really come here for? Of course he killed Boone, I understand that, but why did he waste his time and mine—"

"You let him in," Wolfe said icily. "You did not notify me. You seem to forget—"

"Oh, well," I broke in cheerfully, "it all helps in studying human nature. I helped get him out, didn't I? Now we have work to do, getting ready for the party. How many will there be, around twelve not counting us?"

I got busy on the chair problem. There were six there in the office, and the divan would hold four comfortably, except that in a murder case three days old you don't often find four people connected with it who are still in a frame of mind to sit together on the same piece of furniture. It would be better to have plenty of chairs, so I brought five more in from the front room, the one facing on the street, and scattered them around, not in rows, which would have been too stiff, but sort of staggered and informal. Big as the room was, it made it look pretty crowded. I backed against the wall and surveyed it with a frown.

"What it needs," I remarked, "is a woman's touch."

"Bah," Wolfe growled.

Chapter 9

At a quarter past ten Wolfe was leaning back in his chair with his eyes half closed, taking them in. They had been at it for over an hour.

There were thirteen of them. Thanks to my foresight with the seating arrangements, there had been no infighting. The NIA contingent was at the side of the room farthest from my desk, the side toward the hall door, with Erskine in the red leather chair. There were six of them: the four who had formed the afternoon delegation, including Winterhoff, who had had an appointment he couldn't break, Hattie Harding, and Don O'Neill.

On my side of the room were the BPR's, four in number: Mrs. Boone the widow, Nina the niece, Alger Kates, and a gate-crasher named Solomon Dexter. Dexter was around fifty, under rather than over, looked like a cross between a statesman and a lumberjack, and was the ex-Deputy Director, now for twenty-four hours Acting Director, of the Bureau of Price Regulation. He had come, he told Wolfe, ex officio.

In between the two hostile armies were the neutrals or referees: Spero of the FBI, and Inspector Cramer and Sergeant Purley Stebbins. I had explained to Cramer that I was aware that he rated the red leather chair, but that he was needed in the middle. By a quarter past ten he was about as mad as I had ever seen him, because he had long ago caught on that Wolfe was starting from scratch and had arranged the gathering for the purpose of taking in, not giving out.

There had been one puny attempt to disrupt my seating plans. Mrs. Boone and the niece had come early, before nine, and since there is nothing wrong with my eyesight I had without the slightest hesitation put the niece in the chair—one of the yellow ones from the front room—nearest to mine. When Ed Erskine arrived, alone, a little later, I assigned him to a seat on the NIA side, only to discover, after attending to a couple of other customers, that he had bounced across and was in my chair talking to the niece. I went over and told him:

"This side is for the Capulets. Would you mind sitting where I put you?"

He twisted his neck and lifted his chin to get me, and his focusing was not good. It was obvious that he had been applying the theory of acquired immunity to his hangover. I want to be fair, he was not pie-eyed, but neither was he in danger of desiccating.

He asked me, "Huh? Why?"

"Besides," I said, "this is my chair and I work here. Let's not make an issue of it."

He shrugged it off and moved. I addressed Nina Boone courteously:

"You run into all sorts of strangers in a detective's office."

"I suppose you do," she said. Not a deep remark, nothing specially penetrating about it, but I smiled at her to show I appreciated her taking the trouble to make it when under a strain. She had dark hair and eyes, and was keeping her chin firm.

From the moment, right at the beginning, that Wolfe had announced that he had been retained by the NIA, the BPR's had been suspicious and antagonistic. Of course everyone who reads a newspaper or listens to the radio, which includes me, knew that the NIA hated Cheney Boone and all he stood for, and had done everything possible to get him tossed to the wolves, and also knew that the BPR would gladly have seen the atom bomb tested by bunching the NIA crowd on an island and dropping one on them, but I hadn't realized how it sizzled until that evening in Wolfe's office. Of course there were two fresh elements in it then: the fact that Cheney Boone had been murdered, at an NIA dinner of all places, and the prospect that some person or persons either would or wouldn't get arrested, tried, convicted, and electrocuted.

By a quarter past ten a good many points, both trivial and important, had been touched on. On opportunity, the BPR position was that everyone in the reception room, and probably many others, had known that Boone was in the room near the stage, the murder room, while the NIA claimed that not more than four or five people, besides the BPR's who were there, knew it. The truth was that there was no way of finding out who had known and who hadn't.

Neither hotel employees nor anyone else had heard any noise from the murder room, or seen anybody enter or leave it other than those whose presence there was known and acknowledged.

No one was eliminated on account of age, size, or sex. While a young male athlete can swing a monkey wrench harder and faster than an old female bridge player, either could have struck the blows that killed

Boone. There had been no sign of a struggle. Any one of the blows, from behind, could have stunned him or killed him. G. G. Spero of the FBI joined in the discussion of this point, and replied to a crack from Erskine by stating that it was not a function of the FBI to investigate local murders, but that since Boone had been killed while performing his duty as a government official, the Department of Justice had a legitimate interest in the matter and was acting on a request for co-operation from the New York police.

One interesting development was that it was hard to see how Boone had got killed unless he did it himself, because everybody had alibis. Meaning by everybody not merely those present in Wolfe's office—there being no special reason to suppose that the murderer was there with us—but all fourteen or fifteen hundred at the dinner. The time involved was about half an hour, between seven-fifteen, when Phoebe Gunther left the baby carriage and its contents, including the monkey wrenches, with Boone in the room, and around seven forty-five, when Alger Kates discovered the body. The police had gone to town on that, and everybody had been with somebody else, especially those in the reception room. But the hitch was that all the alibis were either mutual NIA's or mutual BPR's. Strange to say, no NIA could alibi a BPR, or vice versa. Even Mrs. Boone, the widow, for instance—no NIA was quite positive that she had not left the reception room during that period or that she had gone straight from there to the dais in the ballroom. The BPR's were equally unpositive about Frank Thomas Erskine, the NIA president.

There was no evidence that the purpose had been to keep Boone from delivering that particular speech. The speech had been typical Boone, pulling no punches, but had exposed or threatened no particular individual, neither in the advance text distributed to the press nor in the last-minute changes and additions. Nothing in it pointed to a murderer.

The first brand-new ingredient for me, of which nothing had been reported in the papers, was introduced by accident by Mrs. Boone. The only person invited to our party who hadn't come was Phoebe Gunther, Boone's confidential secretary. Her name had of course been mentioned several times during the first hour or so, but it was Mrs. Boone who put the spotlight on it. I had the notion that she did it deliberately. She had not up to that moment got any of my major attention. She was mature and filled-out, though not actually fat and by no means run to seed, and she had been short-changed as to nose.

Wolfe had doubled back to the question of Cheney Boone's arrival at the Waldorf, and Cramer, who was by then in a frame of mind to get it over with and disperse, had said sarcastically, "I'll send you a copy of my notes. Meanwhile Goodwin can take this down. Five of them—Boone and his wife, Nina Boone, Phoebe Gunther, and Alger Kates—were to take the one o'clock train from Washington to New York, but Boone got caught in an emergency conference and couldn't make it. The other four came on the train, and when they reached New York Mrs. Boone went to the Waldorf, where rooms had been engaged, and the other three went to the BPR New York office. Boone came on a plane that landed at LaGuardia Field at six-five, went to the hotel and up to the room where his wife was. By that time the niece was there too, and the three of them went together down to the ballroom floor. They went straight to the reception room. Boone had no hat or coat to check, and he hung onto a little leather case he had with him."

"That was the case," Mrs. Boone put in, "that Miss Gunther *says* she forgot about and left on a window sill."

I looked at the widow reproachfully. That was the first sign of a split in the BPR ranks, and it sounded ominous, with the nasty emphasis she put on *says*. To make it worse, Hattie Harding of the NIA immediately picked it up:

"And Miss Gunther is absolutely wrong, because four different people saw that case in her hand as she left the reception room!"

Solomon Dexter snorted: "It's amazing what—"

"Please, sir." Wolfe wiggled a finger at him. "What was this case? A brief case? A vanity case?"

"No." Cramer was helping out again. "It was a little leather case like a doctor's, and it contained cylinders from a dictating machine. Miss Gunther has described it to me. When she took that baby carriage and other stuff to him Tuesday evening, to the room where he was killed, he told her the conference in Washington had ended earlier than he expected, and he had gone to his office and spent an hour dictating before he took the plane to New York. He had the cylinders with him in that case for her to transcribe. She took it to the reception room when she went back there for a cocktail, and left it there on a window sill. That's the last of it."

"So she says," Mrs. Boone repeated.

Dexter glared at her. "Nonsense!"

"Did *you*," Hattie Harding demanded, "see the case in her hand when she left the reception room?"

All eyes went to the widow. She moved hers and got the picture. One word would be enough. She was either a traitor or she wasn't. Confronted with that alternative, it didn't take her long to decide. She met Hattie Harding's gaze and said distinctly:

"No."

Everybody breathed. Wolfe asked Cramer:

"What was on the cylinders, letters? What?"

"Miss Gunther doesn't know. Boone didn't tell her. No one in Washington knows."

"The conference that ended earlier than Boone expected, what was it about?"

Cramer shook his head.

"Who was it with?"

Cramer shook his head again. G. G. Spero offered, "We've been working on that in Washington. We can't trace any conference. We don't know where Boone was for about two hours, from one to three. The best lead is that the head NIA man in Washington had been wanting to see him, to discuss his speech, but he denies—"

Breslow exploded. "By God," he blurted, "there it is! It's always an NIA man! That's damned silly, Spero, and don't forget where FBI salaries come from! They come from taxpayers!"

From that point on the mud was flying more or less constantly. It wasn't on account of any encouragement from Wolfe. He told Breslow:

"The constant reference to your Association is unfortunate from your standpoint, sir, but it can't be helped. A murder investigation invariably centers on people with motives. You heard Mr. Cramer, early in this discussion, say that a thorough inquiry has disclosed no evidence of personal enemies. But you cannot deny that Mr. Boone had many enemies, earned by his activities as a government official, and that a large number of them were members of the NIA."

Winterhoff asked, "A question, Mr. Wolfe, is it always an enemy who kills a man?"

"Answer it yourself," Wolfe told him. "Obviously that's what you asked it for."

"Well, it certainly isn't always an enemy," Winterhoff declared. "For an illustration, you couldn't say that Mr. Dexter here was Boone's enemy, quite the contrary, they were friends. But if Mr. Dexter had been filled with ambition to become the Director of the Bureau of Price Regulation—and that's what he is at this moment—he might conceivably have taken steps to make the office vacant. Incidentally, he would also have placed under grave suspicion the members of an organization he mortally hates—which also has happened."

Solomon Dexter was smiling at him, not a loving smile. "Are you preferring a charge, Mr. Winterhoff?"

"Not at all." The other met his gaze. "As I said, merely an illustration."

"Because I could mention one little difficulty. I was in Washington until eleven o'clock Tuesday evening. You'll have to get around that somehow."

"Nevertheless," Frank Thomas Erskine said firmly and judicially, "Mr. Winterhoff has made an obvious point."

"One of several," Breslow asserted. "There are others. We all know what they are, so why not out with them? The talk about Boone and his secretary, Phoebe Gunther, has been going on for months, and whether Mrs. Boone was going to get a divorce or not. And lately a reason, a mighty good reason from Phoebe Gunther's standpoint, why Boone had to have a divorce no matter how his wife felt about it. What about it, Inspector, when you're dealing with a murder don't you think it's legitimate to take an interest in things like that?"

Alger Kates stood up and announced in a trembling voice: "I want to protest that this is utterly despicable and beyond the bounds of common decency!"

His face was white and he stayed on his feet. I had not supposed he had it in him. He was the BPR research man who had taken some up-to-the-minute statistics to the Waldorf to be used in Boone's speech and had discovered the body. If my attention had been directed to him on the subway and I had been asked to guess what he did for a living, I would have said, "Research man." He was that to a T, in size, complexion, age, and chest measurement. But the way he rose to protest—apparently he led the BPR, as there represented, in spunk. I grinned at him.

From the reaction he got you might have thought that what the NIA hated and feared most about the BPR was its research. They all howled at him. I caught the gist of only two of their remarks, one from Breslow to the effect that he had only said what everyone was saying, and the wind-up from Don O'Neill, in the accents of The Boss:

"You can keep out of this, Kates! Sit down and shut up!"

That seemed to me to be overdoing it a little, since he wasn't paying Kates's wages; and then Erskine, twisting around in the red leather chair to face the research man, told him cuttingly:

"Since you didn't regard the President of the NIA as a fit person to bring the news to, you are hardly acceptable as a judge of common decency."

So, I thought, that's why they're jumping on him, because he told the hotel manager instead of them. He should have had more sense than to hurt their feelings like that. Erskine wasn't through with him, but was going on:

"Surely, Mr. Kates, you are aware that personal emotions, such as jealousy, revenge, or frustration, often result in violence, and therefore they are proper matters of inquiry when a murder has been committed. It would be proper to ask you, for example, whether it is true that you wanted to marry Boone's niece, and you were aware that Boone opposed it and intended to prevent—"

"Why, you big liar!" Nina Boone cried.

"Whether it is proper or not," Kates said in a high thin voice that was still trembling, "it certainly is not proper for you to ask me anything whatever. If I were asked that by the police, I would reply that part of it is true and part of it isn't. There are at least two hundred men in the BPR organization who wanted, and it is a reasonable assumption that they still want, to marry Mr. Boone's niece. I was not under the impression that Mr. Boone was having anything to say about it one way or another, and, knowing Miss Boone as I do, not intimately but fairly well, I doubt it." Kates moved not his eyes, but his head, to change his target. "I would like to ask Mr. Wolfe, who has admitted that he is in the pay of the NIA, if we were invited here for a typical NIA inquisition."

"And I," Solomon Dexter put in, his voice sounding like a train in a tunnel in contrast to Kates's, "would like to inform you, Mr. Wolfe, that you are by no means the only detective in the employ of the NIA. For nearly a year executives and other BPR personnel have been followed by detectives, and their whole lives have been thoroughly explored in an effort to get something on them. I don't know whether you have taken part in those operations—"

More bedlam from the NIA, taking the form chiefly, as near as I could get it, of indignant denials. At that point, if it hadn't been for my seating arrangements, the two armies would probably have made contact. Wolfe was looking exasperated, but making no effort to stop it, possibly aware that it would take more energy than he wished to spend. What quieted them was Inspector Cramer getting to his feet and showing a palm, officially.

"*I* would like," he barked, "before going, to say three things. First, Mr. Dexter, I can assure you that Wolfe has not helped to tail your personnel or explore their lives, because there's not enough money in that kind of work. Second, Mr. Erskine and you other gentlemen, the police are aware that jealousy and things like that are often behind a murder, and we are not apt to forget it. Third, Mr. Kates, I have known Wolfe for twenty years, and I can tell you why you were invited here this evening. We were invited because he wanted to learn all he could as quick as he could, without leaving his chair and without Goodwin's buying gas and wearing out his tires. I don't know about the rest of you, but I was a sucker to come."

He turned. "Come on, Sergeant. You coming, Spero?"

Of course that ended it. The BPR didn't want any more anyhow, and though the NIA, or part of it, showed an inclination to stay and make suggestions, Wolfe used his veto power on that. With everyone out of their chairs, Ed Erskine crossed the lines again and tried another approach on Nina, but it appeared, from where I stood, that she disposed of that without even opening her mouth. I did much better, in spite of my being associated with Wolfe, who was in the pay of the NIA. When I told her that it was impossible to get a taxi in that part of town and offered to drive her and her aunt to their hotel, she said:

"Mr. Dexter is taking us."

A frank, friendly statement, and I appreciated it.

But after they had all gone and Wolfe and I were alone in the office, it appeared that I wouldn't have been able to go through with it even if she had accepted. I remarked to Wolfe:

"Too bad Cramer bolixed it up like that. If we had been able to keep them here a while, say two weeks, we might have got started somewhere. Too bad."

"It was not too bad," he said testily.

"Oh." I gestured, and sat down. "Okay, then it was a screaming success. Of all our guests, which do you think was the most interesting?"

To my surprise, he answered, "The most interesting was Miss Gunther."

"Yeah? Because?"

"Because she didn't come. You have her address."

"Sure. I sent the telegram—"

"Go and bring her here."

I stared at him, looked at my wrist, and stared at him again. "It is now twenty minutes past eleven."

He nodded. "The streets are less dangerous at night, with the reduced traffic."

"I won't argue." I stood up. "You are in the pay of the NIA, and I am in the pay of you. So it goes."

Chapter 10

I took an assortment of keys along, to simplify things in case 611 East Fifty-fifth Street proved to be an old-fashioned walkup with a locked entrance door, but instead of that it was one of the twelve-story beehives with an awning and hired men. I stepped down the broad hall to the elevator, went in, and said casually:

"Gunther."

Without even glancing at me, the pilot finished a yawn and called out, "Hey, Sam! For Gunther!"

The doorman, whom I had by-passed, appeared and looked in at me. "I'll phone up," he said, "but it's a waste of time. What's your name and what paper are you from?"

Ordinarily I like to save butter, but under the circumstances, with no ceiling on expenses, I saw no reason why he shouldn't be in the pay of the NIA too. So I left the elevator and walked down the hall with him, and when we got to the switchboard I spread out a ten-dollar bill thereon, saying:

"I'm not on a paper. I sell sea shells."

He shook his head and started manipulations at the board. I put a hand on his arm and told him, "You didn't let me finish. That was papa. Here's mamma." I deployed another ten. "But I warn you they have no children."

He only shook his head again and flipped a lever. I was shocked speechless. I have had a lot to do with doormen, and I am certainly able to spot one too honest to accept twenty bucks for practically nothing, and that was not it. His principles didn't even approach as high a standard as that, and he was being pure from some other motive. I emerged from the shock when I heard him telling the receiver:

"He says he sells sea shells."

"The name," I said, "is Archie Goodwin, and I was sent by Mr. Nero Wolfe."

He repeated it to the receiver, and in a moment hung up and turned to me with a look of surprise. "She says go on up. Nine H." He accompanied me toward the elevator. "About papa and mamma, I've changed my mind, in case you still feel—"

"I was kidding you," I told him. "They really have got children. This is little Horace." I handed him two bits and went in and commanded the pilot, "Nine H."

It is not my custom to make personal remarks to young women during the first five minutes after meeting them, and if I violated it this time it was only because the remark popped out of me involuntarily. When I pushed the button and she opened the door and said good evening, and I agreed and removed my hat and stepped inside, the ceiling light right above her was shining on her hair, and what popped out was:

"Golden Bantam."

"Yes," she said, "that's what I dye it with."

I was already understanding, from the first ten seconds, what motive it was that the doorman was being pure from. Her pictures in the papers had been

just nothing compared with this. After we had disposed of my hat and coat she preceded me into the
room, and from the middle of it turned her head to say:

"You know Mr. Kates?"

I thought it had popped out of her as my remark
had popped out of me, but then I saw him, rising to his
feet from a chair in a corner where the light was dim.

"Hello," I said.

"Good evening," he piped.

"Sit down." Phoebe Gunther straightened a corner
of a rug with the toe of a little red slipper. "Mr. Kates
came to tell me what happened at your party this
evening. Will you have some Scotch? Rye? Bourbon?
Gin? Cola?"

"No, thanks." I was getting my internal skull
fixtures jerked back into place.

"Well." She sat on a couch against a nest of
cushions. "Did you come to see what color my hair is or
was there something else?"

"I'm sorry to bust in on you and Mr. Kates."

"That's all right. Isn't it, Al?"

"It is not all right," Alger Kates said, without
hesitation, in his thin voice stretched tight but extremely distinct, "with me. It would be folly to trust
him at all or to believe anything he says. As I told you,
he is in the pay of the NIA."

"So you did." Miss Gunther was relaxing among
the cushions. "But since we know enough not to trust
him, all we have to do is to be a little smarter than he
is in order to get more out of him than he gets out of
us." She looked at me, and seemed to be smiling, but I
had already discovered that her face was so versatile,
especially her mouth, that it would be better not to
jump to conclusions. She told me, possibly smiling, "I
have a theory about Mr. Kates. He talks the way

people talked before he was born, therefore he must read old-fashioned novels. I wouldn't suppose a research man would read novels at all. What would you suppose?"

"I don't discuss people who don't trust me," I said politely. "And I don't think you are."

"Are what?"

"Smarter than me. I admit you're prettier, but I doubt if you're smarter. I was spelling champion of Zanesville, Ohio, at the age of twelve."

"Spell snoop."

"That's just childish." I glared at her. "I don't imagine you're hinting that catching people who commit crimes is work to be ashamed of, since you're smart, so if what you have in mind is my coming here, why didn't you tell the doorman—"

I stopped short because she was possibly laughing at me. I quit glaring, but went on looking at her, which was a bad policy because that was what was interfering with my mental processes.

"Okay," I said curtly, "you got a poke in and made me blink. Round one for you. Round two. Your Mr. Kates may be as loyal as What's-his-name, the boy that stood on the burning deck, but he's a sap. Nero Wolfe is tricky, that I admit, but the idea that he would cover a murderer because he happened to belong to something out of the alphabet that signed checks is plain loony. Look at the record and show me where he ever accepted a substitute, no matter who said it was just as good. Here's a free tip: if you think or know a BPR man did it, and don't want him caught, bounce me out immediately and keep as far away from Wolfe as you can get. If you think an NIA man did it and you'd like to help, put on some shoes and get your hat and coat and come to his office with me. As far as I'm concerned you don't need to bother about the hat." I looked at Kates. "If you did it yourself, with some motive not to be mentioned for the sake of common decency, you'd better come along and confess and get it over with."

"I told you!" Kates told her triumphantly. "See how he led up to that?"

"Don't be silly." Miss Gunther, annoyed, looked at him. "I'll explain it to you. Finding that I am smarter than he is, he decided to pick on you, and he certainly got documentation for his statement that you're a sap. In fact, you'd better be going. Leave him to me. I may see you at the office tomorrow."

Kates shook his head bravely and firmly. "No!" He insisted. "He'll go on that way! I'm not going to—"

He continued, but there's no more use my putting it down than there was his saying it, for the hostess had got up, crossed to a table, and picked up his hat and coat. It seemed to me that in some respects she must have been unsatisfactory as a confidential secretary. A man's secretary is always moving around, taking and bringing papers, ushering in callers and out again, sitting down and standing up, and if there is a constant temptation to watch how she moves it is hard to get any work done.

Kates lost the argument, of course. Within two minutes the door had closed behind him and Miss Gunther was back on the couch among the cushions. Meanwhile I had been doing my best to concentrate, so when she possibly smiled at me and told me to go ahead and teach her the multiplication table, I arose and asked if I might use her phone.

Her brows went up. "What am I supposed to do? Ask who you want to call?"

"No, just say yes."

"Yes. It's right over—"

"I see, thanks."

It was on a little table against a wall, with a stool there, and I pulled out the stool and sat with my back to her and dialed. After only one buzz in my ear, because Wolfe hates to hear bells ring, I got a hello and spoke:

"Mr. Wolfe? Archie. I'm up here with Miss Gunther in her apartment, and I don't believe it's a good plan to bring her down there as you suggested. In the first place she's extremely smart, but that's not it. She's the one I've been dreaming about the past ten years, remember what I've told you? I don't mean she's beautiful, that's merely a matter of taste, I only mean she is exactly what I have had in mind. Therefore it will be much better to let me handle her. She began by making a monkey of me, but that was because I was suffering from shock. It may take a week or a month or even a year, because it is very difficult to keep your mind on your work under these circumstances, but you can count on me. You go on to bed and I'll get in touch with you in the morning."

I arose from the stool and turned to face the couch, but she wasn't there. She was, instead, over toward the door, in a dark blue coat with a fox collar, standing in front of a mirror, adjusting a dark blue contraption on her head.

She glanced at me. "All right, come on."

"Come on where?"

"Don't be demure." She turned from the mirror. "You worked hard trying to figure out a way of getting me down to Nero Wolfe's office, and you did a good job. I'll give you Round Two. Some day we'll play the rubber. Right now I'm taking on Nero Wolfe, so it will have to be postponed. I'm glad you don't think I'm beautiful. Nothing irritates a woman more than to be thought beautiful."

I had my coat on and she had the door open. The bag under her arm was the same dark blue material as the hat. On the way to the elevator I explained, "I didn't say I didn't think you were beautiful. I said—"

"I heard what you said. It stabbed me clear through. Even from a stranger who may also be my enemy, it hurt. I'm vain and that's that. Because it just happens that I can't see straight and I do think I'm beautiful."

"So do—" I began, but just in time I saw the corner of her mouth moving and bit it off. I am telling this straight. If anyone thinks I was muffing everything she sent my way I won't argue, but I would like to point out that I was right there with her, looking at her and listening to her, and the hell of it was that she *was* beautiful.

Driving down to Thirty-fifth Street, she kept the atmosphere as neighborly as if I had never been within ten miles of the NIA. Entering the house, we found the office uninhabited, so I left her there and went to find Wolfe. He was in the kitchen, deep in a conference with Fritz regarding the next day's culinary program, and I sat on a stool, thinking over the latest development, Gunther by name, until they were finished. Wolfe finally acknowledged my presence.

"Is she here?"

"Yep. She sure is. Straighten your tie and comb your hair."

Chapter 11

It was a quarter past two in the morning when Wolfe glanced at the wall clock, sighed, and said, "Very well, Miss Gunther, I am ready to fulfill my part of the bargain. It was agreed that after you had answered my questions I would answer yours. Go ahead."

I hadn't been distracted much by gazing at beauty because, having been told to get it in the notebook verbatim, my eyes had been busy elsewhere. It was fifty-four pages. Wolfe had been in one of his looking-under-every-stone moods, and the stuff on some of the pages had no more to do with Boone's murder, from where I sat, than Washington crossing the Delaware.

Some of it might conceivably help. First and foremost, of course, was her own itinerary for last Tuesday. She knew nothing about the conference which had prevented Boone from leaving Washington on the train with the others, and admitted that that was surprising, since she was his confidential secretary and was supposed to know everything and usually did. Arriving in New York, she had gone with Alger Kates and Nina Boone to the BPR New York office, where Kates had gone into the statistical section, and she and

Nina had helped department heads to collect props to be used as illustrations of points in the speech. There had been a large collection of all sorts of things, from toothpicks to typewriters, and it wasn't until after six o'clock that the final selection had been made: two can openers, two monkey wrenches, two shirts, two fountain pens, and a baby carriage; and the data on them assembled. One of the men had conveyed them to the street for her and found a taxi, and she had headed for the Waldorf, Nina having gone previously. A bellboy had helped her get the props to the ballroom floor and the reception room. There she learned that Boone had asked for privacy to go over his speech, and an NIA man, General Erskine, had taken her to the room, to be known before long as the murder room.

Wolfe asked, "*General* Erskine?"

"Yes," she said, "Ed Erskine, the son of the NIA President."

I snorted.

"He was a B.G.," she said. "One of the youngest generals in the Air Force."

"Do you know him well?"

"No, I had only seen him once or twice and had never met him. But naturally I hate him." At that moment there was no question about it; she was not smiling. "I hate everybody connected with the NIA."

"Naturally. Go ahead."

Ed Erskine had wheeled the baby carriage to the door of the room and left her there, and she had not stayed with Boone more than two or three minutes. The police had spent hours on those two or three minutes, since they were the last that anyone except the murderer had spent with Boone alive. Wolfe spent two pages of my notebook. Boone had been concentrated and tense, even more than usual, which was not remarkable under the circumstances. He had jerked the shirts and monkey wrenches out of the baby carriage and put them on the table, glanced at the data, reminded Miss Gunther that she was to follow a copy of the speech as he talked and take notes of any deviation he made from the text; and then had handed her the leather case and told her to get. She had returned to the reception room and had two cocktails, two quick ones because she felt she needed them, and then had joined the exodus to the ballroom and had found table number eight, the one near the dais reserved for BPR people. She was eating her fruit cocktail when she remembered about the leather case, and that she had left it on the window sill in the reception room. She said nothing about it because she didn't want to confess her carelessness, and just as she was starting to excuse herself to Mrs. Boone and leave the table, Frank Thomas Erskine, on the dais, had spoken into the microphone:

"Ladies and gentlemen, I regret the necessity of giving you this news, thus abruptly, but I must explain why no one can be allowed to leave this room . . ."

It was an hour later when she finally got to the reception room, and the leather case was gone.

Boone had told her the case contained cylinders he had dictated in his Washington office that afternoon, and that was all she knew. It wasn't remarkable that he hadn't told her what the dictation was about, because he seldom did. Since he used other stenographers for all routine stuff, it was understood that any cylinders he turned over to her personally were important and probably confidential. There were twelve such cases in use in Boone's office, each holding ten cylinders, and they were constantly going back and forth among him and her and other stenographers, since Boone had done nearly all of his dictating on the machine. They were numbered, stamped on top, and this one had been number four. The machine that Boone had used was the Stenophone.

Miss Gunther admitted that she had made a mistake. She had not mentioned the missing case to anyone until Wednesday morning, when the police had asked her what had been in the leather case which she had had with her when she came to the reception room for a cocktail. Some NIA louse had of course told the police about it. She had told the police that she had been ashamed to confess her negligence, and anyway her silence had done no harm, since the case could have had no connection with the murder.

"Four people," Wolfe murmured, "say that you took the case with you from the reception room to the ballroom."

Phoebe Gunther nodded, unimpressed. She was drinking Bourbon and water and smoking a cigarette. "You believe them or you believe me. It wouldn't surprise me if four of that kind of people said they looked through the keyhole and saw me kill Mr. Boone. Or even forty."

"You mean NIA people. But Mrs. Boone isn't one."

"No," Phoebe agreed. She lifted her shoulders, kept them up a second, and let them down. "Mr. Kates told me what she said. Mrs. Boone doesn't like me. Yet—I rather doubt if that's true—I think maybe she does like me, but she hated having her husband depend on me. You notice she didn't actually lie about it; she didn't say she saw me have the case when I left the reception room."

"What did Mr. Boone depend on you for?"

"To do what he told me to."

"Of course." Wolfe was merely murmuring. "But

what did he get from you? Intelligent obedience? Loyalty? Comfortable companionship? Happiness? Ecstasy?"

"Oh, for the lord's sake." She looked mildly disgusted. "You sound like a congressman's wife. What he got was first-class work. I'm not saying that during the two years I worked for Mr. Boone I was always fresh out of ecstasy, but I never took it to the office with me, and anyway I was saving it up until I met Mr. Goodwin." She gestured. "You've been reading old-fashioned novels too. If you want to know whether I was on terms of sinful intimacy with Mr. Boone, the answer is no. For one thing, he was too busy, and so was I, and anyhow he didn't strike me that way. I merely worshiped him."

"You did?"

"Yes, I did." She gave the impression that she meant it. "He was irritable and he expected too much, he was overweight and he had dandruff, and he nearly drove me crazy trying to keep his schedule under control, but he was honest clear through and the best man in Washington, and he was up against the dirtiest gang of pigs and chiselers on earth. So since I was born weak-minded to begin with, I merely worshiped him, but where he was getting ecstasy I really don't know."

That would seem to cover the ecstasy angle. It was around that point, as I filled page after page in my notebook, that I took a sounding of how much of it I believed, and when I found my credibility gauge mounting up into the nineties and still ascending, I disqualified myself for bias.

She had a definite opinion about the murder. She doubted if any number of NIA members were in cahoots on it, probably not even two of them, because they were too cagey to conspire to commit a murder that would be a nationwide sensation. Her idea was that some one member had done it himself or hired it done, and it had to be one whose interests had been so damaged or threatened by Boone that he was willing to disregard the black eye the NIA would get. She accepted Wolfe's theory that it was now desirable, from the standpoint of the NIA, that the murderer be caught.

"Then doesn't it follow," Wolfe asked, "that you and the BPR would prefer not to have him caught?"

"It may follow," she admitted. "But I'm afraid that personally I'm not that logical, so I don't feel that way."

"Because you worshiped Mr. Boone? That's understandable. But in that case, why didn't you accept my invitation to come and discuss it last evening?"

She either had it ready or didn't need to get it ready. "Because I didn't feel like it. I was tired and I didn't know who would be here. Between the police and the FBI, I have answered a thousand questions a thousand times each and I needed a rest."

"But you came with Mr. Goodwin."

"Certainly. Any girl who needed a rest would go anywhere with Mr. Goodwin, because she wouldn't have to use her mind." She didn't even toss me a glance, but went on, "However, I didn't intend to stay all night, and its after two, and what about my turn?"

That was when Wolfe looked at the clock and sighed and told her to go ahead.

She shifted in the chair to change pressure, took a couple of sips from her glass and put it down, leaned her head back against the red leather, getting a very nice effect, and asked as if it didn't matter much one way or the other:

"Who approached you from the NIA, what did they say, what have you agreed to do. and how much are they paying you?"

Wolfe was so startled he almost blinked at her. "Oh, no, Miss Gunther, nothing like that."

"Why not?" she demanded. "Then it wasn't a bargain at all."

He considered, realizing what he had let himself in for. "Very well," he said, "let's see. Mr. Erskine and his son, and Mr. Breslow and Mr. Winterhoff came to see me. Later Mr. O'Neill also came. They said many things, but the upshot was that they hired me to investigate. I have agreed to do so and to attempt to catch the murderer. What—"

"No matter who it is?"

"Yes. Don't interrupt. What they pay will depend on the expenses incurred and what I decide to charge. It will be adequate. I don't like the NIA. I'm an anarchist."

He had decided to make the best of it by being whimsical. She ignored that.

"Did they try to persuade you that the murderer is not an NIA member?"

"No."

"Did you get the impression that they suspect any particular person?"

"No."

"Do you think one of the five who came to see you committed the murder?"

"No."

"Do you mean you are satisfied that none of them did commit it?"

"No."

She made a gesture. "This is silly. You aren't playing fair. You say nothing but no."

"I'm answering your questions. And so far I haven't told you a lie. I doubt if you could say as much."

"Why, what did I tell you that wasn't true?"

"I have no idea. Not yet. I will have. Go ahead."

I broke in, to Wolfe. "Excuse me, but I have no precedent for this, you being grilled by a murder suspect. Am I supposed to take it down?"

He ignored me and repeated to her, "Go ahead. Mr. Goodwin was merely making an opportunity to call you a murder suspect."

She was concentrating and also ignored me. "Do you think," she asked, "that the use of the monkey wrench, which no one could have known would be there, proves that the murder was unpremeditated?"

"No."

"Why not?"

"Because the murderer could have come armed, have seen the wrench, and decided to use it instead."

"But it might have been unpremeditated?"

"Yes."

"Has any NIA man said anything to you that indicated that he or any of them might know who took that leather case or what happened to it?"

"No."

"Or where it is now?"

"No."

"Have you any idea who the murderer is?"

"No."

"Why did you send Mr. Goodwin after me? Why me, instead of—oh, anyone?"

"Because you had stayed away and I wanted to find out why."

She stopped, sat erect, sipped at her glass again, draining it, and brushed her hair back.

"This is a lot of nonsense," she said emphatically. "I could go on asking you questions for hours, and how would I know that a single thing you told me was the truth? For instance, I would give I don't know what for that case. You say that as far as you know no one knows what happened to it or where it is, and it may be in this room right now, there in your desk." She looked at the glass, saw it empty, and put it down on the check-writing table.

Wolfe nodded. "That is always the difficulty. I was under the same handicap with you."

"But I have nothing to lie about!"

"Pfui. Everybody has something to lie about. Go ahead."

"No." She stood up and saw to her skirt. "It's perfectly useless. I'll go home and go to bed. Look at me. Do I look like a played-out hag?"

That startled him again. His attitude toward women was such that they rarely asked him what they looked like.

He muttered, "No."

"But I am," she declared. "That's the way it always affects me. The tireder I get the less I look it. Tuesday I got the hardest blow I ever got in my life, and since then I haven't had a decent night's sleep, and look at me." She turned to me. "Would you mind showing me which way to go for a taxi?"

"I'll run you up," I told her. "I have to put the car away anyhow."

She told Wolfe good night, and we got our things on and went out and climbed in. She let her head fall back against the cushion and closed her eyes for a second, then opened then, straightened up, and flashed a glance at me.

"So you took Nero Wolfe on," I remarked, as to a comparative stranger.

"Don't be aloof," she said. She reached to put her fingers around my arm, three inches below the shoulder, and press. "Don't pay any attention to that. It doesn't mean anything. Once in a while I like to feel a man's arm, that's all."

"Okay, I'm a man."

"So I suspected."

"When this is over I'd be glad to teach you how to play pool or look up words in the dictionary."

"Thanks." I thought she shivered. "When this is all over."

When we stopped for a light in the upper Forties she said, "You know, I believe I'm going to be hysterical. But don't pay attention to that either."

I looked at her, and there certainly wasn't any sign of it in her voice or her face. I never saw anyone act less hysterical. When I pulled up at the curb at her address, she hopped out before I could move and stuck her hand in.

"Good night. Or what is the protocol? Does a detective shake hands with one of the suspects?"

"Sure." We shook. It fitted nicely. "To get her off her guard."

She disappeared inside, probably to give the doorman a brief glance on her way to the elevator, to strengthen his motive.

When I got back home, after putting the car away, and stopped in the office to make sure the safe was locked, there was a scribbled note lying on my desk:

Archie: Do not communicate further with Miss Gunther except on my order. A woman who is not a fool is dangerous. I don't like this case and shall decide tomorrow whether to abandon it and refund the retainer. In the morning get Panzer and Gore here.

NW

Which gave me a rough idea of the state of confusion he was in, the way the note contradicted itself. Saul Panzer's rate was thirty bucks a day, and Bill Gore's was twenty, not to mention expenses, and his committing himself to such an outlay was absolute proof that there would be no retainer refund. He was merely appealing for my sympathy because he had taken on such a hard job. I went up two flights to my room, glancing at the door of his as I passed it on the first landing, and noting that the little red light was on, showing that he had flipped the switch for the alarm connection.

Chapter 12

I realized all the more how hard the job was likely to be when, the next morning after Wolfe came down from the plant rooms at eleven o'clock, I heard him giving Saul Panzer and Bill Gore their instructions.

To anyone seeing him but not knowing him, Saul Panzer was nothing but a little guy with a big nose who never quite caught up with his shaving. To the few who knew him, Wolfe and me for instance, those details meant nothing. He was the one free-lance operative in New York who, year in and year out, always had at least ten times more jobs offered him than he had the time or inclination to take. He never turned Wolfe down if he could possibly help it. That morning he sat with his old brown cap on his knee, taking no notes because he never had to, while Wolfe described the situation and told him to spend as many hours or days at the Waldorf as might be necessary, milking and gathering eggs. He was to cover everything and everybody.

Bill Gore was full size and unpolished, and one glance at the top of his head showed that he was doomed. He would be bald in another five years. His immediate objective was the NIA office, where he was to compile certain lists and records. Erskine had been phoned to and had promised co-operation.

After they had departed I asked Wolfe, "Is it really as bad as that?"

He frowned at me. "As bad as what?"

"You know darned well what. Fifty dollars a day for the dregs. Where is there any genius in that?"

"Genius?" His frown became a scowl. "What can genius do with this confounded free-for-all? A thousand people, all with motive and opportunity, and the means at hand! Why the devil I ever let you persuade me—"

"No, sir," I said loudly and firmly. "Don't try it! When I saw how tough this was going to be, and then when I read that note you left for me last night, it was obvious you would try to blame it on me. Nothing doing. I admit I didn't know how desperate it was until I heard you telling Saul and Bill to dive into the holes the cops have already cleaned out. You don't have to admit you're licked. You can wriggle out. I'll draw a check to the NIA for their ten thousand, and you can dictate a letter to them saying that on account of having caught the mumps, or perhaps it would be better—"

"Shut up," he growled. "How can I return money I haven't received?"

"But you have. The check was in the morning mail and I've deposited it."

"Good God. It's in the bank?"

"Yes, sir."

He pushed the button, savagely, for beer. He was as close to being in a panic as I remembered seeing him.

"So you have nothing," I said without mercy. "Nothing whatever?"

"Certainly I have something."

"Yeah? What?"

"Something Mr. O'Neill said yesterday afternoon. Something very peculiar."

"What?"

He shook his head. "Not for you. I'll put Saul or Bill on it tomorrow."

I didn't believe a word of it. For ten minutes I went over in my mind everything I remembered Don O'Neill saying, and then believed it less than ever.

All day Saturday he had no jobs for me connected with the Boone case, not even a phone call to make. The calls all came the other way, and there were plenty of those. Most of them, from newspapers and Cramer's office and so on, were nothing but blah. Two of them were merely comic relief:

Winterhoff, the Man of Distinction, phoned around noon. He wanted something for his money right away. The cops were after him. Many hours of questioning about fourteen people had got it settled that it was he who had suggested the little room near the stage for Boone's privacy and had escorted him there, and he was being harassed. He had explained that his knowledge of the room had come from his participation in previous affairs on those premises, but they weren't satisfied. He wanted Wolfe to certify to his innocence and instruct the police to let him alone. His order wasn't filled.

Just before lunch there was a call from a man with an educated voice who said his name was Adamson, of counsel for the NIA. His tone implied that he wasn't very crazy about Wolfe's being hired anyway, and he wanted practically everything, including a daily report of all actions. He insisted on speaking to Wolfe, which was a mistake on his part, because if he had been willing to talk with me I might at least have treated him with common courtesy.

Another thing the NIA wanted the very day we got their retainer check was something we couldn't have furnished even if we had felt like it. This request was brought by their Hattie Harding in person, in the middle of the afternoon, just after Wolfe went up to the orchids. I took her to the office and we sat on the couch. She was still well put together and well dressed, and her eyes were still competent, but the strain was telling on her. She looked much nearer forty-eight than twenty-six.

She had come to yell for help, though she didn't put it that way. To hear her tell it, there was hell to pay from coast to coast and the end of the world was expected any minute. Public Relations was on its last legs. Hundreds of telegrams were pouring into the NIA office, from members and friends all over the country, telling of newspaper editorials, of resolutions passed by Chambers of Commerce and all sorts of clubs and groups, and of talk in the street. Even—this was strictly off the record—eleven resignations had been received from members, one a member of the Board of Directors. Something had to be done.

I asked what.

Something, she said.

"Like catching the murderer?"

"That, of course." She seemed to regard that as a mere detail. "But something to stop this insane hulla-baloo. Perhaps a statement signed by a hundred prominent citizens. Or telegrams urging sermons tomorrow—tomorrow is Sunday—"

"Are you suggesting that Mr. Wolfe should send

telegraphs to fifty thousand preachers and priests and rabbis?"

"No, of course." Her hands fluttered. "But something—something—"

"Listen, P.R." I patted her on the knee to quiet her. "You are stricken, I appreciate that. But the NIA seems to think this is a department store. Who you want is not Nero Wolfe but Russell Birdwell or Eddie Bernays. This is a specialty shop. All we're going to do is catch the murderer."

"Oh, my God," she said. Then she added, "I doubt it."

"Doubt what?" I stared at her. "That we're going to catch him?"

"Yes. That anyone is."

"Why?"

"I just doubt it." She met my gaze, competently. Then her eyes changed. "Look, this is off the record?"

"Sure, you and me. And my boss, but he never tells anybody anything."

"I'm fed up." She worked her jaw like a man, no lip trembling. "I'm going to quit and get a job sewing on buttons. The day anyone catches the murderer of Cheney Boone, finds him and proves it on him, it will rain up instead of down. In fact it will—"

I nodded encouragingly. "What else will it do?"

She abruptly got to her feet. "I'm talking too much."

"Oh, no, not enough. You've just started. Sit down."

"No, thank you." Her eyes were competent again. "You're the first man I've collapsed in front of for a long, long time. For heaven's sake, don't get the idea that I know secrets and try to dig them out of me. It's just that this thing is more than I can handle and I've lost my head. Don't bother to let me out."

She went.

When Wolfe came down to the office at six o'clock I reported the conversation in full. At first he decided not to be interested, then changed his mind. He wanted my opinion and I gave it to him, that I doubted if she knew anything that would help much, and even if she did she was through collapsing in front of me, but he might have a go at her.

He grunted. "Archie. You are transparent. What you mean is that you don't want to bother with her, and you don't want to bother with her because Miss Gunther has got you fidgeting."

I said coldly, "I don't fidget."

"Miss Gunther has got you on a string."

Usually I stay right with him when he takes that line, but there was no telling how far he might go in the case of Phoebe Gunther and I didn't want to resign in the middle of a murder job, so I cut it off by going to the front door for the evening papers.

We get two of each, to avoid friction, and I handed him his share and sat at my desk with mine. I looked at the *Gazette* first, and on the front page saw headlines that looked like news. It was. Mrs. Boone had got something in the mail.

One detail that I believe I haven't mentioned before was Boone's wallet. I haven't mentioned it because its being taken by the murderer provided no new angle on the crime or the motive, since he hadn't carried money in it. His money had been in a billfold in his hip pocket and hadn't been touched. He had carried the wallet in the breast pocket of his coat and used it for miscellaneous papers and cards, and it had not been found on the body, and therefore it was presumed that the murderer had taken it. The news in the *Gazette* was that Mrs. Boone had received an envelope in the mail that morning, with her name and address printed on it with a lead pencil, and in it had been two objects that Boone had always carried in the wallet: his automobile license and a photograph of Mrs. Boone in her wedding dress. The *Gazette* article remarked that the sender must be both a sentimentalist and a realist; sentimental, because the photo was returned; realist, because the auto license, which was still of use, had been returned, while Boone's operator's license, which he had also kept in the wallet, had not been. The *Gazette* writer was picturesque about it, saying that the operator's license had been canceled with a monkey wrench.

"Indeed," Wolfe said loud enough for me to hear. I saw that he was reading it too, and spoke:

"If the cops hadn't already been there and got it, and if Miss Gunther didn't have me on a string, I'd run up to see Mrs. Boone and get that envelope."

"Three or four men in a laboratory," Wolfe said, "will do everything to that envelope but split its atoms. Before long they'll be doing that too. But this is the first finger that has pointed in any direction at all."

"Sure," I agreed, "now it's a cinch. All we have to do is find out which of those one thousand four hundred and ninety-two people is both a sentimentalist and a realist, and we've got him."

We went back to our papers.

Nothing more before dinner. After the meal, which for me consisted chiefly of thin toast and liver pâté on account of the way Fritz makes the pâté, we had just got back to the office again, a little before nine when a telegram came. I took it from the envelope and handed it to Wolfe, and after he had read it he passed it over to me. It ran:

NERO WOLFE 922 WEST 35 NYC
CIRCUMSTANCES MAKE IT IMPOSSIBLE TO
CONTINUE SURVEILLANCE OF ONEILL BUT
BELIEVE IT ESSENTIAL THIS BE DONE
ALTHOUGH CAN GUARANTEE NOTHING
                              BRESLOW

I put my brows up at Wolfe. He was looking at me with his eyes half open, which meant he was really looking.

"Perhaps," he said witheringly, "you will be good enough to tell me what other arrangements you have made for handling this case without my knowledge?"

I grinned at him. "No, sir. Not me. I was about to ask if you have put Breslow on the payroll and if so at how much, so I can enter it."

"You know nothing of this?"

"No. Don't you?"

"Get Mr. Breslow on the phone."

That wasn't so simple. We knew only that Breslow was a manufacturer of paper products from Denver, and that, having come to New York for the NIA meeting, he was staying on, as a member of the Executive Committee, to help hold the fort in the crisis. I knew Frank Thomas Erskine was at the Churchill and tried that, but he was out. Hattie Harding's number, which was in the phone book, gave me a don't answer signal. So I tried Lon Cohen again at the *Gazette*, which I should have done in the first place, and learned that Breslow was at the Strider-Weir. In another three minutes I had him and switched him to Wolfe, but kept myself connected.

He sounded on the phone just the way he looked, red-faced with anger.

"Yes, Wolfe? Have you got something? Well? Well?"

"I have a question to ask—"

"Yes? What is it?"

"I am about to ask it. That was why I had Mr. Goodwin learn your number, and call it and ask for you, so you could be on one end of the telephone and me on the other end, and then I could ask you this question. Tell me when you are ready, sir."

"I'm ready! Damn it, what is it?"

"Good. Here it is. About that telegram you sent me—"

"Telegram? What telegram? I haven't sent you any telegram!"

"You know nothing about a telegram to me?"

"No! Nothing whatever! What—"

"Then it's a mistake. They must have got the name wrong. I suspected as much. I was expecting one from a man named Bristow. I apologize, sir, for disturbing you. Good-by."

Breslow tried to prolong the agony, but between us we got him off.

"So," I remarked, "he didn't send it. If he did, and didn't want us to know it, why would he sign his name? Do we have it traced? Or do we save energy by assuming that whoever sent it knows about phone booths?"

"Confound it," Wolfe said bitterly. "Probably someone peddling herrings. But we can't afford to ignore it." He glanced at the wall clock, which said three minutes past nine. "Find out if Mr. O'Neill is at home. Just ask him—no. Let me have him."

The number of O'Neill's residence, an apartment on Park Avenue was listed, and I got both it and him. Wolfe took it, and told him about the request from

Adamson, the NIA lawyer, and fed him a long rigma-
role about the inadvisability of written reports.
O'Neill said he didn't care a hang about reports,
written or otherwise, and they parted friends.

Wolfe considered a moment. "No. We'll let him go
for tonight. You had better get him in the morning as
he leaves. If we decide to keep it up we can get Orrie
Cather."

Chapter 13

Tailing as a solo job in New York can be almost anything, depending on the circumstances. You can wear out your brain and muscles in a strenuous ten-hour stretch, keeping contact only by using all the dodges on the list and inventing some more as you go along, and then lose him by some lousy little break that nothing and no one could have prevented. Or you can lose him the first five minutes, especially if he knows you're there. Or, also in the first five minutes, he can take to a chair somewhere, an office or a hotel room, and stay there all day, not giving a damn how bored you get.

So you never know, but what I fully expected was a long day of nothing since it was Sunday. A little after eight in the morning I sat in a taxi which, headed downtown, was parked on Park Avenue in the Seventies, fifty paces north of the entrance to the apartment house where O'Neill lived. I would have given even money that I would still be there six hours later, or even twelve, though I admitted there was a fair chance of our going to church at eleven, or to a restaurant for two o'clock dinner. I couldn't even read the Sunday paper with any satisfaction because I had to keep my eye on the entrance. The taxi driver was my old stand-by Herb Aronson, but he had never seen O'Neill. As the time went by we discussed various kinds of matters, and he read aloud to me from the *Times*.

At ten o'clock we decided to get a bet down. Each of us would write on a slip of paper the time that we thought my man would stick his nose out, and the one that was furthest off would pay the other one a cent a minute for the time he missed it by. Herb was just handing me a scrap he tore from the *Times* for me to write my guess on when I saw Don O'Neill emerging to the sidewalk.

I told Herb, "Save it for next time. That's him."

Whatever O'Neill did, it would be awkward, because his doorman knew us by heart by that time. He had previously signaled to Herb for a customer, and Herb had turned him down. What O'Neill did was look toward us, with me keeping my face in a corner so he couldn't see it if his vision was good for that distance, and speak to the doorman, who shook his head. That was about as awkward as it could get, unless O'Neill had walked to us for a conference.

Herb told me out of the corner of his mouth, "Our strategy stinks. He takes a taxi and we ride his tail, and when he comes home the doorman tells him he's being followed."

"So what was I to do?" I demanded. "Disguise myself as a flower girl and stand at the corner selling daffodils? Next time you plan it. This whole tailing idea has got to be a joke. Start your engine. Anyhow, he'll never get home. We'll pinch him for murder before the day's out. Start your engine! He's getting transportation."

The doorman had been blowing his whistle, and a

taxi on its way south had swerved and was stopping at the curb. The doorman opened the door and O'Neill got in, and the taxi slid away. Herb got into gear and we moved.

"This," Herb said, "is the acme. The absolute acme. Why don't we just pull up to him and ask where he's going?"

"Because," I said, "you don't know an acme when you see one. He has no reason at all to think we're following him unless he has been alerted, and in that case nothing would unalert him and we are lost. Keep back a little more—just enough not to let a light part us."

Herb did so, and managed the light stops as if his heart was in it. With the thin traffic of Sunday morning, there were only two of them before we got to Forty-sixth Street, where O'Neill's cab turned left. One block over, at Lexington Avenue, it turned right, and in another minute it had stopped at the entrance to Grand Central Station.

We were two cars behind. Herb swung to the right and braked, and I stepped out behind a parked car and grinned at him. "Didn't I tell you? He's hopping it. See you in court." As soon as O'Neill had paid his driver and started across the sidewalk I left cover.

I was still selling it short. What I would have settled for at that stage was a ride out to Greenwich to join a week-end party for some drinks and maybe poker. At any rate, O'Neill didn't seem to be in any doubt as to what he would settle for, for he marched down the long corridor and across the concourse of the station like a man with a destination. He gave no sign of suspecting that anyone had an eye on him. Where he finally wound up was not one of the train entrances, but the main parcel room on the upper level. I lingered at a distance, with a corner handy. There were several ahead of him and he waited his turn, then handed in a ticket, and in a minute or so was given an object.

Even from where I stood, about thirty feet off, the object looked as if it might be of interest. It was a little rectangular leather case. He grabbed it up and went. I was now somewhat less interested in keeping my presence undetected, but a lot more interested in not losing him, so I closed up some, and nearly stepped on his heels when he suddenly slowed up, almost to a stop, put the case inside his topcoat, got his arm snugly around it, and buttoned the coat. Then he went on. Instead of returning to the Lexington Avenue entrance he went up the ramp toward Forty-second Street, and when he got to the sidewalk turned left, to where the taxis stop in front of the Commodore Hotel. He still hadn't spotted me. After a short wait he snared a cab, opened the door and got in, and reached to pull the door shut.

I decided that would not do. It would have been nice to know what address he would give the driver if there were no interruptions, but that wasn't vital, whereas if I lost contact with that leather case through the hazards of solo tailing I would have to get a job helping Hattie Harding sew on buttons. So I moved fast enough to use a hand to keep the door from closing and spoke:

"Hello there, Mr. O'Neill! Going uptown? Mind giving me a lift?"

I was on the seat beside him, and now, willing to do my share, pulled the door shut.

I am not belittling him when I say he was flustered. It would have flustered most men. And he did pretty well.

"Why, hello, Goodwin! Where did you come from?

I'm—well, no, the fact is I'm not going uptown. I'm going downtown."

"Make up your mind," the driver growled through at us.

"It doesn't matter," I told O'Neill cheerfully. "I just want to ask you a couple of questions about that leather case that's under your coat." I said to the driver, "Go ahead. Turn south on Eighth."

The driver was glaring at me. "It's not your cab. What is this, a hard touch?"

"No," O'Neill told him. "It's all right. We're friends. Go ahead."

The cab moved. There was no conversation. We passed Vanderbilt and, after waiting for a light, were crossing Madison when O'Neill leaned forward to tell the driver:

"Turn north on Fifth Avenue."

The driver was too hurt to reply, but when we got to Fifth and had a green light he turned right. I said:

"All right if you want to, but I thought we would save time by going straight to Nero Wolfe's place. He will be even curiouser than I am about what's in that thing. Of course we shouldn't discuss it in this taxi, since the driver doesn't like us."

He leaned forward again and gave the driver his home address on Park Avenue. I thought that over for three blocks and voted against it. The only weapon I had on me was a pen-knife. Since I had been watching that entrance since eight o'clock it was unlikely that the NIA Executive Committee was assembled in O'Neill's apartment, but if they were, and especially if General Erskine was with them, it would require too much exertion on my part to walk out of there with that case. So I spoke to O'Neill in an undertone:

"Lookit. If he's a public-spirited citizen, and if he

hears anything that gives him the idea this is connected with murder, he'll probably stop at the first cop he sees. Maybe that's what you want too, a cop. If so you will be glad to know that I don't like the idea of your apartment and if we go there I'll display a license to that doorman, put my arms around you, and make him call the Nineteenth Precinct, which is at 153 East Sixty-seventh Street, Rhinelander four, one-four-four-five. That would create a hubbub. Why not get rid of this eavesdropper and talk it over on a bench in the sunshine? Also I saw the look in your eye and don't try it. I'm more than twenty years younger than you and I do exercises every morning."

He relinquished the expression of a tiger about to leap and leaned forward to tell the driver:

"Stop here."

Although I doubted if he carried shooters, I didn't want him fooling around his pockets, so I settled with the meter myself. We were at Sixty-ninth Street. After the cab had rolled off we crossed the avenue, walked to one of the benches against the wall enclosing Central Park, and sat down. He was keeping his left arm hooked tight around the object under his coat.

I said, "One easy way would be for me to take a look at it, inside and out. If it contains only black market butter, God bless you."

He turned sideways to regard me as man to man. "I'll tell you, Goodwin." He was choosing his words. "I'm not going to try a lot of stuff like indignation about your following me and that kind of stuff." I thought he wasn't choosing very well, repeating himself, but I was too polite to interrupt. "But I can explain how I happen to have this case, absolutely innocently—absolutely! And I don't know any more than you do about what's in it—I have no idea!"

"Let's look and see."

"No." He was firm. "As far as you know, it's my property—"

"But is it?"

"As far as you know it is, and I have a right to examine it privately. I mean a moral right, I admit I can't put it on the ground of legal right because you have offered to refer it to the police and that is of course legally correct. But I do have the moral right. You first suggested that we should go with it to Nero Wolfe. Do you think the police would approve of that?"

"No, but he would."

"I don't doubt it." O'Neill was in his stride now, earnest and persuasive. "But you see, neither of us actually wants to go to the police. Actually our interests coincide. It's merely a question of procedure. Look at it from your personal angle: what you want is to be able to go to your employer and say to him, 'You sent me to do a job, and I have done it, and here are the results,' and then deliver this leather case to him, and me right there with you if you want it that way. Isn't that what you want?"

"Sure. Let's go."

"We will go. I assure you, Goodwin, we will go." He was so sincere it was almost painful. "But does it matter exactly *when* we go? Now or four hours from now? Of course it doesn't! I have never broken a promise in my life. I'm a businessman, and the whole basis of American business is integrity—absolute integrity. That brings us back to my moral rights in this matter. What I propose is this: I will go to my office, at 1270 Sixth Avenue. You will come there for me at three o'clock, or I will meet you anywhere you say, and I will have this leather case with me, and we will take it to Nero Wolfe."

"I don't—"

"Wait. Whatever my moral rights may be, if you extend me this courtesy you deserve to have it acknowledged and appreciated. When I meet you at three o'clock I will hand you one thousand dollars in currency as evidence of appreciation. A point I didn't mention: I will guarantee that Wolfe will know nothing about this four-hour delay. That will be easy to arrange. If I had the thousand dollars with me I would give it to you now. I have never broken a promise in my life."

I looked at my wrist and appealed to him, "Make it ten thousand."

He wasn't staggered, but only grieved, and he wasn't even grieved beyond endurance. "That's out of the question," he declared, but not in a tone to give offense. "Absolutely out of the question. One thousand is the limit."

I grinned at him. "It would be fun to see how far up I could get you, but it's ten minutes to eleven, so in ten minutes Mr. Wolfe will come down to his office and I don't like to keep him waiting. The trouble is it's Sunday and I never take bribes on Sunday. Forget it. Here are the alternatives: You and I and the object under your coat go now to Mr. Wolfe. Or give me the object and I take it to him, and you go for a walk or take a nap. Or I yell at that cop across the street and tell him to call the precinct, which I admit I like least, but you've got your moral rights. Heretofore I've been in no hurry, but now Mr. Wolfe will be downstairs, so I'll give you two minutes."

He wanted to try. "Four hours! That's all! I'll make it five thousand, and you come with me and I'll give it to you—"

"No. Forget it. Didn't I say it's Sunday? Come on, hand it over."

"I am not going to let this case out of my sight."

"Okay." I got up and crossed to the curb and stood so as to keep one eye out for a taxi and one on him. Before long I flagged an empty and it turned in to me and stopped. It had probably been years since Don O'Neill had done anything he disapproved of as strongly as he did of arising and walking to the cab and getting in, but he made it. I dropped beside him and gave the driver the address.

Chapter 14

Ten hollow black cylinders, about three inches in diameter and six inches long, stood on end in two neat rows on Wolfe's desk. Beside them, with the lid open, was the case, of good heavy leather, somewhat battered and scuffed. On the outside of the lid a big figure four was stamped. On its inside a label was pasted:

BUREAU OF PRICE REGULATION
POTOMAC BUILDING
WASHINGTON, D.C.

Before pasting in the label someone had typed on it in caps: OFFICE OF CHENEY BOONE, DIRECTOR.

I was at my desk and Wolfe was at his. Don O'Neill was walking up and down with his hands in his pants pockets. The atmosphere was not hail-fellow-well-met. I had given Wolfe a full report, including O'Neill's last-minute offer to me of five grand, and Wolfe's self-esteem was such that he always regarded any attempt to buy me off as a personal affront, not to me but to him. I have often wondered who he would blame if I sold out once, himself or me.

He had repudiated without discussion O'Neill's claim to a moral right to hear what was on the cylinders before anyone else, and when O'Neill had seen it was hopeless the look on his face was such that I had decided to make sure and had given him a good frisking. He was not packing any tools, but that had not improved the atmosphere. The question then arose, how were we to make the cylinders perform? The next day, a business day, it would have been easy, but this was Sunday. It was O'Neill who solved the problem. The President of the Stenophone Company was a member of the NIA and O'Neill knew him. He lived in Jersey. O'Neill phoned him and, without disclosing any incriminating details, got him to phone the manager of his New York office and showroom, who lived in Brooklyn, and instruct him to go to the showroom, get a Stenophone and bring it to Wolfe's office. That was what we were sitting there waiting for—that is, Wolfe and I were sitting and O'Neill was walking.

"Mr. O'Neill." Wolfe opened his eyes enough to see. "That tramping back and forth is extremely irritating."

"I'm not going to leave this room," O'Neill declared without halting.

"Shall I tie him up?" I offered.

Wolfe, ignoring me, told O'Neill, "It will probably be another hour or more. What about your statement that you got possession of this thing innocently? Your word. Do you want to explain that now? How you got it innocently?"

"I'll explain it when I feel like it."

"Nonsense. I didn't take you for a nincompoop."

"Go to hell."

That always annoyed Wolfe. He said sharply,

"Then you are a nincompoop. You have only two means of restraining Mr. Goodwin and me: your own physical prowess or an appeal to the police. The former is hopeless; Mr. Goodwin could fold you up and put you on a shelf. You obviously don't like the idea of the police, I can't imagine why, since you're innocent. So how do you like this: when that machine has arrived and we have learned how to run it and the manager has departed, Mr. Goodwin will carry you out and set you on the stoop, and come back in and shut the door. Then he and I will listen to the cylinders."

O'Neill stopped walking, took his hands from his pockets and put them flat on the desk to lean on them, and glowered at Wolfe.

"You won't do that!"

"I won't. Mr. Goodwin will."

"Damn you!" He held the pose long enough for five takes, then slowly straightened up. "What do you want?"

"I want to know where you got this thing."

"All right, I'll tell you. Last evening—"

"Excuse me. Archie. Your notebook. Go ahead, sir."

"Last evening around eight-thirty I got a phone call at home. It was a woman. She said her name was Dorothy Unger and she was a stenographer at the New York office of the Bureau of Price Regulation. She said she had made a bad mistake. She said that in an envelope addressed to me she had enclosed something that was supposed to be enclosed in a letter to someone else. She said that she had remembered about it after she got home, and that she might even lose her job if her boss found out about it. She asked me when I received the envelope to mail the enclosure to her at her home, and she gave me her address. I asked her what the enclosure was and she said it was

a ticket for a parcel that had been checked at Grand
Central Station. I asked her some more questions and
told her I would do what she asked me to."

Wolfe put in, "Of course you phoned her back."

"I couldn't. She said she had no phone and was
calling from a booth. This morning I received the
envelope and the enclosure was—"

"This is Sunday," Wolfe snapped.

"Damn it, I know it's Sunday! It came special
delivery. It contained a circular about price ceilings,
and the enclosure. If it had been a weekday I would
have communicated with the BPR office, but of course
the office wasn't open." O'Neill gestured impatiently.
"What does it matter what I would have done or what
I thought? You know what I did do. Naturally, you
know more about it than me, since you arranged the
whole thing!"

"I see." Wolfe put up a brow. "You think I arranged
it?"

"No." O'Neill leaned on the desk again. "I *know*
you arranged it! What happened? Wasn't Goodwin
right there? I admit I was dumb when I came here
Friday. I was afraid you had agreed to frame Boone's
murder on someone in the BPR, or at least someone
outside the NIA. And already, you must have been,
you were preparing to frame someone *in* the NIA!
Me! No wonder you think I'm a nincompoop!"

He jerked erect, glared at Wolfe, turned to glare at
me, went to the red leather chair and sat down, and
said in a completely different voice, calm and con-
trolled:

"But you'll find that I'm not a nincompoop."

"That point," Wolfe said, frowning at him, "is
relatively unimportant. The envelope you received

this morning special delivery—have you got it with you?"

"No."

"Where is it, at your home?"

"Yes."

"Telephone and tell someone to bring it here."

"No. I'm going to have some detective work done on that envelope and not by you."

"Then you won't hear what those cylinders have to say," Wolfe explained patiently. "Must I keep repeating that?"

This time O'Neill didn't try to argue. He used the phone on my desk, dialed, got his party, and told someone whom he called Honey to get the envelope as described from the top of his chiffonier and send it by messenger to Nero Wolfe's office. I was surprised. I would have made it five to one that there was no such envelope, and it was still even money with me that it would be gone from the chiffonier because it must have dropped to the floor and the maid thought it was trash.

When O'Neill was back in the red leather chair Wolfe said, "You're going to find it a little difficult to get anyone to believe that you suspect Mr. Goodwin and me of arranging this. For if that's true, why didn't you insist on going to the police? He wanted to."

"He did not want to." O'Neill was keeping calm. "He merely threatened to."

"But the threat worked. Why did it work?"

"You know damn well why it worked. Because I wanted to hear what's on those cylinders."

"You did indeed. Up to five thousand dollars. Why?"

"Do I have to tell you why?"

"No. You don't have to. You know how it stands."

O'Neill gulped. He had probably swallowed "Go to hell" thirty times in thirty minutes. "Because I have reason to suppose, and so have you, that they are confidential dictation by Cheney Boone, and they may have something to do with what happened to him, and if so I want to know it."

Wolfe shook his head reproachfully. "You're inconsistent. Day before yesterday, sitting in that same chair, your attitude was that you of the NIA had nothing to do with it and it was none of your business. Another thing: you didn't try to bribe Mr. Goodwin to let you hear the cylinders. You tried to bribe him to give you four hours alone with them. Were you trying to scoop all of us—the police, the FBI, and me?"

"Yes, I was, if you want to call it scoop. I didn't trust you before, and now . . ."

Now, from his tone, we were something scraped off the under side of a bridge.

I could report it all, since it's still in the notebook, but it isn't worth it. Wolfe decided, apparently more to kill time than anything else, to put the microscope on the episode of the phone call from Dorothy Unger and the receipt of the envelope. He took O'Neill over it, back and forth and up and down, and O'Neill stayed with him, against his strongest instincts and inclinations, because he knew he had to if he wanted to hear those cylinders. I got so fed up with the repetitions that when the doorbell rang the interruption was welcome in more ways than one.

O'Neill sprang from his chair and came along to the front door. On the stoop was a middle-aged square-faced woman in a purple coat. He greeted her as Gretty, took the envelope she handed him, and thanked her.

Back in the office he let Wolfe and me handle it to

look it over, but stayed close. It was a regulation BPR envelope, New York office, with his name and home address typed. Right in the corner, over the penalty clause, was a three-cent stamp, and a couple of inches to the left were five more three-cent stamps. Beneath them was printed by hand with a blue pencil: SPECIAL DELIVERY. Inside was a mimeographed BPR circular, dated March 27th, regarding price ceilings on a long list of copper and brass items.

When Wolfe handed it back to O'Neill and he stuck it in his pocket I remarked, "The post-office employees get more careless all the time. With that stamp in the corner canceled and the others not."

"What?" O'Neill got it from his pocket and glared at it. "What of it?"

"Nothing," Wolfe said shortly. "Mr. Goodwin likes to brag. It proves nothing."

I saw no reason why I shouldn't help to kill time, and I resent Wolfe's habit of making personal remarks in front of strangers, especially when he's an enemy, so I was opening my mouth to go on with it when the bell rang again. When I went to answer it O'Neill came along. You might have thought he was training for the job.

It was the Stenophone man. O'Neill did the honors, mentioning the president and apologizing for ruining his Sunday and so on, and I helped with the machine. It didn't amount to much, for O'Neill had explained on the phone that we didn't need a recorder. The chassis of the player had casters, and didn't weigh over sixty pounds anyhow. The Stenophone man wheeled it into the office, and was introduced to Wolfe, and in less than five minutes had us all instructed. Then, since he didn't seem disposed to linger, we let him go.

When I returned to the office after showing the

visitor out, Wolfe sent me a certain type of glance to
alert me and said:

"Now, Archie, if you'll get Mr. O'Neill's hat and
coat, please. He is leaving."

O'Neill stared at him a second and then laughed, or
at least made a noise. It was the first downright ugly
noise he had made.

Just to try him for size I took two quick steps
toward him. He took three quick steps back. I stopped
and grinned at him. He tried to look at both Wolfe and
me at once.

"So that's how it is," he said, extremely ugly. "You
think you can double-cross Don O'Neill. You'd better
not."

"Pfui." Wolfe wiggled a finger at him. "I have given
you no assurance that you would be permitted to hear
these things. It would be manifestly improper to
permit an official of the NIA to listen to confidential
dictation of the Director of the BPR, even after the
Director has been murdered. Besides, you're inconsistent again. A while ago you said you didn't trust me.
That could only have been because you considered me
untrustworthy. Now you profess to be shocked to find
that I am untrustworthy. Utterly inconsistent." The
finger wiggled again. "Well, sir? Do you prefer to be
self-propelled?"

"I'm not leaving this room."

"Archie?"

I moved to him. This time he didn't budge. From
the look on his face, if he had had anything at all useful
on him he would have used it. I took him by the arm
and said, "Come on, come with Archie. You must
weigh a hundred and eighty. I don't want to carry
you."

He started a right for my jaw, or at least it seemed

that that was what he thought he was doing, but it was too slow to hit anything that wasn't nailed down. Ignoring it, I started to spin him to attack from the rear, and the son of a gun hauled off and kicked me. He tried to kick high and got my knee. I am not claiming that it hurt much, but I do not like kickers. So I plugged him, with my left because it was handiest, on his soft neck just below the ear, and he teetered over against the bookshelves. I supposed that would explain things to him, but he teetered right back and tried another kick, so I used the right with more in it, also to the neck for the sake of knuckles, and he teetered again and tumbled.

I told Wolfe to buzz Fritz to open the door, saw that Fritz was already there, took my fallen foe by the ankles, and dragged him across to the hall, down the hall to the door, and on out to the stoop. Fritz handed me his coat and hat and I dropped them on him, re-entered the hall, and shut the door.

In the office I asked Wolfe, "Is he on the Executive Committee too, or was he just Chairman of the Dinner Committee? I was trying to remember while I was dragging him."

"I dislike commotion," Wolfe said peevishly. "I didn't tell you to hit him."

"He tried to kick me. He did kick me. Next time you do it."

Wolfe shuddered. "Start that machine going."

Chapter 15

It took more than an hour altogether to run off the ten cylinders, not counting time out for lunch.

I started the first one at the speed recommended by our instructor, but it had been going only a few seconds when Wolfe told me to slow it down. Having heard Cheney Boone on the radio I had expected him to sound about the same, but although there was enough similarity to recognize his voice, this seemed to be pitched higher and the words were more distinct. The first one began:

"Six-seventy-nine. Personal. Dear Mr. Pritchard. Thank you very much for your letter but I have decided not to get a Chesapeake retriever but to try an Irish setter. I have nothing against Chesapeakes and there is no good reason for my decision except the unpredictable vagary of the human mind. Sincerely. Six-eighty. Dear. Mrs. Ambruster. I do indeed remember that pleasant day and evening in St. Louis last fall and I deeply regret my inability to be present at the spring meeting of your fine organization. The next time I get to St. Louis I shall certainly get in touch with you. The material you request will be sent you without delay, and if it fails to arrive promptly be sure to let me know. With best regards and best wishes for the success of your meeting. Sincerely. Six-eighty-one. Memo—no, make it a letter to all regional directors. By name to each. Please return to this office immediately the advance copies of the press release for March 25th regarding household appliances. That release has been canceled and will not be sent out. Paragraph. The premature disclosure of some of the contents of that release by a press association has again raised the question whether advance copies of releases should be sent to regional offices. You are requested to investigate without delay, in your office, the handling of the advance copies of the release in question, and make a full report of the results directly to me. I shall expect this report to reach me not later than March 28th. Sincerely. Six-eighty-two. Dear Mr. Maspero. Thank you very much for your letter of the 16th, and I assure you that its contents will be regarded as confidential. That of course would be impossible if your information were susceptible of use in a legal action that could be undertaken by me in the performance of my duty, but I am fully aware of the difficulties involved in any attempt . . ."

That one went on long enough to fill at least two full pages single-spaced, leaving room on that cylinder only for two more letters and an interoffice memo. When it reached the end I removed it and returned it to its place in the row, and picked up number two, remarking meanwhile:

"I suppose you noticed that Boone apparently sent his letters by rocket and the regional directors were expected to be streaks of lightning."

Wolfe nodded gloomily. "We've been sniggled." He leaned forward to look at his desk calendar. "He couldn't possibly have dictated that the afternoon of the day he was killed, March 26th. He told the regional directors to investigate and get a report to him by March 28th. Since it was to go to all regional directors, the West Coast was included. Even granting the speed of air mail, and allowing only one day for their investigations, which seems meager, that must have been dictated not later than March 23rd, and probably several days earlier."

He sighed deep. "Confound it. I was hoping—" He compressed his lips and frowned at the leather case. "That woman said four, didn't she?"

"Do you mean Miss Gunther?"

"Who the devil do you think I mean?"

"I think you mean Miss Phoebe Gunther. If so, yes. She said there were twelve of those cases, and the one Boone gave her in the murder room had the number four stamped on top, and he told her it contained cylinders he had dictated in his Washington office that afternoon. So it looks as if someone has been playing button button. Are we too discouraged to go on or would we care to hear number two?"

"Go ahead."

I proceeded with the concert. Lunch intervened at the end of the sixth movement, and after a leisurely but not especially gay meal we returned to the office and finished them up. There was nothing spectacular anywhere in the lot, though some of them contained matter that was certainly confidential; and considered as clues that might help solve a murder, I wouldn't have paid a dime for them. In four others besides number one there was evidence, some of it conclusive, that they had been dictated earlier than March 26th.

I couldn't blame Wolfe for being depressed. In addition to all the other complications, there were at least eight possible explanations of how leather case number four happened, when found, to contain cylinders dictated prior to the day of the murder, the simplest of all being that Boone himself had picked up the wrong case when he left his Washington office that afternoon. Not to mention the basic question, for which I didn't have even a guess, let alone an answer: were the cylinders only a side show or were they part of the main performance?

Leaning back in his chair digesting, Wolfe was, to an unaccustomed eye though not to mine, sound asleep. He didn't stir as I wheeled the machine out of the way, over to a corner. Then, as I went to his desk and started to return the cylinders to their nests in the case, his lids opened to make a slit.

He shook his head. "You'd better run them off again and make a transcription of them. Three carbons." He glanced at the wall clock. "I'll be going upstairs in thirty-five minutes. Do it then."

"Yes, sir." I was grim. "I expected this."

"You did? I didn't."

"I don't mean I expected the cylinders to be antiques. I expected this typewriting job. That's the level this case seems to have descended to."

"Don't badger me. I was an ass to undertake it. I have more Cattleyas than I have room for, and I could have sold five hundred of them for twelve thousand dollars." He let his eyes come half open. "When you have finished transcribing these things, take them down to Mr. Cramer and tell him how we got them."

"Tell him everything?"

"Yes. But before you go to him do another typing job. Your notebook. Send this letter to everyone who was here Friday evening." He frowned for words, and in a moment dictated, "'Since you were good enough to come to my office at my invitation Friday evening, and since you were present when it was intimated that Miss Gunther's statement that she had left the leather case on the window sill of the reception room might not deserve credence, I am writing to inform you of a development that occurred today. Paragraph. Mr. Don O'Neill received in the mail a ticket for a parcel that had been checked at Grand Central Station. The parcel proved to be the leather case in question, with the figure four stamped on the lid as described by Miss Gunther. However, most of the cylinders it contained were obviously dictated by Mr. Boone prior to March 26th. I send you this information in justice to Miss Gunther.'"

"That's all?" I inquired.

"Yes."

"Cramer will throw a fit."

"No doubt. Mail them before you go to him, and take him a carbon. Then bring Miss Gunther here."

"Her? Phoebe Gunther?"

"Yes."

"That's dangerous. Isn't it too risky to trust me with her?"

"Yes. But I want to see her."

"Okay, it's on you."

Chapter 16

Two hours and more of back-breaking drudgery. Ten whole cylinders. Three carbons. Not only that, it was new to me and I had to adjust the speed about twenty times before I got the knack of it. When I finally got it finished and the sheets collated, I gave the original to Wolfe, who was back in the office by that time, placed the first two carbons in the safe, and folded the third carbon and stuck it in my pocket. Then there were the dozen letters to be typed and envelopes for same. As Wolfe signed them he folded and inserted them, and even sealed the envelopes. Sometimes he has bursts of feverish energy that are uncontrollable. By that time it was the dinner hour, but I decided not to dawdle through a meal in the dining room with Wolfe and made a quickie of it in the kitchen.

I had phoned the Homicide Squad office to make sure that Cramer would be on hand, to avoid having to deal with Lieutenant Rowcliffe, whose murder I hoped to help investigate some day, and had also called Phoebe Gunther's apartment to make a date but got no answer. Getting the car from the garage, I went first to Eighth Avenue to drop the letters in the post office and then headed south for Twentieth Street.

After I had been in with Cramer ten minutes he said, "This sounds like something. I'll be damned."

After another twenty minutes he said, "This sounds like something. I'll be damned."

That, of course, showed clear as day where he stood—up to his hips in a swamp. If he had been anywhere near dry ground, or even in sight of some, he would have waved his prerogative in front of my nose and cussed Wolfe and me up one side and down the other for withholding evidence for nine hours and fourteen minutes and so forth, including threats, growls, and warnings. Instead of which, at one point it looked as if he might abandon all restraint and thank me. Obviously he was desperate.

When I left Cramer I still had the carbon of the transcription in my pocket, because it was not intended for him. If I was to take Phoebe Gunther to Wolfe it was desirable that I get her before Cramer did, and it seemed likely that he would want to know exactly what was on those cylinders before he started a roundup. So I had kept it sketchy and hadn't told him that a transcription had been made.

Also I wasted no time getting to Fifty-fifth Street. The doorman phoned up, gave me another look of surprise when he turned to tell me I would be received, and called an okay to the elevator. Up at Nine H, Phoebe opened the door and allowed me to enter. I put my coat and hat on a chair and followed her into the room, and there was Alger Kates over in the corner where the light was dim.

I will not deny that I am often forthright, but I would put up an argument if anyone called me crude. Yet, at sight of Kates there again, I said what I said. I suppose it could be interpreted different ways. I do not concede that Phoebe Gunther had me fidgeting on a string, but the fact remains that I stared at Alger Kates and demanded:

"Do you live here?"

He stared back and replied, "If it's any of your business, yes, I do."

"Sit down, Mr. Goodwin." Phoebe possibly smiled. She got against the cushions on the couch. "I'll straighten it out. Mr. Kates does live here, when he's in New York. His wife keeps this apartment because she can't stand Washington. Right now she's in Florida. I couldn't get a hotel room, so Mr. Kates is staying with friends on Eleventh Street and letting me sleep here. Does that clear me? And him?"

Naturally I felt foolish. "I'll take it up," I said, "with the Housing Administration and see what I can do. Meanwhile I may be in a hurry, depending on how urgent Inspector Cramer feels. When I phoned you about an hour ago there was no answer."

She reached for a cigarette. "Why, do I need clearance on that too? I was out for a bite to eat."

"Has Cramer's office called since you returned?"

"No." She was frowning. "Does he want me? What for?"

"He either wants you now or he soon will." It was in the line of duty to keep my eyes fastened to her, to get her reaction. "I just took him that case of cylinders that you left on a window sill Tuesday evening."

I do not believe there was any menace in my tone. I don't know where it would have come from, as I did not at that time regard myself as a menace to Miss Gunther. But Alger Kates suddenly stood up, as if I had brandished a monkey wrench at her. He immediately sat down again. She kept her seat, but stopped her cigarette abruptly on its way to her lips, and the muscles of her neck stiffened.

"That case? With the cylinders in it?"

"Yes, ma'am."

"Did you—what's on them?"

"Well, that's a long story—"

"Where did you find it?"

"That's another long story. We've got to step on it, because Cramer has it now, and he may send for you any minute, or come to see you, or he may wait until he has listened to the cylinders. Anyhow, Mr. Wolfe wants to see you first, and since it was me—"

"Then you don't know what's on them?"

Kates had left his dim corner and moved across to the end of the couch, and was standing there in an attitude of readiness to repel the enemy. I ignored him and told her:

"Sure, I know. So does Mr. Wolfe. We got a machine and ran them off. They're interesting but not helpful. Their outstanding feature is that they weren't dictated on Tuesday, but before that—some of them a week or more. I'll tell—"

"But that's impossible!"

"Nope. Possible and true. I'll—"

"How do you know?"

"Dates and things. Absolutely." I stood up. "I'm getting restless. As I say, Mr. Wolfe wants to see you first. With Cramer there's no telling, especially when he's hanging on by his fingernails, so let's go. Kates can come along to protect you if you want him. I've got a transcription of the cylinders in my pocket and you can look at it on the way, and I'll tell—"

A bell rang. Having, though from the outside, heard it ring twice previously, I knew what it was.

I thought goddam it. I asked her in a whisper, "You expecting anybody?"

She shook her head, and the look in her eyes, straight at mine, said plainly that I could name the tune. But of course it was hopeless. Whoever had got by the doorman had also got information. Even so, there's nothing like trying, so I put a finger to my lips and stood there looking at them—at least I gave Kates a glance. His expression said belligerently, I'm not doing this for *you*, mister. We had held the tableau maybe ten seconds when a voice I knew well, the voice of Sergeant Purley Stebbins, came loud and irritated through the door.

"Come on, Goodwin, what the hell!"

I marched across and opened up. He came in past me rudely, took off his hat, and began to try to pretend he was a gentleman.

"Good afternoon, Miss Gunther. Good afternoon, Mr. Kates." He looked at her. "Inspector Cramer would be much obliged if you'd let me drive you down to his office. He's got some things there he wants you to look at. He told me to tell you they're Stenophone cylinders."

I was at his side. "You come right to the point, don't you, Purley, huh?"

"Oh," he said, pivoting his big fine empty head, "you still here? I supposed you was gone. The Inspector will be glad to know I ran into you."

"Nuts." I dropped him. "Of course you know, Miss Gunther, that you may do as you please. Some people think that when a city employee comes to take them somewhere they have to go. That's a fallacy, unless he has a document, which he hasn't."

"Is that true?" She asked me.

"Yes. That's true."

She had stood up when Purley entered. Now she moved across right to me, facing me, and stood looking up to meet my eyes. It wasn't much of a slant, because her eyes were only about five inches below mine, and therefore it wasn't a strain for either of us.

"You know," she said, "you have a way of suggesting things that appeal to me. With all I know about cops and their attitude toward people with power and position and money, and with the little I know about you, even if your boss has been hired by the NIA, I almost think I would let you hold my purse if I had to fix my garter. So you decide for me. I'll go with you to see Mr. Wolfe, or I'll go with this oversize sergeant, whichever you say."

Whereupon I made a mistake. It isn't so much that I regret it because it was a mistake, since I believe in having my share of everything on my way through life, including mistakes. The trouble was, as I now admit, that I did it not for my sake, or for Wolfe's, or for the good of the job, but for her. I would have loved to escort her down to my car with Purley traipsing along behind growling. Wolfe liked nothing better than to rile Cramer. But I knew if I took her to Wolfe's house Purley would camp outside, and after Wolfe finished with her she would either go on downtown for a night of it, or she would refuse to go, and she would certainly never hear the last of that. So I made the mistake because I thought Miss Gunther should have some sleep. Since she had told me herself that the tireder she got the better she looked, and there I was looking at her, it was evident that she was about all in.

So I said, "I deeply appreciate your confidence, which I deserve. You hold onto the purse while I fix the garter. For the present, I hate to say it, but it would be better to accept Cramer's invitation. I'll be seeing you."

Twenty minutes later I walked into the office and told Wolfe:

"Purley Stebbins arrived at Miss Gunther's before I could get her away, and she likes him better than she does me. She is now down at Twentieth Street."

So not only had I made a mistake, but also I was lying to the boss.

Chapter 17

Monday would fill a book if I let it, and so would any other day, I suppose, if you put it all in.

First thing in the morning Wolfe provided evidence of how we were doing, or rather not doing, by having Saul Panzer and Bill Gore sent up to his room during the breakfast hour for private instructions. That was one of his established dodges for trying to keep me from needling him. The theory was that if I contributed any remarks about inertia or age beginning to tell or anything like that, he could shut me up by intimating that he was working like a demon supervising Saul and Bill, and they were gathering in the sheaves. Also that it wouldn't be safe to let me in on the secret because I couldn't control my face. One reason that got my goat was that I knew that he knew it wasn't true.

The sheaves they had so far delivered had not relieved the famine. The armful of words, typed, printed and mimeographed, that Bill Gore had brought in from the NIA would have kept the *Time* and *Life* research staff out of mischief for a week, and that was about all it was good for. Saul Panzer's report of his weekend at the Waldorf was what you would expect, no man whose initials were not A.G. could have done better, but all it added up to was that no hair of a murderer's head was to be found on the premises. What Wolfe was continuing to shell out fifty bucks a day for was, as I say, presumably none of my business.

Public Relations had tottered to its feet again, taken a deep breath, and let out a battle cry. There was a full page ad in the *Times*, signed by the National Industrial Association, warning us that the Bureau of Price Regulation, after depriving us of our shirts and pants, was all set to peel off our hides. While there was no mention of homicide, the implication was that since it was still necessary for the NIA to save the country from the vicious deep-laid plots of the BPR, it was silly to imagine that it had any hand in the bumping off of Cheney Boone. As strategy, the hitch in it was that it would work only with those who already agreed with the NIA regarding who or what had got the shirts and pants.

One of my Monday problems was to get my outgoing phone calls made, on account of so many coming in the other direction. I started bright and early after Phoebe Gunther and never did get her. First, from the Fifty-fifth Street apartment, I got no answer. At nine-thirty I tried the BPR office and was told she hadn't arrived, and no one seemed to know whether she was expected. At ten-thirty I was informed that she was there, but was in with Mr. Dexter and would I call later. Twice later, before noon, she was still with Mr. Dexter. At twelve-thirty she had gone to lunch; my message for her to call me had been given to her. At one-thirty she wasn't back yet. At two o'clock the word was that she wouldn't be back, and no one that I got to knew where she was. That may all sound as if I am a pushover for a runaround, but I had two strikes on me all the way. Apparently there was nobody at the BPR, from switchboard girls to the Regional Director, who didn't know that Nero Wolfe, as Alger Kates put it, was in the pay of NIA, and they reacted accordingly. When I made an attempt to get connected with Dorothy Unger, the stenographer who had phoned Don O'Neill Saturday evening to ask him to mail her the parcel check which she had enclosed in his envelope by mistake, I couldn't even find anyone who would even admit he had ever heard of her.

What I got for my money on phone calls that day was enough to send Tel & Tel to a new low. On incoming calls the score was no better. In addition to the usual routine on a big case, like newspaper boys wanting a ringside seat in case Nero Wolfe was winding up for another fast one, there were all kinds of client trouble on account of the letters Wolfe had sent about finding the cylinders. The ad in the *Times* may have indicated that the NIA was a united front, but the phone calls didn't. Each one had a different slant. Winterhoff's line was that the assumption in the letter that the manner of finding the cylinders vindicated Miss Gunther was unjustified; that on the contrary it reinforced the suspicion that Miss Gunther was lying about it, since the parcel check had been mailed to Don O'Neill in a BPR envelope. Breslow, of course, was angry, so much so that he phoned twice, once in the morning and once in the afternoon. What had him sore this time was that we had spread the news about the cylinders. In the interests of justice we should have kept it to ourselves and the cops. He accused us of trying to make an impression on the Executive Committee, of trying to show that we were earning our money, and that was a hell of a note; we should have only two things in mind: the apprehension of the criminal and the proof of his guilt.

Even the Erskine family was divided. Frank Thomas Erskine, the father, had no complaint or criticism. He simply wanted something: namely, the full text of what was on the cylinders. He didn't get indignant but he was utterly astonished. To him the situation was plain. Wolfe was doing a paid job for the NIA, and any information he got in the performance of that job was the property of the NIA, and any attempt to exclude them from possession of their property was felonious, malevolent, and naughty. He insisted as long as he thought there was any chance, and then quit without any indication of hard feelings.

The son, Ed, was the shortest and funniest. All the others had demanded to talk to Wolfe, not just me, but he said it didn't matter, I would do fine, all he wanted was to ask a question. I said shoot, and he asked this, "How good is the evidence that O'Neill got the parcel check the way he says he did, in the mail?" I said that all we had, besides a look at the envelope, was O'Neill's say-so, but that of course the police were checking it and he'd better ask them. He said much obliged and hung up.

All day I kept expecting a call from Don O'Neill, but there wasn't a peep out of him.

The general impression I got was that the Executive Committee had better call a meeting and decide on policy.

The day went, and dusk came, and I turned on lights. Just before dinner I tried Fifty-fifth Street, but no Phoebe Gunther. The meal took even longer than usual, which is to be expected when Wolfe is completely at a loss. He uses up energy keeping thoughts out and trying to keep me quiet, and that makes him eat more. After dinner, back in the office, I tried Fifty-fifth Street once more, with the same result. I was stretched out on the couch, trying to work out an attack that would make Wolfe explode into some kind of action, when the bell rang and I went to the front door and swung it wide open without a preliminary peek through the glass. As far as I was concerned anybody at all would have been welcome, even Breslow, just for a friendly chat.

Two men stepped in. I told them to hang up their things and went to the office door and announced:

"Inspector Cramer and Mr. Solomon Dexter."

Wolfe sighed and muttered, "Bring them in."

Chapter 18

Solomon Dexter was a blurter. I suppose, as Acting Director of BPR, he had enough to make him blurt, what with this and that, including things like Congress in an election year and the NIA ad in the morning *Times*, not to mention the unsolved murder of his predecessor, but still Wolfe does not like blurters. So he listened with a frown when, after brief greetings and with no preamble, Dexter blurted:

"I don't understand it at all! I've checked on you with the FBI and the Army, and they give you a clean bill and speak of you very highly! And here you are tied up with the dirtiest bunch of liars and cutthroats in existence! What the hell is the idea?"

"Your nerves are on edge," Wolfe said.

He blurted some more. "What have my nerves got to do with it? The blackest crime in the history of this country, with that unscrupulous gang behind it, and any man, any man whatever, who ties himself up—"

"Please!" Wolfe snapped. "Don't shout at me like that. You're excited. Justifiably excited perhaps, but Mr. Cramer shouldn't have brought you in here until you had cooled off." His eyes moved. "What does he want, Mr. Cramer? Does he want something?"

"Yeah," Cramer growled. "He thinks you fixed that stunt about the cylinders. So it would look as if the BPR had them all the time and tried to plant them on the NIA."

"Pfui. Do you think so too?"

"I do not. You would have done a better job of it."

Wolfe's eyes moved again. "If that's what you want, Mr. Dexter, to ask me if I arranged some flummery about those cylinders, the answer is I didn't. Anything else?"

Dexter had taken a handkerchief from his pocket and was mopping his face. I hadn't noticed any moisture on him, and it was cool out, and we keep the room at seventy, but apparently he felt that there was something to mop. That was probably the lumberjack in him. He dropped his hand to his thigh, clutching the handkerchief, and looked at Wolfe as if he were trying to remember the next line of the script.

"There is no one," he said, "by the name of Dorothy Unger employed by the BPR, either in New York or Washington."

"Good heavens." Wolfe was exasperated. "Of course there isn't."

"What do you mean of course there isn't."

"I mean it's obvious there wouldn't be. Whoever contrived that hocus-pocus about the parcel check, whether Mr. O'Neill himself or someone else, certainly Dorothy Unger had to be invented."

"You ought to know," Dexter asserted savagely.

"Nonsense." Wolfe moved a finger to brush him away. "Mr. Dexter. If you're going to sit there and boil with suspicion you might as well leave. You accuse me of being 'tied up' with miscreants. I am 'tied up' with no one. I have engaged to do a specific job, find a murderer and get enough evidence to convict him. If you have any—"

"How far have you got?" Cramer interrupted.

"Well." Wolfe smirked. He is most intolerable when he smirks. "Further than you, or you wouldn't be here."

"Yeah," Cramer said sarcastically. "Here the other evening, I didn't quite understand why you didn't pick him out and let me take him."

"Neither did I," Wolfe agreed. "For one moment I thought I might, when one of them said something extraordinary, but I was unable—"

"Who said what?"

Wolfe shook his head. "I'm having it looked into." His tone implied that the 82nd Airborne was at it from coast to coast. He shifted to one of mild reproach. "You broke it up and chased them out. If you had acted like an adult investigator instead of an ill-tempered child I might have got somewhere."

"Oh, sure. I bitched it for you. I'd do anything to square it, anything you say. Why don't you ask me to get them all in here again, right now?"

"An excellent idea." Wolfe nearly sat up straight, he was so overcome with enthusiasm. "Excellent. I do ask it. Use Mr. Goodwin's phone."

"By God!" Cramer stared. "You thought I meant it?"

"*I* mean it," Wolfe asserted. "You wouldn't be here if you weren't desperate. You wouldn't be desperate if you could think of any more questions to ask anyone. That's what you came to me for, to get ideas for more questions. Get those people here, and I'll see what I can do."

"Who the hell does this man think he is?" Dexter demanded of Cramer.

Cramer, scowling at Wolfe, didn't reply. After some seconds he arose and, without any alteration in the scowl, came to my desk. By the time he arrived I had lifted the receiver and started to dial Watkins 9–8242. He took it, sat on the corner of the desk, and went on scowling.

"Horowitz? Inspector Cramer, talking from Nero Wolfe's office. Give me Lieutenant Rowcliffe. George? No, what do you expect, I just got here. Anything from on high? Yeah. Yeah? File it under C for crap. No. You've got a list of the people who were here at Wolfe's Friday evening. Get some help on the phones and call all of them and tell them to come to Wolfe's office immediately. I know that, but *tell* them. You'd better include Phoebe Gunther. Wait a minute."

He turned to Wolfe. "Anyone else?" Wolfe shook his head and Cramer resumed:

"That's all. Send Stebbins here right away. Wherever they are, find them and get them here. Send men out if you have to. Yeah, I know, all right, they raise hell, what's the difference how I lose my job if I lose it? Wolfe says I'm desperate, and you know Wolfe, he reads faces. Step on it."

Cramer went back to the red leather chair, sat, pulled out a cigar and sank his teeth in it, and rasped, "There. I never thought I'd come to this."

"Frankly," Wolfe muttered, "I was surprised to see you. With what Mr. Goodwin and I furnished you yesterday I would have guessed you were making headway."

"Sure," Cramer chewed the cigar. "Headway in the thickest damn fog I ever saw. That was a big help, what you and Goodwin furnished. In the first place—"

"Excuse me," Dexter put in. He stood up. "I have some phone calls to make."

"If they're private," I told him, "there's a phone upstairs you can use."

"No, thanks." He looked at me impolitely. "I'll go and find a booth." He started out, halted to say over his shoulder that he would be back in half an hour, and went. I moseyed to the hall to see that he didn't stumble on the sill, and after the door had closed behind him returned to the office. Cramer was talking:

". . . and we're worse off than we were before. Zeros all the way across. If you care for any details, take your pick."

Wolfe grunted. "The photograph and car license mailed to Mrs. Boone. The envelope. Will you have some beer?"

"Yes, I will. Fingerprints, all the routine, nothing. Mailed midtown Friday eight P.M. How would you like to check sales of envelopes in the five-and-dimes?"

"Archie might try it." It was a sign we were all good friends when Wolfe, speaking to Cramer, called me Archie. Usually it was Mr. Goodwin. "What about those cylinders?"

"They were dictated by Boone on March 19th and typed by Miss Gunther on the 20th. The carbons are in Washington and the FBI has checked them. Miss Gunther can't understand it, except on the assumption that Boone picked up the wrong case when he left his office Tuesday afternoon, and she says he didn't often make mistakes like that. But if that was it the case containing the cylinders he dictated Tuesday after-noon ought to be still in his office in Washington, and it isn't. No sign of it. There's one other possibility. We've asked everyone concerned not to leave the city, but on Thursday the BPR asked permission for Miss Gunther to go to Washington on urgent business, and we let her. She flew down and back. She had a suitcase with her."

Wolfe shuddered. The idea of people getting on airplanes voluntarily was too much for him. He flashed a glance at Cramer. "I see you have eliminated nothing. Was Miss Gunther alone on her trip?"

"She went down alone. Dexter and two other BPR men came back with her."

"She has no difficulty explaining her movements?"

"She has no difficulty explaining anything. That young woman has no difficulty explaining period."

Wolfe nodded. "I believe Archie agrees with you." The beer had arrived, escorted by Fritz, and he was pouring. "I suppose you've had a talk with Mr. O'Neill."

"A talk?" Cramer raised his hands, one of them holding a glass of beer. "Saint Agnes! Have I had a talk with that bird!"

"Yes, he talks. As Archie told you, he was curious about what was on those cylinders."

"He still is." Cramer had half emptied his glass and hung onto it. "The damn fool thought he could keep that envelope. He wanted to have a private dick, not you, investigate it, so he said." He drank again. "Now there's an example of what this case is like. Would you want a better lead than an envelope like that? BPR stock, special delivery, one stamp canceled and the others not, typewritten address? Shall I tell you in detail what we've done, including trying a thousand typewriters?"

"I think not."

"I think not too. It would only take all night to tell you. The goddam post office says it's too bad they can't help us, but with all the new girls they've got, stamps canceled, stamps not canceled, you never can tell."

Cramer emptied the bottle into the glass. "You heard that crack I made to Rowcliffe about my losing my job."

"That?" Wolfe waved it away.

"Yeah I know," Cramer agreed. "I've made it before. It's a habit. All inspectors tell their wives every evening that they'll probably be captains tomorrow. But this time I don't know. From the standpoint of a Homicide Squad inspector, an atom bomb would be a baby firecracker compared to this damn thing. The Commissioner has got St. Vitus's Dance. The D.A. is trying to pretend his turn doesn't come until it's time to panel a jury. The Mayor is having nightmares, and he must have got it in a dream that if there wasn't any Homicide Squad there wouldn't be any murders, at least not any involving big-time citizens. So it's all my fault. I mustn't get tough with refined people who have got to the point where they employ tax experts to make sure they're not cheating the government. On the other hand, I must realize that public sentiment absolutely demands that the murderer of Cheney Boone shall not go unpunished. It's six days since it happened, and here by God I sit beefing to you."

He drank his glass empty, put it down, and used the back of his hand for a napkin. "That's the situation, my fat friend, as Charlie McCarthy said to Herbert Hoover. Look what I'm doing, letting you take the wheel is what it amounts to, at least long enough for you to run me in a ditch if you happen to need to. I know damn well that no client of yours has ever been convicted of murder, and in this case your clients—"

"No man is my client," Wolfe interposed. "My client is an association. An association can't commit murder."

"Maybe not. Even so, I know how you work. If you

thought it was necessary, in the interest of the client—I guess here he comes or here it comes."

The doorbell had rung. I went to answer it, and found that Cramer's guess was right. This first arrival was a piece of our client, in the person of Hattie Harding. She seemed out of breath. There in the hall she gripped my arm and wanted to know:

"What is it? Have they—what is it?"

I used the hand of my other arm to pat her shoulder. "No, no, calm down. You're all tense. We've decided to have these affairs twice a week, that's all."

I took her to the office and put her to helping me with chairs.

From then on they dribbled in, one by one. Purley Stebbins arrived and apologized to his boss for not making it quicker, and took him aside to explain something. G. G. Spero of the FBI was third and Mrs. Boone fourth. Along about the middle Solomon Dexter returned, and finding the red leather chair unoccupied at the moment, copped it for himself. The Erskine family came separately, a quarter of an hour apart, and so did Breslow and Winterhoff. On the whole, as I let them in, they returned my greeting as a fellow member of the human race, one word or none, but there were two exceptions. Don O'Neill looked straight through me and conveyed the impression that if I touched his coat it would have to be sent to the cleaners, so I let him put it on the rack himself. Alger Kates acted as if I was paid to do the job, so no embraces were called for. Nina Boone, who came late, smiled at me. I didn't imagine it; she smiled right at me. To repay her, I saw to it that she got the same position she had had before, the chair next to mine.

I had to hand it to the Police Department as inviters. It was ten-forty, just an hour and ten minutes since Cramer had phoned Rowcliffe to get up a party. I stood and looked them over, checking off, and then turned to Wolfe and told him:

"It's the same as last time, Miss Gunther just doesn't like crowds. They're all here except her."

Wolfe moved his eyes over the assemblage, slowly from right to left and back again, like a man trying to make up his mind which shirt to buy. They were all seated, divided into two camps as before, except that Winterhoff and Erskine the father were standing over by the globe talking in undertones. From the standpoint of gaiety the party was a dud before it ever started. One second there would be a buzz of conversation, and the next second dead silence; then that would get on someone's nerves and the buzz would start again. A photographer could have taken a shot of that collection of faces and called it I Wonder Who's Kissing Her Now.

Cramer came to my desk and used the phone and then told Wolfe, leaning over to him, "They got Miss Gunther at her apartment over an hour ago, and she said she'd come immediately."

Wolfe shrugged. "We won't wait. Go ahead."

Cramer turned to face the guests, cleared his throat, and raised his voice:

"Ladies and gentlemen!" There was instant silence. "I want you to understand why you were asked to come here, and exactly what's going on. I suppose you read the papers. According to the papers, at least some of them, the police are finding this case too hot to handle on account of the people involved, and they're laying down on the job. I think every single person here knows how much truth there is in that. I guess all of you feel, or nearly all of you, that you're being pestered and persecuted on account of something that you had nothing to do with. The newspapers have their angle, and you have yours. I suppose it was an inconvenience to all of you to come here this evening, but you've got to face it that there's no way out of it, and you've got to blame that inconvenience not on the police or anybody else except one person, the person who killed Cheney Boone. I'm not saying that person is in this room. I admit I don't know. He may be a thousand miles from here—"

"Is that," Breslow barked, "what you got us here to listen to? We're heard all that before!"

"Yeah, I know you have." Cramer was trying not to sound sour. "We didn't get you here to listen to me. I am now turning this over to Mr. Wolfe, and he will proceed, after I say two things. First, you got the request to come here from my office, but from here on it is not official. I am responsible for getting you here and that's all. As far as I'm concerned you can all get up and go if you feel like it. Second, some of you may feel that this is improper because Mr. Wolfe has been engaged to work on this case by the National Industrial Association. That may be so. All I can say is, if you feel that way you can stay here and keep that in mind, or you can leave. Suit yourselves."

He looked around. Nobody moved or spoke. Cramer waited ten seconds and then turned and nodded at Wolfe.

Wolfe heaved a deep sigh and opened up with a barely audible murmur:

"One thing Mr. Cramer mentioned, the inconvenience you people are being forced to endure, requires a little comment. I ask your forbearance while I make it. It is only by that kind of sacrifice on the part of persons, sometimes many persons, who are themselves wholly blameless—"

I hated to disturb his flow, because I knew from long experience that at last he was really working. He had resolved to get something out of that bunch if he had to keep them there all night. But there was no help for it, on account of the expression on Fritz's face. A movement out in the hall had caught my eye, and Fritz was standing there, four feet back from the door to the office, which was standing open, staring wide-eyed at me. When he saw I was looking at him he beckoned to me to come, and the thought popped into my mind that, with guests present and Wolfe making an oration, that was precisely how Fritz would act if the house was on fire. The whole throng was between him and me, and I circled around behind them for my exit. Wolfe kept on talking. As soon as I made the hall I closed the door behind me and asked Fritz:

"Something biting you?"

"It's—it's—" He stopped and set his teeth on his lip. Wolfe had been trying to train Fritz for twenty years not to get excited. He tried again: "Come and I'll show you."

He dived for the kitchen and I followed, thinking it was some culinary calamity that he couldn't bear up under alone, but he went to the door to the back stairs, the steps that led down to what we called the basement, though it was only three feet below the street level. Fritz slept down there in the room that faced the street. There was an exit through a little hall to the front; first a heavy door out to a tiny vestibule which was underneath the stoop, and then an iron gate, a grill, leading to a paved areaway from which five steps mounted to the sidewalk. It was in the tiny vestibule that Fritz stopped and I bumped into him.

He pointed down. "Look." He put his hand on the

gate and gave it a little shake. "I came to see if the gate was locked, the way I always do."

There was an object huddled on the concrete of the areaway, up against the gate, so that the gate couldn't be opened without pushing the object aside. I squatted to peer. The light there was dim, since the nearest street lamp was on the other side of the stoop, thirty paces away, but I could see well enough to tell what the object was, though not for certain who it was.

"What the hell did you bring me here for?" I demanded, pushing past Fritz to re-enter the basement. "Come with me."

He was at my heels as I mounted the stairs. In the kitchen I detoured to jerk open a drawer and get a flashlight, and then went down the main hall to the front door, out to the stoop and down to the sidewalk, and down the five steps to the areaway. There, on the same side of the gate as the object, I squatted again and switched on the flashlight. Fritz was beside me, bending over.

"Shall I—" His voice was shaking and he had to start again. "Shall I hold the light?"

After half a minute I straightened up, told him, "You stay right here," and headed for the stoop. Fritz had pulled the front door shut, and when I found myself fumbling to get the key in the hole I stood erect to take a deep breath and that stopped the fumbling. I went down the hall to the kitchen, to the phone there, and dialed the number of Dr. Vollmer, who lived down the street only half a block away. There were six buzzes before he answered.

"Doc? Archie Goodwin. Got your clothes on? Good. Get here as fast as you can. There's a woman lying in our areaway, by the gate to the basement, been hit on the head, and I think she's dead. There'll be cops on it,

so don't shift her more than you have to. Right now?
Okay."

I took another breath, filling my chest, then took
Fritz's pad and pencil and wrote:

*Phoebe Gunther is in our areaway dead. Hit on
the head. Have phoned Vollmer.*

I tore off the sheet and went to the office. I suppose
I had been gone six minutes, not more, and Wolfe was
still doing a monologue, with thirteen pairs of eyes
riveted on him. I sidled around to the right, got to his
desk, and handed him the note. He got it at a glance,
gave it a longer glance, flashed one at me, and spoke
without any perceptible change in tone or manner:

"Mr. Cramer. If you please. Mr. Goodwin has a
message for you and Mr. Stebbins. Will you go with
him to the hall?"

Cramer and Stebbins got up. As we went out
Wolfe's voice was resuming behind us:

"Now the question that confronts us is whether it
is credible, under the circumstances as we know
them . . ."

Chapter 19

Thirty minutes past midnight was about the peak. At that moment I was alone in my room, two flights up, sitting in the chair by the window, drinking a glass of milk, or at least holding one in my hand. I do not ordinarily hunt for a cave in the middle of the biggest excitement and the most intense action, but this seemed to hit me in a new spot or something, and anyhow there I was, trying to arrange my mind. Or maybe my feelings. All I knew was that something inside of me needed a little arranging. I had just completed a tour of the battlefield, and at that hour the disposition of forces was as follows:

Fritz was in the kitchen making sandwiches and coffee, and Mrs. Boone was there helping him.

Seven of the invited guests were scattered around the front room, with two homicide dicks keeping them company. They were not telling funny stories, not even Ed Erskine and Nine Boone, who were on the same sofa.

Lieutenant Rowcliffe and an underling with a notebook were in the spare bedroom, on the same floor as mine, having a conversation with Hattie Harding, the Public Relations Queen.

Inspector Cramer, Sergeant Stebbins, and a couple of others were in the dining room firing questions at Alger Kates.

The four-star brass was in the office. Wolfe was seated beside his desk, the Police Commissioner was likewise at my desk, the District Attorney was in the red leather chair, and Travis and Spero of the FBI made a circle of it. That was where the high strategy would come from, if and when any came.

Another dick was in the kitchen, presumably to see that Mrs. Boone didn't jump out a window and Fritz didn't dust arsenic on the sandwiches. Others were in the halls, in the basement, all over; and still others kept coming and going from outdoors, reporting to, or getting orders from, Cramer or the Commissioner or the District Attorney.

Newspapermen had at one time infiltrated behind the lines, but they were now on the other side of the threshold. Out there the floodlights hadn't been removed, and some miscellaneous city employees were still poking around, but most of the scientists, including the photographers, had departed. In spite of that the crowd, as I could see from the window near which my chair was placed, was bigger than ever. The house was only a five-minute taxi ride or a fifteen-minute walk from Times Square, and the news of a spectacular break in the Boone case had got to the theater crowds. The little party Wolfe had asked Cramer to arrange had developed into more than he had bargained for.

A piece of 1 ½-inch iron pipe, sixteen inches long, had been found lying on the concrete paving of the areaway. Phoebe Gunther had been hit on the head with it four times. Dr. Vollmer had certified her dead on arrival. She had also received bruises in falling, one on her cheek and mouth, presumably from the stoop, where she had been struck, to the areaway. The scientists had got that far before they removed the body.

I had been sitting in my room twenty minutes when I noticed that I hadn't drunk any milk, but I hadn't spilled any from the glass.

Chapter 20

My intention was to go back downstairs and re-enter the turmoil when the microscope came. It was expected by some that the microscope would do the job, and it seemed to me quite likely.

I had myself been rinsed out, by Wolfe and Cramer working as a team, which alone made the case unique. But the circumstances made me a key man. The working assumption was that Phoebe had come and mounted the stoop, and that the murderer had either come with her, or joined her near or on the stoop, and had struck her before she had pushed the bell button, stunning her and knocking her off the stoop into the areaway. He had then run down into the areaway and hit her three times more to make sure she was finished, and shoved the body up against the gate, where it could not be seen by anyone on the stoop without leaning over and stretching your neck, and wasn't likely to be seen from the sidewalk on account of the dimness of the light. Then, of course, the murderer might have gone home and to bed, but the assumption was that he had remounted the stoop and pushed the button, and I had let him in and taken his hat and coat.

That put me within ten feet of them, and maybe less, at the moment it happened, and if by chance I had pulled the curtain on the glass panel aside at that moment I would have seen it. It also had me greeting the murderer within a few seconds after he had finished, and, as I admitted to Wolfe and Cramer, I had observed each arriving face with both eyes to discover how they were getting along under the strain. That was another reason I had gone up to my room, to look back on those faces. It didn't seem possible that I couldn't pick the one, or at least the two or three most probable ones, whose owner had just a minute previously been smashing Phoebe's skull with an iron pipe. Well, I couldn't. They had all been the opposite of carefree, showing it one way or another, and so what? Wolfe had sighed at me, and Cramer had growled like a frustrated lion, but that was the best I could do.

Naturally I had been asked to make up a list showing the order of arrivals and the approximate intervals between, and had been glad to oblige. I hadn't punched a time clock for them, but I was willing to certify my list as pretty accurate. They had all come singly. The idea was that if any two of them had arrived close together, say within two minutes or less of each other, the one that entered the house first could be marked as improbable. But not the one that came in second, because the murderer, having finished, and hearing footsteps or a taxi approaching, could have flattened himself against the gate in that dark corner, waited until the arriver had mounted the stoop and been admitted, and then immediately ascended the stoop himself to ring the bell. Anyhow, such close calculation wasn't required, since, as my memory had it, none of the intervals had been less than three minutes.

Of course the position on the list meant nothing. As far as opportunity was concerned, there was no difference between Hattie Harding, who came first, and Nina Boone, who came last.

All the guests had been questioned at least once, each separately, and it was probable that repeat performances would go on all night if the microscope didn't live up to expectations. Since they had all already been put through it, over and over, about the Boone murder, the askers had hard going. The questions had to be about what had happened there that evening, and what was there to ask? There was no such thing as an alibi. Each one had been on the stoop alone between nine-fifty and ten-forty, and during that period Phoebe Gunther had arrived and had been killed. About all you could ask anybody was this, "Did you ring the bell as soon as you mounted the stoop? Did you kill Phoebe Gunther first?" If he said Phoebe Gunther wasn't there, and he pushed the button and was admitted by Mr. Goodwin, what did you ask next? Naturally you wanted to know whether he came by car or taxi, or on foot from a bus or subway, and where did that get you?

Very neat management, I told myself, sitting by the window in my room. Fully as neat as any I remembered. Very neat, the dirty deadly bastard.

I have said that the assumption was that the murderer had remounted the stoop and entered the house, but perhaps I should have said one of the assumptions. The NIA had another one, originated by Winterhoff, which had been made a part of the record. In the questioning marathon Winterhoff had come toward the end. His story had three main ingredients:

1. He (Winterhoff, the Man of Distinction) always had shoe soles made of a composition which was almost as quiet as rubber, and therefore made little noise when he walked.

2. He disapproved of tossing trash, including cigarette butts, in the street, and never did so himself.

3. He lived on East End Avenue. His wife and daughters were using the car and chauffeur that evening. He never used taxis if he could help it, because of the revolutionary attitude of the drivers during the present shortage of cabs. So when the phone call had come requesting his presence at Wolfe's office, he had taken a Second Avenue bus down to Thirty-fifth Street, and walked crosstown.

Well. Approaching Wolfe's house from the east, on his silent soles, he had stopped about eighty feet short of his destination because he was stuck with a cigarette butt and noticed an ashcan standing inside the railing of an areaway. He went down the steps to the can and killed the butt therein, and, ascending the steps, was barely back to the sidewalk when he saw a man dart out from behind a stoop, out of an areaway, and dash off in the other direction, toward the river. He had gone on to Wolfe's house, and had noted that it was that areaway, probably, that the man had darted from, but he had not gone so far as to lean over the stoop's low parapet to peer into the areaway. The best he could do on the darting and dashing man was that he had worn dark clothes and had been neither a giant nor a midget.

And by gosh, there had been corroboration. Of the thousand more or less dicks who had been dispatched on errands, two had been sent up the street to check. In half an hour they had returned and reported that there was an ashcan in an areaway exactly twenty-four paces east of Wolfe's stoop. Not only that, there was a cigarette butt on top of the ashes, and its condition, and certain telltale streaks on the inside of the can, about one inch below its rim, made it probable that the butt had been killed by rubbing it against the inside of the can. Not only *that*, they had the butt with them.

Winterhoff had not lied. He had stopped to kill a butt in an ashcan, and he was a good judge of distances. Unfortunately, it was impossible to corroborate the part about the darting and dashing man because he had disappeared during the two hours that had elapsed.

How much Wolfe or Cramer had bought of it, I didn't know. I wasn't even sure how well I liked it, but I had been below normal since I had flashed the light on Phoebe Gunther's face.

Cramer, hearing it from Rowcliffe, who had questioned Winterhoff, had merely grunted, but that had apparently been because at the moment he had his mind on something else. Some scientist, I never knew which one, had just made the suggestion about the microscope. Cramer lost no time on that. He gave orders that Erskine and Dexter, who were elsewhere being questioned, should be returned immediately to the front room, and had then gone there himself, accompanied by Purley and me, stood facing the assemblage and got their attention, which took no effort at all, and had begun a speech:

"Please listen to this closely so you'll know what I'm asking. The piece of—"

Breslow blurted, "This is outrageous! We've all

answered questions! We've let ourselves be searched! We've told everything we know! We—"

Cramer told a dick in a loud and hard voice, "Go and stand by him and if he doesn't keep his trap shut, shut it."

The dick moved. Breslow stopped blurting. Cramer said:

"I've had enough injured innocence for one night." He was as sore and savage as I had ever seen him. "For six days I've been handling you people as tender as babies, because I had to because you're such important people, but now it's different. On killing Boone all of you might have been innocent, but now I know one of you isn't. One of you killed that woman, and it's a fair guess that the same one killed Boone. I—"

"Excuse me, Inspector." Frank Thomas Erskine was sharp, by no means apologetic, but neither was he outraged. "You've made a statement that you may regret. What about the man seen by Mr. Winterhoff running from the areaway—"

"Yeah, I've heard about him." Cramer was conceding nothing. "For the present I stick to my statement. I add to it that the Police Commissioner has just confirmed my belief that I'm in charge here, at the scene of a murder with those present detained, and the more time you waste bellyaching the longer you'll stay. Your families have been notified where you are and why. One of you thinks he can have me sent up for twenty years because I won't let him phone all his friends and lawyers. Okay. He don't phone."

Cramer made a face at them, at least it looked like it to me, and growled, "Do you understand the situation?"

Nobody answered. He went on, "Here's what I

came in here to say. The piece of pipe she was killed with has been examined for fingerprints. We haven't found any that are any good. The galvanizing was rough to begin with, and it's a used piece of pipe, very old, and the galvanizing is flaking off, and there are blotches of stuff, paint and other matter, more or less all over it. We figure that anybody grasping that pipe hard enough to crack a skull with it would almost certainly get particles of stuff in the creases of his hands. I don't mean flakes you could see, I mean particles too small to be visible, and you wouldn't get them all out of the creases just by rubbing your palms on your clothes. The examination would have to be made with a microscope. I don't want to take all of you down to the laboratory, so I'm having a microscope brought here. I am requesting all of you to permit this examination of your hands, and also of your gloves and handkerchiefs."

Mrs. Boone spoke up, "But, Inspector, I've washed my hands. I went to the kitchen to help make sandwiches, and of course I washed my hands."

"That's too bad," Cramer growled. "We can still try it. Some of those particles might not come out of the creases even with washing. You can give your answers, yes or no, to Sergeant Stebbins. I'm busy."

He marched out and returned to the dining room. It was at that point that I felt I needed some arranging inside, and went to the office and told Wolfe I would be in my room if he wanted me. I stayed there over half an hour. It was one A.M. when the microscope came. Police cars were coming and going all the time, and it was by accident that, through my window, I saw a man get out of one carrying a large box. I gulped the rest of the milk and returned downstairs.

Chapter 21

I might as well have stayed put, because that was where the hand inspecting was done, my bedroom. The laboratory man wanted a quiet spot, and there was still activity everywhere else except Wolfe's room, which, by his instructions, was not to be entered. So the customers, one by one, had to climb the two flights. The apparatus, with its special light plugged in, was set up on my table. There were five of us in the room: the two experts, the dick who brought and took the customers, the current customer, and me sitting on the edge of the bed.

I was there partly because it was my room and I didn't care for the idea of abandoning it to a gang of strangers, and partly because I was stubborn and still couldn't understand why I was unable to pick the face, as I had greeted them at the door, of the one who had just finished killing Phoebe. That was the reason I might have bid as high as a nickel for Winterhoff's man in dark clothes darting and dashing. I wanted another good look at them. I had a feeling, of which I wouldn't have told Wolfe, that if I looked straight at the face of the person who had killed Phoebe, I would know it. It was an entirely new slant on crime detection, especially for me, but I had it. So I sat on the edge of my bed and looked straight at faces while the experts looked at hands.

First, Nina Boone. Pale, tired, and nervous.

Second, Don O'Neill. Resentful, impatient, and curious. Eyes bloodshot.

Third, Hattie Harding. Saggy and very jittery. Eyes nothing like as competent as they had been four days earlier in her office.

Fourth, Winterhoff. Distinguished, sweaty, and worried stiff.

Fifth, Father Erskine. Tense and determined.

Sixth, Alger Kates. Grim and about ready to cry. Eyes backing into his head.

Seventh, Mrs. Boone. Everything coming loose but trying to hang on. The tiredest of all.

Eighth, Solomon Dexter. Sort of swollen, with bags under the eyes. Not worried, but extremely resolute.

Ninth, Breslow. Lips tight with fury and eyes like a mad pig. He was the only one who stared back at me instead of at his own hand, under the light and the lens.

Tenth, Ed Erskine. Sarcastic, skeptical, and hangover all gone. About as worried as a pigeon in the park.

There had been no exclamations of delighted discovery from the experts, any more than from me. They had spoken to the customers, to instruct them about holding still and shifting position when required, and had exchanged brief comments in undertones, and that was all. They had tweezers and pillboxes and other paraphernalia handy, but had made no use of it. When the last one, Ed Erskine, had been escorted out, I asked them:

"Any soap?"

The one without much chin replied, "We report to the Inspector."

"Goodness gracious," I said enviously. "It must be wonderful to be connected with the Police Department, with all the secrets. Why do you think Cramer let me come up and sit here and watch? To keep my mind a blank?"

"No doubt," the other one, the one with a jaw, said grimly, "the Inspector will inform you of our findings. Go down and report, Phillips."

I was beginning to get restless, so, deciding to leave my room to its fate temporarily, I followed Phillips downstairs. If it was a weird experience for me, all these aliens trampling all over the house as if they owned it, I could imagine what the effect must be on Wolfe. Phillips trotted into the dining room, but Cramer wasn't among those present, and I steered him into the office. Wolfe was at his desk, and the P.C., the D.A., and the two FBI's were still there, all with their eyes on Cramer, who stood talking to them. He stopped at sight of Phillips.

"Well?"

"On the microscopic examination of hands the results are negative, Inspector."

"The hell they are. Another big rousing achievement. Tell Stebbins to get all gloves and handkerchiefs from their persons and send them up to you. Including the ladies' bags. Tell him to tag everything. Also from their overcoat pockets—no, send up coats and hats and all, and you see what's in the pockets. For God's sake don't mix anything up."

"Yes, sir." Phillips turned and went.

Not seeing how any good could come of staring straight at the faces of gloves and handkerchiefs, I crossed over to the Police Commissioner and addressed him:

"If you don't mind, this is my chair."

He looked startled, opened his mouth, shut it again, and moved to another seat. I sat down where I belonged. Cramer talked:

"You can do it if you can get away with it, but you know what the law is. Our jurisdiction extends to the limits of the premises occupied by the deceased provided it was the scene of the crime, but not otherwise. We can—"

"That's not the law," the D.A. snapped.

"You mean it's not statute. But it's accepted custom and it's what the courts stand for, so it's law for me. You wanted my opinion, and that's it. I won't be responsible for continued occupation of the apartment Miss Gunther was staying in, and not by my men anyway because I can't spare them. The tenant of the apartment is Kates. Three good searchers have spent an hour and a half there and haven't found anything. I'm willing to let them keep at it all night, or at least until we turn Kates loose, if and when we're through here, but any order for continued occupancy and keeping Kates out"—he looked at the P.C.—"will have to come from you, sir, or," he looked at the D.A., "from you."

Travis of the FBI put in, "I'd advise against it."

"This," the D.A. said stiffly, "is a local problem."

They went on. I started kicking my left ankle with my right foot, and vice versa. Wolfe was leaning back in his chair with his eyes closed, and I was pleased to note that his opinion of high strategy was apparently the same as mine. The P.C., the D.A., and the FBI, not to mention the head of the Homicide Squad, debating where Alger Kates was going to sleep, when he got a chance to sleep, and that after three cops had had the apartment to themselves long enough to saw all the legs off the chairs and glue them back on. It developed that it was the D.A. who was plugging for continued occupancy. I decided to enter the conversation just for the hell of it and was considering which side to be on when the phone rang.

It was from Washington, for FBI Travis, and he came to my desk to take it. The others stopped talking and looked at him. On his part it was mostly listening. When he had finished he shoved the phone back and turned to announce:

"This has some bearing on what we've been discussing. Our men and the Washington police have completed their search of Miss Gunther's apartment in Washington—one large room, bath, and kitchenette. In a hatbox on a shelf in a closet they found nine Stenophone cylinders—"

"Confound it!" Wolfe burst out. "Nine?" He was as indignant and irritated as if he had been served a veal cutlet with an egg perched on it. Everyone stared at him.

"Nine," said Travis curtly. He was justifiably annoyed at having his scene stolen. "Nine Stenophone cylinders. A BPR man was with them, and they are now at the BPR office running them off and making a transcription." He looked coldly at Wolfe. "What's wrong with nine?"

"For you," Wolfe said offensively, "apparently nothing. For me, nine is no better than none. I want ten."

"That's a damn shame. I apologize. They should have found ten." Having demolished Wolfe, he reported to the others, "They'll call again as soon as they get something we might use."

"Then they won't call," Wolfe declared, and shut his eyes again, leaving the discussion of the new development to the others. He was certainly being objectionable, and it wasn't hard to guess why. The howling insolence of committing a murder on his own stoop would alone have been enough, but in addition to that his house was filled from top to bottom with uninvited guests and he was absolutely powerless. That was dead against his policy, his practice, and his personality. Seeing that he was really in a bad way, and thinking it might be a good plan for him to keep himself at least partially informed of what was going on, since he was supposed to have an interest in the outcome, I went to the kitchen to get some beer for him. Evidently he was in too bad a humor even to remember to send for beer, since there were no signs of any.

Fritz and about a dozen assorted dicks were there drinking coffee. I told them:

"You sure are cluttering up the place, but I don't blame you. It isn't often that members of the lower classes get a chance to drink coffee made by Fritz Brenner."

There was a subdued, but close to unanimous, concert of Bronx cheers. One said, "Goodwin the gentleman. One, two, three, laugh."

Another said, "Hey, you know everything. What's the lowdown on this NIA-BPR stuff? Is it a feud or not?"

I was putting six bottles and six glasses on a tray, with Fritz's help. "I'm glad to explain," I said generously. "The NIA and the BPR are in one respect exactly like the glorious PD, or Police Department.

They have esprit de corps. Repeat it after me—no, don't bother. That is a French term, the language spoken by Frenchmen, the people who live in France, the literal translation of which is 'spirit of the body.' In our language we have no precise equivalent—"

The cheers had begun again, and the tray was ready, so I left them. Fritz came to the hall with me, closed the kitchen door, held my sleeve, and told my ear:

"Archie, this is awful. I just want to say I know how awful it is for you. Mr. Wolfe told me when I took up his breakfast this morning that you had formed a passion for Miss Gunther and she had you wound around her finger. She was a beautiful girl, very beautiful. This is awful, what happened here."

I said, "Go to hell," jerked my arm to free my sleeve, and took a step. Then I turned to him and said, "All I meant was, this is a hell of a night and it will take you a week to clean up the joint. Go back and finish that lesson in French I was giving them."

In the office they were as before. I peddled beer around, making three sales to outsiders, leaving three bottles for Wolfe, which was about as I had calculated, went back to the kitchen and got myself a sandwich and a glass of milk, and returned to my desk with them. The strategy council was going on and on, with Wolfe still aloof in spite of the beer. The sandwich made me hungry and I went and got two more. Long after they were gone the council was still chewing the fat.

They were handicapped, of course, by continual interruptions, both by phone and by personal appearances. One of the phone calls was for Travis from Washington, and when he was through with it his face displayed no triumph. The nine cylinders had all been listened to, and there was nothing for us to bite on.

They contained plenty of evidence that they had been dictated by Boone at his Washington office on Tuesday afternoon, but no evidence at all that would help to uncover a murderer. The BPR was trying to hang onto the transcriptions, but the Washington FBI promised to send a copy to Travis, and he agreed to let Cramer see it.

"So," Travis said aggressively, daring us to hint that we were no better off than before, "that proves that Miss Gunther was lying about them. She had them all the time."

"Nine." Wolfe grunted in disgust. "Pfui."

That was his only contribution to their discussion of the cylinders.

It was five minutes past three Tuesday morning when Phillips, the expert with less than his share of chin, entered the office with objects in his hands. In his right was a gray topcoat, and in his left was a silk scarf with stripes of dark brown and terra cotta. It was obvious that even an expert is capable of having feelings. His face showed plainly that he had something.

He looked at Wolfe and me and asked, "Do I report here, Inspector?"

"Go ahead." Cramer was impatient. "What is it?"

"This scarf was in the right-hand pocket of this coat. It was folded as it is now. Unfolding one fold exposes about forty square inches of its surface. On that surface are between fifteen and twenty particles of matter which in our opinion came from that piece of pipe. That is our opinion. Laboratory tests—"

"Sure." Cramer's eyes were gleaming. "You can test from hell to breakfast. You've got a microscope up there, and you know what I want right now. Is it good enough to act on, or isn't it?"

"Yes, sir, it is. We made sure before—"

"Whose coat is it?"

"The tag says Alger Kates."

"Yeah," I agreed. "That's Kates's coat."

Chapter 22

Since they were a strategy council, naturally they didn't send for Kates immediately. They had to decide on strategy first—whether to circle him and get him tangled, or slide it into him gently, or just hit him on the head with it. What they really had to decide was who was going to handle it; that would determine the method, and they started to wrangle about it. The point was, as it always is when you've got a crusher like that scarf in his pocket, which way of using it was most likely to crumble him and get a confession? They hadn't been going long when Travis interposed:

"With all this top authority present, and me not in it officially anyhow, I hesitate to make a suggestion."

"So what is it?" the D.A. asked tartly.

"I would suggest Mr. Wolfe for it. I have seen him operate, and if it means anything I freely admit that he is my superior at it."

"Suits me," Cramer said at once.

The other two looked at each other. Neither liked what he was looking at, and neither liked Travis's suggestion, so simultaneously they said nothing.

"Okay," Cramer said, "let's go. Where do you want the coat and scarf, Wolfe, in sight?"

Wolfe half opened his eyes. "What is this gentleman's name?"

"Oh. Phillips. Mr. Wolfe, Mr. Phillips."

"How do you do, sir. Give the coat to Mr. Goodwin. Archie, put it behind the cushions on the couch. Give me the scarf, please."

Phillips had handed me the coat without hesitation, but now he balked. He looked at Cramer. "This is vital evidence. If those particles get brushed off and scattered . . ."

"I'm not a ninny," Wolfe snapped.

"Let him have it," Cramer said.

Phillips hated to do it. He might have been a mother instructed to entrust her newborn infant to a shady character. But he handed it over.

"Thank you, sir. All right, Mr. Cramer, get him in here."

Cramer went, taking Phillips with him. In a moment he was back, without Phillips and with Alger Kates. We all gazed at Kates as he stepped across and took the chair indicated by Cramer, facing Wolfe, but it didn't visibly disconcert him. He looked to me as he had up in my room, as if he might bust out crying any minute, but there was no evidence that he had done so. After he had sat down all I had was his profile.

"You and I have hardly spoken, have we, Mr. Kates?" Wolfe asked.

Kates's tongue came out to wet his lips and went back in again. "Enough to satisfy—" he began, but his thin voice threatened to become only a squeak, and he stopped for a second and then started over. "Enough to satisfy me."

"But my dear sir." Wolfe was gently reproachful. "I don't believe we've exchanged a word."

Kates did not unbend. "Haven't we?" he asked.

"No, sir. The devil of it is that I can't honestly say that I don't sympathize with your attitude. If I were in your position, innocently or not, I would feel the same. I don't like people piling questions on me, and in fact I don't tolerate it." Wolfe let his eyes open another millimeter. "By the way, I am now, momentarily, official. These gentlemen in authority have deputized me to talk with you. As you doubtless know, that doesn't mean that you *must* tolerate it. If you tried to leave this house before they let you go, you would be arrested as a material witness and taken somewhere, but you can't be compelled to take part in a conversation if you are determined not to. What do you say? Shall we talk?"

"I'm listening," Kates said.

"I know you are. Why?"

"Because, if I don't, the inference will be made that I'm frightened, and the further inference will be made that I am guilty of something that I am trying to conceal."

"Good. Then we understand each other." Wolfe sounded as if he were grateful for a major concession. With casual unhurried movement he brought the scarf out from beneath the rim of the desk, where he had been holding it in his hand, and put it down on the blotter. Then he cocked his head at Kates as if trying to decide where to begin. From where I sat, having Kates's profile, I couldn't tell whether he even gave the scarf a glance. Certainly he didn't turn pale or exhibit any hand-clenching or tremors of the limbs.

"On the two occasions," Wolfe said, "that Mr. Goodwin went to Fifty-fifth Street to see Miss

Gunther, you were there. Were you a close friend of hers?"

"Not a close personal friend, no. In the past six months, since I've been doing confidential research directly under Mr. Boone, I've seen her frequently in connection with the work."

"Yet she was staying in your apartment."

Kates looked at Cramer. "You people have gone over this with me a dozen times."

Cramer nodded. "That's the way it goes, son. This'll make thirteen."

Kates returned to Wolfe. "The present housing shortage makes it extremely difficult, and often impossible, to get a room in a hotel. Miss Gunther could have used her position and connections to get a room, but that is against BPR policy, and also she didn't do things like that. A bed in a friend's apartment was available to me, and my wife was away. I offered the use of my apartment to Miss Gunther coming up on the plane from Washington, and she accepted."

"Had she ever stayed there before?"

"No."

"You had seen her frequently for six months. What did you think of her?"

"I thought well of her."

"Did you admire her?"

"Yes. As a colleague."

"Did she dress well?"

"I never noticed particularly—no, that isn't true." Kates's voice zoomed for a squeak again and he used the controls. "If you think these questions are important and you want full and truthful answers. Considering Miss Gunther's striking appearance and her voluptuous figure, I thought she dressed extremely well for one in her position."

If Phoebe was here, I thought, she'd tell him he talks like an old-fashioned novel.

"Then," Wolfe said, "you did notice what she wore. In that case, when did you last see her wearing this scarf?" He used a thumb to indicate it.

Kates leaned forward to look at it. "I don't remember ever seeing her wear that. I never did." He settled back.

"That's strange." Wolfe was frowning. "This is important, Mr. Kates. Are you sure?"

Kates leaned forward again, saying, "Let me see it," and reached a hand for it.

Wolfe's hand was there before his, closing on it. "No," Wolfe said, "this will be an exhibit in a murder trial and therefore should not be handled indiscriminately." He stretched an arm to give Kates a closer look. Kates peered at it a moment, then leaned back and shook his head.

"I've never seen it before," he declared. "On Miss Gunther or anybody else."

"That's a disappointment," Wolfe said regretfully. "However, it doesn't exhaust the possibilities. You might have seen it before and now not recognize it because your previous view of it was in a dim light, for instance on the stoop of this house at night. I suggest that for your consideration, because clinging to this scarf are many tiny particles which came from the piece of pipe, showing that the scarf was used as a protection in clutching the pipe, and also because the scarf was found in the pocket of your overcoat."

Kates blinked at him. "Whose overcoat?"

"Yours. Get it, Archie." I went for it, and stood beside Kates, holding it by the collar, hanging full length. Wolfe asked, "That's your coat, isn't it?"

Kates sat and stared at the coat. Then he arose,

turned his back on Wolfe, and called at the top of his voice, "Mr. Dexter! *Mr. Dexter! Come in here!*"

"Cut it out." Cramer was up and had him by the arm on the other side. "Cut out the yelling! What do you want Dexter for?"

"Then get him in here. If you want me to stop yelling, get him in here." Kates's voice was trembling. "I told him something like this would happen! I told Phoebe to have nothing to do with Nero Wolfe! I told her not to come here tonight! I—"

Cramer pounced. "When did you tell her not to come here tonight? When?"

Kates didn't answer. He realized his arm was being gripped, looked down at Cramer's hand gripping it, and said, "Let go of me. Let go!" Cramer did so. Kates walked across to a chair against the wall, sat on it, and clamped his jaw. He was breaking off relations.

I said to Cramer, "If you want it, I was there when Rowcliffe was questioning him. He said he was at his friend's apartment on Eleventh Street, where he's staying, and Miss Gunther phoned to say she had just been told to come here and wanted to know if he had been told too, and he said yes but he wasn't coming and he tried to persuade her not to come, and when she said she was going to he decided to come too. I know you're busy, but if you don't read reports you throw wild punches."

I turned to include them all. "And if you want my opinion, with no fee, that's not Miss Gunther's scarf because it's not her style. She wouldn't have worn that thing. And it doesn't belong to Kates. Look at him. Gray suit, gray topcoat. Also a gray hat. I've never seen him in anything but gray, and if he was still speaking to us you could ask him."

Cramer strode to the door which connected with

the front room, opened it a crack, and commanded, "Stebbins! Come in here."

Purley came at once. Cramer told him, "Take Kates to the dining room. Bring the others in here one at a time, and as we finish with them take them to the dining room."

Purley went with Kates, who didn't seem reluctant to go. In a moment another dick entered with Mrs. Boone. She wasn't invited to sit down. Cramer met her in the middle of the room, displayed the scarf, told her to take a good look at it but not to touch it, and then asked if she had ever seen it before. She said she hadn't, and that was all. She was led out and Frank Thomas Erskine was led in, and the performance was repeated. There were four more negatives, and then it was Winterhoff's turn.

With Winterhoff, Cramer didn't have to finish his speech. He showed the scarf and started, "Mr. Winterhoff, please look—"

"Where did you get that?" Winterhoff demanded, reaching for it. "That's my scarf!"

"Oh." Cramer backed up a step with it. "That's what we've been trying to find out. Did you wear it here tonight, or have it in your pocket?"

"Neither one. I didn't have it. That's the one that was stolen from me last week."

"Where and when last week?"

"Right here. When I was here Friday evening."

"Here at Wolfe's house?"

"Yes."

"You wore it here?"

"Yes."

"When you found it was gone, who helped you look for it? Who did you complain to?"

"I didn't—what's this all about? Who had it? Where did you get it?"

"I'll explain in a minute. I'm asking now, who did you complain to?"

"I didn't complain to anybody. I didn't notice it was gone until I got home. If—"

"You mentioned it to no one at all?"

"I didn't mention it here. I didn't know it was gone. I must have mentioned it to my wife—of course I did, I remember. But I have—"

"Did you phone here the next day to ask about it?"

"No, I didn't!" Winterhoff had been forcing himself to submit to the pressure. Now he was through. "Why would I? I've got two dozen scarves! And I insist that—"

"Okay, insist." Cramer was calm but bitter. "Since it's your scarf and you've been questioned about it, it is proper to tell you that there is evidence, good evidence, that it was wrapped around the pipe that Miss Gunther was killed with. Have you any comment?"

Winterhoff's face was moist with sweat, but it had already been that way up in my room when they were examining his hands. It was interesting that the sweat didn't seem to make him look any less distinguished, but it did detract some when he goggled, as he now did at Cramer. It occurred to me that his best friend ought to warn him not to goggle.

He finally spoke. "What's the evidence?"

"Particles from the pipe found on the scarf. Many of them, at one spot."

"Where did you find it?"

"In an overcoat pocket."

"Whose coat?"

Cramer shook his head. "You're not entitled to

that. I'd like to ask you not to do any broadcasting on this, but of course you will." He turned to the dick. "Take him to the dining room and tell Stebbins not to bring any more in."

Winterhoff had things to say, but he was shooed out. When the door was closed behind him and the dick, Cramer sat down and put his palms on his knees, pulled in a deep breath, and expelled it noisily.

"Jee-zuss—Christ," he remarked.

Chapter 23

There was a long silence. I looked at the wall clock. It said two minutes to four. I looked at my wrist watch. It said one minute to four. In spite of the discrepancy it seemed safe to conclude that it would soon be four o'clock. From beyond the closed doors to the front room and the hall came faint suggestions of little noises, just enough to keep reminding us that silence wouldn't do. Every little noise seemed to be saying, come on, it's getting late, work it out. The atmosphere there in the office struck me as both discouraged and discouraging. Some buoyancy and backbone were needed.

"Well," I said brightly, "we've taken a big step forward. We have eliminated Winterhoff's darting and dashing man. I am prepared to go on the stand and swear that he didn't dash into the hall."

That got a rise out of nobody, which showed the pathetic condition they were in. All that happened was that the D.A. looked at me as if I reminded him of someone who hadn't voted for him.

The P.C. spoke. "Winterhoff is a damned liar. He didn't see a man running away from that stoop. He made that up."

"For God's sake," the D.A. burst out ferociously, "we're not after a liar! We're after a murderer!"

"I would like," Wolfe muttered sulkily, "to go to bed. It's four o'clock and you're stuck."

"Oh, we are." Cramer glowered at him. "*We're* stuck. The way you put it, I suppose *you're* not stuck?"

"Me? No, Mr. Cramer. No indeed. But I'm tired and sleepy."

That might have led to violence if there hadn't been an interruption. There was a knock on the door and a dick entered, approached Cramer, and reported:

"We've got two more taxi drivers, the two that brought Mrs. Boone and O'Neill. I thought you might want to see them, Inspector. One is named—"

He stopped on account of Cramer's aspect. "This," Cramer said, "will make you a Deputy Chief Inspector. Easy." He pointed to the door. "Out that way and find someone to tell it to." The dick, looked frustrated, turned and went. Cramer said to anyone who cared to listen, "My God. Taxi drivers!"

The P.C. said, "We'll have to let them go."

"Yes, sir," Cramer agreed. "I know we will. Get 'em in here, Archie."

So that was the state of mind the Inspector was in. As I proceeded to obey his command I tried to remember another occasion on which he had called me Archie, and couldn't, in all the years I had known him. Of course after he had got some sleep and had a shower he would feel differently about it, but I put it away for some fitting moment in the future to remind him that he had called me Archie. Meanwhile Purley and I, with plenty of assistance, herded everybody from the front room and dining room into the office.

The strategy council had left their chairs and collected at the far end of Wolfe's desk, standing. The guests took seats. The city employees, over a dozen of them, scattered around the room and stood looking as alert and intelligent as the facts of the case would permit, under the eye of the big boss, the P.C. himself.

Cramer, on his feet confronting them, spoke:

"We're letting you people go home. But before you go, this is the situation. The microscopic examination of your hands didn't show anything. But the microscope got results. On a scarf that was in a pocket of one of your overcoats, hanging in the hall, particles from the pipe were found. The scarf was unquestionably used by the murderer to keep his hand from contact with the pipe. Therefore—"

"Whose coat was it in?" Breslow blurted.

Cramer shook his head. "I'm not going to tell you whose coat it was or who the scarf belongs to, and I think it would be better if the owners didn't tell, because it would be sure to get to the papers, and you know what the papers—"

"No, you don't," Alger Kates piped up. "That would suit your plans, you and Nero Wolfe and the NIA, but you're not going to put any gag on me! It was my coat! And I've never seen the scarf before! This is the most—"

"That's enough, Kates," Solomon Dexter rumbled at him.

"Okay." Cramer did not sound displeased. "So it was found in Mr. Kates's coat, and he says he never saw the scarf before. That—"

"The scarf," Winterhoff interposed, his voice heavier and flatter than ever, "belongs to me. It was stolen from my overcoat in this house last Friday night. I haven't seen it since, until you showed it to me here. Since you have permitted Kates to make insinuations about the plans of the NIA—"

"No," Cramer said curtly, "that's out. I'm not interested in insinuations. If you people want to carry on your quarrel you can hire a hall. What I want to say is this, that some hours ago I said that one of you killed Miss Gunther, and Mr. Erskine objected. Now there's no room for objection. Now there's no doubt about it. We could take you all down and book you as material witnesses. But being who you are, within a few hours you'd all be out on bail. So we're letting you go home, including the one who committed a murder here tonight, because we don't know which one it is. We intend to find out. Meanwhile you may be expected to be called on or sent for any time, day or night. You are not to leave the city, even for an hour, without permission. Your movements may or may not be kept under observation. That's up to us, and no protests about it will get you anywhere."

Cramer scanned the faces. "Police cars will take you home. You can go now, but one last word. This isn't going to let up. It's bad for all of you, and it will go on being bad until the murderer is caught. So if any of you knows anything that will help, the worst mistake you can make is not to let us have it. Stay now and tell us. The Police Commissioner and the District Attorney and I are right here and you can talk with any of us."

His invitation wasn't accepted, at least not on the terms as stated. The Erskine family lingered to exchange words with the D.A., Winterhoff had a point to make with the P.C., Mrs. Boone got Travis of the FBI, whom she apparently knew, to one side, Breslow had something to say to Wolfe, and Dexter confronted Cramer with questions. But before long they had all departed, and it didn't appear that anything useful had been contributed to the cause.

Wolfe braced his palms against the rim of his desk, pushed his chair back, and got to his feet.

Cramer, on the contrary, sat down. "Go to bed if you want to," he said grimly, "but I'm having a talk with Goodwin." Already it was Goodwin again. "I want to know who besides Kates had a chance to put that scarf in his coat."

"Nonsense." Wolfe was peevish. "With an ordinary person that might be necessary, but Mr. Goodwin is trained, competent, reliable, and moderately intelligent. If he could help on that he would have told us so. Merely ask him a question. I'll ask him myself.— Archie. Is your suspicion directed at anyone putting the scarf in the coat, or can you eliminate anyone as totally without opportunity?"

"No sir twice," I told him. "I've thought about it and gone over all of them. I was moving in and out between bell rings, and so were most of them. The trouble is the door to the front room was standing open, and so was the door from the front room to the hall."

Cramer grunted. "I'd give two bits to know how you would have answered that question if you had been alone with Wolfe, and how you will answer it."

"If that's how you feel about it," I said, "you might as well skip it. My resistance to torture is strongest at dawn, which it is now, and how are you going to drag the truth out of me?"

"I could use a nap," G. G. Spero said, and he got the votes.

But what with packing the scarf in a box as if it had been a museum piece, which incidentally it now is, and collecting papers and miscellaneous items, it was practically five o'clock before they were finally out.

The house was ours again. Wolfe started for the

elevator. I still had to make the rounds to see what was missing and to make sure there were no public servants sleeping under the furniture. I called to Wolfe:

"Instructions for the morning, sir?"

"Yes!" he called back. "Let me alone!"

Chapter 24

From there on I had a feeling that I was out of it. As it turned out, the feeling was not entirely justified, but anyhow I had it.

What Wolfe tells me, and what he doesn't tell me, never depends, as far as I can make out, on the relevant circumstances. It depends on what he had to eat at the last meal, what he is going to have to eat at the next meal, the kind of shirt and tie I am wearing, how well my shoes are shined, and so forth. He does not like purple. Once Lily Rowan gave me a dozen Sulka shirts, with stripes of assorted colors and shades. I happened to put on the purple one the day we started on the Chesterton-Best case, the guy that burgled his own house and shot a week-end guest in the belly. Wolfe took one look at the shirt and clammed up on me. Just for spite I wore the shirt a week, and I never did know what was going on, or who was which, until Wolfe had it all wrapped up, and even then I had to get most of the details from the newspapers and Dora Chesterton, with whom I had struck up an acquaintance. Dora had a way of—no, I'll save that for my autobiography.

The feeling that I was out of it had foundation in

fact. Tuesday morning Wolfe breakfasted at the usual hour—my deduction from this evidence, that Fritz took up his tray, loaded, at eight o'clock, and brought it down empty at ten minutes to nine. On it was a note instructing me to tell Saul Panzer and Bill Gore, when they phoned in, to report at the office at eleven o'clock, and furthermore to arrange for Del Bascom, head of the Bascom Detective Agency, also to be present. They were all there waiting for him when he came down from the plant rooms, and he chased me out. I was sent to the roof to help Theodore cross-pollinate. When I went back down at lunch time Wolfe told me that envelopes from Bascom were to reach him un-opened.

"Hah," I said. "Reports? Big operations?"

"Yes." He grimaced. "Twenty men. One of them may be worth his salt."

There went another five hundred bucks a day up the flue. At that rate the NIA retainer wouldn't last long.

"Do you want me to move to a hotel?" I inquired. "So I won't hear anything unfit for my ears?"

He didn't bother to answer. He never let himself get upset just before a meal if he could help it.

I could not, of course, be really blackballed, no matter what whim had struck him. For one thing, I had been among those present, and was therefore in demand. Friends on papers, especially Lon Cohen of the *Gazette*, thought I ought to tell them exactly who would be arrested and when and where. And Tuesday afternoon Inspector Cramer decided there was work to be done on me and invited me to Twentieth Street. He and three others did the honors. What was eating him was logic. To this effect: The NIA was Wolfe's client. Therefore, if I had seen any NIA person lingering unnecessarily in the neighborhood of Kates's overcoat as it hung in the hall, I would have reported it to Wolfe but not to anyone else. So far so good. Perfectly sound. But then Cramer went on to assume that with two hours of questions, backtracking, leap-frogging, and ambushing, he and his bunch could squeeze it out of me, which was droll. Add to that, that there was nothing in me to squeeze, and it became quaint. Anyhow, they tried hard.

It appeared that Wolfe too thought I might still have uses. When he came down to the office at six o'clock he got into his chair, rang for beer, sat for a quarter of an hour and then said:

"Archie."

It caught me in the middle of a yawn. After that was attended to I said:

"Yeah."

He was frowning at me. "You've been with me a long time now."

"Yeah. How shall we do it? Shall I resign, or shall you fire me, or shall we just call it off by mutual consent?"

He skipped that. "I have noted, perhaps in more detail than you think, your talents and capacities. You are an excellent observer, not in any respect an utter fool, completely intrepid, and too conceited to be seduced into perfidy."

"Good for me. I could use a raise. The cost of living has incr–"

"You eat and sleep here, and because you are young and vain you spend too much for your clothes." He gestured with a finger. "We can discuss that some other time. What I have in mind is a quality in you which I don't at all understand but which I know you have. Its frequent result is a willingness on the part of young women to spend time in your company."

"It's the perfume I use. From Brooks Brothers. They call it Stag at Eve." I regarded him suspiciously. "You're leading up to something. You've done the leading up. What's the something?"

"Find out how willing you can make Miss Boone, as quickly as possible."

I stared. "You know," I said reproachfully, "I didn't know that kind of a thought ever got within a million miles of you. Make Miss Boone? If you can think it you can do it. Make her yourself."

"I am speaking," he said coldly, "of an investigating operation by gaining her confidence."

"That way it sounds even worse." I continued to stare. "However, let's put the best possible construction on it. Do you want me to worm a confession out of her that she murdered her uncle and Miss Gunther? No, thanks."

"Nonsense. You know perfectly well what I want."

"Tell me anyway. What do you want?"

"I want information on these points. The extent of her personal or social contacts, if any, with anyone connected with the NIA, especially those who were here last night. The same for Mrs. Boone, her aunt. Also, how intimate was she with Miss Gunther, what did they think of each other, and how much did she see of Miss Gunther the past week? That would do to start. If developments warrant it, you can then get more specific. Why don't you telephone her now?"

"It seems legitimate," I conceded, "up to the point where we get specific, and that can wait. But do you mean to say you think one of those NIA specimens is it?"

"Why not? Why shouldn't he be?"

"It's so damn obvious."

"Bah. Nothing is obvious in itself. Obviousness is subjective. Three pursuers learn that a fugitive boarded a train for Philadelphia. To the first pursuer it's obvious that the fugitive has gone to Philadelphia. To the second pursuer it's obvious that he left the train at Newark and has gone somewhere else. To the third pursuer, who knows how clever the fugitive is, it's obvious that he didn't leave the train at Newark, because that would be too obvious, but stayed on it and went to Philadelphia. Subtlety chases the obvious up a never-ending spiral and never quite catches it. Do you know Miss Boone's telephone number?"

I might have suspected him of sending me outdoors to play, to keep me out of mischief, but for the fact that it was a nuisance for him to have me out of the house, since he either had to answer the phone himself or let Fritz interrupt his other duties to attend to both the phone and the doorbell. So I granted his good faith, at least tentatively, and swiveled my chair to dial the Waldorf's number, and asked for Mrs. Boone's room. The room answered with a male voice that I didn't recognize, and after giving my name, and waiting longer than seemed called for, I had Nina.

"This is Nina Boone. Is this Mr. Goodwin of Nero Wolfe's office? Did I get that right?"

"Yep. In the pay of the NIA. Thank you for coming to the phone."

"Why—you're welcome. Did you—want something?"

"Certainly I did, but forget it. I'm not calling about what I want or wanted, or could easily want. I'm calling about something somebody else wants, because I was asked to, only in my opinion he's cuckoo. You realize the position I'm in. I can't call you up and say this is Archie Goodwin and I just drew ten bucks from the savings bank and how about using it to buy dinner for two at that Brazilian restaurant on Fifty-second Street? What's the difference whether that's what I want to do or not, as long as I can't? Am I keeping you from something important?"

"No . . . I have a minute. What is it that somebody else wants?"

"I'll come to that. So all I can say is, this is Archie Goodwin snooping for the NIA, and I would like to use some NIA expense money to buy you a dinner at that Brazilian restaurant on Fifty-second Street, with the understanding that it is strictly business and I am not to be trusted. To give you an idea how tricky I am, some people look under the bed at night, but I look *in* the bed, to make sure I'm not already there laying for me. Is the minute up?"

"You sound really dangerous. Is that what somebody else wanted you to do, kid me into having dinner with you?"

"The dinner part was my idea. It popped out when I heard your voice again. As for somebody else—you appreciate that working on this thing I'm thrown in with all sorts of people, not only Nero Wolfe, who is—well, he can't help it, he's what he is—but also the police, the FBI, the District Attorney's outfit—all kinds. What would you say if I told you that one of them told me to call you and ask where Ed Erskine is?"

"Ed Erskine?" She was flabbergasted. "Ask *me* where Ed Erskine is?"

"That's right."

"I'd say he was out of his mind."

"So would I. So that's settled. Now before we hang up, to leave no loose ends hanging, maybe you'd better answer my own personally conducted question, about the dinner. How do you usually say no? Blunt? Or do you zigzag to avoid hurting people's feelings?"

"Oh, I'm blunt."

"All right, wait till I brace myself. Shoot."

"I couldn't go tonight, no matter how tricky you are. I'm eating here with my aunt in her room."

"Then supper later. Or breakfast. Lunch. Lunch tomorrow at one?"

There was a pause. "What kind of a place is this Brazilian restaurant?"

"Okay, out of the way, and good food."

"But . . . whenever I go on the street—"

"I know. That's how it is. Leave by the Forty-ninth Street entrance. I'll be there at the curb with a dark blue Wethersill sedan. I'll be right there from twelve-fifty on. You can trust me to be there, but beyond that, remember, be on your guard."

"I may be a little late."

"I should hope so. You look perfectly normal to me. And please don't, five or ten years from now, try to tell me that I said you look average. I didn't say average, I said normal. See you tomorrow."

As I pushed the phone back I had a notion that a gleam of self-congratulation might be visible in my eyes, so I didn't turn immediately to face Wolfe but found papers on my desk that needed attention. After a moment he muttered:

"This evening would have been better."

I counted ten. Then, still without turning, I said distinctly, "My dear sir, try getting her to meet *you* any time whatever, even at Tiffany's to try things on."

He chuckled. Before long he chuckled again. Finding that irritating, I went up to my room and kept busy until dinnertime, straightening up. Fritz and

Charley hadn't been able to get up that high on account of the condition of the rest of the house, and while the microscope experts had been neat and apparently respectable, I thought a spot inventory wouldn't do any harm.

Toward the end of dinner, with the salad and cheese, a little controversy arose. I wanted to have our coffee there in the dining room and then go straight up to bed, and Wolfe, while admitting that he too needed sleep, wanted the coffee in the office as usual. He got arbitrary about it, and just as an object lesson I sat tight. He went to the office and I stayed in the dining room. When I was through I went to the kitchen and told Fritz:

"I'm sorry you had that extra trouble, serving coffee in two places, but he has got to learn how to compromise. You heard me offer to split the difference and drink it in the hall."

"It was no trouble at all," Fritz said graciously. "I understand, Archie. I understand why you're being erratic. There goes the doorbell."

It was a temptation to let the damn thing ring. I needed sleep. So did Wolfe, and all I had to do was flip the switch there on the kitchen wall to stop the bell ringing. But I didn't flip it. I said to Fritz, "Justice. The public weal. Duty, goddam it," and went to the front and pulled the door open.

Chapter 25

The guy standing there said, "Good evening. I would like to see Mr. Wolfe."

I had never seen him before. He was around fifty, medium-sized, with thin straight lips and the kind of eyes that play poker for blood. The first tenth of a second I thought he was one of Bascom's men, and then saw that his clothes ruled that out. They were quiet and conservative and must have had at least three try-ons. I told him:

"I'll see if he's in. Your name, please?"

"John Smith."

"Oh. What do you want to see him about, Mr. Jones?"

"Private and urgent business."

"Can you be more specific?"

"I can to him, yes."

"Good. Sit down and read a magazine."

I shut the door on him, clear shut, and went to the office and told Wolfe:

"Mr. John Smith, which he must have got out of a book, looks like a banker who would gladly lend you a dime on a cupful of diamonds. I left him on the stoop, but don't worry about him being insulted because he has no feelings. Please don't ask me to find out what he wants because it might take hours."

Wolfe grunted. "What is your opinion?"

"None at all. I am not being permitted to know where we're at. The natural impulse is to kick him off the stoop. I'll say this for him, he's not an errand boy."

"Bring him in."

I did so. In spite of his obnoxious qualities and of his keeping us up, I put him in the red leather chair because that had him facing both of us. He was not a lounger. He sat up straight, with his fingers intertwined in his lap, and told Wolfe:

"I gave the name of John Smith because my name is of no significance. I am merely an errand boy."

Starting off by contradicting me. He went on:

"This is a confidential matter and I must speak with you privately."

Wolfe shook his head. "Mr. Goodwin is my confidential assistant. His ears are mine. Go ahead."

"No." Smith's tone implied, and that settles it. "I have to be alone with you."

"Bah." Wolfe pointed to a picture of the Washington Monument, on the wall fifteen feet to his left. "Do you see that picture? It is actually a perforated panel. If Mr. Goodwin is sent from the room he will go to an alcove around a corner of the hall, across from the kitchen door, open the panel on that side, invisible to us, and watch us and listen to us. The objection to that is that he would be standing up. He might as well stay here sitting down."

Without batting an eye, Smith stood up. "Then you and I will go to the hall."

"No we won't.—Archie. Mr. Smith wants his hat and coat."

I arose and moved. When I was halfway across the

room Smith sat down again. I whirled, returned to my base, and did likewise.

"Well, sir?" Wolfe demanded.

"We have somebody," Smith said, in what was apparently the only tone he ever used, "for the Boone and Gunther murders."

"We? Somebody?"

Smith untangled his fingers, raised a hand to scratch the side of his nose, dropped the hand, and retwined the fingers. "Of course," he said, "death is always a tragedy. It causes grief and suffering and often hardship. That cannot be avoided. But in this case, the deaths of these two people, it has already caused widespread injury to many thousands of innocent persons and created a situation that amounts to gross injustice. As you know, as we all know, there are elements in this country that seek to undermine the very foundations of our society. Death is serving them—*has* served them well. The very backbone of our free democratic system—composed of our most public-spirited citizens, our outstanding businessmen who keep things going for us—is in great and real peril. The source of that peril was an event—now two events—which may have resulted either from the merest chance or from deep and calculated malice. From the standpoint of the common welfare those two events were in themselves unimportant. But overwhelmingly—"

"Excuse me." Wolfe wiggled a finger at him. "I used to make speeches myself. The way I would put it, you're talking about the nation-wide reaction against the National Industry Association on account of the murders. Is that correct?"

"Yes. I am emphasizing the contrast between the

trivial character of the events in themselves and the enormous harm—"

"Please. You've made that point. Go on to the next one. But first tell me, do you represent the NIA?"

"No. I represent, actually, the founding fathers of this country. I represent the best and most fundamental interests of the American people. I—"

"All right. Your next point?"

Smith untwined his fingers again. This time it was the chin that needed scratching. When that was finished he proceeded, "The existing situation is intolerable. It is playing directly into the hands of the most dangerous and subversive groups and doctrines. No price would be too high to pay for ending it, and ending it at the earliest possible moment. The man who performed that service would deserve well of his country. He would earn the gratitude of his fellow citizens, and naturally, especially of those who are being made to suffer under this unjust odium."

"In other words," Wolfe suggested, "he ought to be paid something."

"He *would* be paid something."

"Then it's too bad I'm already engaged. I like being paid."

"There would be no conflict. The objectives are identical."

Wolfe frowned. "You know, Mr. Smith," he said admiringly, "I like the way you started this. You said it all, except certain details, in your first short sentence. Who are you and where do you come from?"

"That," Smith declared, "is stupid. You're not stupid. You can learn who I am, of course, if you want to take the time and trouble. But there are seven respectable—*very* respectable—men and women with whom I am playing bridge this evening. After a dinner party. Which accounts for the whole evening, from seven o'clock on."

"That should cover it adequately. Eight against two."

"Yes, it really should," Smith agreed. He untangled his fingers once more, but not to scratch. He reached to his side coat pocket and pulled out a package wrapped neatly in white paper and fastened with Scotch tape. It was big enough to be tight in his pocket and he had to use both hands. "As you say," he remarked, "there are certain details. The amount involved is three hundred thousand dollars. I have one-third of it here."

I gave it a look and decided it couldn't all be in hundreds. There must have been some five-hundreds and grands.

One of Wolfe's brows went up. "Since you're playing bridge this evening, and since you came here on the assumption that I'm a blackguard, isn't that a little foolhardy? Mr. Goodwin, as I told you, is my confidential assistant. What if he took that away from you and put it in the safe and saw you to the sidewalk?"

For the first time the expression of Smith's face changed, but the little crease that showed in his forehead didn't look like apprehension. "Perhaps," he said, and there was no change in his voice, "you're stupid after all, though I doubt it. We know your record and your character. There isn't the slightest assumption that you're a blackguard. You are being given an opportunity to perform a service—"

"No," Wolfe said positively. "We've had that."

"Very well. But that's the truth. If you ask why you're being paid so large a sum to perform it, here are the reasons. First, everybody knows that you get exorbitant fees for everything you do. Second, from the standpoint of the people who are paying you, the rapidly accumulating public disfavor, which is totally undeserved, is costing them or will cost them, directly or indirectly, hundreds of millions. Three hundred thousand dollars is a mere nothing. Third, you will have expenses, and they may be large. Fourth, we are aware of the difficulties involved, and I tell you frankly that we know of no one except you who can reasonably be expected to solve them. There is no assumption whatever that you're a blackguard. That remark was completely uncalled for."

"Then perhaps I misunderstood the sentence you started with." Wolfe's eyes were straight at him. "Did you say you have somebody for the Boone and Gunther murders?"

"Yes." Smith's eyes were straight back at him.

"Who have you?"

"The word 'have' was a little inexact. It might have been better to say we have somebody to suggest."

"Who?"

"Either Solomon Dexter or Alger Kates. We would prefer Dexter but Kates would do. We would be in a position to co-operate on certain aspects of the evidence. After your plans are made I'll confer with you on that. The other two hundred thousand, by the way, would not be contingent on conviction. You couldn't possibly guarantee that. Another third would be paid on indictment, and the last third on the opening day of the trial. The effect of indictment and trial would be sufficient, if not wholly satisfactory."

"Are you a lawyer, Mr. Smith?"

"Yes."

"Wouldn't you pay more for Dexter than for Kates? You should. He's the Acting Director of the Bureau of Price Regulation. It would be worth more to you."

"No. We made the amount large, even exorbitant, to exclude any bargaining." Smith tapped the package with his finger. "This is probably a record."

"Good heavens, no." Wolfe was mildly indignant, as if it had been intimated that his schooling had stopped at about the sixth grade. "There was Teapot Dome. I could rattle off eight, ten, a dozen instances. Alyattes of Lydia got the weight of ten panthers in gold. Richelieu paid D'Effiat a hundred thousand livres in one lump—the equivalent, at a minimum, of two million dollars today. No, Mr. Smith, don't flatter yourself that you're making a record. Considering what you're bidding for, you're a piker."

Smith was not impressed. "In cash," he said. "For you its equivalent, paid by check, would be around two million."

"That's right," Wolfe agreed, being reasonable. "Naturally that had occurred to me. I'm not pretending you're being niggardly." He sighed. "I'm no fonder of haggling than you are. But I may as well say it, there's an insuperable objection."

Smith blinked. I caught him at it. "What is it?"

"Your choice of targets. To begin with, they're too obvious, but the chief obstacle would be motive. It takes a good motive for a murder, and a really tiptop one for two murders. With either Mr. Dexter or Mr. Kates I'm afraid it simply couldn't be done, and I'll have to say definitely that I won't try it. You have generously implied that I'm not a jackass, but I would be, if I undertook to get either Mr. Dexter or Mr. Kates indicted and tried, let alone convicted." Wolfe looked and sounded inflexible. "No, sir. But you might find someone who would at least attempt it. How about Mr. Bascom, of the Bascom Detective Agency? He's a good man."

"I have told you," Smith said, "that you'll get co-operation on evidence."

"No. The absence of adequate motive would make it impossible in spite of evidence, which would have to be circumstantial. Besides, considering the probable source of any evidence you would be able to produce, and since it would be directed against a BPR man, it would be suspect anyhow. You see that."

"Not necessarily."

"Oh, yes. Inevitably."

"No." Smith's face stayed exactly as before, though he had made a major decision, to show a card. He turned the card over without a flicker. "I'll give you an example. If the taxi driver who brought Dexter here testified that he saw him concealing a piece of iron pipe under his coat, with a scarf wrapped around it, that evidence wouldn't be suspect."

"Perhaps not," Wolfe conceded. "Have you got the taxi driver?"

"No. I was merely giving you an example. How could we go after the taxi driver, or anyone else, before we have come to an agreement on the—on a name?"

"You couldn't, of course. Have you any other examples?"

Smith shook his head. That was one way in which he resembled Wolfe. He didn't see any sense in using a hundred ergs when fifty would do the job. Wolfe's average on head-shaking was around an eighth of an inch to the right and the same distance to the left, and if you had attached a meter to Smith you would have got about the same result. However, Wolfe was still more economical on physical energy. He weighed twice as much as Smith, and therefore his expenditure per pound of matter, which is the only fair way to judge, was much lower.

"You're getting a little ahead," Smith stated. "I said we would confer on aspects of evidence after your plans are made. You will make plans only after you have accepted the offer. Do I understand that you've accepted it?"

"You do not. Not as described. I decline it."

Smith took it like a gentleman. He said nothing. After some long seconds of saying nothing, he swallowed, and that was his first sign of weakness. Evidently he was throwing in his hand and was ready for another deal. When, after another period of silence, he swallowed again, there was no question about it.

"There is another possibility," he said, "that would not be open to the objections you have made. Don O'Neill."

"M-m-m-m," Wolfe remarked.

"He also came in a taxicab. The motive is plain and in fact already established, since it is the motive that has already been accepted, wrongly and maliciously, all over the country. He would not serve the purpose as satisfactorily as Dexter or Kates, but it would transfer the public resentment from an institution or group to an individual; and that would change the picture completely."

"M-m-m-m."

"Also, evidence would not be suspect on account of its source."

"M-m-m-m."

"And therefore the scope of the evidence could be substantially widened. For example, it might be possible to introduce the testimony of a person or persons who saw, here in your hall, O'Neill putting the scarf into the pocket of Kates's overcoat. I understand that

Goodwin, your confidential assistant, was there throughout—"

"No," Wolfe said curtly.

"He doesn't mean I wasn't there," I assured Smith with a friendly grin. "Only that I've already been too damn positive about it. You should have come sooner. I would have been glad to discuss terms. When O'Neill tried to buy me it was Sunday, and I can't be bribed on Sunday—"

His eyes darted at me and through me. "What did O'Neill want you to do?"

I shook my head. Probably a thousand ergs. "That wouldn't be fair. Would you want me to tell him what *you* wanted me to do?"

He was strongly tempted to insist, there was no doubt about his thirst for knowledge, but his belief in the conservation of energy, coupled with the opinion he had formed of me, won the day. He gave it up without another try and returned to Wolfe.

"Even if Goodwin couldn't give it," he said, "there is still a good chance of testimony to that effect being available."

"Not from Mr. Breslow," Wolfe declared. "He would be a wretched witness. Mr. Winterhoff would do fairly well. Mr. Erskine Senior would be admirable. Young Mr. Erskine—I don't know, I rather doubt it. Miss Harding would be the best of all. Could you get her?"

"You're going too fast again."

"Not at all. Fast? Such details are of the greatest importance."

"I know they are. *After* you are committed. Are you accepting my suggestion about O'Neill?"

"Well." Wolfe leaned back, opened his eyes to a wider slit, and brought his finger tips together at the apex of his central bulk. "I'll tell you, Mr. Smith. The best way to put it, I think, is in the form of a message, or rather messages, for Mr. Erskine. Tell Mr. Erskine—"

"I'm not representing Erskine. I have mentioned no names."

"No? I thought I heard you mention Mr. O'Neill, and Mr. Dexter and Mr. Kates. However, the difficulty is this, that the police or the FBI may find that tenth cylinder at any moment, and in all likelihood that would make fools of all of us."

"Not if we have—"

"Please, sir. You have talked. Let me talk. On the hypothesis that you may run across Mr. Erskine. Tell him, that I am grateful for this suggestion regarding the size of the fee I may ask for without shocking him. I'll remember it when I make out my bill. Tell him that I appreciate his effort to pay the fee in a way that would keep it off my income tax report, but that form of skulduggery doesn't appeal to me. It's a matter of taste, and I happen not to like that. Tell him that I am fully aware that every minute counts; I know that the death of Miss Gunther has increased the public resentment to an unprecedented outburst of fury; I read the editorial in today's *Wall Street Journal;* I heard Raymond Swing on the radio this evening; I know what's happening."

Wolfe opened his eyes still wider. "Especially tell him this. If this idiotic flimflam is persisted in there will probably be the devil to pay and I'll be helpless, but I'll send in a bill just the same, and I'll collect it. I am now convinced that he is either a murderer or a simpleton, and possibly both. He is not, thank God, my client. As for you—no, I won't bother. As you say, you are merely an errand boy, and I suppose a reputable lawyer, of the highest standing. Therefore you are a sworn officer of the law. Pfui!—Archie. Mr. Smith is going."

He had indeed left his chair and was upright. But he wasn't quite going. He said, in precisely the same tone he had used at the door when telling me he would like to see Mr. Wolfe:

"I would like to know whether I can count on this being treated as confidential. I merely want to know what to expect."

"You're a simpleton too," Wolfe snapped. "What's the difference whether I say yes or no—to you? I don't even know your name. Wouldn't I do as I please?"

"You think—" Smith said, and didn't finish it. Probably the sentence as conceived might have betrayed a trace of some emotion, like sizzling rage for instance, and that wasn't to be permitted under any circumstances. So I don't think it is exaggerating to say that he was rendered speechless. He stayed that way clear out to the stoop, not even telling me good night.

By the time I got back to the office Wolfe had already rung for beer. I knew that by deduction when Fritz entered almost immediately with the tray. I blocked him off and told him:

"Mr. Wolfe has changed his mind. Take it back. It's after ten o'clock, he had only two hours' sleep last night, and he's going to bed. So are you and either me or I or both."

Wolfe said nothing and made no sign, so Fritz beat it with the tray.

"It reminds me," I remarked, "of that old picture, there was one in our dining room out in Ohio, of the people in the sleigh throwing the baby out to the wolves that were chasing them. That may not strictly apply to Dexter or Kates, but it certainly does to O'Neill. Esprit de corps my eye. Good God, he was the Chairman of the Dinner Committee. I used to worry about that picture. One way of looking at it, it was heartless to toss out the baby, but on the other hand if they hadn't the wolves would eventually have got the whole works, baby, horses, and all. Of course the man could have jumped out himself, or the woman could. I remember I decided that if it was me I would kiss the woman and baby good-by and then jump. I was eight years old at the time, a minor, and I don't regard myself as still committed to that. What do you think of the lousy bastards, anyhow?"

"They're in a panic." Wolfe stood up and pulled his vest down, and maneuvered himself into motion toward the door. "They're desperate. Good night, Archie." From the threshold he rumbled, without turning, "For that matter, so am I."

Chapter 26

The next day, Wednesday, here came the envelopes from Bascom. There were four in the morning mail, three in the one o'clock delivery (as I was later informed for bookkeeping purposes, since I was not there at the time), and in late afternoon nine more arrived by messenger. At that time I hadn't the slightest idea what line the Bascom battalion was advancing on, nor did I know what Saul Panzer and Bill Gore were doing, since their telephoned reports were taken by Wolfe, with me instructed to disconnect. The Bascom envelopes were delivered to Wolfe unopened, as ordered.

I was being entrusted with nothing but the little chores, as for example a phone call I was told to make to the Stenophone Company to ask them to deliver a machine to us on a daily rental basis—one equipped with a loudspeaker, like the one the manager had brought us on Sunday and sent for on Monday. They weren't very affable about it and I had to be persuasive to get a promise of immediate delivery. I followed instructions and got the promise, though it was clear over my head, since we had nothing to play on it. An hour later the machine came and I stuck it in a corner.

The only other Wednesday morning activity in which I had a share was a phone call to Frank Thomas Erskine. I was told to make it, and did so, informing Erskine that expenses were skyrocketing and we wanted a check for another twenty thousand at his early convenience. He took that as a mere routine detail and came back at me for an appointment with Wolfe at eleven o'clock, which was made.

The most noteworthy thing about that was that when they—Breslow, Winterhoff, Hattie Harding, and the two Erskines—arrived, sharp at eleven, they had Don O'Neill with them! That was a fair indication that they had not come to take up where John Smith had left off, since Smith's central idea had been to frame O'Neill for a pair of murders, unless they were prepared to sweeten it up with an offer of a signed confession by O'Neill in triplicate, one copy for our files, and I felt that I knew O'Neill too well to expect anything like that, since he had tried to kick me.

Erskine brought the check with him. They stayed over an hour, and it was hard to guess why they had bothered to come, unless it was to show us in the flesh how harassed they were. No comment remotely touching on the errand of John Smith was made by anyone, including Wolfe. Half of their hour was used up in trying to get from Wolfe some kind of a progress report, which meant it was wasted, and they spent most of the other half in an attempt to pry a prognosis out of him. Twenty-four hours? Forty-eight? Three days? For God's sake, when? Erskine stated categorically that each additional day's delay meant untold damage to the most vital interests of the Republic and the American people.

"You're breaking my heart, Pop," young Erskine said sarcastically.

"Shut up!" his father barked at him.

They scratched and pulled hair right in front of us. The pressure was too much for them, and the NIA was no longer a united front. I sat and looked them over, having in mind Smith's offer of testimony regarding the placing of the scarf in Kates's overcoat pocket, and came to the conclusion that it might be had from any one of them with respect to any other of them, with the possible exception of Erskine vs. Erskine, and even that was not unthinkable. Their only constructive contribution was the announcement that the next day, Thursday, over two hundred morning and evening papers in a hundred towns and cities would run a full page ad offering a reward of one hundred thousand dollars to anyone furnishing information leading to the arrest and trial of the murderer of either Cheney Boone or Phoebe Gunther, or both.

"There should be a healthy reaction to that, don't you think?" Erskine asked plaintively but not too hopefully.

I missed Wolfe's answer, and the rest of it, because I was leaving at that moment, on my way upstairs to run a comb through my hair and maybe wash my hands. I barely had time enough to get the car and be parked at the Forty-ninth Street entrance of the Waldorf at twelve-fifty, and since once in a million years a girl is early instead of late I didn't want to take a chance.

Chapter 27

Nina Boone showed up at fourteen minutes past one, which was par and therefore called for no comment one way or the other. I met her as she emerged, steered her to where I was parked just west of the entrance, and opened the door. She climbed in. I turned to observe, and, as I expected, there one was, looking left and right. He was not an acquaintance and I didn't know his name, but I had seen him around. I crossed to him and said:

"I'm Archie Goodwin, Nero Wolfe's handy man. If you'd been on her heels you'd have seen her get in my car there. I can't ask you to ride with us because I'm working on her, but here's some choices. I'll wait till you get a taxi, and I'll bet you a finiff I lose you in less than ten minutes; or I'll grease you to miss the trail right here. Two bits. Fifteen cents now and the other dime when I see a copy of your report. If—"

"I've been told," he said, "that there are only two ways to deal with you. One is to shoot you, and this is too public. The other—give me the fifteen cents."

"Okay." I fished for three nickels and handed them to him. "It's on the NIA. Actually I don't care. We're going to Ribeiro's, the Brazilian restaurant on Fifty-second Street."

I went and got in the car beside my victim, started the engine, and rolled.

A corner table in the side room at Ribeiro's is a good place to talk. The food is no great treat to one who gets fed by Fritz Brenner three times a day, but it goes down all right, there is no music, and you can wave a fork in any direction without stabbing anybody except your own companion.

"I don't believe," Nina said after we had ordered, "that anyone has recognized me. Anyhow no one is staring at me. I guess all obscure people think it would be wonderful to be a celebrity and have people look at you and point you out in restaurants and places. I know I did. Now I simply can't stand it. It makes me want to scream at them. Of course I might not feel that way if my picture had been in the papers because I was a movie star or because I had done something worth while—you know, remarkable."

So, I thought, she wanted someone besides Aunt Luella to talk to. Okay, let her talk.

"And yet," I told her, "you must have had your share of staring before this happened. You're not actually unsightly."

"No?" She didn't try to smile. "How do you know? The way I look now."

I inspected her. "It's a bad time to judge," I admitted. "Your eyes are puffy and you've been clamping your jaw so much that your chin juts. But still there's enough to go by for an estimate. The cheekbone curve is very nice, and the temples and forehead are way above the average. The hair, of course, has not been affected at all. Seeing you from behind on the sidewalk, one man out of three would walk faster to get a look at you from the side or the front."

"Oh? And the other two?"

"My lord," I protested, "what do you want for nothing? One out of three is tremendous. I was piling it on, merely because your hair happens to appeal to me and I might go so far as to break into a trot."

"Then next time I'll sit with my back to you." She moved her hand to her lap to make room for the waiter. "I've been wanting to ask you, and you've got to tell me, who was it that told you to ask me where Ed Erskine was?"

"Not yet. My rule with a girl is to spend the first fifteen minutes discussing her looks. There's always a chance I'll say something that appeals to her, and then it's smooth sailing. Besides, it wouldn't be in good taste to start working on you while we're eating. I'm supposed to drag everything out of you, so that's what I'll have to do, but I shouldn't start on it until the coffee, and by that time, if I'm any good, I'll have you in a frame of mind to let me even copy down your Social Security number."

"I would hate to miss that." She did try to smile. "It would be interesting to see you do it. But I promised my aunt I'd be back at the hotel by two-thirty—and by the way, I promised to bring you with me. Will you come?"

My brows went up. "To see Mrs. Boone?"

"Yes."

"She wants to see me?"

"Yes. Maybe only for fifteen minutes to discuss her looks. She didn't say."

"With girls over fifty, five is enough."

"She's not over fifty. She's forty-three."

"Five is still enough. But if we only have till

two-thirty I'm afraid we'd better start without taking time to break down your resistance. How do you feel? Have you noticed any inclination to melt or relax or put your head on my shoulder?"

"Not the slightest." Her tone carried conviction. "The only impulse I've had was to pull your hair."

"Then it'll be a wonder," I said regretfully, "if you loosen up enough to tell me what size shoes you wear. However we'll see, as soon as he gets through serving. You haven't finished your cocktail."

She did so. The waiter gave us each a steaming plate of shrimps, cooked with cheese and covered with a spicy sauce, and individual bowls of salad on which he had just sprinkled a thin dressing. Nina speared a shrimp with her fork, decided it was too hot to go in whole, halved it, and conveyed a portion to her mouth. She was in no mood for tasting food, but she tasted that, and immediately got some more on her fork.

"I like this," she said. "Go on and drag things out of me."

I finished chewing my second shrimp and swallowed it. "My technique is a little unusual," I told her. "For instance, not only are all ten of you people being followed around, to see what you're up to now, but also your pasts are being drained through cheesecloth. How do you like this cheese?"

"I like it. I love it."

"Good. We'll come here often. There are probably a hundred men—no, more than that, I forgot how important this case is—investigating your people's pasts, to find out, for example, if Mrs. Boone was having secret trysts with Frank Thomas Erskine on the boardwalk at Atlantic City, or if you and Breslow are champing at the bit until he can get his wife to give him a divorce. That takes time and money, and my technique is different. I prefer to ask you and settle it. Are you?"

"Am I what? Champing?"

"At the bit."

"No. I'm champing shrimps."

I swallowed another one. "You see," I explained, "they're all up a stump, including Nero Wolfe. They're not trying to make it more complicated just for the hell of it. The most satisfactory way out of it, the way that would please nearly everybody most, including the investigators themselves, would be the simplest way, namely that one of those six NIA people killed Cheney Boone for the obvious motive, and then killed Phoebe Gunther for some related reason. But the trouble is that if that's how it was, how are you ever going to find out which one of the six did it, let alone prove it? Apparently not a chance in a billion. The New York police and the FBI have been working on it over a week now, giving it all they've got, and where are they? Tailing *you!*"

"Well." She herded cheese and sauce with her fork. "You're buying me a lunch."

"Certainly, and I'm telling you why, aside from your hair and other personal details. We're all sunk unless we can find a new angle. I came to you because there's a possibility that you know something about such an angle without realizing it. Naturally I'm assuming that you want the murderer found and punished. Otherwise—"

"I do. Of course I do."

"Then suppose we try the direct approach and see how it sounds. Did you know any of these NIA birds personally?"

"No."

"None of those six?"

"No."

"How about any NIA people at all? There were around fifteen hundred of them at that dinner."

"This seems perfectly silly."

"Then let's get it over with. Did you?"

"Maybe a few—or rather, their sons and daughters. I graduated from Smith a year ago, and you meet a lot of people. But if we went back over every minute of it, every word of every conversation, we wouldn't find anything remotely resembling an angle."

"You don't think it would do me any good to probe?"

"No." She glanced at her wrist watch. "Anyway, we haven't time."

"Okay. We can go back to it. How about your aunt? Those trysts with Erskine. Did she have trysts?"

Nina made a noise which, under the circumstances, was a fair substitute for a laugh. "Ask her. Maybe that's what she wants to see you about. If all the pasts are being investigated as you say they are, I should think it would be established by now that Aunt Luella was utterly and exclusively devoted to my uncle, and to everything he did and everything he stood for."

I shook my head. "You don't get it. That's just the point. To illustrate: what if Boone learned something in Washington that Tuesday afternoon about something Winterhoff had done, or something that made him decide to take a certain step affecting Winterhoff's line of business, and what if he told his wife about it when he saw her in their hotel room (which you might also have heard since you were there too), and what if Mrs. Boone happened to know Winterhoff, not for trysting purposes but just knew him, and what if later, in the reception room, she was talking with Winterhoff during her third cocktail, and what if unintentionally she gave him an idea of what was up? That's what I mean by a new angle. I could invent a thousand of them just as I invented that one, but what is needed is one that really happened. So I'm asking about your aunt's circle of acquaintance. Is that malevolent?"

She had been making steady progress with the shrimps, which had now cooled off enough to permit it. "No," she admitted, "but you'd better ask her. All I can tell you is about me."

"Sure. You're virtuous and noble. It shows in your chin. The herald angels sing. A in deportment."

"What do you want?" she demanded. "Do you want me to tell you that I saw my aunt sneaking into a corner with Winterhoff or with any of those apes and whispering to him? Well, I didn't. And if I had—" She stopped.

"If you had would you tell me?"

"No. In spite of the fact that in my opinion my aunt is a pain in the neck."

"You don't like her?"

"No. I don't like her and I disapprove of her and I regard her as a grotesque relic. That's spread all over my past, but it's strictly personal."

"You don't go so far as to accept Breslow's suggestion that Mrs. Boone killed her husband on account of jealousy of Phoebe Gunther, and later, at Wolfe's house, finished up?"

"No, does anybody?"

"I couldn't say." Having disposed of the last shrimp, I started on the salad. "I don't. But it does seem to be a sound idea that Mrs. Boone was jealous of Phoebe Gunther."

"Certainly she was. There are several thousand girls and women working for the BPR, and she was jealous of all of them."

"Yeah. Chiefly on account of her nose, of course. But Phoebe Gunther wasn't just one of thousands. Wasn't she special?"

"She was indeed." Nina flashed me a quick glance which I failed to interpret. "She was extremely special."

"Was she going to do anything as trite as having a baby?"

"Oh, good lord." Nina pulled her salad over. "You pick up all the crumbs, don't you?"

"Was she?"

"No. And my aunt had just as little reason to be jealous of her as of anybody else. Her idea that my uncle had wolf in him was simply silly."

"How well did you know Miss Gunther?"

"I knew her pretty well. Not intimately."

"Did you like her?"

"I—yes, I guess I liked her. I certainly admired her. Of course I envied her. I would have liked to have her job, but I wasn't foolish enough to think I could fill it. I'm too young for one thing, but that's only part of it, she wasn't such a lot older than me. She did field work for a year or so and made the best record in the whole organization, and then she was brought to the main office and before long she was on the inside of everything. Usually when an organization like that gets a new Director he does a great deal of shifting around, but when my uncle was appointed there wasn't any shifting of Phoebe except that she got a raise in pay. If she had been ten years older and a man she would have been made Director when my uncle— died."

"How old was she?"

"Twenty-seven."

"Did you know her before you went to work for the BPR?"

"No, but I met her the first day I went there, because my uncle asked her to keep an eye on me."

"Did she do so?"

"In a way she did, yes, as much as she had time for. She was very important and very busy. She had BPR fever."

"Yeah?" I stopped a forkload of salad on its way to my mouth. "Bad?"

"One of the most severe cases on record."

"What were the main symptoms?"

"It varies with character and temperament. In its simplest form, a firm belief that whatever the BPR does is right. There are all kinds of complications, from bitter and undying hatred of the NIA to a messianic yen to educate the young, depending on whether you are primarily a do-gooder or a fighter."

"Have you got it?"

"Certainly I have, but not in its acute form. With me it was mostly a personal matter. I was very fond of my uncle." Her chin threatened to get out of control for a moment, and she paused to attend to that and then explained, "I never had a father, to know him, and I loved Uncle Cheney. I don't really know an awful lot about it, but I loved my uncle."

"Which complications did Phoebe have?"

"All of them." The chin was all right again. "But she was a born fighter. I don't know how much the enemies of the BPR, for instance the heads of the NIA, really knew about the insides of it, but if their intelligence was any good they must have known about Phoebe. She was actually more dangerous to them than my uncle was. I've heard my uncle say that. A political shake-up might have got him out, but as long as she was there it wouldn't have mattered much."

"That's a big help," I grumbled, "I don't think. It gives precisely the same motive, to the same people, for her as for him. If you call that a new angle . . ."

"I don't call it anything. You asked me."

"So I did. How about dessert?"

"I don't think so."

"You'd better. You're going to have to help me out with your aunt maybe all afternoon, and that will take extra energy since you don't like her. A good number here is walnut pudding with cinnamon."

She conceded that it was a good idea and I passed it on to the waiter. While our table was being cleared and we were waiting for the pudding and coffee, we continued on the subject of Phoebe Gunther, with no revelations coming out of it, startling or otherwise. I introduced the detail of the missing tenth cylinder, and Nina snorted at the suggestion that Phoebe might have had concealed relations with some NIA individual and had ditched the cylinder because it implicated him or might have. I gave her that and asked how about the possibility that the cylinder implicated Solomon Dexter or Alger Kates. What was wrong with that?

With her spoon in her hand ready to start on the pudding, she shook her head positively. She said it was loony. To suppose that Dexter would have done anything to hurt Boone, thereby hurting the BPR also, was absurd. "Besides, he was in Washington. He didn't get to New York until late that night, when he was sent for. As for Mr. Kates, good heavens, look at him! He's just an adding machine!"

"He is in a pig's eye. He's sinister."

She gasped. "Alger Kates sinister?"

"Anyhow, mysterious. Down at Wolfe's house that evening Erskine accused him of killing your uncle because he wanted to marry you and your uncle opposed it, and Kates let it stand that he did want to marry you, along with two hundred other lovesick BPR's, and then later that same evening I learn that he already has a wife who is at present in Florida. A married adding machine does not covet another lovely maiden."

"Puh. He was merely being gallant or polite."

"An adding machine is not gallant. Another thing, where does the dough come from to send his wife to Florida at the present rates and keep her there until the end of March?"

"Really." Nina stopped eating pudding. "No matter what Nero Wolfe charges the NIA, you're certainly trying your best to earn it! You'd just love to clear them completely—and it looks as if you don't care how you do it! Perhaps Mrs. Kates won some money at a church bingo. You ought to check on that!"

I grinned at her. "When your face is flushed like that it makes me feel like refusing to take any part of my salary in NIA money. Some day I'll tell you how wrong you are to suspect us of wanting to frame one of your heroes like Dexter or Kates." I glanced at my wrist. "You just have time to finish your cigarette and coffee.—What is it, Carlos?"

"Telephone, Mr. Goodwin. The middle booth."

I had a notion to tell him to say I had gone, because I had a natural suspicion that it was the creature I had bribed with three nickels merely wanting to know how much longer we were going to be in there, but I thought better of it and excused myself, since there was one other person who knew where I was.

It proved to be the one other person.

"Goodwin talking."

"Archie. Get down here at once."

"What for?"

"Without delay!"

"But listen. We're just leaving, to see Mrs. Boone. I've got her to agree to see me. I'll put her through a—"

"I said get down here."

There was no use arguing. He sounded as if six tigers were crouching before him, lashing their tails, ready to spring. I went back to the table and told Nina that our afternoon was ruined.

Chapter 28

Having delivered Nina at the Waldorf entrance, with my pet bribee on our tail in a taxi, and having crowded the lights and the congested traffic down and across to West Thirty-fifth Street, I was relieved to see, as I reached my destination and braked to a stop at the curb, that the house wasn't on fire. There were only two foreign items visible: a police car parked smack in front of the address, and a man on the stoop. He was seated on the top step, hunched over, looking gloomy and obstinate.

This one I knew by name, one Quayle. He was on his feet by the time I had mounted the steps, and accosted me with what was meant to be cordiality.

"Hello, Goodwin! This is a piece of luck. Don't anybody ever answer the bell here when you're away? I'll just go in with you."

"Unexpected pleasure," I told him, and used my key, turned the knob, and pushed. The door opened two inches and stopped. The chain bolt was on, as it often was during my absence. My finger went to the button and executed my private ring. In a minute Fritz's step came down the hall and he spoke to me through the crack:

"Archie, that's a policeman. Mr. Wolfe doesn't—"

"Of course he doesn't. Take off the bolt. Then keep your eye on us. This officer eagerly performing his duty might lose his balance and fall down the stoop, and I may need you as a witness that I didn't push him. He must be twice my age."

"You witty son of a bitch," Quayle said sadly, and sat down on the step again. I entered, marched down the hall to the office, and saw Wolfe there alone behind his desk, sitting up straight as a ramrod, his lips pressed together in a thin straight line, his eyes wide open, his hands resting on the desk before him with the fingers curved ready for a throat.

His eyes darted at me. "What the devil took you so long?"

"Now just a minute," I soothed him. "Aware that you were having a fit, I made it as fast as I could in the traffic. Is it a pinch?"

"It is insufferable. Who is Inspector Ash?"

"Ash? You remember him. He was a captain under Cramer from 1938 to '43. Now in charge of Homicide in Queens. Tall guy, face all bones, plastic eyes, very incorruptible and no sense of humor. Why, what has he done?"

"Is the car in good condition?"

"Certainly. Why?"

"I want you to drive me to Police Headquarters."

"My God." So it was something not only serious, but drastic. Leaving the house, getting in the car, incurring all the outdoor risks, visiting a policeman; and besides all that, which was unheard of, almost certainly standing up the orchids for the regular four o'clock date. I dropped onto a chair, speechless, and gawked at him.

"Luckily," Wolfe said, "when that man arrived the

door was bolted. He told Fritz that he had come to take me to see Inspector Ash. When Fritz gave him the proper reply he displayed a warrant for me as a material witness regarding the murder of Miss Gunther. He pushed the warrant in through the crack in the door and Fritz pushed it out again and closed the door, and, through the glass panel, saw him walk toward the corner, presumably to telephone, since he left his car there in front of my house."

"That alone," I remarked, "leaving his car in front of your house, shows the kind of man he is. It's not even his car. It belongs to the city."

Wolfe didn't even hear me. "I called Inspector Cramer's office and was told he was not available. I finally succeeded in reaching some person who spoke in behalf of Inspector Ash, and was told that the man they had sent here had reported by telephone, and that unless I admitted him, accepted service of the warrant, and went with him, a search warrant would be sent without delay. I then, with great difficulty, got to the Police Commissioner. He has no guts. He tried to be evasive. He made what he called a concession, stating that I could come to his office instead of Inspector Ash's. I told him that only by using physical force could I be transported in any vehicle not driven by you, and he said they would wait for me until half-past three but no longer. An ultimatum with a time limit. He also said that Mr. Cramer has been removed from the Boone-Gunther case and relieved of his command and has been replaced by Inspector Ash. That's the situation. It is unacceptable."

I was staring incredulously. "Cramer got the boot?"

"So Mr. What's-his-name said."

"Who, Hombert? The Commissioner?"

"Yes. Confound it, must I repeat the whole thing for you?"

"For God's sake, don't. Try to relax. I'll be damned. They got Cramer." I looked at the clock. "It's five past three, and that ultimatum has probably got narrow margins. You hold it a minute and try to think of something pleasant."

I went to the front and pulled the curtain aside for a look through the glass, and saw that Quayle had acquired a colleague. The pair were sitting on the stoop with their backs to me. I opened the door and inquired affably:

"What's the program now?"

Quayle twisted around. "We've got another paper. Which we'll show when the time comes. The kind of law that opens all doors from the mightiest to the humblest."

"To be shown when? Three-thirty?"

"Go suck a pickle."

"Aw, tell him," the colleague growled. "What do you expect to get out of it, fame?"

"He's witty," Quayle said petulantly. He twisted back to me. "At three-thirty we phone in again for the word."

"That's more like it," I declared approvingly. "And what happens if I emerge with a large object resembling Nero Wolfe and wedge him into my car and drive off? Do you flash your first paper and interfere?"

"No. We follow you if it's straight to Centre Street. If you try detouring by way of Yonkers that's different."

"Okay. I'm accepting your word of honor. If you forget what you said and try to grab him I'll complain to the Board of Health. He's sick."

"What with?"

"Sitzenlust. Chronic. The opposite of wanderlust. You wouldn't want to jeopardize a human life, would you?"

"Yes."

Satisfied, I closed the door and returned to the office and told Wolfe, "All set. In spite of our having outriders I'm game either for Centre Street or for a dash for Canada, however you feel. You can tell me after we're in the car."

He started to get erect, his lips compressed tighter than ever.

Chapter 29

You are not an attorney," Inspector Ash declared in an insulting tone, though the statement was certainly not an insult in itself. "Nothing that has been said or written to you by anyone whatever has the status of a privileged communication."

It was not a convention as I had expected. Besides Wolfe and me the only ones present were Ash, Police Commissioner Hombert, and District Attorney Skinner, which left Hombert's spacious and well-furnished corner office looking practically uninhabited, even considering that Wolfe counted for three. At least he was not undergoing downright physical hardship, since there had been found available a chair large enough to accommodate his beam without excessive squeezing.

But he was conceding nothing. "That remark," he told Ash in his most objectionable tone, "is childish. Suppose I have been told something that I don't want you to know about. Would I admit the fact and then refuse to tell you about it on the ground that it was a privileged communication? Pfui! Suppose you kept after me. I would simply tell you a string of lies and then what?"

Ash was smiling. His plastic eyes had the effect of reflecting all the light that came at them from the four big windows, as if their surfaces could neither absorb light nor give it out.

"The trouble with you, Wolfe," he said curtly, "is that you've been spoiled by my predecessor, Inspector Cramer. He didn't know how to handle you. You had him buffaloed. With me in charge you'll see a big difference. A month from now or a year from now you may still have a license and you may not. It depends on how you behave." He tapped his chest with his forefinger. "You know me. You may remember how far you got with that Boeddiker case over in Queens."

"I never started. I quit. And your abominable handling gave the prosecutor insufficient evidence to convict a murderer whose guilt was manifest. Mr. Ash, you are both a numskull and a holligan."

"So you're going to try it on me." Ash was still smiling. "Maybe I won't give you even a month. I don't see why—"

"That will do for that," Hombert broke in.

"Yes, sir," Ash said respectfully. "I only wanted—"

"I don't give a damn what you only wanted. We're in one hell of a fix, and that's all I'm interested in. If you want to ride Wolfe on this case go as far as you like, but save the rest till later. It was your idea that Wolfe was holding out and it was time to put the screws on him. Go ahead. I'm all for that."

"Yes, sir." Ash had quit smiling to look stern. "I only know this, that in every case I've ever heard of where Wolfe horned in and got within smelling distance of money he has always managed to get something that no one else gets, and he always hangs onto it until it suits his convenience to let go."

"You're quite correct, Inspector," District Attorney Skinner said dryly. "You might add that when he does let go the result is usually disastrous for some lawbreaker."

"Yes?" Ash demanded. "And is that a reason for letting him call the tune for the Police Department and your office?"

"I would like to ask," Wolfe put in, "if I was hauled down here to listen to a discussion of my own career and character. This babbling is frivolous."

Ash was getting stirred up. He glared. "You were hauled down here," he rasped, "to tell us what you know, and everything you know, about these crimes. You say I'm a numskull. I don't say you're a numskull, far from it, here's my opinion of you in one short sentence. I wouldn't be surprised if you know something that gives you a good clear idea of who it was that killed Cheney Boone and the Gunther woman."

"Certainly I do. So do you."

They made movements and noises. I grinned around at them, nonchalant, to convey the impression that there was nothing to get excited about, because I had the conviction that Wolfe was overplaying it beyond all reason just to get even with them and it might have undesirable consequences. His romantic nature often led him to excesses like that, and once he got started it was hard to stop him, the stopping being one of my functions. Before their exclamations and head-jerkings were finished I stepped in.

"He doesn't mean," I explained hastily, "that we've got the murderer down in our car. There are details to be attended to."

Hombert's and Skinner's movements had been

limited to minor muscular reactions, but Ash had left his chair and strode masterfully to within two feet of Wolfe, where he stopped short to gaze down at him. He stood with his hands behind his back, which was effective in a way, but it would have been an improvement if he had remembered that in the classic Napoleon stance the arms are folded.

"You either mean it," he said like a menace, "or you don't. If it's a bluff you'll eat it. It is isn't, for once in your life you're going to be opened up." His bony head swiveled to Hombert. "Let me take him, sir. Here in your office it might be embarrassing."

"Imbecile," Wolfe muttered. "Hopeless imbecile." He applied the levers and got himself to his feet. "I had reluctantly accepted the necessity of a long and fruitless discussion of a singularly difficult problem, but this is farcical. Take me home, Archie."

"No you don't," Ash said, even more a menace. He reached and gripped Wolfe's arm. "You're under arrest, my man. This time you—"

I was aware that Wolfe could move without delay when he had to, and, knowing what his attitude was toward anybody's hand touching him, I had prepared myself for motion when I saw Ash grab his arm, but the speed and precision with which he slapped Ash on the side of his jaw were a real surprise, not only to me but to Ash himself. Ash didn't even know it was coming until it was there, a healthy open-palm smack with a satisfactory sound effect. Simultaneously Ash's eyes glittered and his left fist started, and I propelled myself up and forward. The emergency was too split-second to permit anything fancy, so I simply inserted myself in between, and Ash's left collided with my right shoulder before it had any momentum to speak of. With great presence of mind I didn't even bend an elbow, merely staying there as a barrier; but Wolfe, who claims constantly to detest a hubbub, said through his teeth:

"Hit him, Archie. Knock him down."

By that time Hombert was there and Skinner was hovering. Seeing that they were voting against bloodshed, and not caring to be tossed in the coop for manhandling an inspector, I backed away. Wolfe glared at me and said, still through his teeth:

"I am under arrest. You are not. Telephone Mr. Parker to arrange for bail immed—"

"Goodwin is staying right here." Ash's eyes were really nasty. I had never had an impulse to send him a birthday greeting card, but I was surprised to learn how mean he was. "Or rather you're both going with me—"

"Now listen." Skinner had his hands spread out patting air, like a pleader calming a mob. "This is ridiculous. We all want—"

"Am I under arrest?"

"Oh, forget that! Technically I suppose—"

"Then I am. You can all go to the devil." Wolfe went back to the big chair and sat down. "Mr. Goodwin will telephone our lawyer. If you want me out of here send for someone to carry me. If you want me to discuss anything with you, if you want a word out of me, vacate those warrants and get rid of Mr. Ash. He jars me."

"I'll take him," Ash snapped. "He struck an officer."

Skinner and Hombert looked at each other. Then they looked at Wolfe, then at me, and then at each other again. Skinner shook his head emphatically. Hombert regarded Wolfe once more and then turned his gaze on Ash.

"Inspector," he said, "I think you had better leave this to the District Attorney and me. You haven't been in charge of this case long enough to—uh—digest the situation, and while I consented to your proposal to get Wolfe down here, I doubt if you're sufficiently aware of—uh—all the aspects. I have described to you the sources of the strongest pressure to take Inspector Cramer off of the case, which meant also removing him from his command, and therefore it is worth considering that Wolfe's client is the National Industrial Association. Whether we want to consider it or not, we have to. You'd better return to your office, give the reports further study, and continue operations. Altogether, at this moment, there are nearly four hundred men working on this case. That's enough of a job for one man."

Ash's jaw was working and his eyes were still glittering. "It's up to you, sir," he said with an effort. "As I told you, and as you already knew, Wolfe has been getting away with murder for years. If you want him to get away with calling one of your subordinates an imbecile and physically assaulting him, in your own office . . ."

"At the moment I don't care a damn who gets away with what." Hombert was a little exasperated. "I care about just one thing, getting this case solved, and if that doesn't happen soon I may not have any subordinates. Get back on the job and phone me if there's anything new."

"Yes, sir." Ash crossed to Wolfe, who was seated, until their toes touched. "Some day," he promised, "I'll help you lose some weight." Then he strode out of the room.

I returned to my chair. Skinner had already returned to his. Hombert stood looking at the door that had closed behind the Inspector, ran his fingers through his hair, shook his head slowly a few times, moved to his own chair behind his desk, sat, and lifted a receiver from its cradle. In a moment he spoke into the transmitter:

"Bailey? Have that warrant for the arrest of Nero Wolfe as a material witness vacated. Right away. No, just cancel it. Send me—"

"*And* the search warrant," I put in.

"Also the search warrant for Nero Wolfe's house. No, cancel that too. Send the papers to me."

He hung up and turned to Wolfe. "All right, you got away with it. Now what do you know?"

Wolfe sighed deep. A casual glance at his bulk might have given the impression that he was placid again, but to my experienced eye, seeing that he was tapping the arm of his chair with his middle finger, it was evident that there was still plenty of turmoil.

"First," he muttered, "I would like to learn something. Why was Mr. Cramer demoted and disgraced?"

"He wasn't."

"Nonsense. Whatever you want to call it, why?"

"Officially, for a change of scene. Off the record, because he lost his head, considering who the people are that are involved, and took on a bigger load than the Department could handle. Whether you like it or not, there's such a thing as sense of proportion. You cannot treat some people like a bunch of waterfront hoodlums."

"Who brought the pressure?"

"It came from everywhere. I've never seen anything like it. I'm giving no names. Anyhow, that wasn't the only reason. Cramer was muffing it. For the first time since I've known him he got tangled up. Here at a conference yesterday morning he couldn't even discuss the problem intelligently. He had got his mind fixed on one aspect of it, one little thing, and that was all he could think of or talk about—that missing cylinder, the tenth cylinder that may or may not have been in the leather case Boone gave to Miss Gunther just before he was murdered."

"Mr. Cramer was concentrating on that?"

"Yes. He had fifty men looking for it, and he wanted to assign another fifty to it."

"And that was one of your reasons for removing him?"

"Yes. Actually the main reason."

Wolfe grunted. "Hah. Then you're an imbecile too. I didn't know Mr. Cramer had it in him to see that. This doubles my admiration and respect for him. Finding that cylinder, if not our only chance, is beyond all comparison our best one. If it is never found the odds are big that we'll never get the murderer."

A loud disgusted snort came from Skinner. "That's you all right, Wolfe! I suspected it was only fireworks. You said you've already got him."

"I said nothing of the sort."

"You said you know who it is."

"No." Wolfe was truculent. Having been aroused to the point of committing assault and battery, he had by no means calmed down again. "I said I know something that gives me a good clear idea of the murderer's identity, and I also said that you people know it too. You know many things that I don't know. Don't try to pretend that I bulldozed you into ejecting Mr. Ash and releasing me from custody by conveying the impression that I am prepared to name the culprit and supply the evidence. I am not."

Hombert and Skinner looked at each other. There was a silence.

"You impervious bastard," Skinner said, but wasting no energy on it.

"In effect, then," Hombert said resentfully, "you are saying that you have nothing to tell us, that you have nothing to offer, that you can't help us any."

"I'm helping all I can. I am paying a man twenty dollars a day to explore the possibility that Miss Gunther broke that cylinder into little pieces and put it in the rubbish receptacle in her apartment in Washington. That's going to an extreme, because I doubt if she destroyed it. I think she expected to use it some day."

Hombert shifted impatiently in his chair as if the idea of hunting for a lousy cylinder, possibly broken anyhow, only irritated him. "Suppose," he said, "you tell us what it is we all know that gives you a good clear idea of who the murderer is, including the who. Off the record."

"It isn't any one thing."

"I don't care if it's a dozen things. I'll try to remember them. What are they?"

Wolfe shook his head. "No, sir."

"Why not?"

"Because of your idiotic treatment of Mr. Cramer. If it seemed to make sense to you, and I believe it would, you would pass it on to Mr. Ash, and heaven knows what he would do. He might even, by pure chance, do something that would result in his solving the case, and I would stop short of nothing to prevent that outcome." Wolfe's middle finger started tapping again. "Help Mr. Ash to a triumph? God forbid!" He frowned at Hombert. "Besides, I've already given you the best advice I've got. Find that cylinder. Put a hundred men on it, a thousand. Find it!"

"We're not neglecting the damn cylinder. How

about this, do you think Miss Gunther knew who killed Boone?"

"Certainly she did."

Skinner broke in. "Naturally you'd like that," he said pessimistically, "since it would eliminate your clients. If Miss Gunther knew who it was, and it was an NIA man, she would have handed it to us on a platter. So if she did know, it was and is one of the other four—Dexter or Kates or one of the Boone women."

"Not at all," Wolfe contradicted him.

"But damn it, of course!"

"No." Wolfe sighed. "You're missing the whole point. What has been the outstanding fact about this case for a whole week now? What was its peculiar characteristic? This, that the public, the people, had immediately brought the case to trial as usual, without even waiting for an arrest, and instead of the customary prolonged disagreement and dissension regarding various suspects, they reached an immediate verdict. Almost unanimously they convicted—this was the peculiar fact—not an individual, but an organization. The verdict was that the National Industrial Association had murdered Cheney Boone. Now what if you were Miss Gunther and knew who had killed Boone? No matter how you knew, that's another question; the point is that you knew. I think she did know. Let's suppose she knew it was young Mr. Erskine. Would she have exposed him? No. She was devoted to the interests of her own organization, the BPR. She saw the rising tide of resentment and indignation against the NIA, constantly increasing in force and intensity. She saw that it might result, if sustained long enough, in completely discrediting the NIA and its purposes, policies, and objectives. She was intelligent enough to calculate that if an individual, no matter who, were arrested for the murder with good evidence, most of the resentment against the NIA would be diverted away from it as an organization."

Wolfe sighed again. "What would she do? If she had evidence that pointed to Mr. Erskine, or to anyone else, she would suppress it; but she wouldn't destroy it, for she wouldn't want the murderer eventually to escape his punishment. She would put it where it wouldn't be found, but where she could retrieve it and produce it when the time came, when the NIA had been sufficiently damaged. It is not even necessary to assume loyalty to the BPR as her dominating motive. Suppose it was personal devotion to Mr. Boone and a desire to avenge him. The best possible revenge, the perfect revenge, would be to use his death and the manner of it for the discomfiture and the destruction of the organization which had hated him and tried to thwart him. In my opinion Miss Gunther was capable of that. She was a remarkable young woman. But she made the mistake of permitting the murderer to learn that she knew who he was, how is still another question, and that she paid for."

Wolfe raised his hand and let it fall. "However, note this. Her own death served her purpose too. In the past two days the wave of anger against the NIA has increased tremendously. It is going deep into the feeling of the people, and soon it will be impossible to dredge it out again. She was a remarkable woman. No, Mr. Skinner, Miss Gunther's knowing the identity of the murderer would not eliminate my clients. Besides, no man is my client, and no men are. My checks come from the National Industrial Association, which, having no soul, could not possibly commit a murder."

Wolfe cocked an eye at Hombert. "Speaking of

checks. You have seen the NIA advertisement offering a reward of one hundred thousand dollars. You might let your men know that whoever finds the missing cylinder will get that reward."

"Yes?" Hombert was skeptical. "You're as bad as Cramer. What makes you so damn sure about that cylinder? Have you got it in your pocket?"

"No. If I had!"

"What makes you so sure about it?"

"Well. I can't put it in a sentence."

"We've got all the time there is."

"Didn't Mr. Cramer explain it to you?"

"Forget Cramer. He's out of it."

"Which is nothing to your credit, sir." Wolfe rearranged his pressures and angles, shifting the mass to get the center of gravity exactly right for maximum comfort. An unaccustomed chair always presented him with a complicated engineering problem. "You really want me to go into this?"

"Yes."

"Mr. Skinner?"

"Yes."

"All right, I will." Wolfe closed his eyes. "It was apparent from the beginning that Miss Gunther was lying about the leather case. Mr. Cramer knew that, of course. Four people stated that they saw her leaving the reception room with it, people who couldn't possibly have been aware, at the time, that its contents had anything to do with the murder—unless they were all involved in a murder conspiracy, which is preposterous—and therefore had no valid reason for mendacity. Also, Mrs. Boone was barely able to stop herself short of accusing Miss Gunther of falsehood, and Mrs. Boone was at the same table with her in the ballroom. So Miss Gunther was lying. You see that."

"Keep right on," Skinner growled.

"I intend to. Why did she lie about the case and pretend that it had disappeared? Obviously because she didn't want the text of the cylinders, one or more of them, to become known. Why didn't she? Not merely because it contained confidential BPR information or intent. Such a text, as she knew, could safely have been entrusted to FBI ears, but she audaciously and jauntily suppressed it. She did that because something in it pointed definitely and unmistakably to the murderer of Mr. Boone. She——"

"No," Hombert objected. "That's out. She lied about the case before she could have known that. She told us Wednesday morning, the morning after Boone was killed, about leaving the case on the window sill in the reception room, before she had had an opportunity to listen to what was on the cylinders. So she couldn't have known that."

"Yes she could."

"She could tell what was on those cylinders without having access to a Stenophone machine?"

"Certainly. At least one of them. Mr. Boone told her what was on it when he gave her the leather case Tuesday evening, in the room there where he was soon to die. She lied about that too; naturally she had to. She lied about it to me, most convincingly, in my office Friday evening. I should have warned her then that she was being foolhardy to the point of imprudence, but I didn't. I would have wasted my breath. Caution with respect to personal peril was not in her makeup—as the event proved. If it had been, she would not have permitted a man whom she knew to be capable of murder get close to her, alone, on the stoop of my house."

Wolfe shook his head, his eyes still closed. "She was

really extraordinary. It would be interesting to know where she concealed the case, containing the cylinders, up to Thursday afternoon. It would have been too risky to hide it in Mr. Kates's apartment, which might have been searched by the police at any moment. Possibly she checked it in the Grand Central parcel room, though that seems a little banal for her. At any rate, she had it with her in her suitcase when she went to Washington Thursday afternoon, with Mr. Dexter and with your permission."

"Cramer's permission," Hombert grumbled.

Wolfe ignored it. "I would like to emphasize," he said with his voice up a little, "that none of this is conjecture except unimportant details of chronology and method. In Washington Miss Gunther went to her office, listened to the cylinders, and learned which one bore the message that Mr. Boone had told her about. Doubtless she wanted to know exactly what it said, but also she wanted to simplify her problem. It isn't easy to conceal an object the size of that case from an army of expert searchers. She wanted to reduce it to one little cylinder. Another thing, she had contrived a plot. She took the nine eliminated cylinders to her Washington apartment and hid them casually in a hatbox on a closet shelf. She also took ten other cylinders that had been previously used which were there in her office, put them in the leather case, brought it with her when she returned to New York, and checked it in the Grand Central parcel room.

"That was in preparation for her plot, and she probably would have proceeded with it the next day, using the police for the mystification, if it hadn't been for that invitation I sent around for a discussion at my office. She decided to wait for developments. Why she ignored my invitation I don't know, and I shall intrude no guesses. That same evening, Friday, Mr. Goodwin went after her and brought her to my office. She had made a profound impression on him, and she struck me as being of uncommon quality. Evidently her opinion of us was less flattering. She formed the idea that we were more vulnerable to guile than the police; and the next day, Saturday, after she had mailed the parcel room check to Mr. O'Neill and made the phone call to him, giving the name of Dorothy Unger, she sent me a telegram, signing Mr. Breslow's name to it, conveying the notion that observation of Mr. O'Neill's movements might be profitable. We validated her appraisal of us. Mr. Goodwin was at Mr. O'Neill's address bright and early Sunday morning, as Miss Gunther intended him to be. When Mr. O'Neill emerged he was followed, and you know what happened."

"I don't understand," Skinner interposed, "why O'Neill was such an easy sucker for that Dorothy Unger phone call. Didn't the damn fool suspect a plant? Or is he a damn fool or something else?"

Wolfe shook his head. "Now you're asking for more than I've got. Mr. O'Neill is a headstrong and bumptious man, which may account for it; and we know that he was irresistibly tempted to learn what was on those cylinders, whether because he had killed Mr. Boone or for some other reason is yet to be discovered. Presumably Miss Gunther knew what might be expected of him. Anyhow her plot was moderately successful. It kept us all in that side alley for a day or two, it further jumbled the matter of the cylinders and the leather case, and it was one more involvement of an NIA man, without, however, the undesirable result—undesirable for Miss Gunther—of exposing him as the murderer. She was saving that—the disclosure of the murderer's identity and the evidence she had—for the time that would best suit her purpose."

"You've got pictures of all this," Skinner said sarcastically. "Why didn't you call her on the phone or get her in your office and lecture her on the duties of a citizen?"

"It was impractical. She was dead."

"Oh? Then you didn't know it all until after she had been killed?"

"Certainly not. How the devil could I? Some of it, yes, it doesn't matter how much. But when word came from Washington that they had found in Miss Gunther's apartment, perfunctorily concealed, nine of the cylinders Mr. Boone had dictated the afternoon of his death—nine, not ten—there was the whole story. There was no other acceptable explanation. All questions became paltry and pointless except the one question: where is the tenth cylinder?"

"Wherever you start a sentence," Hombert complained grouchily, "it always ends on that goddam cylinder!"

Wolfe opened his eyes enough to pick Hombert out. "You try doing a sentence that makes any sense and leave the cylinder out."

Skinner demanded, "What if she threw it in the river?"

"She didn't."

"Why not?"

"I've already told you. Because she intended to use it, when the time came, to get the murderer punished."

"What if you're making your first and only mistake and she *did* throw it in the river?"

"Drag the river. All the rivers she could reach."

"Don't be whimsical. Answer my question."

Wolfe's shoulders went perceptibly up and down. "In that case we would be licked. We'd never get him."

"I think," Hombert said pointedly, "that it is conceivable that you would like to sell a bill of goods. I don't say you're a barefaced liar."

"I don't say I'm not, Mr. Hombert. We all take those chances when we exchange words with other people. So I might as well go home—"

"Wait a minute," Skinner snapped. "Do you mean that as an expert investigator you advise abandoning all lines of inquiry except the search for that cylinder?"

"I shouldn't think so." Wolfe frowned, considering. "Especially not with a thousand men or more at your disposal. Of course I don't know what has been done and what hasn't, but I know how such things go and I doubt if much has been overlooked in a case of this importance, knowing Mr. Cramer as I do. For instance, that piece of iron pipe; I suppose every possible effort has been made to discover where it came from. The matter of arrivals at my house Monday evening has of course been explored with every resource and ingenuity. The tenants of all the buildings in my block on both sides of the street have naturally been interviewed, on the slim chance, unlikely in that quiet neighborhood, that somebody saw or heard something. The question of opportunity alone, the evening of the dinner at the Waldorf, must have kept a dozen men busy for a week, and perhaps you're still working on it. Inquiries regarding relationships, both open and concealed, the checking and rechecking of Mr. Dexter's alibi—these and a thousand other details have unquestionably been competently and thoroughly attended to."

Wolfe wiggled a finger. "And where are you? So

sunk in a bog of futility and bewilderment that you resort to such monkey tricks as ditching Mr. Cramer, replacing him with a buffoon like Mr. Ash, and swearing out a warrant for my arrest! Over a long period I have become familiar with the abilities and performances of the New York police, and I never expected to see the day when the inspector heading the Homicide Squad would try to solve a difficult murder case by dragging me off to a cell, attacking my person, putting me in handcuffs, and threatening me with mayhem!"

"That's a slight exaggeration. This is not a cell, and I don't—"

"He intended to," Wolfe asserted grimly. "He would have. Very well. You have asked me my advice. I would continue, within reason, all lines of inquiry that have already been started, and initiate any others that offer any promise whatever, because no matter what the cylinder gives you—if and when you find it—you will almost certainly need all available scraps of support and corroboration. But the main chance, the only real hope, is the cylinder. I suggest you try this. You both met Miss Gunther? Good. Sit down and shut your eyes and imagine it is last Thursday afternoon, and you are Miss Gunther, sitting in your office in the BPR headquarters in Washington. You have decided what you are going to do with the leather case and the nine eliminated cylinders; forget all that. In your hand is *the* cylinder, and the question is what to do with it. Here's what you're after: you want to preserve it against any risk of damage, you want it easily accessible should you need it on short notice, and you want to be certain that no matter how many people look for it, or who, with whatever persistence and ingenuity, it will not be found."

Wolfe looked from one to the other. "There's your little problem, Miss Gunther. Anything so simple, for example, as concealing it there in the BPR office is not even to be considered. Something far above that, something really fine, must be conceived. Your own apartment would be merely ridiculous; you show that you are quite aware of that by disposing of the other nine cylinders as you do. Perhaps the apartment of a friend or colleague you can trust? This is murder; this is of the utmost gravity and of ultimate importance; would you trust any other human being that far? You are ready now to leave, to go to your apartment first and then take a plane to New York. You will probably be in New York some days. Do you take the cylinder with you or leave it in Washington? If so, where? Where? Where?"

Wolfe flipped a hand. "There's your question, gentlemen. Answer it the way Miss Gunther finally answered it, and your worries are ended." He stood up. "I am spending a thousand dollars a day trying to learn how Miss Gunther answered it." He was multi-plying by two and it wasn't his money he was spend-ing, but at least it wasn't a barefaced lie. "Come, Archie. I want to go home."

They didn't want him to go, even then, which was the best demonstration to date of the pitiable condition they were in. They certainly were stymied, flummoxed, and stripped to the bone. Wolfe magnanimously accom-modated them by composing a few more well-con-structed sentences, properly furnished with subjects, predicates, and subordinate clauses, none of which meant a damn thing, and then marched from the room with me bringing up the rear. He had postponed his exit, I noticed, until after a clerk had entered to deliver some papers to Hombert's desk, which had occurred just as

Wolfe was telling the P.C. and D.A. to shut their eyes
and pretend they were Miss Gunther.

Driving back home he sat in the back seat, as usual,
clutching the toggle, because of his theory that
when—not if and when, just when—the car took a
whim to dart aside and smash into some immovable
object, your chances in back, hopeless as they were,
were slightly better than in front. On the way down to
Centre Street I had, on request, given him a sketch of
my session with Nina Boone, and now, going home, I
filled in the gaps. I couldn't tell whether it contained
any morsel that he considered nutritious, because my
back was to him and his face wasn't in my line of vision
in the mirror, and also because the emotions that being
in a moving vehicle aroused in him were too overwhelming to leave any room for minor reactions.

As Fritz let us in and we entered the hall and I
attended to hat and coat disposal, Wolfe looked almost
good-humored. He had beaten a rap and was home
safe, and it was only six o'clock, time for beer. But
Fritz spoiled it at once by telling us that we had a
visitor waiting in the office. Wolfe scowled at him and
demanded in a ferocious whisper:

"Who is it?"

"Mrs. Cheney Boone."

"Good heavens. That hysterical gammer?"

Which was absolutely unfair. Mrs. Boone had been
in the house just twice, both times under anything but
tranquil circumstances, and I hadn't seen the faintest
indication of hysteria.

Chapter 30

I had made a close and prolonged study of Wolfe's attitude toward women. The basic fact about a woman that seemed to irritate him was that she was a woman; the long record showed not a single exception; but from there on the documentation was cockeyed. If woman as woman grated on him you would suppose that the most womany details would be the worst for him, but time and again I have known him to have a chair placed for a female so that his desk would not obstruct his view of her legs, and the answer can't be that his interest is professional and he reads character from legs, because the older and dumpier she is the less he cares where she sits. It is a very complex question and some day I'm going to take a whole chapter for it. Another little detail: he is much more sensitive to women's noses than he is to men's. I have never been able to detect that extremes or unorthodoxies in men's noses have any effect on him, but in women's they do. Above all he doesn't like a pug, or in fact a pronounced incurve anywhere along the bridge.

Mrs. Boone had a pug, and it was much too small for the surroundings. I saw him looking at it as he leaned back in his chair. So he told her in a gruff and inhospitable tone, barely not boorish:

"I have ten minutes to spare, madam."

Entirely aside from the nose she looked terrible. She had had a go at her compact, but apparently with complete indifference to the result, and anyway it would have been a job for a make-up artist. She was simply all shot and her face had quit trying to do any pretending about it.

"Naturally," she said, in a voice that was holding up much better than the face, "you're wondering why I'm here.'"

"Naturally," Wolfe agreed.

"I mean why I came to see you, since you're on the other side. It's because I phoned my cousin this morning and he told me about you."

"I am not," Wolfe said curtly, "on the other side or any side. I have undertaken to catch a murderer. Do I know your cousin?"

She nodded. "General Carpenter. That was my maiden name. He is my first cousin. He's in a hospital after an operation, or he would have come to help me when my husband was killed. He told me not to believe anything you said but to do whatever you told me to do. He said that you have your own private set of rules, and that if you are working on a case of murder the only one that can really rely on you is the murderer. Since you know my cousin, you know what he meant. I'm used to him."

She stopped, looked at me and back at Wolfe, and used her handkerchief on her lower lip and at the corners, which didn't improve things any. When her hand went back to her lap it was gripping the handkerchief as if it was afraid that someone was planning to snatch it.

"And?" Wolfe prompted her.

"So I came to see you to get some advice. Or maybe I ought to say make up my mind whether I want to ask your advice. I have to get some from somebody, and I don't know—" She looked at me again, returned to Wolfe, and made a gesture with the hand that wasn't guarding the handkerchief. "Do I have to tell you why I prefer not to go to someone in the FBI or the police?"

"You are under no compulsion, madam, to tell me anything at all. You've already been talking three or four minutes."

"I know. My cousin warned me that you would be incredibly rude.—Then I might as well come right out and say that I think I am responsible for the death of Phoebe Gunther."

"That's an uncomfortable thought," muttered Wolfe. "Where did you get it?"

"That's what I want to tell you, and I suppose I'm really going to or I wouldn't have come here, but while I was sitting here waiting I got up to leave a dozen times and then sat down again. I don't know what to do and last night I thought I was going crazy. I always depended on my husband to make important decisions. I don't want to tell the police or the FBI because I may have committed some kind of a crime, I don't know. But it seems silly to tell you on account of the way my husband felt about the NIA, and of course I feel the same way about them, and you're working for them, you're on their side. I suppose I ought to go to a lawyer, and I know lots of lawyers, but there doesn't seem to be one I could tell this to. They all seem to do all the talking and I never understand what they're saying."

That should have softened Wolfe up. He did get a little more receptive, taking the trouble to repeat that he wasn't on any side. "For me," he stated, "this is not a private feud, whatever it may be for others. What was the crime you committed?"

"I don't know—if it was one."

"What did you do?"

"I didn't do anything. That's the trouble. What happened was that Miss Gunther told me what she was doing and I promised her I wouldn't tell anyone and I didn't, and I have a feeling—"

She stopped. In a moment she went on, "That isn't true, I haven't just got a feeling. I'm sure."

"Sure of what?"

"I'm sure that if I had told the police what she told me she wouldn't have been killed. But I didn't tell, because she explained that what she was doing was helping the BPR and hurting the NIA, and that was what my husband would have wanted more than anything else." The widow was staring at Wolfe's face as if she were trying to see inside. "And she was perfectly correct. I'm still making up my mind whether to tell you about it. In spite of what you say, there's my husband's side and there's the other side, and you're working for the NIA. After I talked with my cousin I thought I'd come and see what you sounded like."

"What do I sound like?"

"I don't know." Her hand fluttered vaguely. "I really don't know."

Wolfe frowned at her in silence, then heaved a sigh and turned to me.

"Archie."

"Yes, sir?"

"Your notebook. Take a letter. To be mailed this evening so it will be delivered in the morning. To the

National Industrial Association, attention Mr. Frank Thomas Erskine.

> "Gentlemen: The course events have taken obliges me to inform you that it will be impossible for me to continue to act in your behalf with regard to the investigation of the murders of Mr. Cheney Boone and Miss Phoebe Gunther. Therefore I enclose herewith my check for thirty thousand dollars, returning the retainer you have paid me and ending my association with you in this matter. Sincerely."

I made the last scratch and looked at him. "Do I draw the check?"

"Certainly. You can't enclose it if it hasn't been drawn." Wolfe's eyes moved to the visitor. "There, Mrs. Boone, that should have some effect on your reluctance. Even accepting your point of view, that I was on the other side, now I am not. What did Miss Gunther tell you she was doing?"

The widow was gazing at him. "Thirty thousand dollars?" she asked incredulously.

"Yes." Wolfe was smirking. "A substantial sum."

"But was that all the NIA was paying you? Just *thirty thousand?* I supposed it was twenty times that! They have hundreds of millions—billions!"

"It was only the retainer," Wolfe said testily. The smirk was gone. "Anyway, I am now a neutral. What did Miss Gunther tell you?"

"But now—but now you're not getting anything at all!" Mrs. Boone was utterly bewildered. "My cousin told me that during the war you worked hard for the government for nothing, but that you charge private people outrageous prices. I ought to tell you—if you don't know—that I can't afford to pay you anything outrageous. I could—" she hesitated. "I could give you a check for a hundred dollars."

"I don't want a check." Wolfe was exasperated. "If I can't have a client in this case without being accused of taking sides in a sanguinary vendetta, I don't want a client. Confound it, what did Miss Gunther tell you?"

Mrs. Boone looked at me, and I had the uncomfortable feeling that she was trying to find some sort of resemblance to her dead husband, he being gone and therefore no longer available for important decisions. I thought it might possibly help if I nodded at her reassuringly, so I did. Whether that broke the tie or not I don't know, but something did, for she spoke to Wolfe:

"She knew who killed my husband. My husband told her something that day when he gave her the leather case, and she knew from that, and also he had dictated something on one of those cylinders that told about it, so the cylinder was evidence, and she had it. She was keeping it and she intended to give it to the police, but she was waiting until the talk and the rumors and the public feeling had done as much damage as possible to the NIA. She told me about it because I went to her and told her I knew she wasn't telling the truth about that leather case, I knew she had had it with her at the table in the dining room, and I wasn't going to keep still about it any longer. She told me what she was doing so I wouldn't tell the police about the case."

"When was that? What day?"

She thought a moment, the crease deepening in her forehead, and then shook her head uncertainly. "The days," she said. "The days are all mixed up."

"Of course they are, Mrs. Boone. It was Friday

evening when you were here with the others the first time, when you almost spoke up about it and changed your mind. Was it before that, or after?"

"It was after. It was the next day."

"Then it was Saturday. Another thing that will help you to place it, Saturday morning you received an envelope in the mail containing your wedding picture and automobile license. Do you remember that? It was the same day?"

She nodded with assurance. "Yes, of course it was. Because I spoke of that, and she said she had written a letter to him—to the man who killed my husband— she knew my husband had always carried the wedding picture in the wallet that was missing—he had carried it for over twenty years—twenty-three years—"

The widow's voice got away from her. She gave it up and gulped, sat without trying to go on, and gulped again. If she lost control completely and started noises and tears there was no telling what Wolfe would do. He might even have tried to act human, which would have been an awful strain on all of us. So I told her gruffly:

"Okay, Mrs. Boone, take your time. Whenever you get ready, what did she write a letter to the murderer for? To tell him to send you the wedding picture?"

She nodded and got enough voice back to mumble, "Yes."

"Indeed," Wolfe said to help out.

The widow nodded again. "She told me that she knew I would want that picture, and she wrote him to say that she knew about him and he must send it to me."

"What else did she write him?"

"I don't know. That's all she told me about it."

"But she told you who he was."

"No, she didn't." Mrs. Boone halted again for a moment, still getting her voice back into place. "She said she wouldn't tell me about that, because it would be too much to expect me not to show that I knew. She said I didn't need to worry about his not being punished, there would be no doubt about that, and besides it would be dangerous for me to know. That's where I now think I did wrong—that's why I said I'm responsible for her death. If it would have been dangerous for me it was dangerous for her, especially after she wrote him that letter. I should have made her tell the police about it, and if she wouldn't do it I should have broken my promise to her and told the police myself. Then she wouldn't have been killed. Anyway she said she thought she was breaking a law, withholding information and concealing evidence, so I have that on my mind too, helping her break a law."

"You can stop worrying about that, at least," Wolfe assured her. "I mean the lawbreaking. That part of it's all right. Or it will be, as soon as you tell me, and I tell the police, where Miss Gunther put the cylinder."

"But I can't. That's another thing. I don't know. She didn't tell me."

Wolfe's eyes had popped wide open. "Nonsense!" he said rudely. "Of course she told you!"

"She did not. That's one reason I came to see you. She said I didn't need to worry about the man who killed my husband being punished. But if that's the only evidence . . ."

Wolfe's eyes had gone shut again. There was a long silence. Mrs. Boone looked at me, possibly still in search of a resemblance, but whatever she was looking for her expression gave no indication that she was finding it. Finally she spoke to Wolfe again:

"So you see why I need advice . . ."

His lids went up enough to make slits. In his place I would at least have been grateful for all the corroboration of the guesses I had made, but apparently he was too overcome by his failure to learn where the cylinder was.

"I regret, madam," he said, without any noticeable tremor of regret or anything like it, "that I can't be of any help to you. There is nothing I can do. All I can give you is what you said you came for, advice, and you are welcome to that. Mr. Goodwin will drive you back to your hotel. Arriving there, telephone the police immediately that you have information for them. When they come, tell them everything you have told me, and answer their questions as long as you can stand it. You need have no fear of being regarded as guilty of lawbreaking. I agree with you that if you had broken your promise to Miss Gunther she would probably not have been killed, but it was she who asked you for the promise, so the responsibility is hers. Besides, she can afford it; it is astonishing, the burden of responsibility that dead people can bear up under. Dismiss that from your mind too if you can." He was on his feet. "Good afternoon, madam."

So I did get to drive a female Boone home from our office, though not Nina. Since it appeared that she had given us all she had and was therefore of no further immediate interest, I didn't even bother to discover whether anyone was on her tail and confined myself to the duties of a chauffeur. She didn't seem to care about conversing, which simplified matters. I delivered her safely at the Waldorf entrance and headed back downtown. Aside from the attention to driving, which was automatic, there was no point in trying to put my mind on my work, since I was being left out in the cold and therefore had no work, so I let it drift to Phoebe

Gunther. I went back to the times I had been with her, how she had talked and acted, with my present knowledge of what she had been doing, and decided she had been utterly all right. I have an inclination to pick flaws, especially where young women are concerned, but on this occasion I didn't have the list started by the time I got back home.

Wolfe was drinking beer, as I observed when I stepped inside the office door merely to tell him:

"I'll be upstairs. I always like to wash my hands after I've been with certain kinds of policemen, meaning Inspector Ash, and I've—"

"Come in here. That letter and check. We'd better get that done."

I gawked. "What, to the NIA?"

"Yes."

"My God, you don't mean you're actually going to send it?"

"Certainly. Didn't I tell that woman I would? Wasn't it with that understanding that she told me things?"

I sat down at my desk and regarded him piercingly. "This," I said sternly, "is not being eccentric. This is plain loony. What about Operation Payroll? And where did you suddenly get a scruple? And anyway, she didn't tell you the one thing you wanted to know." I abruptly got respectful. "I regret to report, sir, that the checkbook is lost."

He grunted. "Draw the check and type the letter. At once." He pointed to a stack of envelopes on his desk. "Then you can go through these reports from Mr. Bascom's office. They just came by messenger."

"But with no client—shall I phone Bascom to call it off?"

"Certainly not."

I went to the safe for the checkbook. As I filled out the stub I remarked, "Statistics show that forty-two and three-tenths per cent of all geniuses go crazy sooner or later."

He had no comment. He merely drank beer and sat. Now that I was to be permitted to know what Bascom's men were doing, he wouldn't even cooperate enough to slit open the envelopes. Whatever it was it must be good, since he evidently intended to go on paying for it with his own dough. I pounded the typewriter keys in a daze. When I put the check and letter before him to be signed I said plaintively:

"Excuse me for mentioning it, but a century from Mrs. Boone would have helped. That seems to be more our speed. She said she could afford it."

He used the blotter. "You'd better take this to the post office. I suspect the evening collection from that box doesn't get made sometimes."

So I had some more chauffeuring to do. It was only a ten-minute walk to the post office on Ninth Avenue and back, but I was in no mood for walking. I only like to walk when I can see some future ahead of me. Returning, I put the car in the garage, since the evening would obviously be a complete blank.

Wolfe was still in the office, outwardly perfectly normal. He glanced at me, then at the clock, and back at me.

"Sit down a moment, Archie. You'll have plenty of time to wash before dinner. Dr. Vollmer is coming to see us later, and you need some instructions."

At least his mind was still functioning enough to send for a doctor.

Chapter 31

Doc Vollmer was due to arrive at ten o'clock. At five minutes to ten the stage was set, up in Wolfe's bedroom. I was in Wolfe's own chair by the reading lamp, with a magazine. Wolfe was in bed. Wolfe in bed was always a remarkable sight, accustomed to it as I was. First the low footboard, of streaky anselmo—yellowish with sweeping dark brown streaks—then the black silk coverlet, next the wide expanse of yellow pajama top, and last the flesh of the face. In my opinion Wolfe was quite aware that black and yellow are a flashy combination, and he used it deliberately just to prove that no matter how showy the scene was he could dominate it. I have often thought that I would like to see him try it with pink and green. The rest of the room—rugs and furniture and curtains—was okay, big and comfortable and all right to be in.

Doc Vollmer, admitted downstairs by Fritz and knowing his way around the house, came up the one flight alone and walked into the room, the door standing open. He was carrying his toolbox. He had a round face and round ears, and two or three years had passed since he had given up any attempt to stand with his

belly in and his chest out. I told him hello and shook
hands, and then he went to the bedside with a friendly
greeting and his hand extended.

Wolfe twisted his neck to peer at the offered hand,
grunted skeptically, and muttered, "No, thank you.
What's the ceiling on it? I don't want any."

Standing at the footboard, I began hastily, "I
should have explained—" but Wolfe broke in, thundering at Vollmer, "Do you want to pay two dollars a
pound for butter? Fifty cents for shoestrings? A dollar
for a bottle of beer? Twenty dollars for one orchid, one
ordinary half-wilted Laeliocattleya? Well, confound it,
answer me!" Then he quit thundering and started
muttering.

Vollmer lowered himself to the edge of a chair, put
his toolbox on the floor, blinked several times at Wolfe,
and then at me.

I said, "I don't know whether it's the willies or
what."

Wolfe said. "You accuse me of getting you here
under false pretenses. You accuse me of wanting to
borrow money from you. Just because I ask you to
lend me five dollars until the beginning of the next
war, you accuse me!" He shook a warning finger in the
direction of Vollmer's round astonished face. "Let me
tell you, sir, you will be next! I admit that I am
finished; I am finally driven to this extremity. They
have done for me; they have broken me; they are still
after me." His voice rose to thunder again. "And you,
you incomparable fool, you think to escape! Archie
tells me you are masquerading as a doctor. Bah!
They'll take your clothes off! They'll examine every
inch of your skin, as they did mine! They'll find the
mark!" He let his head fall back on the pillow, closed
his eyes, and resumed muttering.

Vollmer looked at me with a gleam in his eyes and inquired, "Who wrote his script for him?"

Managing somehow to control the muscles around my mouth, I shook my head despairingly. "He's been like this for several hours, ever since I brought him back home."

"Oh, he's been out of the house?"

"Yes. From three-fifteen till six o'clock. Under arrest."

Vollmer turned to Wolfe. "Well," he said decisively. "The first thing is to get some nurses. Where's the phone? Either that or take him to a hospital."

"That's the ticket," I agreed. "It's urgent. We must act."

Wolfe's eyes came open. "Nurses?" he asked contemptuously. "Pfui. Aren't you a physician? Don't you know a nervous breakdown when you see one?"

"Yes," Vollmer said emphatically.

"What's the matter with it?"

"It doesn't seem to be—uh, typical."

"Faulty observation," Wolfe snapped. "Or a defect in your training. Specifically, it's a persecution complex."

"Who's doing the persecuting?"

Wolfe shut his eyes. "I feel it coming on again. Tell him, Archie."

I met Vollmer's gaze. "Look, Doc, the situation is serious. As you know, he was investigating the Boone-Gunther murders for the NIA. The high command didn't like the way Inspector Cramer was handling it and booted him, and replaced him with a baboon by the name of Ash."

"I know. It was in the evening paper."

"Yeah. In tomorrow's evening paper you'll learn

that Nero Wolfe has returned the NIA retainer and quit."

"For God's sake, why?"

"I'm telling you. Ash's personal attitude toward Wolfe is such that he would rather slice his wrists than slash his throat because it would prolong the agony. Today he got a material witness warrant and Wolfe had to go to Centre Street, me taking him. Hombert had the warrant killed, for various reasons, but the main one was that Wolfe was working for the NIA, and if the NIA gets offended any worse than it is now it will probably fire the Mayor and everyone else and declare New York a monarchy. But. Wolfe no sooner gets home than he breaks off relations with the NIA. They'll get his letter, with check enclosed, in the morning mail. Whereupon hell will pop wide open. What the NIA will do we don't know and maybe we don't care—I should say maybe Wolfe doesn't care. But we know damn well what the cops will do. First, with Wolfe no longer sleeping with the NIA, that motive for tenderness will be gone. Second, they know that Wolfe has never yet had a murderer for a client, and they know what a job it is to pry him loose from money, especially thirty thousand bucks and up, and they will therefore deduce that one of the NIA boys is guilty, and that Wolfe knows it and knows who it is."

"Who is it?"

I shook my head. "I don't know, and since Wolfe's a raving lunatic you can't ask him. With that setup, it's a cinch to read the future. The wagon will be at the door ready for him, with the papers all in order, any time after ten o'clock, possibly earlier. It's a shame to disappoint them, but all I can do is meet them with another kind of paper, signed by a reputable physician, certifying that in Wolfe's present condition it would be dangerous either to move him from his bed or to permit anyone to converse with him."

I waved a hand. "That's how it stands. Five years ago, the time Wolfe did you a little favor when that crook—what was his name? Griffin—tried to frame you on a malpractice suit, and you told Wolfe if he ever wanted anything all he had to do was ask for it, I warned you you might regret it some day. Brother, this is the day."

Vollmer was rubbing his chin. He didn't really look reluctant, merely thoughtful. He looked at Wolfe, saying nothing, and then returned to me and spoke:

"Naturally I have an uncontrollable itch to ask a lot of questions. This is absolutely fascinating. I suppose the questions wouldn't be answered?"

"I'm afraid not. Not by me anyhow, because I don't know the answers. You might try the patient."

"How long will the certificate have to function?"

"I have no idea. Damn it, I tell you I'm ignorant."

"If he's bad enough to prohibit visitors I'll have to insist on calling on him at least twice a day. And to make it good there ought to be nurses."

"No," I said firmly. "I grant there ought to be, but he would run a fever. Nurses are out. As for you, call as often as you want to. I may get lonely. And make that certificate as strong as they come. Say it would kill him if anybody whose name begins with A even looked at him."

"It will be so worded as to serve its purpose. I'll bring it over in ten minutes or so." Vollmer stood up with his toolbox in his hand. "I did say that time, though, that Wolfe would get anything *he* asked for." He looked at Wolfe. "It would be gratifying just to hear you ask me for something. How about it?"

Wolfe groaned. "They come in hordes," he said

distinctly, but in a phony voice. "In chariots with spiked wheels, waving the insolent banners of inflation! Five dollars for a pound of corned beef! Ten dollars for a squab! Sixty cents—"

"I'd better be going," Vollmer said, and moved.

Chapter 32

I didn't get lonely during the two and a half days—Thursday, Friday, and part of Saturday—that the certificate worked. Newspapermen, cops, FBI's, NIA's—they all appreciated that I was holding the fort under trying circumstances and did their best to keep my mind occupied so I wouldn't fret. If ordinarily I earn twice as much as I get, which is a conservative estimate, during those sixty-some hours it was ten times as much at a minimum.

Throughout the siege Wolfe stayed put in his room, with the door locked and one of the keys in my pocket and one in Fritz's. Keeping away from the office, dining room, and kitchen for that length of time was of course a hardship, but the real sacrifice, the one that hurt, was giving up his two-a-day trips to the plant rooms. I had to bully him into it, explaining that if a surprise detachment shoved a search warrant at me I might or might not be able to get him back into bed in time, and besides, Theodore slept out, and while he was no traitor he might inadvertently spill it that his afflicted employer did not seem to be goofy among the orchids. For the same reason I refused to let Theodore

come down to the bedroom for consultations. I told
Wolfe Thursday or Friday, I forget which:

"You're putting on an act. Okay. Applause. Since it
requires you to be out of circulation that leaves it
strictly up to me and I make the rules. I am already
handicapped enough by not knowing one single goddam thing about what you're up to. We had a—"

"Nonsense," he growled. "You know all about it. I
have twenty men looking for that cylinder. Nothing
can be done without that cylinder. It must be found
and it will be. I simply prefer to wait here in my room
instead of in jail."

"Nuts." I was upset because I had just spent a hot
half hour with another NIA delegation down in the
office. "Why did you have to break with the NIA
before you went to bed to wait? Granting that one of
them did it and you know all about it, which everybody
is now sure of but you'll have to show me, that was no
reason to return their money in order to keep from
having a murderer for a client, because you said
yourself that no man was your client, the NIA was.
Why in the name of God did you return their dough?
And if this cylinder gag is not merely a stall, if it's
really it and all the it there is, as you say, what if it
never is found? What are you going to do, stay in bed
the rest of your life, with Doc Vollmer renewing the
certificate on a monthly basis?"

"It will be found," he said meekly. "It was not
destroyed, it exists, and therefore it will be found."

I stared at him suspiciously, shrugged, and beat it.
When he gets meek it is absolutely no use. I went back
to the office and sat and scowled at the Stenophone
machine standing over in a corner. My chief reason for
admitting that Wolfe really meant what he said about

the cylinder was that we were paying a dollar a day rent for that machine.

Not the only reason, however. Bill Gore and twenty Bascom men were actually looking for the cylinder, no question about it. I had been instructed to read the reports before taking them up to Wolfe, and they were quite a chapter in the history of hunting. Bill Gore and another guy were working on all of Phoebe Gunther's friends and even acquaintances in Washington, and two others were doing likewise in New York. Three were flying all over the country, to places where she knew people, on the theory that she might have mailed the cylinder to one of them, though that seemed like a bum theory if, as Wolfe had said, she had wanted to have it easily accessible on short notice. His figure of a grand a day hadn't been so far out after all. One had learned that she had gone to a beauty parlor that Friday afternoon in New York, and he had turned it inside out. Three had started working on parcel rooms everywhere, but had discovered that parcel rooms were being worked by the police and the FBI, armed with authority, so they had switched to another field. They were trying to find out or guess all the routes she had taken on foot and were spending their days on the sidewalks, keeping their eyes peeled for something, anything—a window box with dirt in it, for instance—where she might have made a cache. The rest of them were trying this and that. Friday evening, to take my mind off my troubles, I tried to figure out some possible spot that they were missing. I kept at it an hour, with no result. They were certainly covering the territory.

There were unquestionably twenty-one expensive men on the cylinder chase, but what stuck in my craw was Saul Panzer. No matter what you had on the program Saul rated star billing, and he was not among the twenty-one at all. As far as I was allowed to know he was not displaying the slightest interest in any cylinder. Every couple of hours he phoned in, I didn't know from where, and I obeyed instructions to connect him with Wolfe's bedside extension and keep off the line. Also he made two personal appearances—one at breakfast time Thursday morning and one late Friday afternoon—and each time he spent a quarter of an hour alone with Wolfe and then departed. By that time I was so damn cylinder-conscious that I was inclined to suspect Saul of being engaged in equipping a factory in a Brooklyn basement so we could roll our own.

As the siege continued, my clashes with Wolfe increased both in frequency and in range. One, Thursday afternoon, concerned Inspector Cramer. Wolfe buzzed me on the house phone and told me he wished to have a telephone conversation with Cramer, so would I please dig him up. I flatly refused. My point was that no matter how bitter Cramer might be, or how intensely he might desire to spray Ash with concentrated DDT, he was still a cop, and was therefore not to be trusted with any evidence, as for instance Wolfe's voice sounding natural and making sense, that would tend to cast doubt on Doc Vollmer's certificate. Wolfe finally settled for my getting the dope on Cramer's whereabouts and availability, and that proved to be easy. Lon Cohen told me he had taken a two weeks' leave of absence, for sulking, and when I dialed the number of Cramer's home he answered the phone himself. He kept the conversation brief and to the point, and when I hung up I got Wolfe on the house phone and told him:

"Cramer's on leave of absence and is staying home

licking his wounds, possibly bedridden. He wouldn't say. Anyhow, he can be reached there any time, but he is not affable. I have a notion to send Doc Vollmer to see him."

"Good. Come up here. I'm having trouble with this window again."

"Damn it, you stay in bed and keep away from the windows!"

One feature of the play was that I was not supposed to deny entry to any legitimate caller. That was to convey the impression that our household was not churlish, far from it, but merely stricken with misfortune. Although newspapermen and various other assorted prospectors kept me hopping, the worst nuisances were the NIA and the cops. Around ten Thursday morning Frank Thomas Erskine phoned. He wanted Wolfe but of course didn't get him. I did my best to make the situation clear, but I might as well have tried to explain to a man dying of thirst that the water was being saved to do the laundry with. Less than an hour later here they came, all six of them—the two Erskines, Winterhoff, Breslow, O'Neill, and Hattie Harding. I was courteous, took them to the office, gave them seats, and told them that a talk with Wolfe was positively not on the agenda.

They seemed to be under the impression, judging from their attitudes and tones, that I was not a fellow being but a cockroach. At times it was a little difficult to keep up with them, because they were all full of ideas and words to express them and no one acted as chairman to grant the floor and prevent overlapping. Their main gripes were, first, that it was an act of treachery and betrayal for Wolfe to return their money; second, that if he did it because he was sick he should have said so in his letter; third, that he should immediately and publicly announce his sickness in order to stop the widespread and growing rumor that he broke with the NIA because he got hold of conclusive evidence that the NIA had committed murder; fourth, that if he did have evidence of an NIA man's guilt they wanted to know who and what it was within five minutes; fifth, that they didn't believe he was sick; sixth, who was the doctor; seventh, if he was sick how soon would he be well; eighth, did I realize that in the two days and three nights that had passed since the second murder, Phoebe Gunther's, the damage to the NIA had become incalculable and irretrievable; ninth, fifty or sixty lawyers were of the opinion that Wolfe's abandoning the case without notice would vastly increase the damage and was therefore actionable; tenth, eleventh and twelfth, and so on.

Through the years I have seen a lot of sore, frantic, and distressed people in that office, but this aggregation of specimens was second to none. As far as I could see the common calamity had united them again and the danger of an indiscriminate framing bee had been averted. At one point their unanimous longing to confront Wolfe reached such proportions that Breslow, O'Neill, and young Erskine actually made for the stairs and started up, but when I yelled after them, above the uproar, that the door was locked and if they busted it in Wolfe would probably shoot them dead, they faltered, about-faced, and came back for some more of me.

I made one mistake. Like a simp I told them I would keep a continual eye on Wolfe on the chance of his having a lucid interval, and if one arrived and the doctor permitted I would notify Erskine and he could saddle up and gallop down for an interview. I should have foreseen that not only would they keep the phone humming day and night to ask how about some lucidity, but also they would take turns appearing in person, in singles, pairs, and trios, to sit in the office and wait for some. Which they did. Friday some of them were there half the time, and Saturday morning they started in again. As far as their damn money was concerned, I did at least thirty thousand dollars' worth of entertaining.

After their first visit, Thursday morning, I went up and reported in full to Wolfe, adding that I had not seen fit to inform them that he was keeping the cylinder hounds on the jog at his own expense. Wolfe only muttered:

"It doesn't matter. They'll learn it when the time comes."

"Yeah. The scientific name for the disease you've got is acute malignant optimism."

As for the cops, I was instructed by Wolfe to try to prevent an avalanche by volunteering information without delay, and therefore had phoned the Commissioner's office at eight-thirty Thursday morning, before any mail could have been opened up at the NIA office. Hombert hadn't arrived yet, nor had his secretary, but I described the situation to some gook and asked him to pass it on. An hour later Hombert himself called, and the conversation was almost verbatim what it would have been if I had written it down before it took place. He said he was sorry Wolfe had collapsed under the strain, and that the police official who would shortly be calling to see him would be instructed to conduct himself diplomatically and considerately. When I explained that it was doctor's orders that no one at all should see him, not even an insurance salesman, Hombert got brusque and wanted Vollmer's full name and address, which I obligingly furnished. He wanted to know if I had told the press that Wolfe was off the case, and I said no, and he said his office would attend to that to make sure they got it straight. Then he said that Wolfe's action, dropping his client, put it beyond argument that he knew the identity of the murderer, and was probably in possession of evidence against him, and since I was Wolfe's confidential assistant it was to be presumed that I shared the knowledge and the possession, and I was of course aware of the personal risk incurred by failing to communicate such information to the police immediately. I satisfied him on that point, I don't think. Anyhow I was telling the truth, and since I'm not very good at telling the truth I couldn't very well expect him to believe me.

In less than half an hour Lieutenant Rowcliffe and a detective sergeant showed up and I conducted them into the office. Rowcliffe read Doc Vollmer's certificate thoroughly, three times, and I offered to type a copy for him to take along for further study. He was keeping himself under restraint, since it was obvious that thunder and lightning would be wasted. He tried to insist that it wouldn't hurt a bit for him to tiptoe into Wolfe's room just for a compassionate look at a prostrated fellow citizen, and indeed a professional colleague, but I explained that much as the idea appealed to me I didn't dare because Doc Vollmer would never forgive me. He said he understood my position perfectly, and how about my getting wise to myself and spilling some beans? I was, I told him, fresh out of beans. He came about as close to believing me as Hombert had, but there was nothing he could do about it short of taking me downtown and using a piece of hose on me, and Rowcliffe knew me almost as well as he disliked me, so that didn't strike him as feasible.

When they departed Rowcliffe climbed in the police car and rolled away, and the sergeant began strolling up and down the sidewalk in front of the house. That was sensible. There was no point in hiring a window across the street or some similar subtlety, since they knew that we knew there would be a constant eye on our door. From there on we had a sentry out front right up to the end.

I never did understand why they didn't try quicker and harder to break it up, but I suspect it was on account of friction between Inspector Ash and the high command. Later, after it was all over, I tried to find out from Purley Stebbins what had gone on, but Purley never was willing to contribute more than a couple of grunts, probably because the Ash regime was something he wanted to erase from memory. Doc Vollmer got more of it than I did. He kept me informed when he came to pay visits to his patient. The first one, Thursday morning, I escorted him up to the bedroom, but when Wolfe started to enjoy himself by pointing a shaking finger at the wall and declaring that big black worms covered with dollar signs were crawling down from the ceiling, we both got out of there. Thereafter Vollmer never went near the patient, merely staying in the office chinning with me long enough to make it a call for the benefit of the sidewalk sentry. The police were pestering him, but he was getting a kick out of it. Thursday morning Rowcliffe had called on him right after leaving me, and that afternoon a police doctor had come to his office to get information about Wolfe on a professional level. Friday morning Ash himself had showed up, and twenty minutes with Ash had made Vollmer more enthusiastic

than ever about the favor he was doing Wolfe. Later
Friday afternoon another police doctor had come and
had put Vollmer over some high hurdles. When Vollmer dropped in that evening he was, for the first time,
not completely cocky about it.

Saturday noon the blow fell—the one I had been
expecting ever since the charade started, and the one
Vollmer was leery about. It landed via the telephone,
a call from Rowcliffe at twenty past twelve. I was
alone in the office when the bell rang, and I was even
more alone when it was over and I hung up. I took the
stairs two at a time, unlocked Wolfe's door, entered
and announced:

"Okay, Pagliaccio, luck is with us at last. You are
booked for the big time. An eminent neurologist
named Green, hired by the City of New York and
equipped with a court order, will arrive to give you an
audition at a quarter to six." I glared down at him and
demanded, "Now what? If you try to bull it through I
resign as of sixteen minutes to six."

"So." Wolfe closed his book with a finger in it. "This
is what we've been fearing." He made the book do the
split on the black coverlet. "Why must it be today?
Why the devil did you agree on an hour?"

"Because I had to! Who do you think I am, Joshua?
They wanted to make it right now, and I did the best
I could. I told them your doctor had to be present and
he couldn't make it until after dinner this evening, nine
o'clock. They said it had to be before six o'clock and
they wouldn't take no. Damn it, I got an extra five
hours and I had to fight for it!"

"Quit yelling at me." His head went back to the
pillow. "Go back downstairs. I'm going to have to
think."

I stood my ground. "Do you actually mean you

haven't got it figured out what to do? When I've warned you it would come any minute ever since Thursday morning?"

"Archie. Get out of here. How can I put my mind on it with you standing there bellowing?"

"Very well. I'll be in the office. Call me when you get around to it."

I went out, shut the door and locked it, and descended. In the office the phone was ringing. It was only Winterhoff, inquiring after my employer's health.

Chapter 33

I try, as I go along, not to leave anything essential out of this record, and, since I'm telling it, I regard my own state of mind at various stages as one of the essentials. But for that two hours on Saturday, from twelve-thirty to two-thirty, my state of mind was really not fit to be recorded for family reading. I have a vague recollection that I ate lunch twice, though Fritz politely insists that he doesn't remember it that way. He says that Wolfe's lunch was completely normal as far as he knows—tray taken upstairs full at one o'clock and brought down empty an hour later—and that nothing struck him as abnormal except that Wolfe was too preoccupied to compliment him on the omelet.

What made me use up a month's supply of profanity in a measly two hours was not that all I could see ahead was ignominious surrender. That was a hard dose but by no means fatal. The hell of it was, as I saw it, that we were being bombed out of a position that no one but a maniac would ever have occupied in the first place. I had a right to assume, now that I was reading the reports from Bill Gore and Bascom's men, that I knew exactly what was going on in every sector except the one that was occupied by Saul Panzer, and it was impossible to imagine what Saul could be doing that could justify, let alone necessitate, the gaudy and spectacular stunt Wolfe was indulging in. When Saul phoned in at two o'clock I had a notion to tackle him and try to open him up, but I knew it would be hopeless and put him through to the bedroom. On any list of temptations I have resisted, that one goes first. I was tingling from head to foot with the desire to listen in. But a part of the understanding between Wolfe and me is that I never violate instructions except when circumstances unknown to him, as interpreted by my best judgment, require it, and I couldn't kid myself that that applied here. My instructions were that Saul Panzer was out of bounds for me until further notice, and I put the thing on the cradle and walked up and down with my hands in my pockets.

Other phone calls came, it doesn't matter what, and I did violate another instruction, the one to receive any and all callers. Circumstances certainly justified that. I was in the kitchen helping Fritz sharpen knives, I suppose on the principle that in times of crisis we instinctively seek the companionship of fellow creatures, when the bell rang and I went to the front door, fingered the curtain aside for a peek, and saw Breslow. I opened the door a crack and barked through at him:

"No admittance this is a house of mourning beat it!"

I banged the door and started back to the kitchen, but didn't make it. Passing the foot of the stairs I became aware of sound and movement, and stopping to look up I saw what was making it. Wolfe, covered with nothing but the eight yards of yellow silk it took to make him a suit of pajamas, was descending. I goggled at him. If nothing else, it was unprecedented for him to move vertically except with the elevator.

"How did you get out?" I demanded.

"Fritz gave me a key." He came on down, and I noted that at least he had put his slippers on. He commanded me, "Get Fritz and Theodore in the office at once."

I had never before seen him outside his room in deshabille. It was obviously an extreme emergency. I swung the kitchen door open and spoke to Fritz and then went to the office, buzzed the plant rooms on the house phone, and told Theodore to make it snappy. By the time Theodore trotted down and in, Wolfe was seated behind his desk and Fritz and I were standing by.

"How are you, Theodore? I haven't seen you for three days."

"I'm all right, thank you, sir. I've missed you."

"No doubt." Wolfe's glance went from him to Fritz, then to me, and he said slowly and clearly, "I am a brainless booby."

"Yes, sir," I said cordially.

He frowned. "So are you, Archie. Neither of us has any right, henceforth, to pretend possession of the mental processes of an anthropoid. I include you because you heard what I said to Mr. Hombert and Mr. Skinner. You have read the reports from Mr. Bascom's men. You know what's going on. And by heaven, it hasn't occurred to you that Miss Gunther was alone in this office for a good three minutes, nearer four or five, when you brought her here that evening! And it occurred to me only just now! Pfui! And I have dared for nearly thirty years to exercise my right to vote!" He snorted. "I have the brain of a mollusk!"

"Yeah." I was staring at him. I remembered, of

course, that when I had brought Phoebe that Friday night I had left her in the office and gone to the kitchen to get him. "So you think—"

"No. I am through pretending to think. This makes it untenable. —Fritz and Theodore, a young woman was in here alone four minutes. She had, in her pocket or her bag, an object she wanted to hide—a black cylinder three inches in diameter and six inches long. She didn't know how much time she would have; someone might enter any moment. On the assumption that she hid it in this room, find it. Knowing the quality of her mind, I think it likely that she hid it in my desk. I'll look there myself."

He shoved his chair back and dived to pull open a bottom drawer. I was at my own desk, also opening drawers. Fritz asked me, "What do we do, divide it in sections?"

"Divide hell," I told him over my shoulder. "Just start looking."

Fritz went to the couch and began removing cushions. Theodore chose, for his first guess, the two vases on top of the filing cabinet which at that season contained pussy willows. There was no more conversation; we were too busy. I can't give a detailed report of the part of the search conducted by Fritz and Theodore because I was too intent on my own part of it; all I had for them was occasional glances to see what they were covering; but I kept an eye on Wolfe because I shared his opinion of the quality of Phoebe's mind and it would have been like her to pick Wolfe's own desk for it provided she found a drawer which looked as if its contents were not often disturbed. But he drew a blank. As I was opening the back of the radio cabinet, he slid his chair back into position, got comfortable in it, muttered, "Confound that woman," and surveyed us like a field commander directing his troops in action.

Fritz's voice came, "Is this it, Mr. Wolfe?"

He was kneeling on the rug in front of the longest section of bookshelves, and stacked beside him were a dozen volumes of the bound *Lindenia*, with a big gap showing on the bottom shelf, which was only a few inches above the floor. He was extending a hand with an object in it at which one glance was enough.

"Ideal," Wolfe said approvingly. "She was really extraordinary. Give it to Archie. Archie, roll that machine out. Theodore, I'll be with you in the potting room possibly later today, certainly tomorrow morning at the usual hour. Fritz, I congratulate you; you tried the bottom shelf first, which was sensible."

Fritz was beaming as he handed me the cylinder and turned to go, with Theodore following him.

"Well," I remarked as I plugged the machine in and inserted the cylinder, "this may do it. Or it may not."

"Start it," Wolfe growled. He was tapping on an arm of his chair with a finger. "What's the matter? Won't it go?"

"Certainly it will go. Don't hurry me. I'm nervous and I have the brain of a—I forget what. Mollusk."

I flipped the switch and sat down. The voice of Cheney Boone came to our ears, unmistakably the same voice we had heard on the other ten cylinders. For five minutes neither of us moved a muscle. I stared at the grill of the loud-speaker attachment, and Wolfe leaned back with his eyes closed. When it came to the end I reached and turned the switch.

Wolfe sighed clear to the bottom, opened his eyes, and straightened up.

"Our literature needs some revision," he declared.

"For example, 'dead men tell no tales.' Mr. Boone is dead. Mr. Boone is silent. But he speaks."

"Yep." I grinned at him. "The silent speaker. Science is wonderful, but I know one guy who won't think so, goddam him. Shall I go get him?"

"No. We can arrange this, I think, by telephone. You have Mr. Cramer's number?"

"Sure."

"Good. But first get Saul. You'll find him at Manhattan five, three-two-three-two."

Chapter 34

By ten minutes to four our guests had all arrived and were collected in the office. One of them was an old friend and enemy: Inspector Cramer. One was an ex-client: Don O'Neill. One was merely a recent acquaintance: Alger Kates. The fourth was a complete stranger: Henry A. Warder, Vice-President and Treasurer of O'Neill and Warder, Incorporated. Don O'Neill's vice. Saul Panzer, who had retired to a chair over in the corner behind the globe, was of course not regarded as a guest but as one of the family.

Cramer was in the red leather chair, watching Wolfe like a hawk. O'Neill, entering and catching sight of his Vice-President, who had arrived before him, had immediately hit the ceiling, and then had just as immediately thought better of it, clamped his mouth shut, and congealed. The vice, Henry A. Warder, who was both broad and tall, built like a concrete buttress, looked as if he could use some buttressing himself. He was the only one whose demeanor suggested that smelling salts might be called for, being obviously scared silly. Alger Kates had not spoken a word to anyone, not a word, not even when I let him in. His basic attitude was that of a Sunday School teacher in a den of thieves.

Wolfe had clothes on for the first time since Wednesday evening. He sat and did a circle with his eyes, taking them in, and spoke:

"This is going to be disagreeable, gentlemen, for all three of you, so let's make it as brief as we can. I'll do my share. The quickest way is to begin by letting you listen to a Stenophone cylinder, but first I must tell you where I got it. It was found in this room an hour ago, behind the books"—he pointed—"on that bottom shelf. Miss Gunther placed it there, hid it there, when she came to see me Friday evening a week ago—a week ago last evening."

"She wasn't here," O'Neill rasped. "She didn't come."

Wolfe regarded him without affection. "So you don't want this to be brief."

"You're damn right I do! The briefer the better!"

"Then don't interrupt. Naturally everything I'm saying is not only true but provable, or I wouldn't be saying it. Miss Gunther came that evening, brought by Mr. Goodwin, after the others left, and happened to be alone in this room for several minutes. That I did not remember that sooner and search the room was inexcusable. It was an appalling failure of an intellect which has sometimes been known to function satisfactorily.

"However." He made a brusque gesture. "That is between me and the universe. We shall now listen to that cylinder, which was dictated by Mr. Boone his last afternoon at his office in Washington. Do not, I beg you, interrupt it. Archie, turn it on."

There were murmurs as I flipped the switch. Then Cheney Boone, the silent speaker, had the floor:

Miss Gunther, this is for no one but you and me. Make sure of that. One carbon only, for your locked file, and deliver the original to me.

I have just had a talk in a hotel room with Henry A. Warder, Vice-President and Treasurer of O'Neill and Warder. He is the man who has been trying to reach me through you and refusing to give his name. He finally got me directly, at home, and I made this appointment with him, for today, March 26th. He told me the following—

Warder catapulted out of his chair and started for the machine, screaming, "Stop it!"

It would be more in keeping with his size and appearance to say that he roared or blared, but it literally was a scream. Having anticipated some such demonstration, I had placed the machine at the end of my desk, only four feet from me, and therefore had no difficulty intercepting the attack. I planted myself in Warder's line of approach, reached back of me to turn the switch, and spoke firmly:

"Nothing stirring. Back up and sit down." From my coat pocket I produced an automatic and let it be seen. "All three of you are going to like it less and less as it goes along. If you get a simultaneous idea and try to act on it, I'll wing you and it will be a pleasure."

"That was under a pledge of confidence!" Warder was trembling from head to foot. "Boone promised—"

"Can it!" Cramer had left his chair and was beside Warder. He asked me, "They haven't been gone over, have they?"

"They're not gunmen," Wolfe snapped. "They merely club people on the head—or one of them does."

Cramer paid no attention to him. He started with

Warder, gave him a quick but thorough frisking, motioned him back, and said to O'Neill, "Stand up." O'Neill didn't move. Cramer barked at him, "Do you want to get lifted?" O'Neill stood up and did some fancy breathing while Cramer's expert hands went over him. When it was Alger Kates's turn no pressure was required. He looked dazed but not even resentful. Cramer, through with him and empty-handed, moved across to the machine and stood with a hand resting on its frame. He growled at me:

"Go ahead, Goodwin."

Not being a Stenophone expert and not wanting to damage the cylinder, I started it over at the beginning. Soon it was at the point where it had been interrupted:

He told me the following. Warder has known for several months that the president of his company, Don O'Neill, has been paying a member of the BPR staff for confidential information. He did not discover it by accident or any secret investigation. O'Neill has not only admitted it, but bragged about it, and Warder, as Treasurer, has been obliged to supply corporation funds for the purpose through a special account. He has done so under protest. I repeat that this is Warder's story, but I am inclined to believe it as he tells it because he came to me voluntarily. It will have to be checked with the FBI to find out if they have had any lead in the direction of O'Neill and Warder and specifically Warder, but the FBI must not be given any hint of Warder's communicating with me. I had to give him my pledge on that before he would say a word, and the pledge must be kept absolutely. I'll talk this over with you tomorrow, but I have a hunch—

you know how I have hunches—that I want to get it on a cylinder without delay.

Cramer made a little noise that was part snort and part sneeze, and three pairs of eyes went to him as if in irritation at his interfering with a fascinating performance. I didn't mind so much because I had heard it before. What I was interested in was the audience.

Warder said that to his knowledge the payments began last September and that the total paid to date is sixteen thousand five hundred dollars. The reason he gave for coming to me is that he is a man of principle, so he put it, and he violently disapproves of bribery, especially bribery of government officials. He was not in a position to take a firm stand with O'Neill because O'Neill owns over sixty per cent of the corporation's stock and Warder owns less than ten per cent, and O'Neill could and would throw him out. That can easily be checked. Warder was extremely nervous and apprehensive. My impression is that his story is straight, that his coming to me was the result of his conscience gnawing at him, but there is a chance that his real motive is to build a fire under O'Neill, for undisclosed reasons. He swore that his only purpose was to acquaint me with the facts so I can put a stop to it by getting rid of my corrupted subordinate, and that is substantiated by his exacting a pledge beforehand that makes it impossible for us to touch O'Neill in the matter.

This will be a surprise to you—I know it was to me—the man O'Neill has bought is Kates, Alger Kates. You know what I have thought of

Kates, and, so far as I know, you have thought the same. Warder claims he doesn't know exactly what O'Neill has got for his money, but that isn't important. We know what Kates has been in a position to sell—as much as any man in the organization outside of the very top ranks—and our only safe assumption is that he has given it all to O'Neill and that O'Neill has passed it on to the whole rotten NIA gang. I don't need to tell you how sick I am about it. For a miserable sixteen thousand dollars. I don't think I would mind quite so much being betrayed by a first-class snake for something up in the millions, but this just makes me sick. I thought Kates was a modest little man with his heart in his work and in our objectives and purposes. I have no idea what he wanted the money for and I don't care. I haven't decided how to handle it. The best way would be to put the FBI on him and catch him with O'Neill, but I don't know whether my pledge to Warder would permit that. I'll think it over and we'll discuss it tomorrow. If I were face to face with Kates right now I don't think I could control myself. Actually I don't ever want to see him again. This has gone pretty deep and if he entered this room now I think I'd get my fingers around his throat and choke him to death. You know me. That's the way I talk.

The important thing is not Kates himself, but what this shows. It shows that it is simply insanity for me to put complete trust in anybody, anyone whatever except Dexter and you, and we must install a much better system of checks immediately. To some extent we can continue to let the FBI handle it, but we must reinforce that with a setup and personnel that will work directly under us. I want you to think it over for tomorrow's discussion, to which no one will be invited but Dexter. The way it strikes me now, you'll have to take this over and drop everything else. That will leave me in a hole, but this is vitally important. Think it over. I have to appear before the Senate Committee in the morning, so I'll take this to New York and give it to you, and you can run it off while I'm up on the Hill, and we'll get at it as early in the afternoon as possible.

The voice stopped and was replaced by a faint sizzling purr, and I reached to flip the switch.

There was complete dead silence.

Wolfe broke in. "What about it, Mr. Kates?" he asked in a tone of innocent curiosity. "When you entered that room, taking Mr. Boone material for his speech, and he found himself face to face with you, did he get his fingers around your throat and try to choke you?"

"No," Kates squeaked. He sounded indignant, but that may have been only because squeaks often do.

O'Neill commanded him: "You keep out of this, Kates! Keep your mouth shut!"

Wolfe chuckled. "That's marvelous, Mr. O'Neill. It really is. Almost verbatim. That first evening here you admonished him, word for word, 'You can keep out of this, Kates! Sit down and shut up!' It was not very intelligent of you, since it sounded precisely like a high-handed man ordering an employee around, as indeed it was. It led to my having a good man spend three days trying to find a link between you and Mr. Kates, but you had been too circumspect." His eyes darted back to Kates. "I asked about Mr. Boone's choking you because apparently he had it in mind, and also because it suggests a possible line for you—self-defense. A good lawyer might do something with it—but then of course there's Miss Gunther. I doubt if a jury could be persuaded that she too tried to choke you, there on my stoop. By the way, there's one detail I'm curious about. Miss Gunther told Mrs. Boone that she wrote a letter to the murderer, telling him that he must return that wedding picture. I don't believe it. I don't think Miss Gunther would have put anything like that in writing. I think she got the picture and the automobile license from you and mailed them to Mrs. Boone herself. Didn't she?"

For reply Alger Kates put on one of the strangest performances I have ever seen, and I have seen plenty. He squeaked, and this time there was no question about the indignation, not at Wolfe but at Inspector Cramer. He was trembling with indignation, up on his feet, a retake in every way of the dramatic moment when he had accused Breslow of going beyond the bounds of common decency. He squeaked, "The police were utterly incompetent! They should have found out where that piece of pipe came from in a few hours! They never did! It came from a pile of rubbish in a basement hall in the building on Forty-first Street where the NIA offices are!"

"For Christ's sake," Cramer rumbled. "Listen to him! He's sore!"

"He's a fool," O'Neill said righteously, apparently addressing the Stenophone. "He's a contemptible fool. I certainly never suspected him of murder." He turned to look straight at Kates. "Good God, I never thought you were capable of that!"

"Neither did I," Kates squeaked. He had stopped

trembling and was standing straight, holding himself stiff. "Not before it happened. After it happened I understood myself better. I wasn't as much of a fool as Phoebe was. She should have known it then, what I was capable of. I did. She wouldn't even promise not to tell or to destroy that cylinder. She wouldn't even promise!" He kept his unblinking eyes on O'Neill. "I should have killed you too, the same evening. I could have. You were afraid of me. You're afraid of me right now! Neither of them was afraid of me, but you are! You say you never suspected me of murder when you knew all about it!"

O'Neill started a remark, but Cramer squelched him and asked Kates, "How did he know all about it?"

"I told him." If Kates's squeak was as painful to perform as it was to listen to he was certainly being hurt. "Or rather I didn't have to tell him. He arranged to meet me—"

"That's a lie," O'Neill said coldly and precisely. "Now you're lying."

"Okay, let him finish it." Cramer kept at Kates, "When was that?"

"The next day, Wednesday. Wednesday afternoon. We met that evening."

"Where?"

"On Second Avenue between Fifty-third and Fifty-fourth. We talked there on the sidewalk. He gave me some money and told me that if anything happened, if I was arrested, he would furnish whatever I needed. He was afraid of me then. He kept watching me, watching my hands."

"How long were you together?"

"Ten minutes. My estimate would be ten minutes."

"What time was it?"

"Ten o'clock. We were to meet at ten o'clock and I

was on time, but he was late about fifteen minutes because he said he had to make sure he wasn't being followed. I don't think an intelligent man should have any trouble about that."

Wolfe broke in. "Mr. Cramer. Isn't this a waste of time? You're going to have to go all over it again downtown, with a stenographer. He seems to be ready to co-operate."

"He is ready," O'Neill put in, "to get himself electrocuted and to make all the trouble he can for other people with his damn lies."

"I wouldn't worry too much about that if I were you." Wolfe regarded O'Neill with a glint in his eyes. "He is at least more of a philosopher than you are. Bad as he is, he has the grace to accept the inevitable with a show of decorum. You, on the contrary, try to wiggle. From the glances you have been directing at Mr. Warder, I suspect you have no clear idea of where you're at. You should be making up with him. You're going to need him to look after the business while you're away."

"I'm seeing this through. I'm not going away."

"Oh, but you are. You're going to jail. At least that seems—" Wolfe turned abruptly to the Vice-President. "What about it, Mr. Warder? Are you going to try to discredit this message from the dead? Are you going to repudiate or distort your interview with Mr. Boone and have a jury vote you a liar? Or are you going to show that you have some sense?"

Warder no longer looked scared, and when he spoke he showed no inclination to scream. "I am going," he said in a firm and virtuous voice, "to tell the truth."

"Did Mr. Boone tell the truth on that cylinder?"

"Yes. He did."

Wolfe's eyes flashed back to O'Neill. "There you are, sir. Bribery is a felony. You're going to need Mr. Warder. The other matter, complicity in murder as an accessory after the fact—that all depends, mostly on your lawyer. From here on the lawyers take over. —Mr. Cramer. Get them out of here, won't you? I'm tired of looking at them." He shifted to me. "Archie, pack up that cylinder. Mr. Cramer will want to take it along."

Cramer, moving, addressed me: "Hold it, Goodwin, while I use the phone," so I sat facing the audience, with the automatic in my hand in case someone had an attack of nerves, while he dialed his number and conversed. I was interested to hear that his objective was not the Homicide Squad office, where Ash had been installed, nor even the Chief Inspector, but Hombert himself. Cramer did occasionally show signs of having more brain than a mollusk.

"Commissioner Hombert? Inspector Cramer. Yes, sir. No, I'm calling from Nero Wolfe's office. No, sir, I'm not trying to horn in, but if you'll let me . . . Yes, sir, I'm quite aware it would be a breach of discipline, but if you'd just listen a minute— certainly I'm here with Wolfe, I didn't break in, and I've got the man, I've got the evidence, and I've got a confession. That's exactly what I'm telling you, and I'm neither drunk nor crazy. Send—wait a minute, hold it."

Wolfe was making frantic gestures.

"Tell him," Wolfe commanded, "to keep that confounded doctor away from here."

Cramer resumed. "All right, Commissioner. Send up—oh, nothing, just Wolfe raving something about a doctor. Were you sending him a doctor? He don't need one and in my opinion never will. Send three cars and six men to Wolfe's address. No, I don't, but I'm bringing three of them down. You'll see when I get there. Yes, sir, I'm telling you, the case is finished, all sewed up and no gaps worth mentioning. Sure, I'll bring them straight to you. . . ."

He hung up.

"You won't have to put handcuffs on me, will you?" Alger Kates squeaked.

"I want to phone my lawyer," O'Neill said in a frozen voice.

Warder just sat.

Chapter 35

Skipping a thousand or so minor details over the weekend, such as the eminent neurologist Green—no one having bothered to stop him— showing up promptly at a quarter to six, only a few minutes after Cramer had left with his catch, and being informed, in spite of his court order, that the deal was off, I bounce to Monday morning. Wolfe, coming down from the plant rooms at eleven o'clock, knew that he would have a visitor, Cramer having phoned for an appointment, and when he entered the office the Inspector was there in the red leather chair. Beside him on the floor was a misshapen object covered with green florist's paper which he had refused to let me relieve him of. After greetings had been exchanged and Wolfe had got himself comfortable, Cramer said he supposed that Wolfe had seen in the paper that Kates had signed a full and detailed confession to both murders.

Wolfe nodded. "A foolish and inadequate man, that Mr. Kates. But not intellectually to be despised. One item of his performance might even be called brilliant."

"Sure. I would say more than one. Do you mean his

leaving that scarf in his own pocket instead of slipping it into somebody else's?"

"Yes, sir. That was noteworthy."

"He's noteworthy all right," Cramer agreed. "In fact he's in a class by himself. There was one thing he wouldn't talk about or sign any statement about, and what do you suppose it was, something that would help put him in the chair? Nope. We couldn't get anything out of him about what he wanted the money for, and when we asked if it was his wife, trips to Florida and so forth, he stuck his chin out and said as if we was worms, 'We'll leave my wife out of this, you will not mention my wife again.' She got here yesterday afternoon and he won't see her. I think he thinks she's too holy to be dragged in."

"Indeed."

"Indeed yes. But on the part that will do for him he was perfectly willing to oblige. For instance, with Boone there at the hotel. He entered the room and handed Boone some papers, and Boone threw it at him, what he had found out, and then told him to beat it and turned his back on him, and Kates picked up the monkey wrench and gave it to him. Kates tells us exactly what Boone said and what he said, and then carefully reads it over to be sure we got it down right. The same way with Phoebe Gunther here on your stoop. He wants the story straight. He wants it distinctly understood that he didn't arrange to meet her and come here with her, when she phoned him, he merely waited in an areaway across the street until he saw her coming and then joined her and mounted the stoop with her. The pipe was up his sleeve with the scarf already wrapped around it. Three days before that, the first time they were here, when he swiped the scarf out of Winterhoff's pocket, he didn't know then what he would be using it for, he only thought there might be some way of planting it somewhere to involve Winterhoff—an NIA man."

"Naturally." Wolfe was contributing to the conversation just to be polite. "Anything to keep eyes away from him. Wasted effort, since my eye was already on him."

"It was?" Cramer sounded skeptical. "What put it there?"

"Mostly two things. First, of course, that command Mr. O'Neill gave him here Friday evening, indubitably a command to one from whom he had reason to expect obedience. Second, and much more important, the wedding picture mailed to Mrs. Boone. Granted that there are men capable of that gesture, assuredly none of the five NIA men whom I had met had it in them. Miss Harding was obviously too cold-blooded to indulge in any such act of grace. Mr. Dexter's alibi had been tested and stood. Mrs. Boone and her niece were manifestly not too suspected, not by me. There remained only Miss Gunther and Mr. Kates. Miss Gunther might conceivably have killed Mr. Boone, but not herself with a piece of pipe; and she was the only one of them who could without painful strain on probability be considered responsible for the return of the wedding picture. Then where did she get it? From the murderer. By name, from whom? As a logical and workable conjecture, Mr. Kates."

Wolfe fluttered a hand. "All that was mere phantom-chasing. What was needed was evidence—and all the time here it was, on that bookshelf in my office. That, I confess, is a bitter pill to swallow. Will you have some beer?"

"No, thanks, I guess I won't." Cramer seemed to be nervous or uneasy or something. He looked at the clock and slid to the edge of the chair. "I've got to be going. I just dropped in." He elevated to his feet and shook his pants legs down. "I've got a hell of a busy day. I suppose you've heard that I'm back at my desk at Twentieth Street. Inspector Ash has been moved to Richmond. Staten Island."

"Yes, sir. I congratulate you."

"Much obliged. So with me back at the old stand you'll have to continue to watch your step. Try pulling any fast ones and I'll still be on your neck."

"I wouldn't dream of trying to pull a fast one."

"Okay. Just so we understand each other." Cramer started for the door. I called after him:

"Hey, your package!"

He said over his shoulder, barely halting. "Oh, I forgot, that's for you, Wolfe, hope you like it," and was on his way. Judging from the time it took him to get on out and slam the door behind him, he must have double-quicked.

I went over and lifted the package from the floor, put it on Wolfe's desk, and tore the green paper off, exposing the contents to view. The pot was a glazed sickening green. The dirt was just dirt. The plant was in fair condition, but there were only two flowers on it. I stared at it in awe.

"By God," I said when I could speak, "he brought you an orchid."

"Brassocattleya thorntoni," Wolfe purred. "Handsome."

"Nuts," I said realistically. "You've got a thousand better ones. Shall I throw it out?"

"Certainly not. Take it up to Theodore." Wolfe wiggled a finger at me. "Archie. One of your most serious defects is that you have no sentiment."

"No?" I grinned at him. "You'd be surprised. At

this very moment one is almost choking me—namely, gratitude for our good luck at having Cramer back, obnoxious as he is. With Ash there life wouldn't have been worth living."

Wolfe snorted. "Luck!"

Chapter 36

Sooner or later I had to make it plain to him that I was not a halfwit. I was waiting for a fitting moment, and it came that same day, Monday afternoon, about an hour after lunch, when we received a phone call from Frank Thomas Erskine. He was permitted to speak to Wolfe, and I listened in at my desk.

The gist of it was that a check for one hundred thousand dollars would be mailed to Wolfe that afternoon, which would seem to be enough gist for one little phone call. The rest was just trivial. The NIA deeply appreciated what Wolfe had done for it and was utterly unable to understand why he had returned its money. It was paying him the full amount of the reward at once, as offered in its advertisement, in advance of the fulfillment of the specified conditions, because of its gratitude and its confidence in him, and also because Kates's signed confession made the fulfillment of the conditions inevitable. It would be glad to pay an additional amount for expenses incurred if Wolfe would say how much. It had discussed the matter with Inspector Cramer, and Cramer had disavowed any claim to any part of the reward and insisted that it all belonged to Wolfe.

It was a nice phone call.

Wolfe said to me with a smirk, "That's satisfactory and businesslike. Paying the reward without delay."

I leered at him. "Yeah? Little does Mr. Erskine know."

"Little does he know what? What's wrong now?"

I threw one knee over the other and settled back. The time had come. "There are," I stated, "several ways of doing this. One would be to put a hunk of butter in your mouth and see if it melted. I prefer my way, which is just to tell you. Or I should say ask you, since I'll put it in the form of questions, only I'll supply the answers myself."

"What the devil are you talking about?"

"No, the questions originate with me. Number one: when did you find the cylinder? Saturday afternoon, when you waddled in here in your pajamas, belittling your brains? Not a chance. You knew where it was all the time, at least for three or four days. You found it either Tuesday morning, while I was down at Cramer's office being wrung out, or Wednesday while I was up having lunch with Nina Boone. I lean to Tuesday, but I admit it may have been Wednesday."

"You shouldn't," Wolfe murmured, "leave things teetering like that."

"Please don't interrupt me. Number two: why, if you knew where the cylinder was, did you pester Mrs. Boone to tell you? Because you wanted to make sure she *didn't* know. If she had known she might have told the cops before you decided to let loose, and the reward would have gone to her, or anyway not to you. And since Phoebe Gunther had told her a lot she might have told her that too. Also, it was part of your general plan to spread the impression that you didn't know where the cylinder was and would give an arm and several teeth to find it."

"That was actually the impression," Wolfe murmured.

"It was indeed. I could back all this up with various miscellaneous items, for instance your sending for the Stenophone Wednesday morning, which is the chief reason I lean to Tuesday, but let's go on to number three: what was the big idea? When you found the cylinder why didn't you say so? Because you let your personal opinions interfere with your professional actions, which reminds me I must do some reading up on ethics. Because your opinion of the NIA coincides roughly with some other people's, including my own, but that's beside the point, and you knew the stink about the murders was raising cain with the NIA, and you wanted to prolong it as much as possible. To accomplish that you even went to the length of letting yourself be locked in your room for three days, but there I admit another factor enters, your love of art for art's sake. You'll do anything to put on a good show, provided you get top billing."

"How long is this going on?"

"I'm about through. Number four, why did you drop the client and return the dough, is easy. There's always a chance that you may change your mind some day and decide you want to go to heaven, and a plain unadulterated double cross would rule it out. So you couldn't very well have kept the NIA's money, and gone on having it for a client, while you were doing your damnedest to push it off a cliff. Here, however, is where I get cynical. What if no reward had been publicly offered? Would you have put on the show just the same? I express no opinion, but boy, I have one.

Another thing about ethics—exactly what is the difference between having a client and taking a fee, and accepting a reward?"

"Nonsense. The reward was advertised to a hundred million people and the terms stated. It was to be paid to whoever earned it. I earned it."

"Okay, I merely mention the point. I don't question your going to heaven if you decide you want in. Incidentally, you are not absolutely watertight. If Saul Panzer was put under oath and asked what he did from Wednesday to Saturday, and he replied that he kept in touch with Henry A. Warder to make sure that Warder could be had when needed, and then if you were asked where you got the idea that you might need Henry A. Warder, mightn't you have a little trouble shooting the answer? Not that it will happen, knowing Saul as I do. —Well. Let's see. I guess that's about all. I just wanted you to know that I resent your making contemptuous remarks about your brain."

Wolfe grunted. There was a silence. Then his eyes opened half way and he rumbled:

"You've left one thing out."

"What?"

"A possible secondary motive. Or even a primary one. Taking all that you have said as hypothesis—since of course it is inadmissible as fact—look back at me last Tuesday, six days ago, when—by hypothesis—I found the cylinder. What actually would have taken precedence in my mind?"

"I've been telling you. Not what would have, what did."

"But you left one thing out. Miss Gunther."

"What about her?"

"She was dead. As you know, I detest waste. She had displayed remarkable tenacity, audacity, and even imagination, in using the murder of Mr. Boone for a purpose he would have desired, approved, and applauded. In the middle of it she was herself murdered. Surely she deserved not to have her murder wasted. She deserved to get something out of it. I found myself—by hypothesis—in an ideal position to see that that was taken care of. That's what you left out."

I stared at him. "Then I've got a hypothesis too. If that was it, either primary or secondary, to hell with ethics."

The World of Rex Stout

Enjoy a peek into the life of Nero Wolfe's creator, Rex Stout, courtesy of the Stout Estate. Pulled from Rex Stout's own archives, here are rarely seen memorabilia.

The Silent Speaker

Even though the rationing of World War II was over, there was still a shortage of many needed materials in 1946, the year of *The Silent Speaker*'s publication. Following is a letter from Rex Stout's publisher describing the scarcity of metals necessary for the printing of books, and Stout's response.

Rinehart
& COMPANY · INCORPORATED
Publishers

232 MADISON AVENUE · NEW YORK 16 · N. Y.

28 October 1946

Dear Rex:

    Our printer has told us that there is
an acute metal shortage, particularly of lead,
expected in the near future and while there is
no moral or legal obligation on your part to
consent, they would like to melt the plates of
ALPHABET HICKS for the salvage value in scrap
metal. I am wondering whether you will have
any objection. Certainly we have no intention
of doing anything about it until we have heard
from you and as you are undoubtedly aware, should
there be a new demand for the book, it can always
be reproduced by photography or by re-setting.

    Will you let us know?

        Sincerely yours,

        Ted

        Frederick R. Rinehart
FRR:em   Vice-President

P.S. We find that we have your name on our
list again for HAND IN THE GLOVE, LEAGUE OF
FRIGHTENED MEN. Could you let us know about
those, too?

November 6 1946

Mr. Frederick R. Rinehart
232 Madison Avenue
New York City 16

Dear Ted:

    A session with the flu has delayed
a reply to yours of October 28th. No,
I have no objection to melting the plates
of ALPHABET HICKS, THE HAND IN THE GLOVE
and THE LEAGUE OF FRIGHTENED MEN. As
you say, when the throngs demanding new
editions clog Madison Avenue, we can
set it again.

                    Yours,

Not for publication
Confidential Memo
From Rex Stout
September 15 1949

DESCRIPTION OF NERO WOLFE

Height 5 ft. 11 in. Weight 272 lbs. Age 56.
Mass of dark brown hair, very little greying, is not
parted but sweeps off to the right because he brushes
with his right hand. Dark brown eyes are average in
size, but look smaller because they are mostly half
closed. They always are aimed straight at the person
he is talking to. Forehead is high. Head and face
are big but do not seem so in proportion to the whole.
Ears rather small. Nose long and narrow, slightly
aquiline. Mouth mobile and extremely variable; lips
when pursed are full and thick, but in tense moments
they are thin and their line is long. Cheeks full but
not pudgy; the high point of the cheekbone can be seen
from straight front. Complexion varies from some
floridity after meals to an ivory pallor late at night
when he has spent six hard hours working on someone.
He breathes smoothly and without sound except when he
is eating; then he takes in and lets out great gusts of
air. His massive shoulders never slump; when he stands
up at all he stands straight. He shaves every day. He
has a small brown mole just above his right jawbone,
halfway between the chin and the ear.

DESCRIPTION OF ARCHIE GOODWIN

Height 6 feet. Weight 180 lbs. Age 32. Hair is
light rather than dark, but just barely decided not to
be red; he gets it cut every two weeks, rather short,
and brushes it straight back, but it keeps standing up.
He shaves four times a week and grasps at every excuse
to make it only three times. His features are all regular, well-modeled and well-proportioned, except the
nose. He escapes the curse of being the movie actor
type only through the nose. It is not a true pug and
is by no means a deformity, but it is a little short
and the ridge is broad, and the tip has continued on
its own, beyond the cartilage, giving the impression
of startling and quite independent initiative. The eyes
are grey, and are inquisitive and quick to move. He is
muscular both in appearance and in movement, and upright
in posture, but his shoulders stoop a little in unconscious
reaction to Wolfe's repeated criticism that he is too
self-assertive.

DESCRIPTION OF WOLFE'S OFFICE

The old brownstone on West 35th Street is a double-
width house. Entering at the front door, which is seven
steps up from the sidewalk, you are facing the length of

a wide carpeted hall. At the right is an enormous coat
rack, eight feet wide, then the stairs, and beyond the
stairs the door to the dining room. There were originally two rooms on that side of the hall, but Wolfe had
the partition removed and turned it into a dining room
forty feet long, with a table large enough for six (but
extensible) square in the middle. It (and all other
rooms) are carpeted; Wolfe hates bare floors. At the
far end of the big hall is the kitchen. At the left of the
big hall are two doors; the first one is to what Archie calls
the front room, and the second is to the office. The front
room is used chiefly as an anteroom; Nero and Archie do
no living there. It is rather small, and the furniture
is a random mixture without any special character.

The office is large and nearly square. In the far
corner to the left (as you enter from the hall) a small
rectangle has been walled off to make a place for a
john and a washbowl — to save steps for Wolfe. The door
leading to it faces you, and around the corner, along its
other wall, is a wide and well-cushioned couch.

SKETCH OF OFFICE

In furnishings the room has no apparent unity
but it has plenty of character. Wolfe permits nothing
to be in it that he doesn't enjoy looking at, and that
has been the only criterion for admission. The globe
is three feet in diameter. Wolfe's chair was made by
Meyer of cardato. His desk is of cherry, which of
course clashes with the cardato, but Wolfe likes it.
The couch is upholstered in bright yellow material
which has to go to the cleaners every three months.
The carpet was woven in Montenegro in the early nineteenth century and has been extensively patched. The
only wall decorations are three pictures: a Manet, a
copy of a Corregio, and a genuine Leonardo sketch. The
chairs are all shapes, colors, materials, and sizes.
The total effect makes you blink with bewilderment at
the first visit, but if you had Archie's job and lived
there you would probably learn to like it.